# Buck's eyes seemed to focus on her mouth

"In that case, I'll come inside with you. While you put the things you bought away, I'll make us some instant coffee. I could do with a cup."

Alex's heart thumped. This was something she knew she should avoid, but after all he'd done for them, she didn't dare offend him. "Well...I won't say no to that."

As they went inside with her packages, the feeling grew stronger that she'd been on a date with him, and now they were coming home to spend the rest of the evening together. But she had to remember this was the middle of the afternoon and it wasn't a date!

For one thing, he was probably ten years younger than she, despite his maturity. For another, in the absence of Jenny's father, it was Buck's job to make certain this turned into a real vacation for her granddaughter, nothing more. She wished to heaven she could see it that way, but he'd managed to get under her skin. The only way to get him out was to leave Wyoming, but she and Jenny had only just arrived!

Dear Reader,

In *Home to Wyoming*, our bachelor hero rancher cannot believe that the gorgeous woman who comes to the Daddy Dude Ranch is a grandmother, raising her adorable seven-year-old granddaughter. Her age may not concern ex-marine Buck Summerhayes, but Alexis Wilson's engagement to another man does! What can he do to convince Alex she is the woman for him?

I hope you'll read this novel and experience all the thrills and chills of this love affair involving an unlikely couple who discover they are made for each other.

Enjoy!

Rebecca Winters

# HOME TO WYOMING

—

## REBECCA WINTERS

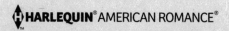

Recycling programs
for this product may
not exist in your area.

ISBN-13: 978-0-373-75471-7

HOME TO WYOMING

Copyright © 2013 by Rebecca Winters

**Printed in U.S.A.**

## ABOUT THE AUTHOR

Rebecca Winters, whose family of four children has now swelled to include five beautiful grandchildren, lives in Salt Lake City, Utah, in the land of the Rocky Mountains. With canyons and high alpine meadows full of wildflowers nearby, she never runs out of places to explore. These spaces, plus her favorite vacation spots in Europe, often end up as backgrounds for her romance novels. Writing is her passion, along with her family and church. Rebecca loves to hear from readers. If you wish to email her, please visit her website, www.cleanromances.com.

### Books by Rebecca Winters

#### HARLEQUIN AMERICAN ROMANCE

*Undercover Heroes
**Daddy Dude Ranch

Dedicated to all the selfless, wonderful, heroic grandmothers raising grandchildren after raising their own children. What greater love can there be?

# Chapter One

The station wagon pulled up to the curb in front of the airport in Colorado Springs. "Son, won't you please consider coming back home? I mean…for good."

He knew what she meant. Buck Summerhayes stared into his mother's pleading eyes before releasing the seat belt. They'd been through this half a dozen times since last March when he'd been given a medical discharge from Walter Reed National Military Medical Center in Bethesda, Maryland. The military had flown him home, where his family had been waiting to welcome him.

"You know I can't do that, Mom," he said, breaking into a cough. "I've made a commitment to Carson and Ross. I only flew here for a three-day break. Now I have to get back to Wyoming. Another family of a fallen soldier from California will be arriving in Jackson this evening. The guys and I take turns. This family will be my main responsibility for the next week, so I have to be there to pick them up."

"I realize that, but you have no idea how much we all miss you. Your father and brothers could use you in the business. At his last physical, the doctor told Dad he needed to slow down."

"Is it anything serious?" Buck asked in alarm.

"No, darling. He's just getting older, and all I'm saying is that Summerhayes Construction could use your help." Her face took on a sad expression. "Is it possible you're still staying away because of Melanie?"

A mother wasn't a mother for nothing. There was no point in avoiding the subject of Melanie Marsden, his high school girlfriend and the woman he'd hoped to marry after college.

But after his oldest brother, Pete, told him she and his brother Sam had fallen in love while Buck had been away at school and that they were afraid to tell him, he wished them all the best. After their wedding, he'd joined the marines and it would have become his lifelong career if he hadn't been diagnosed with acute dyspnea.

He frowned. "That might have been the case twelve years ago, but the war changed my life. When you see your buddies blown up in front of your face, it changes the way you think about things. I got over it a long time ago. Don't you remember? When I was first sent overseas, I wrote them a letter telling them how happy I was for them?"

"Yes, of course. They told me what you did after you were deployed and it meant the world to them, but I was just afraid that because you haven't met a woman to settle down with—"

"You thought I was still pining for her?" He cut her off. Incredulous, he said, "Mom—put your fears away. That's in the long-forgotten past. There've been many women since then and there will be many more to come. Jackson Hole is a mecca for Western goddesses decked out in cowboy hats and spurs."

His comment caused her to laugh. "If you want to know the truth, I love what I'm doing *now*. I need it."

She patted his cheek. "I believe you."

"I'm glad you do, because you don't know what survivor's guilt is like. When I was in the hospital, it tore me apart to think that some of our buddies didn't make it home to their wives and children. My friends and I decided the only way to get over it was to find a way to help people. Carson came up with the idea of turning his ranch into a dude ranch to give some of the victims' families a vacation. It struck a chord with Ross and me."

"It's a very noble idea, but what about your health?"

"We all see the doctor regularly. It could've been a lot worse. We like to think of it as our mark of bravery for breathing all that nasty stuff over in Afghanistan."

She leaned across and gave him a big hug and a kiss. "I love you, honey." Her voice was filled with tears.

Emotion swamped him as he reciprocated. "I love you, too. Stop worrying so much. I'll see you in six weeks."

He was saying that now, but he couldn't guarantee it. Their dude-ranch business for regular tourists was growing faster than they'd anticipated. As for their first experiment entertaining a war widow and her son, it had gone so well that Carson had just married Tracy Baretta, and her six-year-old son Johnny was the cutest little kid Buck had ever seen.

It seemed unbelievable that she'd flown out from Ohio at the beginning of June and now they were man and wife and raising a child together. It was only the third week of July. Johnny would be celebrating his seventh birthday next Thursday night. Carson and Tracy were in the middle of planning a big party for him.

In truth, Buck was envious of Carson. Bachelorhood was all right until the right woman came along, but Buck could see how fulfilling it would be to be a father and he felt that yearning growing stronger. Johnny had gotten to Buck in a big way.

Buck smiled when he thought about Carson. The second he'd laid eyes on Tracy, the ultimate bachelor cowboy was a goner. He couldn't be happier for his friend, but his nuptials had cut their numbers to an overall bachelor status of two.

After getting out of the car, he reached for his duffel bag on the backseat. "Drive safely, Mom. You're the only mother I've got. And please, don't worry. One day the right woman will come along and I'll get married and give you grandchildren."

"Oh, you." She chuckled. "Take care, my brave boy."

He was still her boy instead of a thirty-five-year-old vet with an annoying disease. As for *brave,* there were degrees of bravery. Like the heroism of one of their buddies who volunteered to be a target to save half a dozen of their platoon. He'd saved Buck's life. Now, *that* was brave.

Buck shook his head after watching his mother pull away, and then he hurried inside to make his afternoon flight to Jackson via Denver.

His forty-minute trip went smoothly, but after changing planes for the second leg, the pilot made an announcement. Bad weather and high winds over Wyoming meant their flight had to be diverted to Salt Lake.

Terrific.

Once he arrived at Salt Lake International to check his bag, he phoned Carson and Ross, but got voice mail for both and had to leave messages. Frustrated, he called the front desk at the ranch and was able to reach Willy and tell him about the delay. The part-time apprentice mechanic who alternated shifts with Susan and Patty told him not to worry. Alexis and Jenny Forrester—the mother and daughter he was supposed to meet—would probably be late, too. But no matter when they arrived, someone on staff would pick them up. Buck was to give them a call whenever he touched down.

Rather than sit it out in the passenger waiting area, he found a Starbucks on the lower level and grabbed a sandwich and coffee and a copy of *The Salt Lake Tribune.* The place was packed with tourists. A lot of flights had been delayed. After he'd eaten, he went back upstairs and walked behind the last row of lounge seats until he came to the end where he found a free one. In the next chair was a blonde girl, maybe six or seven years old, curled up asleep next to her mother.

After sitting, he opened his newspaper to the business section. Unlike many other states, Utah was experiencing some growth of new housing in an otherwise depressed economy. He hoped things would pick up in Colorado, but it probably wouldn't happen for some time.

Beside him, Buck could hear the mother talking to someone on her cell phone. "I know a week seems like a long time, but it's something I feel I had to do for a lot of reasons….You know why….Please try to understand, Frank….Love you, too."

The call ended just as Buck had finished the editorial

page. When he felt a spasm coming on, he coughed into the newspaper to muffle the sound, hoping he hadn't startled the little girl, who straightened in her seat and rubbed her eyes.

"Now that you're awake, let's go to the restroom, sweetheart," the mother said in a well-modulated voice. Buck would bet it wasn't a coincidence that she'd made the suggestion at that particular moment. Chagrined to think he was probably the reason they got up, he kept his face hidden behind the paper and flipped to the financial section.

The guys had joked about wearing signs that said their coughs weren't contagious; maybe it wasn't such a bad idea.

When he'd finished reading the paper, he tucked it between him and the side of the chair. As he sat leaning forward with his hands clasped between his knees, waiting for the announcement that his flight was now boarding, the little girl walked in front of him to take her seat.

Behind her came the most gorgeous pair of long legs he'd ever seen on a woman. Her linen-colored skirt fit snugly around shapely hips and legs to flare at the knee, and she was wearing beige wedge sandals.

Compelled to look up, he took in the top half of her shapely body clothed in a summery crocheted top. Her wavy chestnut-colored hair hid her profile as she sat down next to her daughter. Surprised by his strong reaction to the stranger, it took all the willpower he possessed not to stand so he could get a better look at her. No one appreciated a beautiful woman more than he did.

When he'd told his mom there'd been many women

in his life, he hadn't exaggerated, which was why he was so surprised that this particular female had so captured his attention. It appeared that she and her daughter were taking his flight, but that didn't mean Jackson was their final destination. The mother and daughter he was supposed to meet were flying in from Sacramento, California—could they have been rerouted to Salt Lake City, as well?

In the middle of his reverie, he heard the announcement that his flight was ready for boarding. The woman and her daughter had already gone ahead to join the lineup. He was the last one to board the midsize passenger plane. Since his flight had been diverted, he was the last to be given a seat assignment and had to sit at the rear of the plane.

Before he reached his seat, he spotted the mother who'd caught his eye sitting on the left a couple of rows ahead. She was helping her daughter with the seat belt. He noted there was no wedding ring on her left hand. She could still be married, he surmised, or then again Frank—the man she'd been talking to on the phone earlier—could be a boyfriend. Buck was forced to keep moving down the aisle and he still didn't get a look at her face, because her hair had fallen forward.

The flight was a short one, but bumpy toward the end. After the plane landed, three-fourths of the passengers got off, but he saw no sign of the woman and her daughter. Oddly disappointed, he made his way over to the baggage claim to retrieve his duffel bag and call the ranch.

"Buck!"

He wheeled around to see Willy carrying a sign for the Teton Valley Dude Ranch. "Hey, Willy."

The twenty-six-year-old pushed his cowboy hat back on his head. "I didn't know you'd be on this flight. You didn't by any chance see a woman and little girl on board, did you? The Forresters didn't come in on the last flight. I was supposed to pick them up in front, but they weren't outside, so I figured they'd be in here getting their luggage. Some of the bags still haven't been claimed."

So the woman and her daughter were the Forresters!

After overhearing part of her phone conversation with "Frank," he'd pretty much ruled her out as possibly being the widow of Daniel Forrester.

The marine's heroism had been lauded after he'd taken a grenade to save members of his platoon from certain death. He'd been buried only nine months ago. Not that his wife couldn't have found herself in another relationship this fast. The woman was a raving beauty.

Come to think of it, Melanie and Buck's brother had gotten close much faster than that while he'd been away at school. But Melanie hadn't lost a husband in the war. Somehow, Buck would have expected a grieving widow to take a little longer to recover. The woman had already removed her wedding ring. Still, it was none of his business.

"I sat next to a mother and daughter in the airport lounge in Salt Lake, but I had no idea they were the family we're hosting. Unfortunately, I was the last one off the plane." He frowned, wondering if the turbulence had made one of them ill. They were his responsibility, after all. "Maybe they're in the restroom. Stay here."

He started across the terminal lounge to look around when he saw them come out of an alcove and head for the luggage carousel. The little girl clung to her mother's hand. Buck closed in on them.

"Mrs. Forrester?"

She swung halfway around, giving him the frontal view he'd been trying to glimpse earlier. Midnight-blue eyes connected with his. He thought she looked surprised to see him. She probably hadn't expected the man with the cough at the Salt Lake airport to be the one greeting her.

She was maybe thirty. A generously curved mouth and high cheekbones were set in an oval face. Her classic features appealed to him as much as the rest of her. She was a very attractive woman. He thought of Carson and the way he'd felt when he'd first laid eyes on Tracy.

*Damn.*

He looked down at her daughter, who showed all the promise of growing up to be a beauty herself. "I'm Buck Summerhayes, one of the partners at the dude ranch. Welcome to Teton Valley." He shook her hand.

"Thank you, Mr. Summerhayes. We're very happy to be here." Although her tone sounded cordial enough, she seemed a bit subdued. Maybe the flight had made her ill.

"Let me introduce Willy Felder. He's one of our staff and will be taking us back to the ranch."

"My name's Alex. How do you do?" She shook hands with him.

"If you'll tell Willy which of those bags are yours, he'll take them out to the van."

"They're the red ones."

"Red's my favorite color," the little girl piped up.

Buck smiled. "So I can see." He squatted in front of her. She was wearing jeans and a red top with a princess on the front. "It's nice to meet you, Jennifer. I'm glad you're coming to the ranch. I forget—are you six or seven?"

"Seven."

"Jenny had a birthday last week," her mother explained.

"Well, congratulations, Jenny!" he said. "The owner of the dude ranch, Carson Lundgren, has a son named Johnny who's going to turn seven next Thursday. You'll meet him at breakfast in the morning. He'll want to show you his pony, Goldie."

"I've never seen a real pony."

"We've got four of them."

"Can I have a ride on one?"

He smiled. "You can pick your favorite and start riding first thing in the morning. Do you know you have the prettiest green eyes?"

"So do you." Her comment took him by surprise. She seemed so grown up for a seven-year-old. "My daddy's were green, too."

"That explains their color." A lump lodged in his throat. This was Daniel Forrester's little girl, who would have to live without him for the rest of her life. "Your daddy was a very brave man. We invited you to the ranch as our way of honoring him."

Her features sobered, but she didn't tear up. "Were you in the war?"

"Yes."

"How come you're not there now?"

"That's a good question. It's because I got sick while

I was in Afghanistan and had to come home. So did my friends Carson and Ross who run the ranch. They have coughs, too."

"I heard you coughing at the airport."

"I saw you sleeping, and I'm sorry if I woke you up. I cough a lot, but just remember you can't catch it from me."

"Why not?" She was curious like Johnny, a trait he found endearing.

"Because it's not a cough from a cold. It's from breathing the bad air in the war."

She looked up at her mother with an anxious expression. "Do you think Daddy got that cough, too?"

"I don't think so, or he would have said something in his emails."

Jenny looked a trifle pale. The mention of her father must have upset her. "Let's get going to the ranch. It's only a short drive away. I'm sure you're tired and hungry."

"I got sick on the plane."

That explained her pallor. "I'm sorry about that. Our plane did get bounced around, but we're on the ground now. Are you thirsty?"

"Not yet."

Buck got to his feet and turned to the girl's mother. "Are you ready to go?"

"Yes, thank you."

He guessed that she couldn't wait to get to the ranch and put her daughter to bed. "Then let's go. The van's right outside."

When they exited the terminal into the darkness, the wind was blowing so fiercely it was a good thing he wasn't wearing his cowboy hat. He saw lightning flashes followed by thunder. It was going to rain before they reached the ranch. Willy opened the van door to help Jenny and her mother get in. A strong gust caused her skirt to ride up those fabulous legs just as Buck climbed in behind her. Once behind the wheel, Willy pulled away. Two minutes later, the downpour started.

"Where's that big mountain?" Jenny wanted to know. She rested her head against her mother, who had a protective arm around her. He noticed she squeezed her daughter harder every time there was another clap of thunder.

"The Grand Teton is to the right of us, but with the storm, you won't be able to see it until tomorrow."

"I'm scared."

Willy had turned on the windshield wipers, but it was still hard to see.

"You don't need to be, Jenny. We're perfectly safe in the van, and in a few minutes we'll have you tucked in bed in our cabin. You'll be as cozy as the red squirrel who lives in a hole in the fir tree near the main ranch house."

"It's really red?"

When Buck smiled, Jenny's mother reciprocated. "Not exactly like your top. More of a burnt-orange-red color. Moppy likes pine nuts."

"Moppy?" Jenny squealed in delight, her fear forgotten for the moment.

"That's Carson's name for her."

"I want to see her."

"Tomorrow she'll be running up and down the tree,

chattering her head off. You won't be able to miss her. She has a huge bushy tail."

"What if it's still raining tomorrow and she doesn't come out?"

"By morning, this storm will be long gone."

"Promise?"

Buck had checked his smartphone for the weather report before he'd exited the plane. He caught her mother's eye before he said, "I promise the sun will be out."

She kissed her daughter's forehead. "If Mr. Summerhayes made a promise, then you can believe it, sweetheart."

"Please, call me Buck."

"That sounds like a horse's name."

Jenny's comment made him laugh and brought on a cough. When it subsided, he said, "A lot of people say that and you're absolutely right, but I was named Bradford after my great grandfather. My dad nicknamed me Buck because his grandfather liked the Buck Rogers comic books and thought I looked like him."

"Who was Buck Rogers?"

"A spaceman."

The girl glanced at her mom. "Have you heard of Buck Rogers?"

"Yes. I loved science fiction growing up."

Buck had been enjoying their conversation so much, he didn't realize they'd driven up in front of the guest cabin until Willy turned off the engine.

He leaned toward the two of them. "The worst of the storm has passed. I'll unlock the cabin door and then you make a run for it so you don't get too wet. Willy will bring in your luggage. But before we go in, I have to put on an oxygen mask."

Jenny looked startled. "How come?"

"Because housekeeping has made a fire for you and smoke hurts my lungs. The guys and I have started carrying an oxygen apparatus in all our vehicles because we never know when we'll need it." He opened the small locker on the floor and pulled out a mask and canister. "Don't be scared."

"I won't."

"If my great grandfather saw me now, he'd think I really was Buck Rogers from outer space." He put on the mask and turned on the oxygen before leaving the van. In a minute, he had the cabin door unlocked.

Jenny and her mother hurried over the threshold into the living room where the glow from the hearth illuminated their faces. Judging by their expressions, they found the cabin welcoming and moved closer to the heat source.

When he and the guys had built the cabins, they'd decided on wood-burning fireplaces for their authenticity.

"Ooh, this feels good, doesn't it, sweetheart?"

"I wish our house had a fireplace."

Pleased with their response to their temporary home away from home, Buck helped Willy take the bags into one of the two bedrooms adjoined by a bathroom. "Ladies," he said as he came back to the living room, "you have all the comforts of home here. There's a coffeemaker and microwave. The fridge is stocked with drinks and there's a basket of fruit, along with packets of hot chocolate and snacks on the table. If you'll look in the closets, there are extra pillows and blankets."

"This is wonderful," she exclaimed, looking around at the rest of the room, her eyes landing on the state-of-the-art entertainment center.

"If you need anything, just dial zero on the house phone by your bed and the front desk will let me know, no matter the hour." He studied his guests. "Is there anything I can get you before I say good-night?"

Jenny stared up at him with a worried expression. "Do you feel okay?"

"I feel fine. Do I look too frightening?"

"No, but I feel bad for you. Where do you live?"

"In the main ranch house. It's close by, but you couldn't see it in the storm. I hope your stomach will feel better by morning. We serve breakfast in the big dining room from six to nine. Lunch is from twelve to two and dinner from five to eight."

"Will you be there?"

"I wouldn't be anywhere else."

"That's good." Jenny's quiet response touched him. "Do you have to wear the mask at the ranch house?"

"Only if they make a fire in the big fireplace, which doesn't happen very often."

"You're brave."

"No. Your dad was the one who was brave. If you've noticed, the thunder and lightning have already moved on. It isn't scary anymore. I bet Moppy is already peeking out of her hole and planning her breakfast for tomorrow. The rain will have made a lot of pine nuts fall to the ground."

The little girl's face broke into a sweet smile. Daniel Forrester's daughter was a treasure. It tore him up to think she'd lost her father. "I want to watch."

He cleared his throat. "She'll be up early."

"I don't know if we can say the same thing for us," her mother remarked.

Buck was trying hard not to think too much about Daniel's wife and his unwanted attraction to her. He threw her a glance. "Tomorrow will be your first day here. After coming from Sacramento, you need to get used to the altitude."

"You can certainly tell the air is thinner here."

"It's a bit of a change and that flight had to be unsettling to a lot of the passengers. Jenny? You're a courageous girl to have handled it. Something tells me you're just like your daddy."

When she didn't say anything, he glanced at her mother and saw tears pooling in her dark blue eyes. "You don't know how true that is." Her comment piqued his curiosity, but now wasn't the time to probe.

"Good night."

"Good night, Mr. Summerhayes."

"Buck."

"Yes, Buck. Sorry."

"No problem. What would you like me to call you?"

"Alex. It's short for Alexis," Jenny volunteered. "Frank calls her that, but she doesn't like it."

*"Jenny—"*

Amused, Buck's gaze swerved back to the seven-year-old. "Who's Frank?" Might as well learn the truth right now. Hopefully it would help kill his interest in her.

"He's going to be my new grandpa."

"You mean, your grandmother is getting married to Frank?"

"Yes. After we get back from our trip."

"That's an exciting thing to look forward to."

The little girl's face crumpled. "No, it isn't." Before he could blink, she ran out of the living room into the bedroom where he'd put their bags and shut the door.

Alex looked shattered. "I'm sorry. She's been upset lately, but never around anyone other than me."

"It's probably just because she's not feeling well and the storm scared her. I'll leave so you can take care of her. I can show you around the ranch tomorrow."

"Please don't go yet. There's something you need to know. I was going to tell you at the airport, but it didn't feel like the right time. Jenny needs to cry this out and she'll be fine by herself for a few minutes. I'm afraid this can't wait."

He felt her urgency. "What is it?"

"Do you mind if we sit down?"

Wondering what this was all about, Buck sat in one of the chairs, while she took the end of the couch. "I'll make this as short as possible. My name is Alex Wilson. I'm Jenny's grandmother, *not* her mother."

Buck shot up from the chair. *Grandmother?* It wasn't possible. She looked so young! His mind had to do a complete thought reversal.

"Two months after Daniel was killed, my daughter, Christy, died. She'd suffered from leukemia for a short time before her passing. I became Jenny's legal guardian."

A slug to the gut couldn't have come as more of a shock.

"When the letter arrived from the Teton Valley Dude Ranch inviting Christy and Jenny to come, I was so touched you couldn't imagine. But the invitation was meant for my daughter." He heard tears in her voice.

"I called Daniel's commanding officer so he could explain my situation to Mr. Lundgren—Carson—and tell him the reason why we couldn't accept such a great honor. He told me that since I was Jenny's legal guardian and had virtually raised her since Christy fell ill, no one had more of a right to come and bring Jenny than I did.

"I struggled with it. In fact, up to a week ago, I was ready to call the ranch and tell you about my daughter's death. I wanted you to give this honor to a well-deserving widow and her child. But the commanding officer wouldn't hear of it. By that time Jenny was so excited to come, I couldn't disappoint her. With both her parents' deaths, she's been through so much grief. But I wanted you to know the truth."

Buck couldn't begin to fathom it. "I'm glad he insisted you come. After hearing what you've told me, I speak for Carson and Ross when I say we couldn't be happier that Daniel Forrester's daughter and mother-in-law have accepted our invitation. He was a real hero. We're hoping this trip will let Jenny know how special we thought her father was."

Her eyes glazed over. "You're very kind, Buck. Daniel was a terrific son-in-law. My daughter couldn't have chosen better. Which brings me to what happened tonight. I'm planning to be married to a man I met over two years ago. He's been careful because of Jenny's feelings and has only proposed recently.

"Jenny knows we're planning marriage and I'd hoped she was getting used to the idea, but tonight's outburst has shown me she's not ready to share me with Frank yet. To be truthful, he was worried about my bringing her on this trip and is still unhappy about it. She adored her daddy and Frank thought meeting more ex-marines might be too painful a reminder of her loss.

"But she acted so excited about coming here that I couldn't disappoint her. I'm embarrassed for the way she acted out just now. If I see any more of this behavior while we're here, we'll have to leave, and I'll reimburse you for the airline tickets and any expense you've gone to for us."

"I'm sure that won't be necessary. Once she meets Johnny, she'll be so preoccupied that she'll forget to be upset. There's something about this ranch that gives people a new perspective."

She stood and walked over to the door. "I hope you're right. I can tell you one thing. You knew exactly how to calm Jenny's fears tonight. For that, I'm indebted to you. Thank you for inviting us here. You'll never know what that letter from the ranch did for me and Jenny. At a very dark hour for her, it gave us the hope that a brighter future was in store."

Buck could hardly swallow for the sorrow he was feeling for their family. "I'm so glad it did that for you. Good night, Alex. See you in the morning."

Without lingering, he hurried outside and whipped off his mask. After the rain, the scent of sage hung heavy in the air. Willy was waiting for him in the van. "Everything all right, Buck? You look…disturbed."

He put his apparatus back in the locker. "To be honest, disturbed doesn't come close to what I'm feeling." His thoughts were in chaos.

Willy started driving them along the puddled dirt

road toward the parking area at the side of the main ranch house. "Mrs. Forrester is a knockout."

That she was. "Just so you know, her name is actually Alex Wilson. She's Jenny Forrester's grandmother."

*"Grandmother—"* At that revelation, Willy pressed on the brakes and looked at him. "Come on… You're joshing me, right? How could she be a grandmother?"

Buck's eyebrows lifted. "I don't know. I've been trying to do the math. Her granddaughter just turned seven." He could hear Willy's brain working.

"She would have to be forty or damn near close."

"Yep." But she could pass for ten years younger and was planning to get married. "Her daughter died soon after Daniel Forrester was killed by a grenade."

Quiet reigned until they reached the ranch house. "That's awful. The poor little kid."

"You can say that again." They'd both suffered too many losses. Buck opened the door. "Thanks for the lift, Willy. See you tomorrow."

Buck entered the ranch through the front door, coughing his way back to the office to find the guys. What he had to tell them would blow their minds. During those weeks in the hospital when they'd come up with the idea to run a dude ranch to honor soldiers' families, Buck could never have dreamed up a scenario like this one.

# *Chapter Two*

Relieved that Buck Summerhayes knew the truth about everything, Alex locked up and walked back to the bedroom. Jenny was lying on top of one of the twin beds with her head buried in the pillow. Alex sat at her side and started rubbing her back.

"Did Buck leave?"

"Yes."

"I wish he didn't have to go. He's nice."

"I agree, but it's late. He needs his sleep and so do you. Before he left, I told him about your mom."

"I'm so glad we came. Do you think he's in pain?"

"No. As long as he doesn't breathe smoke, I'm sure he's fine."

"I like him."

"I know."

"He has pretty green eyes. They're lighter than Daddy's."

"You're right."

With his full head of thick light brown hair and his well-defined physique, Buck Summerhayes was undeniably an attractive man—and he had a way about him that had charmed her granddaughter. She suspected he charmed most females. Alex hadn't seen a wedding band. Since he hadn't mentioned a wife or children, Alex presumed he was still a bachelor.

"I have something to tell you that will make you happier, but you have to turn over so we can look at each other."

Jenny flipped over on her back. "What is it?"

"When we go home, I'm going to tell Frank I'm not ready to marry him yet."

She sat up straight. "You're not?"

"No. You and I need more time." Tonight's outburst in front of a stranger had given her ample proof that it was too soon for any more changes in Jenny's life.

The girl's slim arms caught Alex around the neck in a powerful hug. "I love you, Nana!"

"I love you too, sweetheart. How does your tummy feel now? Would you like a soda?"

"Yes, please."

"Good. I'll see what I can find."

Alex went in the other room and opened the mini-fridge. There were a variety of drinks. She drew out a ginger ale and a cola. Before she went back to the bedroom, she checked on the fire. It was burning down. With the screen in place, she didn't need to worry about sparks catching something on fire.

"Here you go." Alex sat on the other twin bed and pulled out the brochure that had been included with the letter she'd received from the dude ranch. Together they made plans for the next day while they drank their sodas.

She knew Frank was waiting for her to call him, but for the first time, she didn't feel like talking to him. He hadn't wanted her to come to the ranch, and Jenny was thrilled to be there. Alex felt as if she was in a tug-of-war. It took too much emotional energy. Instead of calling, she reached for her cell phone and texted him that they'd arrived safely but were exhausted. She'd phone him tomorrow. Alex meant it about being worn out.

With that decision made, she and Jenny opened their suitcases to get out the things they'd need for bed, including the framed photograph of Jenny's parents that Alex placed on the telephone table for her.

"We'll put everything else away in the morning," she said. After brushing their teeth, they said their prayers, and then she turned out the lights and they climbed under their comfy quilts. Alex liked their yellow-and-white-checkered design. The whole log cabin had a cheery ambience. There was no doubt that she and Jenny needed a little cheer in their lives.

In her heart of hearts, she was relieved about the decision she'd made where Frank was concerned. Alex had refused to wear his engagement ring yet because deep down she'd known Jenny wasn't ready. She'd seen the signs, but tonight's incident had crystallized things for her.

Marriage was a big step for anyone, but an even bigger one for a woman who'd be forty-one in a few months and had never been married. Frank was fifty-five but looked fifty because he played a lot of tennis and kept fit. They'd met when she'd started working at the bank where he was the vice president. After he lost his wife to cancer, they became friends. That friendship deepened following Christy's death and they fell in love.

She liked his two married children and grandchildren. He had a maturity and stability that were especially appealing to her. Jenny liked him fairly well, but the mention of marriage was something else. Obviously it was too soon after her daddy's death for her to imagine a man living with them under the same roof.

Alex knew it would come as a blow when she got home and told Frank she couldn't marry him yet. For her, intimacy was out of the question until their wedding, because she refused to anticipate their vows as she'd done with Kyle when she was seventeen.

Although she hated the thought of disappointing Frank further, Jenny had to come first. Alex had raised one daughter, and now she was raising another. The responsibility was enormous. Frank would help her, but not until Jenny was ready. And as much as Alex was looking forward to marriage, they had to get past this problem first. She guessed she was going to find out how patient Frank could be.

With a troubled sigh, she turned on her other side. When Jenny had been in the first grade, Alex had arranged various playdates for her. One girl named Mandy was turning into a friend Jenny really liked. They got along great, but she needed more friends. She hoped that she would make some friends at the ranch for the time that they were there. Maybe there would be some other families with a girl. And Buck had mentioned a boy....

She and Jenny had been through so much in the past year, but if there was any consolation, it was that her daughter and Daniel were together in heaven. Alex loved her granddaughter and was determined they were going to have a wonderful life and enjoy this special week, which had come as an unexpected gift.

To her surprise, her thoughts drifted to the handsome

ex-marine who'd flown on the plane with them to Jackson. Who would have guessed he was one of the owners of the dude ranch.

Buck's words rang in her ears: *There's something about this ranch that gives you a new perspective.* She had the feeling he'd been speaking from personal experience and prayed it would be equally true for her and Jenny.

"NANA? Somebody's knocking at the door. Do you think it's Buck?" Jenny asked with an eagerness that surprised Alex.

"I have no idea." Alex had awakened thinking about him and how good he'd been with Jenny last night. She knew married men who didn't handle their own children's fears as well as the way he'd handled Jenny's. She shot up in bed and brushed the hair out of her eyes to check her watch. It was five after eight.

There was another knock. "Can I get it?"

"Go ahead." Alex had slept in her sweats and felt decent enough as she followed Jenny into the other room. Her granddaughter had inherited the best features from both Christy and Daniel. She looked so cute in her Sleeping Beauty pajamas. Alex thought she was the most adorable girl on the planet.

When Jenny opened the door, they were met by a brown-eyed, brown-haired boy in a black Stetson and cowboy boots. He wore a holster around his hips and was holding a cap gun in one hand. Alex decided she was looking at the most adorable *boy* on the planet.

"Hi! I'm Johnny Lundgren. Are you Jenny?" Her granddaughter's green eyes widened in astonishment before she nodded. "Do you want to have breakfast with me?"

She turned to Alex. "Would that be okay with you, Nana?"

"Of course." She moved to the door. "Hi, Johnny. I'm Alex."

"I know. You're her grandmother."

Alex couldn't help smiling. He had amazing confidence for his age. "That's right. Last night Buck told us you're Mr. Lundgren's son."

"Yep."

"We're very pleased to meet you." She shook his hand. "We understand you have a pony named Goldie."

"Yep. I'll show you to her after breakfast. Do you want to see me ride her?"

"Yes. I want to ride, too."

"Okay. We'll go after we eat. I like Fruit Loops. What about you?"

Jenny thought for a minute. "Do they have Boo Berry?"

"I think so, but it makes your mouth blue."

"I know." Both children laughed at the same time. A small miracle had occurred with her granddaughter. Buck Summerhayes wasn't the only male around the ranch who had charm. "Come on in, Johnny. We'll be ready in a few minutes."

"Thanks."

"Where did you get your cap gun?"

"In Jackson. Maybe your nana will buy one for you." Jenny turned to her. "Would you?"

"We'll see. First we need to get dressed."

"Okay."

Alex hustled Jenny into the bedroom. They took turns quickly showering, and then both dived into their suitcases for jeans and tops. She guessed that Buck was behind this and knew what he was doing. Here Alex had been hoping there'd be a girl for Jenny to play with, but Johnny Lundgren was so cute and interesting that he had her granddaughter mesmerized. Better strike while the iron was hot.

In fewer than twenty minutes, they'd freshened up and brushed their hair. "I think we're ready." They joined Johnny and the three of them stepped out of the cabin. The Teton mountain range rose majestically in the distance. The sight of it in the sunshine took Alex's breath away. You would never have known there'd been a storm last night.

"There's the big mountain!" Jenny cried, pointing to it. You couldn't miss it.

"Yep. That's the Grand Teton."

"What does *Teton* mean?" The question didn't surprise her. Her granddaughter was the most observant, curious person Alex had ever known.

Johnny looked puzzled. "I'll have to ask Dad."

"Have you ever seen anything more beautiful, sweetheart?"

"I didn't know it was so tall!"

Alex looked all around. There were a few other cabins besides their own, and they were all surrounded by sagebrush. A distance away, she could see the main ranch house—a big rustic two-story affair with a copse of trees to the side. It was the type of home the man on the horse in the Great American Cowboy ad might live in. Alex was being fanciful, but this ranch was the kind of place dreams were made of.

The children moved ahead of her as they walked along the road.

Johnny turned to Jenny. "Do you want to camp out on the mountain?"

"Have you done it?"

"A couple of times."

"Is it scary?"

"Only once, when we got caught in a storm."

"I don't like storms."

"It was okay. Dad was with me. We stayed in our tent and drank hot chocolate until it was over."

Alex caught up to them. "That sounds fun."

Jenny's expression sobered. "I don't have a dad anymore."

"I know."

Her blond head lifted. "You do?"

"Yep. I know all about you. Your daddy was a marine like mine, and they both got killed in the war."

"But I thought you said you went hiking with your dad."

"I meant my *new* dad."

After a pause, Jenny said, "Your mom got married again?"

"Yep. To Carson."

"Do you like him?"

"He's my favorite person in the whole world besides my dad."

Alex knew what her granddaughter was thinking. Frank wasn't her favorite person in the world, but she didn't say it out loud, for which Alex was grateful.

Suddenly a lovely blonde woman in a blouse and jeans came walking around the side of the building where Alex could see half a dozen vehicles of different kinds were parked. "There you are, Johnny. I was just coming to look for you."

"I'm afraid it's our fault." Alex smiled at her. "Jenny and I needed to get showered and dressed while he waited for us. You must be Johnny's mother."

"Yes. I'm Tracy Lundgren and you have to be Alex Wilson. Welcome to the ranch." They shook hands.

"Thank you. Your son makes a wonderful guide. We're thrilled to be here."

"No more than we are to have you." She walked over to Jenny. "Buck told us you just had your seventh birthday. Johnny's turning seven next week. It's an amazing coincidence. You'll have to come to his party. We're going to go into Jackson to the Funorama. They have all kinds of slides and games, and you can eat all the pizza you want."

Johnny eyed Jenny. "Do you like pizza?"

She nodded. "It's my favorite food."

"Mine, too."

"I like pepperoni."

"Me, too."

Alex and Tracy exchanged amused glances. Johnny's mother was probably in her late twenties and seemed so friendly. Christy would have liked her. Alex's heart ached for what her daughter was missing, but today wasn't the time to be sad. Johnny's arrival at their front door had brought its own brand of sunshine, something they badly needed.

"Which tree does Moppy live in?"

Johnny looked surprised. "How do you know about her?"

"Buck told me last night."

He ran over to a big fir. "See that hole?"

Jenny moved closer. "Do you think she's inside?"

"I don't know. When she hears voices, she hides. We'll come back after breakfast and sneak up on her."

"Okay."

They rounded the corner to enter the main doors of the lobby. Suddenly Jenny cried, "Look, Nana—"

Alex turned in time to see what had to be the biggest moose head ever. It was mounted above the door frame. "My heavens—he's enormous."

Johnny tilted his hat back. "Dad calls him Mathoozela."

*"Mathoozela?"* At this point Jenny's eyes had rounded. "I never heard that name before."

"It's because he was so old when he died."

By now Tracy's shoulders were shaking along with Alex's. She put an arm around her granddaughter's shoulders. "The Bible says Methusela was the oldest man who ever lived."

"Yep. Dad says he lived to be 969 years. He thinks maybe that's how old this moose got to be."

"Maybe he's even older," sounded a male voice behind them.

"Dad!"

Alex watched as the attractive dark blond Stetson-wearing cowboy gave his stepson a bear hug before picking him up. "So, introduce me."

"This is Jenny Forrester and that's her nana, Alex. My dad's name is Carson."

Carson Lundgren smiled, his eyes a bright blue. "Welcome to the ranch." He coughed. "We've been waiting for you, especially when we found out your granddaughter was the same age as Johnny. The more kids around here, the better."

Alex agreed. "We're very excited to be here." What wasn't there about these people to like?

"Our other partner Ross would be here, but he's on an overnight pack trip with some of our guests. You'll meet him tomorrow."

After the greetings were over, Carson put Johnny back down and curled an arm around his wife's waist. They appeared to be crazy about each other. Alex remembered being in love like that with Christy's father once, but once she told him she was pregnant, she never saw him again.

Jenny looked up at him. "Is Buck here?"

"Did I hear someone say my name?"

At the sound of the deep, familiar male voice, Alex spun around to see the former marine walk toward them from a doorway beyond the front-desk area. Last night he'd been wearing a jacket and chinos. This morning he was dressed in cowboy boots, a Western shirt and jeans that molded his powerful thighs. His rugged good looks caused her pulse to race for no good reason.

"*I* did." Jenny smiled up at him. "But we didn't see Moppy this morning."

"Don't worry. We'll catch her after dinner when she doesn't think anyone is watching. Have you had breakfast yet?" Jenny shook her head. "Are you hungry?" She nodded. "Good. Then let's go in the dining room. We could eat the three big trout I caught early this morning."

"You did?" Jenny looked amazed.

"Do you know what a trout is?" Johnny asked her.

"Yes, it's fish."

Alex was glad her granddaughter could hold her own on something. Mirth filled Buck's green eyes as he lifted them to Alex, bringing on an unexpected rush of adrenaline. What on earth was wrong with her? "How about you?"

"One medium trout sounds delicious."

His low chuckle traveled to her insides. "I caught a couple of those, too." He turned to Carson. "Are you going to join us?"

"I'm afraid I've got a meeting with the stockmen, but I'll try to catch up with you at the barn later in the day." Alex remembered reading that the dude ranch was also a cattle ranch. These men led busy lives. He hugged Johnny again. "Have you got a pony picked out for Jenny yet?"

He whispered to his father. Carson nodded. "Good choice."

"Hey, Dad? Jenny wants to know what *Teton* means."

Suddenly both men broke out in wide grins. "I'll leave that to your mom to explain. Got to run."

"Coward," Tracy said to her husband with a grin as he kissed her. "Come on, everyone. We need to eat breakfast while we still can."

The five of them walked through the great room with its floor-to-ceiling fireplace and entered the main dining room. Wagon-wheel chandeliers hung from the ceiling. Alex saw several families seated with older teenagers. Only one table was empty. All of them were covered in

red-and-white-checked cloths with white daisies forming the centerpieces. Alex loved the decor.

Once they were seated and had been served their orders, Buck looked at Alex and Jenny. "Last night you
were too tired for me to tell you much about the ranch.
Carson Lundgren's great-great-grandfather purchased
this land in 1908 and turned it into the Teton Valley
Ranch where they ran cattle and we still do, today.

"His grandparents raised him and he became a rodeo
champion known as 'King of the Cowboys.' Since I went
into business with him and Ross Livingston, we've also
begun operating the ranch as a dude ranch for tourists
who make reservations with us and are paying guests.
But once a month we use part of the money to invite
one war widow and her children to stay with us. You
two are our honored guests for this week and have access to all the facilities free of charge."

"We're thrilled to be here," Alex exclaimed. "Jenny
and I read the brochure. You offer so many activities
we can't believe it. I think it would be impossible to do
them all."

He chuckled. "Most everyone wants to try horseback riding, so you'll probably want to invest in some
Western gear. We also offer fishing. If you want to go
down the Snake River in a raft or a kayak, we'll take
you. Some people want to do mountain climbing or go
hiking.

"We also have a swimming pool off the games room
on the other side of the dining room. Ping-Pong, cards,
television—it's all at your disposal. We plan pack trips
to the lake for overnight campouts and there are hot-air-
balloon rides you can enjoy over Jackson Hole. You can

also attend the Jackson Rodeo if that appeals to you. If you need a car, we'll provide you with one so you can go into town to shop, see a movie or try out one of the restaurants.

"Housekeeping makes up your cabins and supplies you with laundry service. Just put what needs washing or cleaning in the laundry bag under the sink and leave it on the peg of the door. It'll be returned to you later in the day.

"As the brochure explained, this is also a cattle ranch with a foreman and stockmen. They work up on the mountain with the cattle. If Jenny wants to see the herd, that can be arranged, too."

Alex smiled at him. "I'm still trying to take it all in."

"What do you think you want to do first?"

Jenny glanced at Alex. "Can we go buy me a cap gun like Johnny's?"

Buck chuckled. "Sure we can. I'll drive us into Jackson and we'll get you some other stuff, too."

"Can I go?" Johnny eyed his mother for permission.

"If it's all right with Buck."

"We couldn't get along without him."

"Be sure to mind Buck and be helpful." Tracy gave her son a kiss and excused herself. "I'm overseeing some heavy-duty cleaning. I'll see all of you later."

She left and Buck finished off a second trout and hash browns with another cup of coffee. Alex was already full from her fish and biscuits. "That was delicious."

"That's good," Buck said, smiling at her. "Johnny? Are you about ready to go?"

"Yep."

"Why don't you come and help me unload some supplies from the truck? Then we'll pick you ladies up at
your cabin in, say, half an hour."

Alex nodded. "That sounds perfect." She needed to
phone Frank before they went into town.

Johnny slid off his chair. "See you guys soon."

"Okay." Jenny ate her last spoonful of cereal. "We'll
be ready."

"Hey—you've got blue teeth."

They both giggled.

Alex hadn't heard such a happy sound come out of
her granddaughter in a long time. She herself felt lighter
as the four of them parted company outside and they
made their way back to the cabin.

"Why didn't Johnny's dad tell us what *Teton* means?"

She remembered the way Buck's eyes lit up *and* the
way it made her feel—as if little sunbursts had exploded
inside her. "Well, it's only a guess, but I imagine the
range got its name from the Indians and early trappers
who thought those peaks reminded them of a woman.
You know what I mean?"

Alex had learned early that the unvarnished truth
was the only way to get her granddaughter off a subject. Euphemisms didn't work with her.

"Oh." Jenny's eyes twinkled as she looked at Alex.
Sometimes, she seemed older than seven. "Do you think
Johnny knows?" They'd reached the cabin and went
inside.

"No, or he wouldn't have asked his father in front of
everyone. One day his dad will tell him."

In the midst of their illuminating conversation, her
phone rang, interrupting a special moment. *Frank.* He

had to be wondering why she hadn't phoned him yet. It was because Johnny had wakened them out of a sound sleep and they'd rushed to make breakfast on time.

"Jenny? Be sure to brush your teeth."

"I will. Nana? Will you tell Frank what we talked about last night?"

*Oh, Jenny.* Nothing got past her granddaughter.

JOHNNY HELPED BUCK unload some supplies at the new house Carson was having built on the property for his family down near the Snake River. So far everyone was living in the ranch house with Buck and Ross upstairs, and Carson and his family on the main floor.

Buck had been overseeing the construction. After the foundation had been poured, he'd spent the next three days on a brief vacation in Colorado Springs with his family while he waited for it to settle. He hadn't seen his parents since March. Now it was back to work.

He talked with the construction workers who'd already started the framing. When everything appeared under control, he shoved his cowboy hat back on his head and turned to Johnny. "Come on. Let's go get the girls." They walked back to the truck and climbed in.

"Jenny's nana isn't a girl."

"You're right, but she doesn't look like any grandma I ever met."

"I know. My Grandma Baretta looks a lot, lot older."

Buck was having a devil of a time coming to grips with that fact. He started the engine and they took off.

"Hey—can we go to town in the Jeep? It's more fun."

"Sure."

"Will you take the top off?"

"Why not." According to the weather forecast, they wouldn't have to worry about rain for at least three or four days. Buck drove them to the parking area at the side of the ranch house and they got in the Jeep. But before they went anywhere, he had to remove the soft top at the garage south of the house.

Once that was accomplished, they set out for the Forrester cabin. The second they pulled up in front, Johnny threw open the door. "I'll get them."

"You do that." The less involvement he had with Alex Forrester, the better. After they got back from town, he'd turn them over to Carson for the horseback-riding lesson while he helped with the framing. Ross could take them fishing in the morning. A good rotational plan was called for if he wanted to survive this week with his emotions intact.

He didn't have to wait long for their guests. The ladies came right out. Correction, Jenny practically flew down the steps, her blond ponytail swaying back and forth. "I've never ridden in a Jeep before!"

"It's cool!" Johnny raced after her. "Can we sit in back, Uncle Buck?"

"Uncle—"

"He's not really my uncle. Neither is Ross. But Daddy told me I could call them that if I wanted."

"You must love them a lot."

"I love them as much as my uncles in Cleveland, but don't tell my mom I told you that."

The things Johnny said got to Buck's heart. More and more, he found himself wanting to be a father. "Ross and I love you, too. Now, make sure your seat belts are fastened."

"We will," they said in unison.

Buck stepped down and walked around to help Alex in the front passenger seat. She was wearing a crewneck sweater in a sage-green color with khaki pleated trousers. Although her legs were covered today, the length of them combined with her womanly hips and generous curves made nonsense of his intentions to remain indifferent.

Her fragrance put him in mind of a vale of spring wildflowers, adding to the assault on his senses. Damn. Frank had more than one reason to wish the two of them hadn't come on this trip. Buck knew he wouldn't have been able to handle it.

"Thank you," she said as he shut the door.

He nodded and took his place behind the wheel. "Before we leave, did anyone forget anything? Now is the time to speak up."

Alex glanced at him with a mysterious smile. "Or forever hold our peace?"

Buck could feel himself falling into those eyes that looked like impossibly dark blue pools. "Something like that," he murmured.

"Thanks, Buck, for taking us into town," she said. "You've been so wonderful to us and this is such a beautiful day. I can't believe there was ever a storm last night. It's getting hot already."

"It's always that way here in the mountains."

"Yep," Johnny piped up from the back as they drove off. He had big ears. As usual, he was multitasking and could take in every word the grown-ups had to say, while maintaining a conversation with his new friend. "Hey, Jenny? Do you want to go swimming later?"

"Yes. I love swimming."

Buck smiled to himself. "You mean, after you've shown her your pony?"

"Yeah. I think she should ride Mitzi. Have you ever been riding?"

"Yes."

"Do you like it?"

"It's okay, but the horses are so big. Frank's friend owns horses and he's taken us a lot of times."

"Oh. Who's Frank?"

"Nana's boyfriend."

"I didn't know grandmas had boyfriends."

Buck burst into laughter. He couldn't help it. Thankfully, Alex joined him.

Buck heard whispering coming from the backseat. Alex turned her head. "Jenny? It's not polite to whisper in front of other people."

"I'm sorry."

Johnny had always amused Buck, but he couldn't remember ever being this entertained before. He turned onto the highway leading into the town of Jackson. The place was crowded with every kind of four-wheel-drive vehicle loaded up with kayaks, bikes and rafts. After he made a left down one of the streets, they passed a movie theater.

"Hey—" Johnny cried out. "Can we go see that after we get her a cap gun?"

"Could we, Nana? See *The Big Blue Macaw?* It's that show about those birds from Brazil! My teacher said we should go."

"Sweetheart, we came to a dude ranch. Buck has more exciting things for us to do than watch a movie."

"Actually I haven't been to see a movie in a theater in years. It sounds fun."

"Yippee!" Johnny exclaimed.

"Mandy says it's really good."

"Who's Mandy?"

"One of my friends from school. But we've been off track for a week and I haven't seen her. I have to go back to school after our trip."

"My school doesn't start for another month."

"You're lucky."

Alex shot Buck a glance. "Do you think the theater would even be open this time of day?"

He nodded. "They have matinees. You'd be surprised how many guests at the dude ranch take in a show while they're in town. When you're on vacation, you should be able to do whatever you want." For the moment, this was exactly what Buck wanted to do.

One more corner and they came to the Boot Corral. He shut off the engine and they all climbed out. Johnny led the way inside the store. The college-aged girl at the counter broke into a smile when she saw Buck. "Hello again, you guys."

"Hi," Johnny greeted her. Buck followed suit.

The brunette was cute and flirted with him every time he came in, but there was no chemistry and she was too young for him. "Today we need a cap gun, a holster and enough ammo to last a week."

"It's for Jenny," Johnny explained.

"I see. Well, let's get her outfitted. Is there anything else you need while I'm at it?"

"Do you have any cowboy boots?" Johnny asked Jenny.

"No."

"Then she needs boots and a hat!" Johnny was starting to sound more like Carson every day.

"Could I have a white one?"

"I think there's one your size."

"Maybe I'll get some cowboy boots, too," Alex spoke up.

Buck had been on the verge of suggesting it.

"Great. Come on and follow me to the other end of the store."

Before long, they'd bought everything they needed. Buck enjoyed sitting back while he watched Alex try on several different kinds of boots. With those legs...

When all the decisions had been made, he threw in a white hat for her. "Now you and Jenny will be the good guy twins."

After flashing him a smile that lit her eyes, she walked to the front desk and pulled out her credit card.

"Sorry." Buck picked it up and handed it back to her. He felt her warmth when their hands brushed in the process. "These purchases are compliments of the ranch. They go with the territory."

She shook her head. "I don't feel right about it."

"Too bad, because that's the way it is." He turned to the clerk. "Put it on my bill."

"You bet."

"Would it be all right if we leave the bags here? We'll come back for them a little later."

"No problem. I'll leave them behind the counter."

"Thank you." Excited for what was to follow, Buck left his cowboy hat with their purchases and walked the four of them out to the Jeep. When he'd flown into Jackson last evening anticipating the Forresters' arrival, he couldn't have imagined this happy scene or a woman like Alex. Although Frank was waiting in the background, Buck refused to think about that right now.

## Chapter Three

Alex had noticed the way the clerk who'd waited on them only had eyes for Buck. That didn't surprise her. There were a lot of guys walking around the store and out on the streets, but none of them had captured Alex's attention, either.

And although he was nice to the attractive girl who'd looked to be in her early twenties, he didn't give off any signals that he was interested. If Alex had been that clerk, it would have been disappointing not to make any headway with him. A man with his appeal and charisma didn't come along often.

Alex couldn't remember the last time she'd found a younger man so attractive. In fact, it frustrated her that he'd been on her mind this much since their arrival in Jackson.

After Christy was born, Alex had lived with her parents and had gotten a job so she could afford day care for her baby. Later on, when Christy started kindergarten, Alex went to college on student loans at night and worked during the day while still living at home.

Once she'd graduated with a degree in finance, she started a new job at a bank near her parents' house and eventually earned enough money to move into an apartment with Christy. Over those years, she'd dedicated herself to her child and her work. She'd gone out on the occasional date, but getting married hadn't been her focus.

Her teenage love affair resulting in a child had changed her life and priorities. She'd worked so hard at everything and was so grateful for her parents' help that her mind hadn't been on guys. To her chagrin, her teenage daughter fell in love at seventeen, too. Since she and Daniel wanted to get married, Alex gave her permission. It was a good thing because they had a baby right away and Alex helped them all she could so they'd have a stable home. Soon after Jenny came along, Daniel joined the marines.

It was about the same time that Frank lost his wife. While Alex commiserated with him at work, their friendship grew. Then came double tragedy. Alex lived to console her granddaughter and give her the life she deserved. Frank was there to talk to and filled a huge void in her life.

In time, she fell in love with him and was thrilled when he proposed. To have a wonderful, constant man in her life and Jenny's meant everything. But when she'd broached the idea of marriage with Jenny, it hadn't gone as she'd hoped.

Her granddaughter's feelings seemed all mixed up inside. Some days she was angry and threw her Lego bricks all over her room. Other times, Alex found her by the window in her bedroom after school, so lonely and quiet it pierced her heart. Last week, she'd talked constantly about her daddy and cried because he and her mommy were gone.

The invitation to spend an expense-free week at the dude ranch had brought the only light to Jenny's eyes in the past year. When Frank drove them to the airport to come on this trip, Jenny had acted as if he wasn't there. Alex was mortified over her behavior and suspected her granddaughter was glad they were getting away from him for a week. He *had* to have noticed, but there was nothing to be done about it.

But since their arrival in Jackson last night, Jenny had been acting like a normal girl again. Alex had a hunch Buck's entry into their lives had something to do with Jenny's lighter spirits. The man sure knew how to make everything exciting.

Frank wasn't exciting in the same way to Jenny, because he was older. Of course, it wasn't only that. Frank had a completely different personality. But the aspects Alex loved about him didn't do it for Jenny. He was too set in his ways for her and not spontaneous enough.

Buck, on the other hand, appeared ready to do anything and delighted the kids by getting them hot dogs and popcorn to eat during the movie. Alex felt like a kid herself as they entered the crowded theater with their food. Johnny spotted four seats together three-fourths of the way back and urged Jenny to follow him. Alex and Buck joined them. The film had a clever story and some catchy music. But as much as Alex enjoyed it, she was far too aware of the man seated on her left to be able to concentrate fully.

He smelled good and looked fantastic. Buck Summerhayes was a man in his prime who was plagued by a cough he'd inherited from the war. Like her son-in-law, Daniel, he'd done something exceptional with his life by fighting for his country. He and his friends were still doing something exceptional in their own way by making this trip possible for her and Jenny.

Her eyes smarted at the dedication of these men who had to keep oxygen on hand, yet didn't let it bother them. Johnny obviously admired Buck who could be fun and kind, yet firm when necessary. Jenny had liked him right off. That never happened with strangers.

Alex couldn't remember the last time she'd felt this carefree. When she got home, she would have to write to Daniel's commanding officer and thank him for urging her to bring Jenny on this trip.

"Are you all right?" Buck whispered.

Besides everything else, he was sensitive, too. "Yes," she whispered back. "I was just thinking how glad I am we came. Already you've made my granddaughter so happy."

"That's Johnny's doing."

"I think she feels an affinity with him because they've both lost their fathers, but he's had help from you and your friends. You're all true heroes."

After a long silence, he asked, "What about you? How are you holding up? I've never been a parent, but I know it had to be devastating for you to lose your daughter."

Her throat swelled. "I wouldn't have made it if I didn't have Jenny to raise. She gives me a reason to get up every morning."

"For what it's worth, your devotion to her is heroic. Carson's grandfather raised him after his parents died. I see how he turned out and can only marvel over the older man's ability to be there for Carson in every way.

He left this ranch to him. It's now Carson's goal to make the ranch successful and pay back the man who was a hero, just like you."

Tears escaped her closed lids. She wiped them away. "Don't praise me. My work has barely begun."

"That's what I'm talking about." His deep tone flowed through her. "You'll be there for her all your life. After what you've had to endure, I admire you more than you know."

"Thank you."

Deeply touched, she remained silent for the rest of the film. When it was over, they left and drove to the Boot Corral for their packages. On the way back to the ranch, Jenny got out her new gun. Johnny showed her how to fill the cartridge with a roll of caps. Pretty soon they were both firing their weapons at imaginary bad guys.

The noise didn't seem to bother Buck. Frank would have asked them to stop until they got home. He was so different from Buck, who seemed to say and do all the right things around Jenny. But it wasn't fair to compare them. Frank was probably twenty years Buck's senior.

He drove them to her cabin, and then looked over his shoulder at the kids. "What do you want to do now?"

"Play cowboys!" Jenny spoke up. She and Johnny scrambled out of the back and ran around the side of the cabin, whooping it up.

Buck's lips twitched, mesmerizing Alex. "I thought he wanted to go riding, but those cap guns are a strong draw."

"Jenny's never had one. The novelty will wear off, but I'm just glad she's having a great time with Johnny. Since I know your work is never done here on the ranch, why don't you go and do what needs doing. I'll watch both of them and walk Johnny back to the ranch house later."

From beneath the rim of his Stetson, he gazed at her through shuttered eyes. Jenny had been correct about their color. In the sunlight they were the shade of new spring grass. "You're right about the never-ending work, but my main responsibility is to take care of you this week. Behind the scenes, we've nicknamed this place the Daddy Dude Ranch for obvious reasons."

And they did the daddy part better than she could have imagined. "Then I'll relieve you of that awesome responsibility for a little while, because you deserve some rest."

"Well, thank you, ma'am," he drawled. His eyes seemed to focus on her mouth. "In that case, why don't I come inside with you? While you put the things you bought away, I'll make us some instant coffee. I could do with a cup."

Alex's heart thumped. This was something she knew she should avoid, but after all he'd done for them, she didn't dare offend him. "Well…I won't say no to that."

As they went inside with her packages, the feeling grew stronger that she'd just been on a date with him, and now they were coming home to spend the rest of the evening together. She had to remember this was the middle of the afternoon and it wasn't a date!

For one thing, he was probably ten years younger than she was, despite his maturity. For another, in the absence of Jenny's father, it was Buck's job to make certain this turned into a real vacation for her granddaughter, nothing more. She wished to heaven she could see it that way, but he'd managed to get under her skin. The only way to get him out was to leave Wyoming, but she and Jenny had only just arrived.

On her way into the bedroom with their packages, her cell phone rang. She glanced at the caller ID. It was Frank calling her back. She'd tried to reach him earlier that morning, but he'd been in a meeting. Guilt pricked her when she thought about Buck being in the next room. The fact that she felt any guilt told her she was in trouble.

"If you'll excuse me, I need to answer my phone."

"Take all the time you need. I'm not going anywhere."

She shivered, knowing it was true. After shutting the door, she sank down on the side of her twin bed to talk. "Frank?"

"Finally! I waited for your call this morning, but when it didn't come, I had a business conference to attend. How are you?"

"Good." Better than good, but he wouldn't like hearing her say that, since he hadn't wanted her to leave Sacramento. He was afraid it would open up old wounds for her and Jenny by being around the marines who'd invited them. To her surprise, it was doing the exact opposite. But after meeting Buck, she felt...vulnerable. She could never remember feeling that way before.

"I miss you more than I can say, Alexis." He'd always called her that at the bank and it had stuck.

When she thought about it, she hadn't had time to miss him and that made her feel guiltier. "I miss you too. Will you be seeing Cindy and the kids soon?"

"I'm going over there for dinner tonight."

"I'm glad."

"Where are you right now?"

"At the cabin. We've just come home from town with cowboy boots and a cap gun."

"Cap gun?"

"Yes. There's a boy here, Jenny's age, who has one. They're outside, running around with them. In a few minutes we're going to the barn to see his pony. Frank— I-I'm afraid I can't talk any longer," she stammered, aware Buck was waiting for her. She couldn't think with him inside her cabin. "Call me tonight when you're back from Cindy's and we'll talk."

"I should be home by ten at the latest."

"Talk to you then."

"Alexis?"

"Yes?"

"I love you. Let's hope this trip does Jenny a world of good, because we have plans to make when you get back."

"We'll talk about that tonight. Love you, too." She hung up and hurried back into the living room.

Buck was standing on the front porch with a coffee mug, obviously keeping an eye on the kids. He'd made coffee for her. She pulled it out of the microwave and joined him. "Sorry. That was a phone call I had to take. Thanks for the coffee." She took a sip.

He eyed her over his mug. "You're welcome. Everything okay?"

She took a steadying breath. She wasn't okay, not really. Frank would be horribly hurt and upset by what she had to tell him. She was upset, too. "Yes."

He turned toward the main ranch house. "They've

gone to see if they can spot Moppy. If they're not back in a few minutes, I'll go get them."

"I suspect they ran out of caps."

"You're right." He chuckled. "But they decided to take a detour before they loaded up again so they wouldn't scare the squirrel."

"Johnny seems to be a busy bee. I think Jenny has met her match."

"Soul mates at seven," he mused aloud. "Wouldn't that be something?"

"Did you ever meet yours?" The question flew out of her mouth before she could prevent it. She shouldn't have asked him anything that personal, but couldn't seem to help herself.

"I thought I had in high school. But when I went away to college, she didn't wait for me."

"Is that when you joined the marines?"

"Am I that transparent?"

"Not at all. But getting away from the pain is probably something I would have done in your position."

He gave her a penetrating glance. "What about your soul mate?"

"I met Christy's father when we were in high school. We were both seventeen. Like you and the girl you loved, I thought we'd be together forever. But when he found out I was pregnant, all that ended. I wanted the baby more than anything, and he didn't, so we parted ways. His family moved and I never saw him again."

"Your daughter never knew her father, then?"

"No."

His features sobered. "How did you manage?"

"My parents were terrific and still are. They helped

me. I got a job. After Christy was born, I put her in day care and paid for my share at home. When she started school full-time, I went to college at night and kept working. After I got my degree in finance, I started working for a bank and moved us to an apartment. Christy was seventeen when she fell in love with Daniel."

He smiled in understanding, but she was embarrassed because she knew she'd been babbling. He was easy to talk to, but it was still no excuse.

"They wanted to get married. I talked with his aunt and uncle who'd raised him. Knowing how Daniel and Christy felt about each other, we all agreed to give them our permission. It was a good thing. Before long, Jenny was born. For a few years, life was wonderful for all of us."

Buck studied her with a compassion she could feel. "Take it from me, it will be again."

"It already is with Frank in my life. As for this trip, it's doing wonders for Jenny, thanks to you and your friends. I know I keep repeating myself, but your invitation came at just the right time."

She finished her coffee and relieved him of his empty mug, which she took inside. He followed her. "Since they haven't come back, let's get in the Jeep and find them. It's hot. Johnny probably took her into the house for a drink."

"I don't want her to be a nuisance."

"That would be impossible, but now would be a good time to pick them up and drive over to the barn to see the ponies. It's only a short distance from the house.

Later on, there'll be a barbecue out on the patio by the swimming pool."

"That sounds terrific."

Alex was much more excited than she should have been over their plans. Although she could come up with several reasons why, she knew Buck was at the center of the unexpected charge of energy she felt. Considering their age difference and the situation, it was ridiculous. He'd done nothing to make her think he was attracted to her. This was all on her side and it needed to be squelched.

BUCK STAYED INSIDE the corral while Jenny got used to her saddled pony. Johnny rode around, and soon both of them were doing figure eights, playing follow the leader.

Alex stood outside the fence to watch. She'd put one leg on the lower bar and rested against the top, beaming at her granddaughter and taking pictures with her cell phone. Her femininity stood out a mile. The blond streaks in her hair caught the light.

"Hey—you're a pretty good rider!" Johnny called to Jenny, drawing Buck's attention away from her grandmother.

"Thanks. So are you. I wish I could take Mitzi home with me."

"That's what Rachel said."

"Who's she?"

"A girl from Florida who came to the ranch last month. She was nine."

"Was she a good rider?"

"Yep."

"Better than me?"

Buck already felt an attachment to Jenny and was all set to pipe in with something positive when Johnny said, "Nope." Sometimes he sounded exactly like Carson. The one syllable answer brought a smile to Jenny's face.

"Why don't you guys walk the ponies around the outside of the fencing for a little while."

At his suggestion, Johnny led them out of the corral and they started making broader circles. Buck walked over to Alex.

"Your granddaughter has been taught well. I'm almost as impressed as Johnny, who's so surprised he can hardly talk right now."

She chuckled softly. "Frank's friend Hugh has had horses for years. He taught his own children and grandchildren and has been happy to give her pointers."

"It appears she was an apt pupil. So was Johnny. When he came out here with Tracy last month, he'd never been on a horse. Carson was a rodeo champion and is teaching him one step at a time."

"It shows. See the way he holds himself in the saddle? Wearing that cowboy hat, he already has the look of a junior champion."

"That's Johnny's dream. Would you like to ride with them? I'll ask Bert to saddle one of the mares for you. He's been running the stable for years."

"Thank you, but I'll wait till tomorrow. Right now I'm just enjoying watching the kids having a great time."

Johnny rode up to them. "We're going to ride over to the ranch house to see Moppy. She ran away from us before. We'll be right back."

"I think it's a little too soon for that," Buck stated.

"But I can do it!" Jenny insisted.

"That's not the point, sweetheart," Alex intervened. "Buck's right about your staying close to the corral until your pony is used to you and trusts you. When you ride her again tomorrow, she'll be more comfortable with you. Remember what Hugh told you about trust?"

"Hey—" Johnny cried. "That's what Dad says."

Alex smiled. "Since your father was a rodeo champion, he knows what he's talking about."

"Your dad's a champion?" Jenny's voice was full of wonder.

"Yep. I'll show you his belt buckles and pictures."

"Belt buckles?"

"Those are the prizes he won."

"How funny."

Buck's chuckle over their conversation turned into a cough. "Tomorrow we'll go on a ride. For now, why don't you head into the barn. Bert will help you down. Then we'll start back to the ranch house for dinner. How does that sound?"

"What are we going to have?"

"It's Saturday-night barbecue out by the pool."

"Oh, yeah. I forgot. Come on, Jenny. If we hurry, we can go swimming before we eat."

"I'll have to get my suit."

"Me, too."

Maybe after dinner Buck could talk Alex into a game of water volleyball. The Lundgren family against... He realized he'd gotten awfully possessive over two females who'd been strangers on his flight fewer than twenty-four hours ago. He had to stop his thoughts right there.

By tacit agreement, they walked over to the Jeep. The children came running and he started the engine. Within a few minutes they'd made the trip to the ranch house. "Be sure to let your mom know you're back, Johnny."

"I will."

After the boy disappeared, Buck left for the Forresters' cabin. When Alex got out, she darted him a glance. "Jenny and I want to thank you for a fabulous day and all the gifts."

Her granddaughter nodded. "The movie was really fun. I love my cap gun."

"I'm glad, but just remember this day isn't over yet." He was determined about that.

"See ya later, Buck."

"You can count on it," he murmured. With reluctance, he looked away from Alex before driving straight to the building site by the river. He'd expected to see Carson at the barn, but maybe he'd gone to see the progress on his new home.

The work crews had left for the evening, but sure enough, he spied Carson's truck and discovered him walking around inspecting everything. Relieved to find him alone, Buck jumped down from the Jeep and joined him.

"What do you think?"

Carson smiled. "It's exciting to see how fast the framing is coming along."

"I've been pushing them."

"Everything looks good."

"You'll be moved in here before long."

"Frankly, I can't wait to have some real privacy, if you know what I mean." Buck could only imagine. "How did it go with Johnny?"

"He and Jenny have hit it off. She's a pretty good

little rider for her age." For the next few minutes, Buck gave him a rundown of their day, including the moment when Johnny had said he didn't know grandmas had boyfriends. That brought a roar of laughter from Carson.

"My new son still has a lot to learn. Tracy and I love his innocence, but we know he's growing up a little more every day and will lose it eventually."

"Jenny seems a little further along in that department, but then she's had to be." In the next breath, Buck found himself telling Carson about Alex's life and her struggles.

When he'd finished, his friend let out a low whistle. "That family has really been through it. No wonder Jenny's not ready to let Frank into her life. Sharing her grandmother will be another kind of loss she's not prepared for yet."

"I think having lost both parents in such a short period of time has made her extra afraid," Buck theorized.

Carson's blue eyes searched his. "According to my wife, it appears she doesn't have a problem sharing her nana with *you*."

He'd hit a nerve, causing Buck's head to rear. "What are you saying, Carson? Hell—leave me out of this! They just got here and Alex is on the verge of marrying Frank. But she can't until Jenny learns to accept him."

"Hey—take it easy. All I meant was, isn't it a good thing Jenny doesn't resent you being around her nana, since you'll be hosting this family until they leave?"

Buck eyed him warily. "That wasn't all you meant, but I'll let it go for now."

"Hey, buddy—it's me. Carson. For what it's worth, if I were in your shoes and hadn't met Tracy, I'd be walking around like a shell-shock victim, too. In a word, Alex is breathtaking. Ross will have a heart attack when he meets her. How old is she?"

"I didn't ask. It's none of my business."

"Whatever you say," he said with a sly grin. "Come on. Let's head back. Tracy's expecting me to help with the barbecue."

Feeling out of sorts after his conversation with Carson, Buck got in the Jeep and started out for the ranch house. Carson followed in his truck. By the time they reached the parking area, he'd gotten himself under control. He was taking all of this way too seriously and Carson had just been teasing him.

*Chill out, Summerhayes.*

Taking a deep breath, he exited the Jeep. While Carson hurried inside to find his wife, Buck walked around the other side of the house to see what was going on. Sounds of shouts and laughter came from the pool area where tables of food had already been set up on the patio. Some of the guests were eating and others were in the pool, Tracy among them.

He would have been all right if he hadn't seen Ross cleaving the water to bear down on Alex, ready to dunk her. Buck didn't know Ross had returned from the overnight campout.

She screamed, laughing, trying to get away from the inevitable. Watching his friend horse around with her should have made him laugh. Instead he was knocked sideways. Ross usually swam laps in the pool before calling it a night, but he did it when the guests weren't around.

Buck hadn't known a feeling like this since he'd first

learned about Melanie and his brother. How could he possibly be jealous? Ross was one of the greatest guys he knew.

As for Alex, she'd arrived only last night and would soon belong to another man. She and Ross were just fooling around and having fun. Last night, Alex had told him that fun was exactly what she and Jenny needed. But Buck had no other answer for what was bothering him. There had to be something seriously wrong with him.

"Buck—come and help us!" Jenny cried out the second she saw him. At least Buck had one fan: a precious little girl who was making inroads into his heart.

Johnny's brown head bobbed next to hers. "We're having a water fight with Ross. Come and be on our side!"

Whatever he was feeling, he needed to put it away for now. "I'll get on my suit and be right out."

"Yippee!" the kids cried.

He dashed through the side doors of the games room into the hall and hurried up the stairs to his bedroom to change. Once he'd put on his trunks, he grabbed a towel and rushed outside again. He'd be all right if he stayed with the children.

*Ignore what's going on with Grandma and the thirty-year-old ex-marine who ought to know better.*

Except that Ross probably didn't know the whole story about Alexis Wilson.

Taking a running leap, Buck did a cannonball in front of the kids that spread water in every direction like a tidal wave. Their screams of delight were followed by more screams as Carson plunged in, practically emptying the pool. When he surfaced, he was holding a ball. "Okay, everybody. It's the girls against the guys for a game of volleyball. Girls over there." He pointed to the shallow end.

Buck didn't put it past Carson to have seen Ross zero in on Alex and decide to do something about it. Whatever. Buck joined his friends and a couple of the older teenage boys. Johnny swam over to their side.

"Hey, sport." Carson immediately put Johnny on his shoulders while Ross spiked the ball to the other side.

One of the older teenage girls returned it and the game was on, but Buck had trouble concentrating. Alex's hair was in a braid she'd pinned to the top of her head. The style emphasized her angelic face. When she jumped to hit the ball, he caught a glimpse of her shapely body in her two-piece emerald suit. His lungs gave out in reaction, leaving him coughing up a storm.

The battle wore on for ten minutes. "Give up yet?" Carson called out with a gloating expression.

"Never!" Tracy retorted and spiked a ball that Buck never saw coming because he was looking somewhere else.

Carson turned to him. "Hey, buddy. We're supposed to be throttling them." But his eyes were crinkled with laughter, conveying a private message that he knew exactly what was going on with Buck.

Making a quick recovery, Buck served a fast ball that had the girls scrambling. Within minutes it was all over. Thirty-one to nine in favor of the guys.

"It's not fair," Jenny complained when Buck swam over to her. She looked so cute in her red suit, but she was so upset that he needed to turn things around for her.

"I know, but there's something we *can* do to make things equal. If you get on my shoulders, we'll have a water fight with Carson and Johnny."

"Goody!" She'd adopted one of Johnny's words. In the next instant, she flew toward Buck so he could lift her onto his shoulders. Ignoring Alex, who was treading water while she watched them, he headed for the other end. Johnny saw them coming and yelped.

"I hope you guys are ready, because Jenny and I are going to whomp you."

"Oh, yeah?" Carson countered.

"Start chopping the water, Jenny."

"Okay."

The game was on while the kids fought like warriors. Buck and Carson were laughing so hard, they started coughing and Johnny got dumped in the water by accident.

"We won!" Jenny squealed, hugging Buck around the neck so hard he almost choked.

Johnny hung on to his daddy's arm. "We'll get you tomorrow night."

"No, you won't. Buck and I are the best!"

Yeah. Buck loved it.

By now everyone had gotten out of the pool, including Alex. She was covered in a beach robe that hid her exquisite figure and long legs from view. She stood at the edge of the pool to throw another large beach towel around Jenny who bragged to her grandmother about winning the contest against Carson and Johnny.

"You two deserve a prize."

"What kind?" she wanted to know immediately.

"I don't know yet." Those deep blue eyes found Buck's. Maybe it was the exertion from the water fight that caused adrenaline to pump through him, but he doubted it. "I'll have to think about it while we eat. Come on."

Buck ran back inside the house to change into jeans and a polo shirt. Once dressed, he came out to help himself to steak and corn on the cob. Jenny waved him over to one of the candlelit tables where she and Alex were sitting with Carson's family and Ross. He was telling them about the elk his group had seen while camping.

"You know something, Johnny? I believe it was the same elk as the one on the dude ranch brochure."

"You mean, the one with the giant antlers?" He nodded. "I bet that's another one of your fish stories, Uncle Ross."

"I swear, it isn't! I took a picture with my phone."

"Dad doesn't think it's around anymore."

"Then maybe it's his brother."

"His brother?" Jenny laughed over the comment, causing Buck to smile. Despite all the pain she'd lived through, Alex's granddaughter had a great sense of humor. His heart warmed to her more and more.

"Where's your phone?" Johnny asked.

"In my bedroom."

"Could I go get it?"

"Sure. It's on the top of the dresser."

"It can wait," Tracy reminded her son. "Ross can show it to us at breakfast. Right now let's all finish our dinner."

"Your mother's right," Carson backed her up.

Johnny turned to Buck with pleading brown eyes. "If it's the granddaddy elk, can we go on a campout tomorrow in the same place? I want to see it." He glanced at Jenny. "You want to see it, too, don't you? It's *huge*."

"I know. I saw it on the brochure." She turned to Alex. "Can—I mean—may we go see it, Nana? Please?"

"Maybe in a few days, sweetheart. Remember what Buck said? You and the pony need to get used to each other. After a few days of short rides, you'll be ready for a longer ride. Doesn't that make sense?"

"I guess."

"But what if the elk isn't there by then?"

Carson put an arm around Johnny. "You have the rest of your life to find him."

"Yeah, but Jenny will be going home pretty soon and might not see it."

"I don't want to go home," she piped up out of the blue.

Alex looked chagrined. She put her fork down and got to her feet. "You know what, sweetheart? You sound tired. So am I. Let's thank everyone for this delicious meal and go back to the cabin."

Jenny mumbled her thanks before standing up. "Good night everybody. It's been really fun."

"Good night," Johnny muttered back, clearly unhappy. "See you in the morning. We'll go hunting for bad guys with our guns."

"Buck? Can we ride back to the cabin with you?"

It thrilled him that Jenny wanted his company. He got up from the deck chair. "I was just going to suggest it. The air is cooling down too fast for you to have to walk in your swimsuit. Even though the Jeep will be cold, we'll get there faster. But as soon as we arrive, I'll start a fire and make the cabin cozy for you."

Jenny hurried around the table toward Buck with a smile that reached down inside him.

"Can I come with you?" Johnny was already on his feet.

Tracy put the kibosh on that idea. "Not tonight. You've had a big day and need a good sleep, too."

Good. Buck wanted to be alone with Alex and Jenny. In Afghanistan he'd been around a lot of buddies who were family men and talked about their wives and children. During that period, Buck found himself wanting the same thing but he hadn't met the right woman yet.

When the guys had been hospitalized and they'd conceived of the idea of a daddy dude ranch, he'd had many fantasies about being married and having a family. Now that Alex and Jenny had arrived on the ranch, he found himself hungering for the experience.

But to fantasize about the three of them being a family was wrong. She'd pledged herself to another man. Buck needed to remember that or he'd go a little insane.

# *Chapter Four*

Troubled by the direction of the conversation in the past few minutes, Alex said good-night and followed Jenny and Buck around the side of the ranch house. But Jenny didn't wait for Alex to catch up. To her dismay, she saw her granddaughter reach for Buck's hand the way she might have done with her father.

It all happened naturally. That was because he took such good care of them and made Jenny feel safe, just the way Daniel had done. Though that was his job while they were here, she knew instinctively that Buck would always be attentive and fun that way. Being there at the ranch, she could see the contrast between him and Frank, who'd already raised a family and had grandchildren. Frank was good to Jenny, but it was different because Frank was more attentive to Alex.

When they reached the Jeep, Alex climbed in front and settled Jenny on her lap to help keep her warm. Buck drove them to the cabin in record time. After putting on another oxygen mask he kept in the Jeep, he got a fire going while they showered and washed their hair.

After dressing in their pajamas, they went back to the living room to dry their hair in front of the fire with the bathroom towels. Buck checked their stock of supplies while Alex put Jenny's hair in a ponytail.

Her granddaughter stared at Buck, seemingly fascinated by everything about him. "Do you have to leave now?"

"In about three more minutes. That's when my oxygen runs out."

"I wish you could stay longer." She looked up at Alex. "Tomorrow night let's not have a fire. Then Buck won't have to leave."

"He might have other plans, sweetheart."

Jenny's eyes switched to Buck with a worried expression. "*Do* you?"

"I was thinking that after dinner tomorrow we could watch a movie here with Johnny. There are a half dozen family DVDs in that armoire."

"Could we, Nana?"

It wouldn't be wise for Alex to spend any more time in Buck's company if she wanted to forget he existed, but it would mean the world to her granddaughter. "Sure. Maybe we can get Tracy and Carson to come, too. It sounds like fun. You and Johnny can pick the movie."

"Then it's a date."

Not that kind of a date. No, no, no.

Buck got to his feet and moved his hard-muscled frame to the door. Alex averted her gaze to avoid feasting her eyes on him. "I'll see you lovely ladies at breakfast tomorrow. Afterward we'll go fishing with anyone who wants to come."

"I want to catch a big one!"

"Then we'll do it." He grinned. "And you'll have to eat it."

"I'll get Johnny to help me."

"Good thinking." He started for the door. Jenny darted after him. "Good night, Buck."

"Good night, Red."

She laughed. "Red—"

"That's your favorite color, right?" She nodded. He sent Alex a brief glance before shutting the door.

Alex knew the unexpected nickname had slipped out in the same natural way Jenny had reached for his hand earlier. She could see Buck and Jenny bonding before her eyes and moaned inwardly.

The second he left, Alex hurried over to lock the door, but she found her fingers trembled.

"Do I have to go to bed yet?"

"You can stay up until I finish doing my hair." Alex dried it a little more before securing it at the nape with an elastic.

"You're going to talk to Frank tonight, huh?"

Her heart pounded harder. "Yes."

"Is he mad at me?"

"Of course not!" Alex picked her up and hugged her.

"I wish you didn't like him so much."

They'd been over this many times before. Alex could see how much Jenny needed reassurance of her love. "It's because of all the good things he does. But don't you know there's nobody in the whole world more important to me than you? I love you with all my heart."

Jenny clung to her. "I love you, too. I wish we could stay here forever."

That was the second time in an hour her granddaughter had expressed the same sentiment. "I love it here, too, and I know exactly how you feel, sweetheart. Everyone needs to go on vacation once in a while. You forget all your problems and just have fun."

"Do you think Buck goes on vacation sometimes?"

Alex groaned. Buck again. Where had that question come from? "I'm sure he does. Now, let's go in the bedroom. It's time to get some sleep."

Tears escaped Alex's lids when her granddaughter ended her prayer by asking God to cure Buck's disease. Jenny had a tender heart made much more sensitive by the loss of her parents. Alex supposed it was possible Jenny worried Buck might die because of his condition. The thought was too terrible to contemplate.

Once she'd gone to sleep, Alex went back to the living room and stretched out on the floor in front of the fire. She checked her watch. It was twenty after ten. There was an hour's time difference between Wyoming and California. Frank might be home from his daughter's by now, but there was time to spare before she needed to phone him.

Unfortunately the longer she put off making the call, the guiltier she would feel. Turning on her side, she pressed the speed dial for his number. He picked up before the second ring. "I've been waiting to hear your voice."

"Hi. I just got Jenny to bed. How was your dinner?"

"My daughter's a great cook. Phil got a promotion, which is good news, but I want to know about you. I keep thinking about you being there without me. I have to tell you I'm having a hard time. Work isn't the same."

"I know what you mean. It's too bad you can't be here. You'd love it."

"I've been to the Tetons several times in my life. It's a beautiful place, no doubt about it. Does Jenny like it?"

*If he only knew.* "Yes. She spent all day with Johnny, that boy I told you about. His father was a marine who lost his life, so they have that bond between them." But Jenny had formed another bond, too. That was the one that made Alex break out in a cold sweat.

"If you think it's helping, then I'm glad you went."

"To be honest, I haven't seen her this carefree since before Daniel's death. Tomorrow we're all going fishing."

"Who all?"

Her pulse picked up speed when she thought of Buck. "Different members of the staff and guests. Today Jenny rode one of the ponies."

"They have ponies?"

"Yes. Thanks to Hugh, she was able to ride around with a lot of confidence." After a pause she said, "Frank, tonight she opened up to me about some of her feelings. We have to talk about it."

"I can hear you hesitating. What's wrong?"

Alex closed her eyes tightly. "She isn't ready for me to get married yet."

"That's not news. Will she ever be? Honestly?"

"I realize that's the last thing you want to hear, but it's clear she's not over Christy's death."

"Alexis—"

She sat up. "I know what you're going to say. We've been over this before, so here's my idea. When we fly back to Sacramento, I'm going to get us into counseling. When Daniel died, I was advised to seek help and I would have, but then Christy got so ill, I put it off."

"Counseling could take months."

"Maybe, maybe not. The point is, I can't marry you until she's able to accept it, otherwise we'll have a nightmare on our hands. I'm so sorry it has to be this way. You *have* to know this isn't what I want."

"But let's be truthful about one thing. She has resented me from the beginning and is holding you hostage."

Alex bristled. "It's not personal, Frank. She's scared she's going to lose me. She'd feel that way about any man I wanted to marry."

"In that case, I have an idea. Why don't you stay there one more day and have fun, then fly home and start your counseling. I'll go with you."

In her head, his idea made a lot of sense. The sooner Jenny got professional help, the sooner their marriage could take place. But in Alex's heart of hearts, she knew her granddaughter too well. To leave the ranch before their time was up next Saturday was unthinkable. "Jenny's planning on us being here the full week. I can't disappoint her."

"You never disappoint her and she takes advantage of that fact because she knows she's the apple of your eye."

His resentment had been growing, and now he couldn't hold it back. "Frank—"

She heard a labored sigh. "All right. I'll leave it alone, but I don't like it. I miss you too much."

To her horror, she couldn't tell him the same thing. "I'll phone you tomorrow night about the same time."

"Alexis?"

"What is it?"

"You seem different."

"I do?"

"Yes, but I can't put my finger on it."

"I don't mean to be. Jenny's still going through a difficult time."

"It's this separation. I'm afraid I'm not used to you being gone. I love you."

"I love you, too," she said honestly. That would never change, but circumstances had. "We'll talk tomorrow. Good night." She ended the call, thankful not to have to discuss this any further tonight.

Alex *did* love him, but coming to the ranch had given her a perspective she wouldn't have imagined, just as Buck had said it would. Being away from everything familiar had already put a different slant on things for her and Jenny.

For so long, their lives had been wrapped up in Christy and Daniel, with Frank playing a growing part in the background. But for a little while, this trip had taken them out of that sad world and was bringing Jenny some real happiness. If Alex were honest with herself, she could admit she liked this feeling of freedom, too. It was as if she'd put her worries on hold and could be a free agent with no deadlines, no one to answer to.

When Frank had suggested she fly home in another day, she'd rebelled at the idea. Not just for Jenny's sake, but for her own. She recognized that she'd desperately needed this time away, but she would never have taken it if it hadn't have been for that letter from the ranch.

She still had it in her purse. It was lying on the table. Compelled to read it again, she got up and pulled it out. The fire was burning down, but she could still make out the words.

Dear Mrs. Forrester,

My name is Carson Lundgren. You don't know me, but I served as a marine in Afghanistan before I got out of the service.

Along with Buck Summerhayes and Ross Livingston, also former marines, I own the Teton Valley Dude Ranch. We put our heads together and decided to contact the families of the fallen soldiers from our various units.

Your courageous husband, Daniel Forrester, served our country with honor and distinction. Now we'd like to honor him by offering you and your daughter, Jennifer, an all-expenses-paid, one-week vacation at the dude ranch anytime in July or August. We'll pay for your airfare and any other travel expenses.

You're welcome to contact your husband's division commander. His office helped us obtain your address. If you're interested or have questions, please phone our office at the number below. We've also listed our web address. Click on it to see the brochure we've prepared. We'll be happy to email you any additional information.

Please know how anxious we are to give something back to you after his great sacrifice.

With warmest regards,
Carson Lundgren

Tears gushed down Alex's cheeks. She'd been touched when she'd first read it, but nothing compared to the feelings she had now. These men, suffering from an awful disease, were breaking their backs and their pocketbooks to bring joy to families who'd been torn apart by war. Their selflessness was beyond description.

The image of Buck wearing his oxygen mask refused to leave her. In order for them to enjoy a fire in their own fireplace, he'd put himself in jeopardy because he'd wanted to make Jenny feel welcome.

Christy would have been overwhelmed by their kindness. Alex hoped she and Daniel were looking down and knew what was going on.

Finally exhausted from crying, she put the letter back in her purse and went to bed. That letter would go in a scrapbook after they got home, along with a lot of pictures Alex was taking of everyone, including Buck, when Jenny wasn't looking.

ALEX HEARD THE house phone ringing and it brought her fully awake. Her watch said it was a quarter to eight. She turned on her other side to pick it up, aware of her pulse beating faster at the thought that it might be Buck on the other end. Maybe there'd been a change in plans for the morning. "Hello?"

"Hi, Alex. It's Johnny!"

He had more personality than any child she'd ever known. "Hi! How are you this morning?"

"I'm good. Can I speak to Jenny?"

Her mouth broke into a smile. "Sure. Just a minute." She handed the receiver to her granddaughter. "It's for you."

Jenny sprang out of bed. "Hello?"

Alex got up and loosened the hair from her elastic while she listened to Jenny's end of the conversation.

"Nana? Can I go over to the ranch house right now? Johnny has to clean his room before he can go anywhere. He wants me to help him so he can go fishing with us and Buck. His mom said it's all right. Can I? Please?"

"You mean, *may* I?" Alex tried to use any teaching moment to correct her granddaughter's grammar.

"I forgot. May I?"

She chuckled, never having seen Jenny this excited to help with chores. "If that's what you want to do."

"Thanks." A smile broke out on her precious face before she spoke into the phone again. "Nana says I can come. I'll hurry. Bye." She hung up and dashed into the bathroom to brush her teeth. When she hurried back in the room for a clean pair of jeans and a top, she said, "He wants me to wear my holster and cowboy stuff." In a flash, she was ready.

"Just a minute, young lady. Let me do your hair."

"I don't want a ponytail. Sometimes the elastic hurts."

"Then I'll just brush it out." Her silky blond hair had a lot of natural curl like her mother's and Alex's. It was a trait that spanned three generations. "There." She put the white cowboy hat on her head. "Do you know what? In that getup and with those fancy cowboy boots, you look like a real cowgirl." She kissed her cheeks. "As soon as I'm dressed, I'll walk over to the ranch house to eat. Come and find me in the dining room for breakfast."

"We will." She fastened her cap gun in her holster before racing out the door. The famous Road Runner from the cartoon couldn't have moved any faster. If

Frank could see the change in Jenny, he wouldn't believe it. And Alex guessed that, while he'd be happy for her, he wouldn't like it because it meant Jenny wasn't getting any closer to accepting him.

More guilt consumed Alex, as she found herself looking forward to seeing Buck. On a whim, she put on her new cowboy boots and hat, more gifts from him. Why not? They were going fishing and horseback riding today. She might as well look the part.

WHEN ALEX WALKED into the dining room, looking like a rodeo queen, Buck's heart did a fierce kick. In fact, every male in the room appeared to freeze, including Ross, who'd stopped munching on his toast. "Last night she could have been a mermaid," he murmured. "This morning…"

Buck didn't want to hear the rest. "Damn—I just remembered I need to talk to the contractor at the building site about something urgent before the crews get started." He got up from the table. "Do me a favor and take Alex and her granddaughter fishing after breakfast? I'll be back soon to relieve you, but this can't wait."

Ross eyed him with a puzzled expression. "Sure. They can come with my group."

"I owe you."

Hoping Alex hadn't seen him yet, he escaped through the swinging doors into the kitchen and headed for the other exit. No sooner had he reached the back hallway than the children's cries forced him to spin around. "Hey, you two—what's going on?"

With her eyes shining, Jenny ran up to him. "I just finished helping Johnny clean up his room. It was a big mess. While we were changing the water in his baby garter snake's aquarium, it got out and we had to look for it."

Buck chuckled. "Did you find it?"

Johnny nodded. "It was curled up in my laundry bag. Fred likes to hide."

"It's a good thing you found him before your mom did."

"She would have freaked."

"He put him back and gave him water," Jenny explained. "His mom did her inspection and said we were free to go fishing."

"Have you had breakfast?"

She shook her head. "We're going to eat right now."

"Then it's good timing, because your nana just walked into the dining room. While you go find her, I have an errand to run at the building site."

"Buck is helping build our brand-new house," Johnny informed her.

Her eyes rounded. "You can build a house?"

"I learned how from my father. While I'm gone, Ross will get you guys outfitted with a rod and bait. I'll join you in a little while."

A frown appeared on the girl's face. "I'd rather come with you."

"I'll take you to the new house another time when it's not so dangerous."

"How come it's dangerous?"

Jenny Forrester looked so cute in her cowgirl outfit, Buck felt his heart melt. He hunched down in front of her. "A lot of men are carrying big long boards around. They have to wear hard hats in case they get hit by accident. Sometimes they still get hurt and I don't want anything to happen to you."

She stared into his eyes. "Do you wear a hard hat, too?"

"Yes."

"Do you promise to keep it on the whole time?"

"I promise."

Her sweetness and caring haunted him all the way to the site. He had eight nephews and nieces and loved them all, but they didn't tug at him emotionally the way Jenny did. She'd been deprived of her daddy. He suffered to think about the pain she'd gone through losing her mother, too.

Buck's mother and father had always been there for him. He hadn't been deprived of anything. He thought about Alex, who'd raised her daughter alone and was now raising her granddaughter by herself. That woman's strength awed him.

Needing an outlet for the nervous energy building inside him, he helped the guys haul lumber for the next two hours to give himself a workout. But when he left and caught up to everyone at the river, he didn't see Alex or the kids.

Surprised, he got out of the Jeep and wandered over to Ross, who was helping with some of the guests. "What happened to our family? Didn't they come with you?"

Ross gave him a speculative glance. "Jenny decided she'd rather play Ping-Pong with Johnny in the games room." His eyebrows lifted. "I think we know why, so I decided not to push it."

"What are you talking about?"

"Johnny whispered to me that Jenny had her heart set on you helping her catch a big one. I'd say she has a little crush on you. Kind of reminds me of the way Johnny ignored everyone but Carson after he got here. As you remember, that relationship happened fast. I'm beginning to feel like the invisible man." He said it with a smile, but Buck worried there might be some truth behind his words.

As much as it pleased him that Jenny had been enjoying herself when he was around, the last thing he wanted to do was make the situation harder for Alex where Frank was concerned. That was why he'd asked Ross to take over for a couple of hours.

"Thanks for being willing to help out."

"Any time. You know that."

He nodded. "See you later."

In a different frame of mind since learning what had happened, Buck drove back to the ranch house and went inside. Some of the teenagers were in the games room, but there was no sign of the kids or Alex in there or out by the pool.

"Susan?" The part-time redheaded receptionist looked up from the computer. "You wouldn't by any chance know where Johnny and Jenny have gone, would you?"

"Tracy took them into town with her. She needed to mail a couple of packages to her in-laws. Johnny's grandpa has a birthday coming up. She said something about eating lunch there, but they ought to be back pretty soon."

"Did Jenny's grandmother go with them?"

"I'm not sure."

"What about Carson?"

"He's gone to the upper pasture."

"Okay. Thanks for the info. Call me on the cell if you need me."

"Will do."

Buck had planned to take everyone riding, but that would have to wait till later. He made a beeline for the kitchen, where he fixed himself a sandwich and grabbed a couple of doughnuts. After leaving the table earlier without finishing his breakfast, he was starving.

Still feeling at loose ends, he left the ranch house, figuring he'd drive back to the building site. But after he started up the Jeep, he found himself headed for the Forrester cabin. It was probably a wasted trip, but something nagged at him to find out if Alex was inside, so he could explain.

After a few knocks, Alex opened the door to him. Her fragrance assailed him along with her beauty. He heard a quiet gasp, revealing her surprise at seeing him. "Buck—"

"I'm sorry about this morning, but something came up at the building site that I needed to see to." Buck didn't consider it an outright lie. After all, he'd manufactured it as a preventative measure. If he hadn't shown up at her door just now, he might have actually believed his own explanation.

"Johnny told me you're supervising the construction of his family's new house. You don't need to apologize for that."

"Yes, I do. Jenny was counting on us going fishing."

"When I explained, she understood."

He was knee-deep in guilt about now. "When Ross

told me what happened, I didn't know if you'd gone to town with Tracy or not. In case you were here, I decided to see if there was anything you needed."

When she shook her head, her dark hair flounced back and forth across her shoulders. "Jenny begged to go with them, so I decided to take advantage of the peace and quiet and write a letter to Daniel's commanding officer. If I hadn't listened to him, Jenny and I wouldn't be having this vacation of a lifetime. That's what it is, you know."

Buck braced his body against the door frame. "Living in the shadow of the Grand Teton is a vacation for me, too. I have to tell you, it's indecent to enjoy your work as much as I do. Just so you know, I'm free for the rest of the day if you and Jenny want to go riding later."

"Jenny will be thrilled."

*She's not going to invite you in, Summerhayes. What in the hell is wrong with you?*

"Call the front desk when you're ready, and I'll swing by for you." He pivoted and reached the Jeep in a couple of strides.

Ross had implied Jenny had a crush on him. He could relate to that. He wished a crush was all he had on Alex, but he knew in his gut his feelings were involved and went deeper than that, but he couldn't begin to describe what made meeting her different from all the other women he'd met in his life.

Alex was committed to the man she'd been seeing for two years. They had a long history and worked at the same bank, where according to Johnny, Frank was the vice president. He'd been there to support her through both losses and had watched out for Jenny. They were planning to be married. So how could he stand on that porch, hoping she'd ask him to stay and talk for a while? What kind of a person was he?

For the first time in years he had a different take on what had happened when Melanie and his brother had found themselves attracted to each other during Buck's absence. Strong chemistry could draw you to another person against your will, no matter how hard you fought it or didn't want it. Before they realized they were playing with fire, they'd been burned by it. He understood that now. He got it.

Good grief. He'd seen Alex's legs walking in front of him at the airport lounge. By the time he'd come face-to-face with her in the terminal, something profound had happened to him. Nothing but chemistry could explain such a powerful physical reaction. But in two days it had gone beyond that, even though he knew that she and Frank were a couple.

Buck didn't know if she felt that same chemistry for him. He couldn't tell. If she did, he envied her ability to hide it.

But the more he reflected, the more he realized that this was completely different from what had gone on with Melanie and his brother years ago. Then, there'd been no child involved whose feelings had to be considered. Jenny came first with Alex. Her granddaughter's existence complicated an already complex situation for her and Frank.

As Buck had told Carson yesterday, Buck wanted to be left out of that equation, despite how much he was attracted to Alex or cared for Jenny. He'd meant it then, and meant it even more so now. Somehow he had to find a way to insulate himself until they left the ranch and she and Jenny went back to Frank and a future that didn't include Buck.

His first rule of thumb—don't ever be alone with her.

Second rule—don't involve yourself if you don't have to.

Third rule—keep Johnny close.

## Chapter Five

Alex moved over to the window and watched him drive away. Would he have stayed if she'd invited him inside?

*For what, Alex?* So they could talk?

She didn't have an answer for that, because she didn't know what she wanted.

*Oh, yes, you do.*

Simply put, she had the hots for Buck Summerhayes.

The signs had been there from the night she'd seen him walking toward her in the Jackson airport. It made no sense. It hadn't made any sense when she'd met Kyle and had been struck by an energy she couldn't explain. But that was twenty-four years ago and she'd long since given up believing such a thing would ever happen again. She didn't want it to happen again, considering Kyle didn't turn out to have staying power.

It was as if a bolt of lightning during that summer storm over the Tetons had struck her, charging every atom of her body when she'd least expected it. She hadn't been the same since.

Earlier on the phone, Frank had told her she seemed different.

Yes, she was....

When Buck appeared at the cabin door just a few

minutes ago, her body had sizzled at the very sight of him. She couldn't do anything about the feelings he aroused in her without even trying. They were a fact of life. If she ran away to the other side of the earth, they'd still be with her.

If Frank were here kissing her right this very minute, she wouldn't be able to feel it, not since her body had been ignited by this new energy radiating from Buck.

So deep was her fear of her feelings that she didn't realize Jenny had come back from town and was trying to get her attention. "Nana? Can't you hear me?"

Startled, Alex spun around. "Sweetheart—"

"What's wrong?"

"Nothing." Heat swept through her. "I was thinking about something else." Someone else. "I'm sorry. Did you have a good time?"

"Yes, and guess what? It's Buck's birthday on Friday. He'll be thirty-six. Johnny says he's older than Carson or Ross."

Adrenaline coursed through her body. "I didn't know that." Johnny knew just about everything that went on around the ranch. Buck was closer to her age than she'd assumed. He'd insisted that losing the girl he'd loved hadn't played a part in his decision to join the armed forces, but Alex marveled he hadn't fallen in love with someone else since then and wasn't married by now.

"Johnny's mom says we're going to celebrate it on Johnny's birthday the day before so it will be a surprise," she chattered away. "She let me and Johnny pick out a present for Buck and she'll wrap it for us. It's a T-shirt."

Alex took an extra breath. "What does it look like?"

"We went to a shop where they put on whatever you tell them. It's a dark green one with the Grand Teton on it, and we had them put Super Dad on it."

Of course. The Daddy Dude Ranch. How absolutely perfect for the man who was being a super dad to Johnny and Jenny and would definitely be a super dad if he had his own children one day.

"Do you think we could go into town to that same shop and make a T-shirt for Johnny? But it will have to be a secret."

"Of course. Since we have the use of a car while we're here if we want it, we can drive into Jackson tomorrow before breakfast. Do you have an idea what you'd like his shirt to say?" Interestingly enough, Alex had been thinking about buying matching T-shirts for Jenny and Buck for winning the water-fight contest last night.

"Not yet."

She squeezed her granddaughter. "Well, you've got plenty of time to decide."

"Can we go riding now? Buck's going to take us."

*I know.* "I was planning on it. Have you eaten lunch?"

"Yes. Johnny's mom bought us hamburgers and milk shakes."

"Lucky you!"

"She's really nice and fun. I wish we lived here all the time."

"I know you do. Hurry and freshen up, and then we'll walk to the barn. It's not that far."

"Okay. Be sure and wear your hat, just like in the cowboy movies. Johnny says his dad has a DVD we have to watch. Have you ever heard of Hopalong Cassidy?"

"I have. When I was little, I saw a few of his movies."

"Was Hopalong really his name?"

"I think so."

"That's funny. Wait till I tell Johnny—"

Alex chuckled and put the hat on her head. One thing she wouldn't do was phone the desk to reach Buck. No doubt he would find out Johnny was back and would meet them at the corral. The stable manager would help get their animals saddled.

When Jenny was ready, Alex grabbed a granola bar and an apple from the basket and they left the cabin. She munched her way along the road, so filled with a sense of well-being in spite of her guilt that she didn't notice her cowboy boots touching the ground.

They arrived at the barn to find Johnny already astride his pony. "What took you guys so long?"

She smiled at the boy who'd quickly become Jenny's friend. "It's such a beautiful day that we decided to stretch our legs."

Bert led Mitzi outside and saddled her. Jenny looked around while she was waiting, and then the older man helped her on. "Thanks, Bert. Where's Buck?" There was no sign of the Jeep.

They all heard a cough. "I'm right here."

"Goody!"

Alex felt as if she was falling into space when he emerged from the shadows of the barn, leading a saddled horse by the reins. In his hat and jeans and wearing a Western shirt that accentuated the size of his chest, he looked sensational.

He raised his head, causing their gazes to collide. Buck had to know she'd been staring at him, because he'd caught her before she could look away. One side of his compelling mouth turned up, giving her senses a jolt. "This is Blossom. She's a mare you can trust."

*Don't touch me, Buck. Don't come near me.*

But it was too late, because he steadied the horse while she climbed onto the saddle and his hard-muscled arm brushed hers, sending liquid fire through her body. "Thank you," she said in an unsteady voice.

"You're welcome."

While she attempted to recover, he went back to the barn and rode out on a dark brown horse.

Jenny made an excited sound. "What's his name?"

"Dopey."

She laughed hilariously. "No, it isn't."

"Buck's just teasing," Johnny explained. "His real name is Dynamite. Can we ride to the new house so Jenny can see it?"

"Sure. It's midafternoon. The workmen should be gone by the time we get there. Why don't you lead the way?"

"Okay. Let's go."

Alex hurriedly drew alongside him with Jenny on his other side and they were off. Buck brought up the rear. It had seemed like a good idea to go ahead with the children, but she couldn't forget that he was right behind them. Alternating thrills and chills bombarded her as they left the sagebrush and entered a forested area filled with the sound of insects and birds whirring about.

The children talked incessantly, but their voices couldn't drown out the sound of her own heart pounding mercilessly in her chest. Alex breathed in the fresh smell of pine and simply absorbed the wonder of her surroundings, made more intoxicating by the man trailing them.

When they came out of the trees into a clearing near the river, the skeleton of a house appeared before them. Beyond it, the Grand Teton stood like a sentinel. Alex had never seen anything so spectacular.

"What a beautiful house!"

"Yep. Uncle Buck built it."

Alex turned to look at Buck. "I thought you were a rancher."

"I grew up learning how to do construction. My father and brothers run Summerhayes Construction in Colorado Springs."

"Why didn't you go back to the business after you left the military?"

"I met the guys in the hospital. We had a lot of time to talk and think about our lives once we were no longer deployed. Compared to what we'd lived through, Carson's life as a rancher sounded like a piece of heaven. It got to me and Ross.

"We were filled with guilt that we'd survived the war and others hadn't. The idea of turning his ranch into a dude ranch for helping children who'd lost their dads in the war grew on us until we couldn't think about anything else. I figured I could put all the training I'd learned from my father to work building cabins and remodeling the ranch house. One thing led to another."

"And now he's built us our house! He made the loft just for me!" Johnny declared with a happy face.

Alex smiled. "Well, aren't you just the luckiest boy

in the world to have a daddy like Carson and an uncle like Buck."

"Buck can do anything!" Jenny exclaimed.

"I know," Johnny said in that way of his. He rode over to a nearby stand of jack pines and dismounted by himself. Jenny needed help. While Buck jumped down to assist her, Alex swung her leg over and got down from Blossom. They tied the reins to tree trunks and started walking around. Johnny pointed out where every room would be.

"Mine's going to be in the loft. How long before I can go up there to look around, Uncle Buck?"

He was already inspecting the work. "In a few more days." The last word came out on a cough.

"That long? I want Jenny to be able to see it." Alex expected some kind of remark from her granddaughter about not wanting to go home, but oddly enough she remained quiet and kept following Johnny around. "We're going to go down by the river and watch the beavers."

"Don't get too close," Buck warned.

"We won't."

As they ran off, Buck came to stand by her. She turned to him. "It's going to be spectacular when it's finished. Paradise for a boy like Johnny."

"Carson hired an architect to design something contemporary. There'll be a lot of glass. He and Tracy want as much light as possible."

"I'd want the same thing so I could enjoy every season here. With a view like this, it will be beautiful in winter, sitting in front of a fire." The second the words came out, she cried, "Oh, no—I forgot."

He smiled. "We'll be putting in a fireplace, but it

will be more for effect. Whether gas log or wood, the smoke is real."

"I'm so sorry you have to suffer," she whispered.

"It's a small price to pay to be alive." Shadows marred his features. "Daniel's death shouldn't have happened," he said in a hushed tone.

"Even so, he chose to go into the marines and knew it was possible he wouldn't come home. What no one expected was the sudden illness that attacked Christy and took her life. If I've learned anything so far, it's that life is precious and fragile. Coming to the ranch has taught me something else. You need to make every moment count in case it's your last."

He eyed her beneath the rim of his Stetson. "You sound as if you've made some kind of decision."

"I have. Last night Frank asked me to cut our vacation short and return home to get started on some counseling I'd planned for me and Jenny. You know, to help her adjust to our impending marriage. But watching her smile and laugh again, I know I don't want to leave until our vacation is over. Truth be told, Frank didn't want me to bring Jenny to the ranch in the first place."

Buck's eyebrows met in a frown. "Why not?"

"Since you're all marines, he worried she'd think too much about her father's death and it wouldn't help her to get on with her life." Alex swallowed hard. "But I haven't found that to be true. In fact, it's just the opposite because Johnny lost his father, too, and they talk about it. I think it's been healthy for her."

"For Johnny, as well," Buck concurred. "Kids have their own system for relating. Carson's been worried about Johnny since he and Tracy got married. He knew it would be a big adjustment for him even though he does love Carson."

"Well, you can tell Carson for me, that boy is one of the happiest, cutest, most well-adjusted children I've ever met. I know Tracy has a lot to do with it, but Johnny told me himself that Carson was his favorite person in the whole wide world besides his birth father."

Buck inhaled sharply. "That'll make his day."

"I guess it doesn't come as any surprise that Jenny thinks the world of you." He had to have seen the way Jenny was smiling at him earlier.

"I'm flattered, but the truth is, every child enjoys attention." Apparently, Buck didn't do well with compliments. His modesty was one more thing to add to the list of his virtues.

"That's true, but she's given you a lot of thought, like, for example, do you ever go on a vacation?"

His eyes darted to hers in surprise. "Why do you think she would ask that?"

"Maybe she worries you'll leave while she's still here."

"I just got back from the only vacation I've taken since I got out of the hospital."

"Where did you go?"

"Colorado Springs to see my family. I was only there three days. My mother wished it had been longer, but I told her I had to get back to host the new family flying in."

"Do you have a large family?" Alex couldn't learn enough about him fast enough.

"Pretty big. Four brothers, all married with children, and lots of extended family. I'll always like working with my hands the way they do, but you can't beat ranch living. I'm here to stay."

Alex knew she was taking a big chance to ask her next question, but something had come over her and she decided to risk it. "If you'd married your soul mate, would you be working with your father today?"

He slanted a look at her, one she couldn't decipher. "I'll never know the answer to that. The girl I loved married my brother, Sam."

No-o. *"Buck—"*

"Take that devastated look off your face. It happened twelve years ago while I was attending the University of Colorado at Boulder on scholarship. They didn't mean for it to happen. I'm glad they got together before we ever made it to the altar. It saved everyone a world of pain and trouble."

Even so, she was sick for the hurt he'd had to endure at the time.

"I can read your mind, Alex, but seeing Melanie and Sam together has nothing to do with my only staying in Colorado for a few days."

"I believe you."

"By the time I'd been deployed to Afghanistan, I'd gotten over it and gave them my full blessing. It's ancient history and there've been plenty of women since then."

Alex didn't doubt it.

"Melanie was my high school love, but we were never meant to be. Not very many high school affairs last."

"I know what you're saying. Kyle and I had no destiny. At the time it killed me, but it's amazing how time heals those wounds."

"Amen to that. The only reason I didn't take a week off to be with the family is because the guys and I are doing everything possible to make our venture work. I love my family and during the winter when we don't have so many guests, I'll spend more time with them."

"Thanks for telling me, Buck. When Jenny learns you don't have plans to leave the ranch anytime soon, she'll stop fretting. Since her mother and father died, she's turned into a worrywart."

"I've noticed. This morning when I bumped into her and Johnny in the back hall, they wanted to drive to the building site with me. I told them they couldn't because the workers were there and it was in the hard-hat stage. She promptly asked me if I wore one. When I said yes, she made me promise to keep it on the whole time. She's a sweetheart."

Her darling granddaughter was watching out for him. Jenny had never shown that kind of worry over Frank when he'd had a bad case of bronchitis, or when he'd slipped on the tennis court and had to be hospitalized for a torn leg muscle.

While she was cogitating on that fact, they both heard Johnny's blood-curdling cry for help, followed by Jenny's screams. Buck took off so fast Alex didn't have time to blink. With her heart in her throat, she raced after him. A dozen horrifying scenarios passed through her mind, giving her feet wings.

Buck was already there. Jenny was standing on top of a big beaver dam while Johnny stood on the grassy bank beside it. It appeared as if Jenny's leg had gone through part of the wooden structure. "I can't get out!" she cried in a terrified voice. "It hurts! Come and get me, Buck! Come and get me!" Tears streamed down her cheeks.

He was already in the water. Alex could imagine him as a frogman, swimming against the fast current toward her granddaughter with torpedo-like strength. "I'm almost there. Easy does it, Jenny. Don't move."

Alex ran down to Johnny and put her arms around him, hugging him tight. "She's going to be all right."

Johnny had gone pale. "I was going to come and get you, but she begged me not to leave her."

"You did exactly the right thing."

"I told her she shouldn't walk on it, but she wouldn't listen to me. She lost her hat when her leg fell through. It's floating down the river."

"Don't worry about that. We can always get her a new one. What's important is that she's going to be okay." Knowing Buck was there made all the difference. Without him, Alex would be hysterical.

"Dad said it was dangerous. He wasn't kidding!"

"No, he wasn't, and now I'm afraid Jenny's had to learn a lesson the hard way."

"Are you mad at her?"

"Oh, no, honey. Accidents happen."

"You're nice." He hugged her hard.

"So are you," she whispered. Alex loved this boy who'd been through the same grief as Jenny.

For the next few minutes, Alex held her breath while Buck dug through the debris on his stomach to reach Jenny and extricate her leg. When he got her free, she howled in pain. He comforted her the best he could while he swam with her to the shore with her arms clutched around his neck.

"Alex?" he called to her. "Phone the ranch and tell someone to come in one of the vans stat! We need to get her to the hospital pronto. She's injured her ankle."

Alex did his bidding, and in a minute she got Tracy who said she'd be right there. By the time the van arrived, Buck had brought Jenny to shore and carried her up the incline to the road leading into the building site.

While Johnny climbed in front with his mom, Alex sat on the bench in back next to a dripping wet Buck and Jenny. Jenny lay across them with a pinched white face, still hugging Buck for dear life. Alex supported her legs. Her right cowboy boot was still on, but the left boot was missing and her ankle looked swollen.

"It hurts so much, Nana."

"I know it does, brave girl, but thanks to Buck nothing worse has happened. The doctor will fix you up in no time."

"Try to lie still," Buck encouraged her. "You know something?" He kissed her cheek. "The next time I see that beaver, I'm going to have to teach him how to build a better dam so there won't be any holes in it."

Jenny actually giggled before she started crying again. Before long they reached the hospital in Jackson.

An attendant brought over a gurney and Jenny was wheeled inside a cubicle. Soon she was getting fed through an IV and given something for her pain. The nurse changed her out of her wet clothes and put her in a hospital gown. After the initial examination by the doctor, she was taken to X-ray. Alex had to stay behind. The wait seemed to take forever until she was wheeled back in.

"Nana—"

"I'm right here, sweetheart." Alex sat on a chair next to her and held the hand that was free of the IV. "I love you and I think you were very courageous while you waited for Buck to rescue you."

"It doesn't hurt as much now. Where is he?" She sounded sleepy.

Alex had no idea. "I'm sure he'll be back in a few minutes."

"Okay." Her eyes closed.

Tracy peeked around the curtain and came in. Alex got up and they hugged. "Thank you for bringing the van so fast."

"I'm just glad I was available to help. Are you all right, Alex?" she asked quietly.

"Yes, but we wouldn't be without Buck. I don't know what I would have done if we'd been alone. That darling son of yours yelled loud enough for us to hear him. You never saw anyone react to an emergency so fast or expertly as Buck."

"As we both know, that comes from his military training."

"Where is he?"

"He took Johnny with him to give the information to triage. He knew Jenny wouldn't want you to leave her side."

"Oh, Tracy, I'm so thankful for him," she whispered. "When I think what could have happened…"

"But it didn't."

She wiped her eyes. "He just dived into that water—wallet, cell phone, watch and all."

"Those things are replaceable."

"I know, b-but he needs a change of clothes." Alex felt jittery.

"I've already talked to Carson. He'll be here shortly with some things for him and Jenny."

"Oh, thank you. I only remembered now that we left the horses at the building site."

"Ross is taking care of that. You just concentrate on Jenny. I'm going to slip out and see if they've arrived yet. I'll be right back."

Alex sat back down and clung to Jenny's hand. In a minute the doctor came in. "Mrs. Wilson? Your granddaughter has an ankle fracture. The good news is, the fracture isn't badly displaced, so we'll splint her instead of applying a cast. That way it will allow more room for swelling, should it continue."

"Thank goodness it's not too serious."

"We'll keep her overnight. You can ask for a cot to be brought into the room for you."

"I appreciate that."

"In the morning we'll send her home with crutches. Keep her leg elevated as much as possible for the first twenty-four hours. Apply cold compresses at intervals if necessary. She can take ibuprofen and return to normal activity, except for sports, in another day."

"How long will she have to use crutches?"

"We'll want to see her in outpatient in ten days, and then we can tell you better. Most ankle injuries take four to eight weeks to heal. She's young, so she'll probably recover faster than an adult."

"I surely hope so."

"You're welcome to stay while we splint her."

"Thank you so much."

Twenty minutes later Jenny was ready to be wheeled out of the E.R. and into a private room. When Alex emerged from the cubicle, Buck was there waiting for them, dressed in dry jeans and a T-shirt. No one had ever looked so wonderful to her. His compassionate eyes sought hers before he leaned over Jenny and kissed her forehead.

"Hey, Red—"

Alex watched her granddaughter's eyelids flutter open. "Buck—"

"How are you doing?"

Tears filled her eyes. "The doctor says I can't go home until tomorrow. Will you stay with me and Nana?"

"What do *you* think?"

Jenny sniffed, struggling to hold back from crying. Alex was struggling herself.

The orderlies wheeled Jenny along until they arrived at her room and transported her to the bed. A different nurse came in to elevate her leg and make her comfortable.

After she left, Jenny asked, "Is Johnny here?"

"No," Buck answered. "His parents took him home, but we'll see him tomorrow."

"I wish he didn't have to go. The accident was my fault."

"You know what? I always did want to walk on top of the dam so I could watch that beaver. It's a good thing I didn't. Otherwise I'd have fallen right through it." A wan smile came and went. "Was it fun before you got trapped?"

"No. It was scary. Is my cowboy boot still stuck in the dam?"

"Afraid so. We'll get you another pair. I think you're the bravest girl I've ever known."

"Thanks, but I shouldn't have done it. Johnny told me not to. Thanks for saving me."

"It was my pleasure."

"You looked like a fish coming through the water."

He grinned. "Yeah?"

"But I wasn't scared, because I knew it was you." Buck could do no wrong.

The nurse chose that moment to come in again with some apple juice for Jenny. She looked at Alex. "We're serving dinner now, if she's hungry. I can bring it out to you."

"I can't believe it's that late already. Thank you— that sounds great."

The nurse returned a few minutes later with two trays. Buck arranged the chairs on both sides of the bed and the three of them settled down to eat.

"Does this roll look good? You can have it. I'll get myself another one," Buck said.

Jenny nodded and bit into it. "It tastes nummy. Thanks."

Her granddaughter might not have wanted it if Alex had been the one to offer it. She could see the hero worship in Jenny's eyes as she gazed at Buck.

"Do you know something?" he said. "You don't look sick. In fact, you don't look like you should be in the hospital."

"You were in a hospital, too, huh?"

"Yes. That's where I met Ross and Carson."

"I know. Did you have to be in it a long time?"

"Five weeks."

Jenny made a face. "I get to go home tomorrow."

"That'll make Johnny happy."

"Buck, do you have a girlfriend? Johnny says you have lots of them."

Alex almost choked on her roast beef.

"Yes. In fact, I've got a special one now."

His answer trapped Alex's lungs in a vise.

"You do? What's her name?"

"Red."

Jenny giggled, but after she quieted down, she looked at him with a serious expression. "Are you ever going to get married? Johnny heard his parents say you're getting old."

"Johnny shouldn't repeat everything he hears," Alex muttered, but no one was listening because Buck had broken into laughter. It rebounded off the hospital room walls.

"You're never too old to get married, Jenny."

"My daddy got married at seventeen."

"Sometimes you meet the right woman fast. Sometimes it takes a long time to meet her."

"Johnny asked me how old Frank was. I told him fifty-five. He said that's as old as his Grandpa Baretta."

Alex couldn't take any more of this conversation. "Jenny? Are you hungry for anything more?"

"No."

"In that case, I'm going to lower the head of your bed so you can relax and go to sleep. You've had a big day and need your rest so that ankle will get better faster."

"The doctor said I have to see him in ten days. That means we'll have to stay at the ranch longer."

Sensing where this conversation was headed, Alex

said, "We'll talk about all that tomorrow. Say good-night to Buck."

"But I thought he was going to stay with us tonight."

"He can't, sweetheart." She spoke before Buck could. "He has work to do back at the ranch. Carson and Ross are relying on him."

Buck put his tray on the cart and leaned over her. "I'll be here in the morning to drive you home. How does that sound?"

"Good," she answered in a tremulous voice, and kissed his cheek. "Thank you for saving me. I love you."

*No-o.* The words had slipped out from Jenny's heart. She'd never said them to Frank. Alex groaned because she had the strongest conviction she never would.

"I love you, too. You're my best girl, remember?"

"Yes."

He stood. "Good night, Alex. Call if you need anything." She watched his tall form disappear out the door, leaving her in utter turmoil.

## Chapter Six

"There she is in a wheelchair!"

His pulse raced. *And there's Alex.*

Buck had prevailed on Tracy to let Johnny come in the van with him. She said she was afraid to take advantage of him, but he insisted Johnny was a joy to be around, which was the truth. He could also cheer Jenny up better than anyone. And from a selfish standpoint, Johnny would provide the buffer Buck needed to keep his emotional distance from Alex.

He understood why she wanted to marry Frank. In addition to love and affection, he could offer her stability. He was a bank vice president and could provide her with a nice home, spending money and all the benefits that came with marriage.

When Jenny had brought up the question of a girl-friend last night, he realized he was hardly in a position to ask anyone to marry him. He was a vet with a disease, only a small nest egg and a job that might turn into a lifelong career as a rancher, but these were early days. He lived upstairs in the ranch house. Had no place of his own.

It was a good life, but hardly one he could share with

a woman who wanted and needed all the things a man like Frank could supply.

That time he'd spent in the hospital with the guys had given him focus and a reason to get on with life. He'd been doing fine since coming to Wyoming. There'd been women. There'd be more of them as soon as Alex and Jenny went back to Sacramento.

Only four more days left to endure this fatal attraction. He could handle that. Stick to groups. Keep Johnny close. Not spend any alone time with her. Then she'd be out of sight. Hopefully, after a while, she'd be out of mind. It terrified him that he might not be able to forget her.

Buck pulled up to the entrance. "Johnny? If you'll open the back door, I'll lift Jenny inside."

"Okay." The boy jumped down from the passenger side, while Buck got out of the van and went around.

"Good morning, you two."

Both females flashed him a smile. "Thanks for coming to get me, Buck."

"I couldn't wait." It was the truth. He'd spent a restless night anticipating the morning to come.

Johnny looked at the splint. "Does it hurt?"

"A little bit."

"Come on. Let's get you inside so we can all go home."

The nurse steadied the wheelchair for Buck while he picked Jenny up and placed her on the seat. Alex climbed in back next to Jenny, carrying a plastic bag that probably held her other clothes. He fastened Jenny's seat belt, taking care with her injured ankle. There was nothing he'd rather do than fasten her nana's, but that was out of the question.

Johnny climbed in and sat opposite them while Buck shut the door. Getting behind the wheel, he called out, "Who wants doughnuts?"

"I do!" the kids shouted at once.

He headed for the drive-through and picked up half a dozen doughnuts before they drove back to the ranch. The conversation between the kids was hilarious and prevented Buck from having to say anything. By the time he pulled up to the cabin, the doughnuts had been eaten and everyone was happy to go inside.

Jenny looped her arms around Buck's neck as he carried her into the living room and laid her down on the couch. Alex propped up her leg and head with pillows. Johnny brought in the crutches and tried using them. After a couple of failures, he got the knack.

"Hey—this is easy."

"Jenny can try it tomorrow. Today she needs to rest."

Johnny laid the crutches on one of the chairs and walked over to her. "Do you want to watch cartoons or movies?"

"Can you get that Hopalong DVD?"

"Yeah! I'll go get it right now."

"I'll drive you," Buck volunteered. It was time to get out of there before he started enjoying himself too much.

"Can't you stay?"

He'd expected that from Jenny. "I'll come back with lunch for everybody. Right now, I've got to get some work done."

"Okay, but hurry."

"You know I will. Come on, Johnny."

He left without looking at Alex, but she followed him out to the van. "Wait—"

Buck rolled down the window. "What's wrong? If there's something you need, say the word and I'll get it."

"I know you will. That's what's wrong." Her incredible blue eyes searched his as if she were looking for something, but couldn't find it. "I'm afraid the Forrester family has turned into the ranch's biggest liability. My debt to you and your partners has gotten out of hand with her hospitalization, for which I refuse to let your insurance pay. I have insurance.

"Last night while Jenny was asleep, I looked into flights leaving for Salt Lake. Jenny and I are taking the 10:00 a.m. flight out tomorrow morning and we'll make a connecting flight to Sacramento. Frank is meeting us at the airport."

Buck froze. "Your vacation isn't over until Saturday morning. Yesterday you told me you planned to stay the whole week."

She moistened her lips—out of nerves, he presumed. "It ended when she got hurt. I thought if I gave you a heads-up, you'd be able to plan accordingly. We'll need to be at the airport by eight-thirty."

"Alex—"

"The accident disrupted everyone," she interrupted. "We're leaving so this cabin can go to the next lucky child on your list who'll be able to enjoy everything this dude ranch has to offer."

What she was saying didn't sound like the Alex he'd come to know. The woman who'd been so grateful for the opportunity afforded them that she'd expressed her gratitude constantly.

Something else was behind her sudden decision to go back to California and she was using Jenny's accident as the excuse. Frank hadn't wanted her to come in the first place. If he was behind this, she'd never tell Buck.

"Alex—tomorrow she'll be able to get around on her crutches. We have several cars here for the benefit of the guests. You can keep one and use it to take her places. That way you won't be inconveniencing anyone."

"I can't ask that."

"Not even for your granddaughter?" Maybe if he played on her guilt. "Jenny hasn't begun to see everything yet. We've planned an overnight campout at Secret Lake, Johnny's favorite spot. The drive is beautiful, and she'll be able to sit on a lounge chair and fish to her heart's content."

Alex rubbed her temples, leading him to believe she had a headache. He would be amazed if she didn't have one after yesterday's trauma. "I appreciate what you're saying and it all sounds amazing, but I've already made plane reservations."

He bit down so hard, he almost severed his tongue. "I'm sorry to hear that."

"I—I need to ask something else of you." Her voice faltered. "It'll be the last favor, I promise."

Buck struggled to keep his emotions under some semblance of control. "What is it?"

Her chest rose and fell as if what she was about to say was causing her great distress. "I would rather you didn't bring us lunch. Jenny thinks you're her personal genie. We had a good breakfast at the hospital. When we're hungry again, I'll walk to the ranch house and get us some food. Johnny will stay with her long enough for that."

Before Buck could get another word out, she hurried up the steps into the cabin and shut the door.

He closed his eyes tightly for a minute before starting the engine. Halfway to the ranch house, he felt something stir at his side.

Damn if it wasn't Johnny, who'd been sitting next to him quietly the whole time, listening. Buck slammed on the brakes. When he looked over, he saw tears in the boy's soulful brown eyes. "I don't want Jenny to leave."

"You're not the only one, sport, but you heard her nana."

"Can't you make her stay?"

After a burst of coughing, he said, "Could you have stopped Jenny from climbing on the beaver dam?"

"I could have tackled her."

He probably could have, being a little taller and heavier than Jenny. Despite his pain, Buck laughed. "You think that's what I ought to do? Tackle Alex?" The thought brought on a whole fantasy he needed to delete from his mind forever.

"We've got to do something! Jenny loves it here! She told me she never wants to go home."

Johnny was as upset as Buck.

"There's a reason why I can't stop her. She and Jenny came on vacation, but Jenny can't do any sports for a while."

"That doesn't matter."

"It does to Alex. She would rather take care of her granddaughter at home where she has all her things to keep her entertained. She doesn't want to be a burden around here." *And there was always Frank waiting in the wings.* Buck's hands gripped the steering wheel so tightly, it was a miracle he didn't break it.

"What's a *burden?*"

"She doesn't want us waiting on them when we have other things to do."

"What other things?"

Another laugh escaped his lips. Oh, to be a child again where everything was so simple.

"If they go, she'll miss my birthday party. Mom's got all this stuff planned. We're going to the Funorama. Jenny would love it there."

"I'm as sorry as you are, Johnny. You have no idea."

On that note, he drove the rest of the way to the ranch house and pulled onto the parking area to let Johnny out. "Let your mom know you're back before you go looking for that DVD. I'm headed for the building site."

"Okay." He got out of the Jeep and started walking. There was a slump to his young shoulders. Johnny looked the way Buck felt.

When Alex had asked him not to bring them lunch, she'd really been telling him he'd done enough for them. Other than giving them a ride to the airport in the morning, she didn't expect to see him again. He understood she didn't want to make things more difficult for Jenny.

Buck got it, and he'd honor her wishes. But he didn't have to like it.

AFTER TURNING ON a cartoon for Jenny to watch, Alex went into the bathroom to shed the clothes she'd slept in at the hospital and take a shower. Her body trembled beneath the water as she washed her hair.

That speech she'd made to Buck before she could take the words back had been one of the hardest things she'd ever had to do in her life. But last night, while she'd tossed and turned on that hospital cot, she'd had an epiphany and a clear grasp of her situation.

If she loved Frank the way she'd thought she loved him before arriving at the ranch, then meeting Buck wouldn't have made any kind of impact. But the truth was, she was conflicted about her feelings because of Buck. For him to affect her this fast and this strongly made Alex realize she wasn't in love with Frank the way she needed to be and couldn't possibly marry him.

For both their sakes, their relationship needed to end immediately so he could meet someone else. Frank had enjoyed a happy marriage and wanted to have that again. Naturally, he did.

Alex had been alone for so long, it had felt good to have a man she cared about and trusted in her life. She'd wanted to get married and would have done so when Jenny was more amenable.

But then she'd met Buck Summerhayes. He had had such a profound effect on her already that she was shaken to the core. Through no fault of his own, Buck had been the catalyst that reminded Alex of the girl she'd once been. The girl with stars in her eyes who'd once been passionately in love. Being with him these past few days had brought back all those intense feelings of breathlessness and excitement, the element of wonder and the anticipation of new possibilities that made you thankful to be alive.

All of that had been missing from her life since Kyle had abandoned her, only to be resurrected by one ex-marine who was carving out a new life for himself in the Tetons with his partners. It was clear from their conversation that he wasn't ready for marriage yet. He had girlfriends and was still enjoying his bachelor life.

If Buck could produce these feelings in her without even trying or being aware of it, then so could another man, but she needed to put herself in a position to find him. On this trip Alex had found out she *wanted* to experience those feelings again.

Last night she'd done a lot of heavy thinking. If she lived to be eighty or even ninety, then she needed to fill the next forty or fifty years with new adventures. She had no idea when or if this special man would come along, but she planned to find out.

First of all, she was going to give her two weeks' notice at the bank. She had enough savings for her and Jenny to live off while she looked for a new job. Something different that would challenge her and give her a new perspective.

That was what Buck had done after returning from war. Instead of going back to the family business, he'd joined forces with Carson and Ross. Anyone could see how happy and fulfilled he was.

Maybe it would require a move to a different city. Her parents had been retired for a few years and lived on the California side of Lake Tahoe. They came every three weeks or so for a visit. Maybe Alex would look for work there. Jenny would be so glad she wasn't marrying Frank, and she'd love being closer to her great-grandparents.

Once Alex had finished getting dressed and had

blow-dried her hair, she walked into the living room. "Sweetheart? How's the pain?"

"It doesn't hurt now. I wish I could get up."

"I'm glad your leg's feeling better. If you rest today, then tomorrow you can use your crutches to get around. Do you mind if I turn off the TV? I want to talk to you before Johnny comes back."

"What about?"

Alex shut the television off with the remote and sat in a chair next to her. "I've got a plan, but you need to listen until I'm through talking. Will you do that for me?"

A worried look crossed over her granddaughter's face before she nodded.

"First of all, you need to know we're flying back to Sacramento tomorrow." Instantly, tears sprang from the girl's eyes. "Here's the reason why."

Without discussing Buck, Alex laid it out that she wasn't going to marry Frank after all. "And I'm going to make you a promise. As soon as your splint comes off, we'll fly back here and finish the rest of our vacation. I bet it can come off in a month. We'll bring some presents for Johnny and throw him a surprise birthday party. But it will be our secret for now. Okay?"

That brought a glimmer to her eyes. After a long silence, she said, "You really promise?" Her question told her that Jenny was overjoyed Frank wouldn't be in their lives anymore. It also meant she'd accepted the change in plans to leave tomorrow instead of Saturday.

"I've never lied to you, have I?"

"No." Her answer coincided with a knock on the door.

"That'll be Johnny. I'll get it." Alex hurried to open

it and discovered Tracy had come with her son. She was carrying a sack.

"Hi! I came to see how our famous patient is doing."

"She's fine. Please, come in."

"Johnny and I decided to bring Popsicles and potato chips. We also brought a couple of his board games and some DVDs."

"Fantastic. I'll put the Popsicles in the freezer for now."

Tracy walked over to the couch. "How are you feeling, honey?"

"Good. My leg doesn't hurt."

"That's the best news we've heard."

"Do you want to watch Hopalong?" Johnny asked.

"Yes."

"Well, have fun, everyone. I'll come back in a while and see how you're all doing."

Alex walked her to the door. When they were out of earshot of the children, Tracy turned to her. "Is it true you're leaving tomorrow?"

"Yes. I need to get her home and check in with the doctor there. Her friend Mandy will be happy to see her."

"I understand there's a man in your life. No doubt he'll be anxious to have you back, too."

Alex nodded, not wanting to get into it. She had to end it with Frank before she told anyone else, except Jenny of course. "I talked to my parents early this morning. They're going to come and stay at the house with us for a week."

"I'm happy for you, but sorry for Johnny. He's taken

such a liking to Jenny. We've got a whole month before he's back in school and able to make new friends."

"I know how that goes, and the feeling's mutual, believe me, but under the circumstances it's for the best we get back home. You have to know we've had the time of our lives here. What your husband and the others are doing for children like Jenny is so noble, I tear up thinking about it."

"I felt the same way when I got the letter. It was overwhelming."

Alex nodded. "And look what happened when you brought your Johnny to the ranch." She smiled at Tracy, who blushed.

"From anguish to pure joy. That was how it felt after I met Carson."

"They're remarkable men. Buck was positively heroic yesterday. This grandma will never forget what he did." Alex emphasized the word *grandma* to help keep her mental distance from the man who'd lit up her life over the past few days.

Tracy shook her head. "No one would believe you're a grandmother. My husband says you're way too young and beautiful."

"He doesn't see me when I first wake up in the morning." They both chuckled.

"Jenny and I will never be able to thank him or the rest of you enough."

"It's been our pleasure. Send Johnny home when he's worn out his welcome. He can talk your ear off," Tracy said with a laugh before she left.

Alex leaned against the closed door. Johnny usually had a lot to say, but not right now. Both children watched the cowboy video without saying a word. It was Alex's fault, and yet the strongest emotion she felt at the moment was relief that she'd set their plans in motion and Jenny wasn't fighting her.

AFTER A SLEEPLESS night, Buck needed coffee. He leaped down the stairs three at a time and headed for the kitchen. Pouring himself a cup, he strode through the hall to the office. He didn't know if Alex had asked for a wheelchair, but in case she hadn't, he'd called the airport to reserve one for her ahead of time.

"Morning."

He reared his head when he discovered he wasn't alone. "Hey, guys." Carson and Ross were both drinking coffee, too.

Carson flashed him a curious glance. "You weren't at dinner last night and we didn't hear you come in."

"I searched along the river for Jenny's cowboy hat. I thought if I found it downstream, I'd give it to her for a souvenir, but I didn't have any luck."

"Some guest from the ranch will probably fish it out next spring," Ross murmured.

By then it would be too late. Far too late.

"How soon will you be taking our guests to the airport?"

He eyed Carson. "Their plane leaves at ten. I'll call her at seven-thirty to alert her." It was almost that time now. "We'll leave at eight."

"With Johnny's birthday coming up, it's a shame to see them go so soon. Tracy has already put plan B into action by arranging for Cory, his favorite cousin in Cleveland, to fly out and stay for a week. Hopefully the surprise will offset his disappointment."

Disappointment didn't begin to cover what Buck was feeling. "Does Johnny want to come to the airport with me?"

"That's up to you."

"The more the merrier."

"I'll tell him to get dressed and eat some breakfast quick. Be right back."

Buck felt Ross's eyes on him after Carson walked out. "What?"

"How come you're letting her leave?"

He swallowed the rest of his coffee. "What are you talking about? She's a grown woman who came at our invitation and now she's going home to marry her boyfriend. She wants to get Jenny back in familiar surroundings."

"And that's okay with you."

Ross could be relentless. This time he'd struck a nerve. "Frank's waiting for her."

"Frank wasn't on her mind when I took dinner to her and Jenny. Last night she opened her door expecting to see you. If you could have seen the look of pain in her eyes..."

"Shut up, Ross."

"It's the kind I see in yours right now," he persisted. "Why in the hell aren't you going to do something about it?"

"Like what?" he bit out angrily.

"Tell her how you feel!"

"I would if she'd given me *one* signal."

"She's been throwing them out right and left, but for

some reason I can't understand, you've refused to read anything into them. What are you afraid of?"

"The truth is, I don't want to be the guy responsible for interfering with her relationship with Frank. I was on the receiving end of a similar situation once, remember?" The guys had shared everything when they'd been hospitalized together. There were few secrets left.

"This is different. And Alex doesn't have a ring on her finger yet."

"So that makes her fair game?"

"You know it does!"

Maybe, but that wasn't all of it. Buck hadn't had these kinds of feelings for a woman since Melanie. The idea of risking everything again only to be rejected, terrified him. "I don't want to talk about it."

"That's too bad. I feel for you. Let me know if there's anything I can do." He started out the door.

At the last second, Buck called after him. "Ross?" His friend hesitated. "Thank you."

"Don't mention it."

No sooner had he left than Johnny came running in. "Dad said I could go with you. Is that okay?"

He gave Johnny a hug. "I want you to come. It'll make it more fun for Jenny." *And save my life.* "We'll take the van so she can prop her foot on the seat. First I have to let Alex know we're coming."

"Okay."

Buck picked up the house phone receiver and rang through to the cabin. It wasn't long before she answered. "Hello?" He felt her voice snake through him.

"Alex? It's Buck. How's Jenny this morning?"

"She's doing better than expected."

"And you?"

"I'm fine." Code for any number of things she wasn't about to reveal to him.

"That's good. Have you eaten breakfast?"

"We filled up on fruit and granola bars. I even stuffed some of those homemade packets of pine nuts in our pockets."

"Those nuts are addictive." He couldn't handle this unsatisfying conversation any longer. "If you're ready, Johnny and I will come by for you."

"I'm glad he's coming. I think we're all packed."

"Then we'll be there shortly." He hung up. "Let's go!"

Within a few minutes, he'd started up the van and they headed for the cabin. Buck tried not to think that when they got back from the airport, another guest would take up residence and there'd be no evidence that the Forrester family had ever stayed there. At the thought, the hollow feeling inside threatened to envelop him.

Once he pulled up in front, Johnny scrambled out of the front seat and ran up to the door. Buck followed, but his legs felt like lead.

When Alex opened the door, she was dressed in the outfit she'd worn on the plane, looking elegant and completely gorgeous. He quickly averted his eyes and walked over to Jenny who was half lying on the couch.

"Hey, Red. Guess what? It's beautiful weather outside. No storm anywhere. When you fly out, you'll be able to see the mountains and the ranch. I'll be watching from the building site when your plane takes off. Look out the window at five after ten and I'll wave to you. When you see me, wave back."

She smiled. "I will."

"Promise?" he teased.

"Yes."

"Okay. Put your arms around my neck and I'll carry you out to the van. You should save using your crutches until you're back home in Sacramento."

Johnny helped Alex carry out their two bags and the crutches. Buck helped settle them in the back. When everyone was strapped in, he swung the van around and they drove out to the highway. He avoided looking through the rearview mirror in case he wouldn't be able to take his eyes off Alex.

The kids talked about the ponies and Moppy, while Buck and Alex put in a word here and there.

"I never got to see her."

"Maybe she's been playing with some squirrels in the other trees."

"But I didn't see any other squirrels."

As soon as Buck pulled up to the terminal, he told everyone to stay put while he went to get the wheelchair. It was such a novelty, the children were excited. After Buck had helped Jenny into it, Johnny volunteered to push her inside. Buck grabbed the bags and the four of them entered the terminal.

"Hey, Buck!"

Out of the corner of his eye, he saw Janie Olsen smiling at him. She worked for one of the airlines. They'd had a couple of dinner dates, but he hadn't followed up.

"How are you doing, Janie?" he said, but he kept walking past her to the counter where he checked in Alex's bags and the crutches. In return, he got their boarding passes. They had an hour's wait.

A TV was playing in the lounge. Since no one was watching, Buck flipped the channel to the cartoon network for the kids. Jenny shared her pine nuts with Johnny while they laughed at the antics on screen.

Buck looked down at Alex, who'd taken a seat next to her granddaughter. "If you'll tell me what airline you'll be connecting with in Salt Lake, I'll ask the employee at the counter to arrange ahead for a wheelchair at both ends."

Her eyes were a more intense blue than usual. "That's so thoughtful of you, Buck. It's Skyways."

"I'll be right back."

With that errand taken care of, he returned and pulled one of the seats around so they could talk. He handed her the passes. "How are you going to manage work with Jenny incapacitated?"

"My parents are coming from Lake Tahoe tomorrow to help for a while."

He knew next to nothing about her parents. They were Jenny's great-grandparents. Amazing. There was still so much he didn't know about her life. *And never would.* He coughed. "I'm glad you're going to have help."

"I'll phone her friend Mandy's mom and see if she can't spend some with Jenny, but I know she's going to really miss Johnny. Tracy came over yesterday morning and we both agreed the children had a great time together. Too much of a great time, perhaps," she said on a nervous laugh. "My granddaughter decided to show off in front of Johnny, to her peril."

Buck cocked his head. "Things like that happen when you're really having fun."

"I suppose."

The children grew bored and Johnny started pushing Jenny around in the wheelchair. "Look at them."

She nodded. "They're a pair, aren't they?" After a silence, she added, "Thank heaven you were there, Buck." It came out as a sudden torrent of words. "She's the luckiest little girl in the world to have been rescued by you. My heart almost failed me when I saw her on top of that dam. If she'd fallen off into the current…"

"She couldn't have. Her boot was wedged in that hole too tightly."

"But you knew exactly what to do, while I stood there in absolute panic. You have my undying gratitude for everything you've done for us from the moment you picked us up here. We'll never forget you. As for Jenny, you have a special place in her heart." Her voice wobbled.

"That goes both ways."

"Except for her daddy and my father, she's never told another man she loved him. So you see, that letter from the ranch inviting us here truly did bring her great happiness despite her accident. The Daddy Dude Ranch achieved its objective. Please let Ross and Carson know that."

It was a good thing their flight was announced right then because Buck's endurance had worn out. He got up and went over to the children. "It's time for you to board."

"I wish you didn't have to go," Johnny said, taking hold of one of the wheelchair's handles. Buck took the other and they rolled her to the entrance where one of the attendants took over. Other passengers had queued up. "See ya, Jenny."

"See ya, Johnny." Her eyes filled with tears. "Bye, Buck."

"So long, Red." He kissed her on the forehead. "Take care of that ankle."

"I will."

Alex grabbed Johnny and gave him a big hug. When she lifted her head, her wet eyes met Buck's. "*You* take care of that cough."

Twenty minutes later Buck watched the jet take off from the building site and waved. The pain in his gut was unreal.

## Chapter Seven

The orthopedic surgeon reentered the examination room, smiling at Alex and Jenny. "Are you two ready for the good news?" Jenny nodded. "I've seen the X-ray we just took and your ankle has healed beautifully. We can take off the splint."

Jenny beamed.

He put her up on the end of the exam table and proceeded to remove it. Then he helped her down and asked her to walk around. "Your leg's like brand-new. No more need for crutches."

"Can I ride my pony again?"

*My* pony—

Alex gasped quietly, realizing her granddaughter had been living for this day for a month. She now expected Alex to honor her promise to take them back to the Tetons. Jenny's recovery had happened even faster than Alex had anticipated. The rapid rise of her pulse made her dizzy with excitement when she imagined seeing Buck again.

"I didn't know you had one."

"Her name is Mitzi."

"Well, the answer to your question is yes. You can do everything you did before the accident."

Alex shook his hand. "Thank you for all your help, Doctor."

"Good luck to you."

Jenny thanked him, too, and they left the office, but as Alex walked down the corridor, it was *her* legs that felt unsteady. Her granddaughter kept up as if the accident had never happened. On their way to the car, Alex turned to her. "Do you think Johnny's back in school yet?"

It was August 23. "Probably not for a few more days."

"Can we fly to the ranch today?"

"Sweetheart—I don't know if we could get a flight that soon. I don't even know if there'd be a guest cabin free when we get there."

"Couldn't we stay at a motel? Johnny's grandma and grandpa stayed at one when they visited him."

Alex couldn't believe how much those two children had shared. But she had to admit the mention of a motel sounded like a good idea. That way they wouldn't be putting anyone out at the ranch.

When she thought about it, she realized it *was* a Friday. If they went for this weekend plus another day, Jenny would only miss school today and Monday. Her job hunt wasn't going well. There was nothing in Lake Tahoe that interested her. Four more days over a weekend before she renewed her search in the Sacramento area wouldn't make any difference.

After they got in the car, she said, "I'll call and see if we can get a flight." It was nine-thirty. There'd be a lot of flights to Salt Lake before evening. Most likely one of them would have seats available. The problem was trying to connect to a flight leaving for Jackson that wouldn't require a long layover.

Her hand actually shook as she called information for Skyways. She found out they could take a flight out at two and make a connecting flight that would put them in Jackson at 6:10 p.m. They'd need a rental car when they got there.

It meant they'd have to be at the airport in two and a half hours. If they threw a few things in one suitcase and locked up the house, they could manage it and park her car in short-term parking until they got back.

The biggest problem was finding a place to stay. After an exhaustive search of every hotel or motel in the area, she was able to reserve a room for three nights at a place called the Teton Shadows. Unfortunately it was still high season with summer rates, but she'd promised Jenny. After thinking it over, she decided this would be the best time to leave Sacramento.

If Frank broke down again and came over to see her this weekend, he wouldn't find her home. That was a good thing. He'd taken her rejection extremely hard and still called her, begging her to reconsider. She assured him she still loved him in her own way, but she would never change her mind about marrying him.

It astounded her that she hadn't missed him at all this past month. To her shame, her thoughts had been all about Buck. She'd had more sleepless nights than she cared to remember wondering how he spent his evenings.

Alex remembered the attractive woman at the airport counter in Jackson. She'd devoured Buck with her eyes when they'd wheeled Jenny into the terminal. Something in her look told Alex she'd been with Buck before. Wherever he went, women noticed him or went out of their way to get his attention. The poor girl at the Boot Corral....

That night at the pool, the female guests hadn't been able take their eyes off him. Alex was one of those guests. She'd been the worst.

Though they were returning to the ranch because she'd made a deal with Jenny, Alex could no longer lie to herself about Buck. She wanted to see him again and hopefully be alone with him, if only to find out if this longing was all on her part.

The trickle-down effect of Kyle's rejection had done its damage in her early years, but that period had long since passed. She didn't know if she could say the same thing when it came to Buck. If she learned he was already in a relationship with someone new, she might never recover and wondered if it were possible to die of jealousy.

*What is wrong with you?* She was a grandmother, not a starry-eyed teenager. But right now Alex didn't feel any older than seventeen with her hormones firing on all cylinders.

She hung up the phone. "Guess what, sweetheart? It looks like we're going to the Tetons. We'll have to rush home and get packed."

"I'm glad we already have Johnny's present."

"He'll love it." The first week after getting back home, they'd bought a tan T-shirt featuring a snake. It had been Jenny's idea to have the words Fred's Dad printed on it. So silly and funny. Just the kind of thing to make Johnny laugh. Those two found the same things amusing and were in tune with each other on a level that surprised Alex.

But she had a secret she'd kept from her granddaughter. She'd had two T-shirts made up for Jenny and Buck, both in red. On the front, the white lettering said: Teton Valley Ranch Water Fight Champions.

"I can't wait to go back, Nana."

"Neither can I." *Neither can I.*

By a quarter to seven that evening, they'd checked in to their motel. Jenny wanted to call Johnny and surprise him. That was fine with Alex. She used the landline so the motel number would show up on the caller ID and pressed the digits for the ranch. Then she handed the receiver to Jenny.

Her eyes twinkled as she looked at Alex. "Hi—I want to speak to Johnny Lundgren." After a pause she said, "It's Jenny Forrester." Another pause. "Yes. My ankle's all better now." One more pause. "Me, too. But don't tell him it's me."

She held the receiver to her chest. "It was Willy at the desk. He said to wait just a minute."

Alex bet Willy couldn't believe who was calling. "Okay. Then you listen and wait."

Jenny nodded.

Alex was so nervous, she jumped up from the side of the bed and started pacing.

THE GUYS HAD formed a line moving boxes of possessions into the Lundgrens' new house from the last truckload for the day. Tonight, Carson's family would be sleeping under their new roof for the first time. Not everything was done yet, but the house was ready enough for them to move in and be comfortable.

Johnny was in the kitchen with Tracy, putting the kitchen utensils away in drawers. Buck was happy for Carson's family and secretly envious of their joy. He knew Ross was, too. But no matter how many hours of hard work Buck had put in during the past month so he wouldn't let his mind wander, his emptiness had grown. Something had to be done about his mental state.

While he and Carson were carrying in the last heavy case of books, Carson's cell phone rang. They lowered the box to the floor so he could answer the call.

Buck saw a surprised look cross over his friend's face. "Hey, Johnny—the phone's for *you*."

He came running. "Is it Cory or Grandpa Baretta?"

"Neither. Willy says it's a girl."

He frowned. "A girl?"

The guys grinned. At this point they were all curious.

"Here." He handed the phone to him.

"Hello?"

As he listened, there was an instant change in the boy's expression. His brown eyes rounded before he looked up at Carson in disbelief. "It's *Jenny!* Her leg's all better. She's in Jackson at a motel!"

Buck's next heartbeat practically knocked him to the floor. Alex had said she didn't want to inconvenience the staff any more than necessary. That had been a month ago. It appeared she still meant it. His thoughts spun out of control.

"Well, keep talking to her, sport," he said, eyeing Tracy with a grin. Between them and Ross, they were trying hard not to laugh at Johnny's excitement.

After a minute, he said, "Hey, mom—can she have a sleepover with me tonight in the loft? We'll be good and go right to sleep."

Carson burst into laughter because Johnny was so predictable. It spread like contagion, pulling Buck out of his shock. He joined in with the others, but in letting go like that, the guys paid the price by ending up with coughs. For a minute it sounded like their former hospital ward.

With a tender smile, Tracy walked over to her son. "Ask Jenny to put Alex on the phone, honey."

"Okay, but please, please, please tell her she has to let Jenny come."

Buck watched Tracy wander into the kitchen out of earshot.

"Dad—" Johnny jumped up and down holding on to his arm. "The doctor said she can ride Mitzi again. Yippee!" He was so happy, he did a little dance in front of them.

Buck knew exactly how he felt. He'd given up on ever seeing that family again. In the past month, no one on the ranch had received word from Alex. It was as if she and Jenny had disappeared off the face of the earth. The past thirty days without them had been brutal.

"How many more signals do you need?" Ross had come up behind him.

"It's a moot point if she's officially engaged," Buck muttered, his body in turmoil. He was still reeling to think Alex was actually in Jackson.

Tracy came back in the room and walked over to Johnny. "Her grandma said yes. I told her we had a guest room for her to stay in, but she turned me down."

Another clap of thunder resounded in Buck's chest. She handed the phone to Carson. "Alex has a rental car. She'll drive them here in a few minutes."

"Does she know I'm at my new house?"

"Yes. But I need you to keep something in mind."

"What?"

"They can only stay until Monday."

Johnny's face fell like a loose shingle off a roof. "How come?" Buck could relate. They were both suffering from too much good and bad news in the same breath.

"It has to be a quick trip for them, honey. You know Alex has to work, and Jenny's been in school since she went home. But before they left the ranch, Alex promised that once her ankle was better, she'd bring Jenny back to finish their vacation." Alex never told Buck that! "They missed your birthday party and wanted to make sure they celebrated with you another time."

"Hooray!"

"Evidently, the splint was just removed this morning and they decided this weekend would be the best time for them to come."

Was that because Alex was eager to get back here, too? Or had Jenny finally accepted Frank into their lives and this was the duty visit Alex had promised her granddaughter before they got married? How soon would it happen? Until Buck had answers, his emotions would be all over the place.

"But that's not long enough, Mom."

*You can say that again.*

"By then you'll be in school, too, honey."

Carson reached for Johnny and hoisted him on his

shoulders. "We'd better get your bed made up for her. We'll put down the air mattress and sleeping bag for you."

"I don't know where that stuff is."

"We'll find it in one of the boxes. Let's go."

"I'll help look," Buck offered, needing to channel his energy before he jumped out of his skin waiting for Alex to get there.

THE AIR FELT a little cooler than a month ago. Jenny and Alex decided to dress in matching navy turtleneck cotton sweaters and jeans to keep them warm. Alex left her hair loose and Jenny copied her. On their way out of town, she found the drive-through they'd been to before and picked up a dozen chocolate doughnuts with chocolate icing, the kind she knew Buck liked.

After learning Tracy and her family had been moving in to their new house all day, Alex had said she wouldn't dream of interfering with their first night. But Tracy insisted that everyone was thrilled to know they were there and that it would make Johnny's night to have Jenny sleep over. Alex caved and realized they'd all be hungry for a treat. It was the least she could do.

The sight of the Grand Teton ruling over the Snake River valley with the starlit sky overhead was so beautiful it hurt. What a difference from a month ago when they'd flown in with the storm. She still couldn't believe that Buck had just been sitting a few rows behind them on the plane, but they'd had to land before he'd introduced himself. While Alex drove, Jenny talked nonstop about how he'd saved her from falling in the current. She wondered where her cowboy hat had gone and chatted about Moppy and the ponies. When they entered the dude ranch property, the feeling of coming home was so overpowering, Alex only took in a portion of what her granddaughter was saying.

Would Buck treat her the same way as before?

*Of course he would.*

The morning Alex and Jenny had left the ranch, he didn't know she was going home to end her relationship with Frank. But he'd never given her a clue as to how he really felt about her. Alex's fears didn't stop there. He would never have feelings for her if his mind wouldn't allow him to see her as anything but Jenny's grandmother!

As her father would say, Buck played his cards close to the chest. So close it had given her terrible angst. Once he learned Frank was no longer part of her life, he might still treat her like the woman at the airport counter, or the girl at the Boot Corral. The thought was so crushing, Alex couldn't bear it.

She took the last curve on the dirt road that wound through the trees. Blood hammered in her ears as they came out on the other side where the newly constructed house was all lit up. It was a masterpiece of rustic and contemporary. There were several trucks and cars parked in front.

"Nana—their house is all done!"

She parked the car and turned off the ignition. "Can you believe it's finished already?" Before she could hear Jenny's answer, Johnny came running down the porch steps toward them. For once, he wasn't wearing his cowboy gear. Her granddaughter scrambled out of the front seat.

"Hi!"

"Hey—you can walk! Come on in the house and I'll show you where we're going to sleep."

Just like that, they were off in their own world. Alex got out of the car and reached in back for the box of doughnuts and the plastic bag with the things Jenny would need for the night.

"Would you like some help?"

Attractive as he was, the wrong man had appeared out of nowhere. *You've got your answer about Buck. Keep smiling.* She shut the door. "How are you, Ross?"

"Couldn't be better." He walked into the house with her. "You should have heard Johnny when he found out Jenny was in town."

"It was the same excitement on my end when she talked to him."

Tracy hurried over to give her a hug. "Welcome back. We're so thrilled you're here."

"So are we." She handed her the doughnuts. "These are for you."

"Thank you. You couldn't have brought us anything we'd love more right now."

"That's what I was hoping."

"Nana?" Alex looked up to see Jenny in the loft overhang. "You've got to come up and see Johnny's room. It's huge!"

"Okay. I'm coming."

Once she reached the top of the stairs, she could see Carson making up the queen-size bed. Not until she took a few more steps did she spy Buck on the other side. He was sitting against the far wall with his long, rock-hard legs extended, blowing up an air mattress. While the kids ran around, she felt his piercing gaze travel up her body until their eyes met.

"It's good to see you again, Alex." That deep voice of his was unforgettable.

Her heart throbbed in her throat, making it difficult to talk. "It's wonderful to see all of you." Her smile took in Carson.

"Your arrival has made this a red-letter night for our son."

"We had no idea your house would be finished this soon."

He flashed Buck a glance. "The taskmaster made certain the job got done in record time."

She didn't doubt it. "That's what best friends are for. Your home is breathtaking." Unfortunately she was out of breath and needed to go back downstairs away from Buck where she could get a grip. "I brought doughnuts in case you'd like some."

"In case?" Carson laughed. "Did you hear that, Buck?"

The gorgeous male in question was still filling the mattress with air and simply nodded. She didn't wait to watch anymore and hurried to join Tracy in the kitchen below. "Can I do anything to help?"

"Thank you, but no. We've all had it." She finished off her doughnut. "Come and sit down in the living room. As soon as Carson has Johnny's room sorted out, we'll get the kids to bed. Whether they can stop talking long enough to go to sleep is anyone's guess, however."

Alex chuckled. "They're a riot together. Oh, Tracy, you must be so happy to be in your new house at last!"

"It's a dream come true. But I was just watching

Jenny dash up the stairs and can only imagine your relief that she's made a full recovery."

"You'll never know, but I'm nervous she'll forget and do something that injures it again."

"I have the same fear with Johnny. He keeps trying to imitate Carson's trick riding stunts. One of these days it'll be our turn to rush him to the hospital with a broken leg or arm."

"Let's hope not."

While they laughed, the men came down the stairs to the living room with the kids. Carson sat next to Tracy and pulled her to him, giving her a kiss. "The loft is ready for occupancy."

Alex looked at Jenny. "Did you hear that? No doubt everyone is exhausted and anxious to go to bed. Come here, sweetheart. Your jammies and toothbrush are inside the bag. Why don't you run in the bathroom and change before I leave for the motel."

"Okay."

Tracy eyed her son. "Now's a good time for you to do the same thing."

"I'll be right back."

Johnny bounded up the stairs and returned in record time, wearing camouflage pajamas. Pretty soon Jenny came back in. Alex got to her feet and gave her a hug. "Be sure to mind Tracy and Carson. They've had a long day moving and everyone's tired."

"I know."

"I'll miss you."

"Me, too."

"Tomorrow I'll drive to the ranch house for breakfast and we'll make plans for the day." They kissed each other. "Have fun. Good night, sweetheart."

"See you in the morning, Nana."

Alex gave Johnny a quick hug. "Good night."

Once the children disappeared upstairs, Alex turned to the others. "Thank you for making her feel so welcome. Since I know you weren't expecting visitors, I'm going to leave now. I'm in room fourteen at the Teton Shadows if you need to get ahold of me."

Carson gave Buck an odd glance before he and Tracy got up and walked her to the front door. Ross and Buck brought up the rear. Both of them were eating doughnuts. She heard Buck's voice. "I'll follow you back to town, Alex."

Her heart pounded with unmerciful force. "Thank you, but I'll be fine."

His eyes blazed an intense green in the porch light. "You're still my responsibility while you're here at our invitation. We don't want you driving the ranch roads alone this late at night."

Except that she wasn't staying at the ranch now. But to argue with him in front of the others would only create a fuss for nothing. He'd offered because it was his duty. No one else thought anything about it.

"If you're sure, then I'd appreciate it. See all of you tomorrow."

After everyone said good-night, she stepped off the porch and walked to her rental car. Once she'd started the engine, she noticed Buck climb in one of the trucks. Soon it was just the two of them making their way to Jackson in the moonlight.

Knowing it was his headlights reflected in the mirror,

a rush of heat invaded her body. But her euphoria over being alone with him didn't last long. The thought occurred to her that he could have a late date in town with some beautiful girl and would have been driving there anyway. For the rest of the short trip, she tried without success not to think about his love life.

Jackson was lit up for the weekend with tourists. It was stop-and-go traffic until she reached the motel. When she'd been told she could have a room for all three nights, she should have known it would be on the ground floor at the end. Some guys were partying outside one of the rooms. They saw her pass in the car and let out with wolf whistles and catcalls.

To her chagrin, someone had taken her parking space in front of the door. She had no choice but to park farther away. Buck pulled up next to her and got out. The catcalls ended when he walked over to her wearing a black T-shirt and jeans. It was a sin for any man to look so good.

"I'll go inside with you to make sure you're safe." A familiar cough punctuated his declaration. The silent exchange between Carson and Buck was no longer a mystery. There was a reason why Alex had been able to get a motel for three nights during high season. It also explained why Buck had decided to follow her.

At times he had an authoritative way about him. This was the second time tonight she chose not to challenge one of those moments. "Thank you."

Alex rummaged in her purse for the key and they headed for her room. When they reached the door, he took it from her fingers and inserted it in the lock. The door opened to generic knotty pine walls and two double beds.

She laid her purse on the counter by the TV before turning to him with a smile. "As you can see, there's nothing sinister here."

"It's not what's on the inside that bothers me. Those guys are out for a good time and they'll come around when they know I'm not here."

"I appreciate your concern, but I'll be fine."

His expression remained sober. He lounged against the closed door, scrutinizing her. "I had no idea you were coming back to finish your vacation with us. It's been a while. How's the situation with Jenny? Is she learning to accept Frank?"

Frank who?

Alex was so aware of him, she could hardly breathe. "No."

Buck's brow furrowed. "I'm sorry to hear that. It must be very hard on all of you."

Alex folded her arms against her waist. "When we went home, I ended our relationship."

The man staring at her didn't move a muscle, but his eyes suddenly charged with a new energy. "Why?"

She took another quick breath. "On the first night at the cabin, you told me there's something about being at the ranch that gives you a new perspective. After Jenny and I flew back to California, I realized what you'd said was true.

"When I saw Frank again, certain things were made clear to me that had nothing to do with Jenny's lack of acceptance. We'd both been friends who'd leaned on each other while we went through our grieving periods. He surprised me by asking me to marry him. I did love him, but I wasn't in love with him. Otherwise I wouldn't have let Jenny's objections stand in the way."

"It must've been devastating for him."

"It was bad," she admitted. "He still hasn't accepted it and keeps calling. Needless to say, Jenny couldn't be happier it's over."

He straightened. "Do you still work at the bank with him?"

She shook her head. "After we got back, I gave the manager my two weeks' notice. He knew how difficult it was for me to be in the same building with Frank and let me go after a week. Since then, I've been looking for another kind of job, even in Lake Tahoe where my parents live, but I haven't found one that appeals to me yet. Knowing the statistics about the process taking six months to two years, I'm not too hopeful about it happening anytime soon."

"Are you going to be all right financially?"

"Yes. I'll keep hunting for a job until I find something suitable. That's why I decided to take advantage of this weekend so Jenny could enjoy the rest of her vacation. She was having the time of her life here—it seems so cruel what happened."

"I would wager that the mood couldn't be happier at the Lundgren house tonight." She felt his gaze on her mouth. "I'm glad you came back, Alex." His voice sounded husky and made her feel light-headed.

"I am, too."

"Let's get out of here. I know a place where we can have a drink and listen to a live band."

As good as that sounded, she would have rather been alone with him. "You don't have other plans?"

"There's no woman in my life at the moment if that's what you mean."

It was exactly what she meant. "You're not too exhausted after the big move?"

He inhaled sharply, bringing on a cough. "No, but it sounds like you're tired after your flight and want to call it a night."

"You've misunderstood me. I just didn't want you to feel you had to entertain me."

"What if I want to?"

That was the first overt sign that he felt something for her that was separate from his job as her host. Her body trembled. "Then, with Jenny safe and sound at the Lundgrens', I'd love to go with you. Do I need to change?"

"No. You're perfect just as you are."

*So are you.*

He opened the door. "We'll go in the truck."

She grabbed her purse and walked out. He pulled the door closed and locked it. The party crowd had moved on. Alex was finally going on a date with the man she'd been fantasizing about for over a month. Their arms brushed while he was helping her into the truck's cab. It felt like liquid fire.

Once they left the motel, he maneuvered them through the maze of vehicles lining the streets, but they eventually got stuck in a traffic jam. "I'm taking you to the Million Dollar Cowboy Bar, if we can ever get there. You sit on a saddle to have a drink at the bar. There's a stuffed grizzly bear. It's a must-see for out-of-towners like yourself."

"Do you go there a lot?"

"I've been once."

"Then once was obviously enough and it's not your thing." He shot her a surprised glance. "I'd rather do something you'd like. What's *your* idea of a good time, Buck?"

"That depends on the female."

"Seriously, if you had your druthers."

"My druthers?" His brows lifted. "That would be telling secrets."

She smiled. "Don't hold back on me. Nothing you could say would surprise me. I'm a grandma and have lived longer than you."

Tension filled the cab. "Is that really how you see yourself?"

"It's what I am and you're evading my question."

"Right. My idea would be to camp out under the stars with the smell of pine filling the breeze. A beautiful woman would be in my arms and we'd have a whole night with nothing to do but enjoy each other."

"That sounds amazing." The tremor in her voice infuriated her.

"There were times overseas, breathing those toxic fumes, when I would have killed for one night like that."

"No wonder you got so excited about the idea of coming to work at the ranch." She shifted in her seat. "Buck? It's so busy here. When we get to the corner, let's go back to the motel, and I'll buy you a soda from the machine." At least they could have privacy, even if the surroundings left a lot to be desired.

"You really don't want to go to the bar? There's line dancing."

"Not tonight." She didn't want noise or other people around. She only wanted time alone with him.

## Chapter Eight

*Did he just blow it?* It was time to try another tack.

"I've got an even better idea. Let's check you out of there. We'll grab your suitcase and head for the ranch." His jaw tightened. "That motel is no place for a good-looking woman on her own, let alone for Jenny. I'll follow you to the ranch in your rental car. You can park around the side with the other cars."

"But where will Jenny and I stay? You weren't expecting us."

"You saw Johnny's new furniture at the house. His old room still has the twin beds and matching dresser. Carson wants it to be used as an extra guest room when we have an overflow. I can't think of anyone better than you to christen it."

It would mean being in the ranch house with Buck until Monday. She got a fluttery sensation in her chest. "If you're sure."

He made no further comment. By the time they reached the motel, it was out of her hands. Buck waited for her to gather up her things, and then he walked to the office with her while she checked out. For the second time that night, she found herself en route to the ranch, but this time Buck was driving right behind her and she felt as though she was floating.

She reached the parking area and locked up the car. Buck was there waiting for her and took her suitcase. "Tell me what kind of job you're looking for."

Alex didn't want to think about that tonight, but he'd asked. "I don't know. Something different. A new adventure. Breaking up with Frank has given me a sense of freedom I haven't known before. Now that Jenny is in school full-time, I don't want to do the same thing anymore. Would you think it odd if I told you I've left my old life behind and am ready to begin the next phase? It's kind of exciting to think about since I have no idea what's ahead."

Alex felt his eyes on her. "Would you believe I said those exact words to my parents after I got home from the hospital? The world I'd left behind no longer appealed in the same way. If anyone understands how you feel, *I* do."

She breathed in the scent of sage, something she would always associate with the ranch. "You've found a wonderful life here." The moon over the Grand Teton made the scene surreal.

"Would you be willing to uproot if you had to?"

"You mean, sell the house and put Jenny in a different school?"

He nodded.

"If I found the right job and situation, I'd do it in a heartbeat. My granddaughter is so happy with the way things have turned out, I'm sure she'd be amenable to a move if it meant Frank couldn't drop by unexpectedly anymore."

"Has he done that since you ended it?"

"Yes, but this weekend he won't find me home. Of course, my parents would like me to keep looking in the Tahoe area. But to be honest, after staying there for a few days while I searched for work, I realized it's their retirement dream, not mine."

"You've got years before you have to think about retirement."

"According to the great thinkers of our country, we should be worrying about it from the time we get our first paycheck."

Buck laughed softly as they made their way around the corner of the house. "It looks like we're alone tonight, because I don't see Ross's truck. If he's gone out, who knows when he'll be back."

"Is he involved with anyone special?"

"Nope."

"The bachelor life. I never thought it fair that the powers that be set it up so the guy had to be the one to make things happen."

His lips twitched in reaction. "It's not all joy. The female can choose not to cooperate."

"I don't imagine you or Ross have run into that experience often."

"What makes you say that?"

"Just an observation. I remember two women in particular when I was here last month who were just waiting for you to do more than simply acknowledge them."

"Is that right?"

"I notice you're not denying it."

His veiled eyes revealed little. "We'll go in through the rear door. Except for Willy manning the front desk, we have the place all to ourselves—a new experience for me now that Carson's moved out. I'll fix you a cup of coffee in the kitchen."

"That sounds better than any drink at a bar."

"My sentiments exactly."

He let her in through the back door. This was a portion of the ranch house she'd never seen before. After locking it, he led her down a hallway in the dark. "I feel like we're playing house," she said.

"That's the idea." He put the suitcase down in the hall outside what she presumed was Johnny's old bedroom. Before she could take another breath, he grasped her upper arms and backed her against the wall. "Since Ross could come home at any time, let's take advantage of our privacy. I'd like to properly welcome you back to the Tetons, if that's okay with you."

"It's okay with me," she answered with a boldness she'd blush over tomorrow. She wanted his kiss so badly she could taste it before his beautiful mouth closed over hers.

She moaned as he wrapped his arms around her and pulled her against his rock-hard body.

There was no space between them. His male scent mixed with the faint smell of the soap intoxicated her to the core of her being. Her heart thundered against his while they kissed with sensuous abandon, the way they couldn't have done if they'd gone dancing in public.

Alex had dreamed of this moment for so long and now she found herself going with it, praying he'd never stop. His lips and hands brought pleasure to die for. This was ecstasy so beyond anything she'd felt at seventeen that she was in shock.

He finally lifted his head enough for them to breathe. "I've been wanting to do this since I first saw you in the airport."

A little cry escaped her. "Would you think I was terrible if I admitted to the same thing? I tried to fight what I was feeling. You can't imagine my guilt."

His hands tightened on her shoulders. "Frank has to be out of his mind with pain over losing you. It's no wonder he hasn't given up yet." He kissed her again with near-primitive passion.

If she didn't miss her guess, Buck was under a false impression about her relationship with Frank. This time she was the one to pull away first, but he didn't give her up willingly. "We never slept together," she admitted on a ragged breath.

A stillness surrounded them. His eyes traveled over her features. "But you were together for two y—" A cough cut his words off.

"We were friends for most of it," she explained. "I told him I wouldn't sleep with him until we were married."

He blinked. "Then all these years—"

"I've been the virgin grandma." She half laughed. "Even though I made the mistake with Kyle that resulted in my pregnancy, I still felt virginal. The truth is, we only made love one time before my parents found out and put an end to it. I'm afraid the experience was experimental at best."

A tremor passed through Buck's solid frame before he drew her back in his arms, burying his face in her hair. "You've had a rocky path for too many years."

"That's why I've decided I'm due for a change. Coming here again marks the beginning of my new adventure."

She heard him utter her name before pressing kisses over her hair and face. Once again, he found her mouth. Alex helped him, because her hunger matched his and had grown beyond caution. His short, rough beard was a reminder of his masculinity and whipped up her senses. In the middle of her delirium, a light went on in the hall. She heard footsteps.

"Hey, buddy—I saw your truck around the side." Ross's voice galvanized her into action and she tried to tear her lips from Buck's. "What are you doing back here? I figured you'd still be in—"

Too late, he saw them in an embrace. Buck let her go with reluctance and turned to Ross with a calm that astonished her. "After I saw what was going on in town, I decided to put Alex and Jenny up in Johnny's old room. The Teton Shadows leaves a lot to be desired on a Friday night, if you follow my meaning."

"Carson and I weren't thrilled to hear you were staying there, either." He drew closer. "Welcome to the ranch house, Alex. All day, Buck and I wondered how we were going to handle being orphans in this big old place." A smile lit up his eyes. "Now we don't have to worry."

She edged away from Buck. "You're all so nice, you would never admit that my surprise visit disrupted you."

Ross shot Buck another mysterious glance. "We like surprises. Ask Johnny."

For a little while she'd actually been able to forget about the kids. "Did they ever settle down?"

"No. They were still talking a mile a minute when I left."

"That's what I was afraid of."

Buck grinned. "Want to join us for a cup of coffee before we all turn in?"

"Not me. I've had enough for tonight. See you guys in the morning." He disappeared behind a door down at the other end of the hall.

As much as Alex didn't want to say good-night to Buck, Ross's unexpected appearance had brought her to her senses. He had to have seen how they were clinging to each other. Left alone with Buck again, she knew she'd lose control. This wasn't the time or the place. He'd had a long, tiring day and they couldn't be private in the ranch house. Carson could decide to come back for something.

She looked up at him. "Buck?"

"I know what you're going to say, and I'm way ahead of you," his voice rasped. "I wanted an excuse to be with you any way I could, but it's best you go to bed now while I'm still willing to let you." His words thrilled her. "Housekeeping gave Johnny's room and bathroom a thorough cleaning. The beds have been freshly made up. You'll be comfortable and safe."

"Thank you," she whispered.

"Don't look at me like that or I'll forget every good intention. If you should get hungry or thirsty during the night, help yourself to anything in the kitchen." She nodded and he added, "Have breakfast with me in the morning." She smiled. "I'll look for you in the dining room. Good night."

When she could no longer hear his footsteps, she went inside Johnny's room and got ready for bed. Her body was so wired, she knew it would be a long time before she fell asleep.

After she got into bed, she noticed how a shaft of moonlight fell across the wood floor. She loved everything about the ranch and the house itself. Built in true Western style, Carson had inherited a fabulous legacy, one he was sharing with Ross and Buck and, ultimately, the lucky guests like Alex and her granddaughter.

She lay back against the pillow, still tasting Buck on her lips. If it had been a mistake to kiss him tonight because she wouldn't be seeing him after Monday, she didn't regret it. He'd made her come alive so she didn't even recognize herself anymore.

Her thoughts stretched back to her early years. She'd been five years old when Buck was born. They'd gone through life with a five-year age difference. Even if they'd attended the same high school, she would have graduated before he'd started his sophomore year. It took growing up and becoming adults for the disparity in their ages to no longer matter.

Alex marveled over the painful twists and unexpected turns of both their lives that had brought them together at this particular moment in time. All because of Jenny. But for her father who'd been killed in war, Alex would never have met Buck or his partners.

She made a promise to herself to enjoy the few days she had left with Buck to the fullest.

*Don't think beyond Monday, Alex. Just don't think.*

BUCK TURNED OUT the lights in the hall and walked up the stairs. Each step took him farther away from her, but he had little choice. Tomorrow night he'd get her alone where there was no possibility of anyone bothering them.

Ross heard him coming and walked out in the hall. They eyed each other before Buck said, "Can I talk to you for a minute?"

"If you didn't want to talk, I couldn't have handled it because I'm already exploding with curiosity. Come on in." They both went inside Ross's room. Buck hooked a leg around one of the chairs and sat backward while Ross sank down on the side of his bed to stretch his limbs. "Have you recovered from shock yet?"

He shook his head. "When I heard it was Jenny, calling from a motel in Jackson no less, you could have knocked me over."

"That made two of us. So cut to the chase. What's going on with her and Frank?"

Buck's head flew back. "He's permanently out of the picture."

"Yeah?" Ross grinned. "The news gets better and better."

"She gave up her job at the bank and is looking for a new one, not necessarily in banking. She's even willing to uproot herself and Jenny if she can find the right situation. I'm going to stick my neck out here and ask what you'd think if we hired her to take Susan's place at the front desk.

"Since she left for college, we've been lucky Willy has volunteered to help out until we find a replacement. But let me assure you, Alex has no idea that I've been thinking about asking her."

Ross's smile faded. "You're serious about this."

"I've never been so serious in my life. Whether she'd

be interested is an entirely different matter. The pay wouldn't be near what she's been making as a loan officer. Chances are, she won't even consider it. She has a granddaughter to raise and get through college."

Unable to sit still, Buck got up from the chair. "I wanted to talk to you about it before I run it by Carson. Naturally we'd all have to be in agreement before the position was offered to her."

"You're talking permanent, like as in full time, year round."

Year-round forever. "Yes. But that brings us to another problem. We won't know if we'll have broken even for at least a year. And we still haven't decided if we're going to keep the ranch open as a dude ranch through the winter. If not, we wouldn't need anyone at the desk."

"True. We're still in the experimental stage." Streams of unspoken messages passed between them before Ross whistled.

"I know," Buck muttered as he walked over to the doorway. "While your mind is considering all the logistics, my mind has been making its own list of imponderables. It's a mile long already."

Ross got up from the bed and looked him squarely in the eyes. "I like her a lot. Even if you have to work things out a different way and she gets a job in town, if it's what you want, I'm all for it. You know that. Good luck getting to sleep tonight."

"That's not going to happen, but thanks for your vote of confidence, Ross. It means everything. See you in the morning."

To Buck's surprise, he actually did get some sleep, but he was awake by six-thirty. Knowing Alex was under the same roof caused his adrenaline to kick in and gave him a reason to spring out of the sack.

After a shower and shave, he put on a polo shirt and a pair of jeans. The last thing he did was pull on his cowboy boots. He'd be taking Alex and Jenny on an overnight campout, but he didn't know if it would be today or tomorrow. They still had plans to make. In any case, they'd do some riding both days.

He heard a knock on the door. "Uncle Buck?"

Who else but Johnny. "Are you up already?"

"Yep. Jenny's with me. We've got to talk to you. Can we come in?"

Something was cooking. It always was with Johnny. "Sure."

His young gunslingers walked in looking so cute he couldn't believe it. There was no sign Jenny had ever hurt her ankle. "Hey—I like those new cowboy boots you've got on."

"Nana bought them for me. Hi, Buck!" She ran over and gave him a big hug that warmed his heart.

"Hi, Red." He kissed her forehead. "How was the sleepover?"

A smile broke out on her face. "Really fun."

"I wish we could do it every night."

Johnny was so predictable. Buck had to be careful not to laugh out loud. "I hear you, sport. So tell me what's on your mind."

"We want to camp out at Secret Lake tonight, but mom says everyone's too tired after yesterday's move. Are you too tired?"

"No, but your folks are, so I have a better idea. They

need a day to rest, so let's plan to take the horses up there tomorrow and camp out. Today we'll do something else. How does that sound?"

"I guess that's okay. Can Jenny see the cows after breakfast?" She nodded with a look of anticipation.

A drive up to the pasture with Alex would give him time alone with her while the kids sat in the back of the truck. "Sounds like a plan. After we get back, there's plenty for you guys to do around here."

"We want to ride our ponies and catch bad guys."

"And then we'll go to Funorama!" Jenny looked up at Buck with imploring eyes. "Are you going to eat with us?" She had on another princess top with a ruffle over the waistband of her jeans. This one was pink.

"I'm right behind you. Lead the way."

"Goody!" they said in unison.

There was a full house in the dining room. Business was booming. After being open for only three months, it was the best of signs and proved they were attracting business. In time, their experiment might really grow into something. Nothing would make Buck happier. The thought of doing any other kind of work at this point was anathema to him.

He spotted Ross, who'd beaten him downstairs and was sitting at one of the tables with Alex. Buck's heart practically stopped beating. She'd caught her hair on top of her head with a clip and was dressed in a cream-colored Western shirt with fringe. Ross couldn't take his eyes off her and no wonder.

"That's a sensational outfit," Buck murmured after

sitting down next to her. He saw the pulse at the base of her throat start to throb.

"I just finished telling her the same thing," Ross said.

"I bought the shirt at the Boot Corral on the way in to town. We're staying at a dude ranch so I figured I'd better look the part."

"Nana bought me some new cowboy boots. See?" Jenny walked around the table so Ross would take notice.

"You and your nana light this place up like a Christmas tree."

Johnny giggled. "You're silly, Uncle Ross."

Since the surprise arrival of their guests last night, a whole new mood of excitement permeated the place. Halfway through their meal, Carson and Tracy walked in. The waitress took their orders.

"Excuse us for being late." They'd had the house to themselves on their first morning in their new home. Carson finally had his privacy and looked beyond happy. So did Tracy.

"Guess what?" Johnny exclaimed. "Uncle Buck's going to drive us to the pasture after breakfast."

Buck glanced at Alex. "Want to come?"

Her eyes met his. "I'd love to see more of the ranch." Then she looked around. "Since we're discussing plans, now might be the time to invite everyone to a party at the Funorama at five this afternoon. Jenny and I made the reservation to celebrate Johnny's birthday. We're sorry we had to miss his first one."

"Huh?" Johnny's eyes rounded. "Another party?"

Alex smiled at him. "Absolutely. Turning seven is a big deal and it's on us. Pizza and presents."

Buck wished he could have recorded Johnny's yelp of joy.

"I got you my present last month," Jenny informed him.

"You did? Will I like it?"

Buck was afraid to look at the others while he tried to control his amusement.

She giggled. "Yes. It's funny."

"Can I open it now?"

"Johnny Lundgren—" This from Tracy. "Where are your manners?"

"Sorry."

Carson grinned. "We'll all have to wait in suspense until the party. I've got to hurry and get my work done before then."

"How come you always have to work?" Johnny had posed a rhetorical question so full of disappointment it made everyone burst into laughter.

Alex had to wipe her eyes before she got up from the table. "Jenny? If we're going on a drive, we'd better freshen up first."

"I'll pick you up in front in ten minutes," Buck said.

She nodded and left the dining room with Jenny. His gaze followed her out of the room. Then it switched to Carson.

"Can I talk to you in private for a moment?"

"Sure."

"Come on, Johnny." Tracy was a quick study. "You need to visit the restroom before you leave."

"Thanks, Tracy."

He wanted to broach his idea to Carson while his partner was still available. After telling Ross to stay put, he related what he'd told Ross last night and asked him how he'd feel about offering Alex the front-desk job.

"I want your gut response, but I don't need an answer right now. If Johnny hadn't been around, I would have asked your wife to stay to give her input. Just think about it and talk it over with her and Ross. Alex knows nothing about this and she never will if you don't feel good about it."

The waitress refilled their coffee. Carson took a few sips. "This is déjà vu for me. I wanted to keep Tracy and Johnny around and offered them the use of one of the cabins while we got to know each other better. Instead we got married, but there's no reason why Alex and Jenny can't stay in one of the cabins for a temporary period whether she works for us or not."

"If things worked out that way, I've got a little money put away and would take less of a salary so it wouldn't hurt the business."

Carson studied him for a minute. "Just so you guys know, I've been looking over the books, and I say we keep the dude ranch open over the winter and see what happens. We've already had guests call us about doing some hunting in the winter months and have booked a couple of the cabins."

"That's the kind of news I've been hoping for." He knew Ross felt the same way.

"Heaven knows the staff needs the work in this economy. Any one of them would help run the desk. As for

Alex, it's *your* life we're talking about here. I don't need to think about it. Do you, Ross?"

He shook his head. "I gave him my seal of approval last night."

"Johnny's is a given," Carson added with an infectious grin.

Buck's throat clogged up. "Thanks. It was my lucky day when I was sent to that hospital and got you two for roommates." He finished off his coffee and rose to his feet. "See you guys later." Now that he had the all-clear, he could choose the moment to feel her out. Maybe tomorrow night under the stars.

He made a detour to the kitchen and chatted with the cook while he put some bottles of water and apples in a bag. With that accomplished, he went out to the truck and swung by the barn where they stored the hay on pallets for the winter. Buck threw half a dozen of the smaller bales into the back of his truck. The kids could sit on a couple of them during the drive. As for the rest, the hands working the herd could spread it around.

After wishing Alex would come back every day for the past month, he found it difficult to believe it was really her and Jenny waiting in front of the ranch house with Johnny and Tracy. He jumped down from the cab and lowered the tailgate so he could lift the children inside.

"Do you need a ride back home, Tracy?" he asked as he closed the gate.

"No, thanks. I brought the car." She looked up at Johnny. "Be sure to mind Buck and Alex. I'll meet you back here at lunch."

Buck heard Johnny say okay, but the kids were already trying to choose which bale to sit on and weren't paying attention.

"Hey, guys. You need to sit where you can hold on to the side of the truck. All we need is for one of you to flip out and break another ankle."

"I'll be careful," Jenny promised him.

"I know you will, Red."

"So will *I*," Johnny assured him.

"I can always count on you, sport. If you get thirsty or hungry, there are snacks in that plastic bag."

"Thanks!"

He waved Tracy off and climbed back in the driver's seat. Alex smelled delicious, like a fresh wild strawberry warmed by the sun. The day was heating up, and the most beautiful woman he'd ever met was strapped in next to him. A sage-scented breeze wafted through the windows. Carson wanted to keep the ranch open year round, for this year at least. What more could a man ask for, he thought to himself, as they reached the forest and headed up the mountain.

Unfortunately, the answer that came back was *a lot more*.

The possibility that Alex wouldn't be interested in his proposition was enough for him to keep his boots planted on the ground. While he was experiencing alternating feelings of euphoria and fear, he heard her cell phone ring.

"That's probably my parents." She reached in her purse and checked the caller ID, and then put the phone back.

"Frank?"

She nodded. "He called earlier, but I didn't pick up.

One of these days he'll have to give up, but I hate hurting him."

"It would have been worse to marry him and then discover it was a mistake."

"You're so right."

"I've learned the hard way that when something's truly over, it can't be resurrected, and you have to move on for your own sanity."

"Agreed."

They could hear the kids' talking in the back, mostly Johnny's. "By the time we reach the herd, Jenny's going to be a living encyclopedia of knowledge."

Alex had a warm laugh he loved. "I have to say, the boy's an original and a constant source of fascination."

They drove deeper into the forest. "While we're alone to talk, have you given any more thought to what you'd like to do for a living?"

"It's on my mind constantly," she said. "If we moved, I'd still need hours that coincided with Jenny's school day, and I'd want to live close by. If I could do it all over again, I would have gone into teaching."

"You still could." He said it without enthusiasm.

She sighed. "Yes, but that would mean several more years of college to get a teaching certificate. I'll worry about it after we get home. It's not your problem."

The hell it wasn't! "What about a job in a different bank?" he persisted. They had banks in Jackson.

"Buck…" She chuckled. "Didn't you hear what I said?"

"Yes, but you've got all that schooling in finance that shouldn't go to waste."

"True, but I'd want part-time work until Jenny's out

of high school. To my knowledge, it's the rare bank manager who would hire anyone part-time regardless of their years of experience."

He didn't doubt that she was right, but it wouldn't hurt to inquire. The guys did all their business at the Moran Bank of Wyoming. Buck knew the bank manager well and could find out if they hired part-time employees. It was worth a shot.

"I'm going to make sure I know what's going on in Jenny's life so I can guide her. It's a promise I made to Christy before she died. I want to sign her up for piano lessons, dance, art lessons, all of it, so she gets exposed to lots of different things.

"By the time she's in high school, I'd like to see her involved in working on the school newspaper. Or I'd love to see Jenny on the debate team. She's smart and could work toward a scholarship. Maybe the third time's the charm for the females in our family and Jenny will wait till she's in her twenties before she wants to get married."

"I'm afraid she's already cursed with that Wilson-Forrester beauty, so I wouldn't hold my breath." Johnny had fallen under her spell. When he darted her a glance, he saw that color had crept into her cheeks. "Do you have a picture of your daughter?"

As she pulled a wallet out of her purse, he stopped for a minute. She handed him two photos. "That's Christy at seventeen. The other one shows her with Daniel, holding Jenny after she was born."

Buck heard the love in her voice. "She's lovely, just like you and your granddaughter."

"Hey—" Johnny cried out. "What's wrong?"

"We're just looking at a picture of Jenny when she was born," Buck called back.

"I have a baby monkey face in that picture," Jenny said.

"A monkey?" Johnny laughed. "I want to see it, Uncle Buck."

"Later, guys." He handed Alex the photos and started driving again.

It was clear to Buck that Jenny was Alex's raison d'être. That promise to her daughter was sacrosanct. Jackson was a small community. No doubt the schools offered some of the opportunities she'd mentioned, but not on the larger scale available in a city like Sacramento. The winters could be brutal here. Both she and Jenny would hate the isolation. Neighbors might be next door, but they were separated by acres of ranch land. The front-desk job would never satisfy a woman with her curiosity and education.

No matter how much he wanted her in his life, he had nothing to offer her at the moment, only the good will of Carson and Ross. A year from now, he hoped to be in a different place financially, but no one could predict the future.

Last week his father had phoned, urging him to come home at the end of the summer and join the family business. There was more behind the call. Buck knew his father needed to slow down. The conversation had come at the precise moment when Buck had been missing Alex like crazy and was at a low point. He'd told his dad that if it appeared the dude ranch project was losing too much money, he would have to end the partnership and return to Colorado.

When they emerged from the trees and came to the pasture, Buck was asking himself what in the hell he'd been thinking, imagining that he and Alex could have a good life living together at the ranch.

In a different mood than when they'd started out, he lowered himself from the truck and helped the children down. Johnny led Jenny around to look at the new calves. Alex followed and acted interested, but Buck wasn't an idiot. One trip up here to see the herd was more than enough. By Monday, she would have seen all the sights the dude ranch had to offer and be glad she was flying home to civilization.

## Chapter Nine

The difference in Buck from last night to right now was palpable. She'd been breathless when he'd walked in the dining room this morning and had sat next to her. The smoldering look in his eyes had sent a wave of heat through her she could still feel.

So what had happened on the drive over to make him withdraw from her?

Alex walked through a section of the herd with him and the children, but that feeling of emotional intimacy was gone. Vanished! She kept running their conversation through her mind, trying to pinpoint the moment everything changed.

It had to have been the photographs.

They were a graphic reminder that she'd been a mother and was now a grandmother. Buck was a red-blooded, virile bachelor who last night in the dark had succumbed to the novelty of indulging himself with an older woman until Ross had interrupted them. But in the light of day, reality had asserted itself and it was back to the business of being the congenial host until she and Jenny left the ranch.

That was how gorgeous bachelors like Buck and Ross survived to live another day. They were the opposite of

Frank who should have known better than to go after a woman years younger, but at least he'd wanted to get married. She couldn't fault him for that. In Buck's case, a serious relationship wasn't a priority and hadn't been, not since the woman he'd loved had married his brother.

"Have you guys seen enough?" he asked.

"Yes," Johnny said. "But Jenny wishes we could take a calf home with us."

"The calf's mother wouldn't let us. She loves her too much."

"Oh," Jenny murmured.

"Can we go riding now, Uncle Buck?"

"We'll do whatever you guys want." They started back to the truck.

"Nana? Can I ride in front with Buck on the way home?"

He had to be relieved to hear that. "If it's all right with him."

"I was just going to tell you to hop in, Red."

There was her answer.

"Johnny and I will sit in back and see who can spot the most animals," Alex said. "How about the winner has to give the other one a treat."

"Yippee!" Johnny cried. The boy was always up for a competition. Buck lowered the tailgate and gave Alex an impersonal leg-up before lifting Johnny into the truck bed. In a few seconds they were off.

By the time they'd driven through the forest and reached the sagebrush, they'd counted a total of twenty-three animals, with Johnny spotting the most. He'd spotted a rabbit in the underbrush she hadn't seen.

She smiled at him. "What kind of a treat would you like?"

"Could I have another roll of caps for my gun? Or do they cost too much?"

"That's an easy request to grant."

"Thanks."

Unbeknownst to him she'd already bought a box of caps for him for the belated birthday party. He stared at her for a second. "Hey, Alex?"

Uh-oh. His tone had a serious inflection. "Yes?"

"Do you like it here?"

"I love it." *I love it more than you can imagine.*

"Jenny wants to live here."

"I know."

"Could you move here? My mom and I did."

Oh, boy. The children had been doing a lot of talking. But this was Buck's territory, with a no-trespassing sign he'd erected on the drive over.

"I'm afraid we can't. Remember, I'll be getting a job pretty soon. But maybe you and your parents could come down to Disneyland before Christmas and we could meet you there. Jenny would love that."

Before she could get an answer out of him, they'd pulled to a stop in the parking area outside the ranch house. Buck came around to lower the tailgate. "Time for lunch before we do anything else."

"Yum! I'm hungry." Johnny was such a character, it killed her. "Thanks for taking us, Uncle Buck."

Alex added her voice to his. "We had a wonderful time."

"So did I," Johnny said.

While Buck lifted him to the ground, Alex jumped

down so he wouldn't be forced to help her. She started walking around the front of the ranch house with Jenny. "After playing with those calves, we need to wash our hands."

"They were so cute."

"Not as cute as you," Buck said loud enough for her to hear.

"Thanks." Her granddaughter loved his attention. Who wouldn't?

Alex led her to the rear of the ranch house.

"I've never been in here before."

"Carson and his family lived back here before they moved. This is Johnny's old room. Buck moved us out of the motel so we could sleep in here until we have to leave. Go ahead and use the bathroom first, then we'll eat."

In a few minutes they went back to the dining room to join Buck and Johnny. "We're staying in your bedroom," Jenny announced. "Which bed was yours?"

"I slept in both of them!"

Johnny's answer was so unexpected that the adults broke out laughing.

"No, you didn't." She giggled.

"Actually he did, but not at the same time, of course," Buck explained after a cough.

Jenny's eyes widened. "Why?"

"'Cause it's fun."

More laughter ensued while they ate lunch. Afterward, they walked to the barn and went riding. When everyone was good and hot, they decided to go swimming. Tracy brought Johnny's suit over and swam with them, while Buck disappeared.

Alex had been trying to ignore the change in him, but it was impossible. After last night, she was devastated to think he could shut off his feelings so quickly. He probably thought, now that she was free of Frank, she'd turned to Buck on a rebound. It was too embarrassing.

Having a baby at seventeen and the challenging years that followed had prevented her from enjoying a normal social life. She didn't know how to act around Buck. It sickened her to think she was giving off needy vibes that he'd picked up on without her realizing it. The way she'd clung to him last night must've made her seem desperate.

She'd prided herself on being mature and in charge of her life, but in that one area where she'd made her first mistake by getting involved with a guy way too early, she still hadn't learned anything. A smart woman would have recognized what was going on with Frank and wouldn't have allowed things to progress as far as they did. She could have saved all of them a lot of grief.

An even smarter woman would have said "No thank you" to Buck when he'd suggested they leave the motel and go get a drink. He was a typical single guy who went through women like water. It wouldn't have bothered him if she'd said she was too tired. *But you wanted to be with him any way you could.* In the end he'd gotten what he wanted and it was enough for him. To her humiliation, it wasn't enough for her, but today he'd made it clear it *had* to be.

She swam over to Jenny. "Come on, sweetheart. It's after three. We need to shower and wash our hair. After we're ready, we'll drive over to Funorama to set everything up for the party." Alex was glad she had the rental car and they could leave on their own without asking Buck for a ride.

On the night they'd flown in, they'd done a few errands that had included buying some extra balloons to be blown up. She'd also ordered a birthday cake from the Millhouse Bakery that needed to be picked up. She'd gone to the extra trouble because she and Jenny were crazy about Johnny. It was also her way of thanking Carson and his partners for inviting them to the ranch in the first place.

Jenny was excited and looked around for Johnny. "I have to go in now!" she shouted. "See ya at Funorama."

"Okay! See ya later!" Tracy waved in acknowledgment.

FUNORAMA WAS A noisy place with rides and slides and games for kids. The party rooms were down the corridor. A teenager at the front counter showed Buck where to go. He'd come into town early to buy Johnny another gift and figured a water gun would be fun for him to have at the lake tomorrow. He'd bought one for Jenny, too, but was saving it until they got up there.

Once the party was over, he assumed Jenny would ride back to the ranch with Carson's family and spend another night in the loft. That would give Buck time to follow Alex to the car-rental place and return her vehicle. Then he'd get her alone and they'd have a serious talk. All day he'd gone back and forth about her and needed to speak his mind to her tonight. As Carson had said, Buck's whole life was at stake here. To put it off until tomorrow night would be pure torture.

When he entered, everyone else was already there.

The room had been decorated to the hilt with balloons. He put his gift for Johnny on the table with the others, and then looked over at Alex, who'd changed into a yellow pullover and jeans. She'd washed her hair and tied it back at the nape. Another stunning look for her.

Their gazes met for a brief moment. He couldn't read what was in those beautiful eyes before she clapped her hands. "Now that we're all here, Jenny and Johnny want to eat now and then play. So, everyone, please be seated and we'll let the festivities begin. The decorations were all her idea." Everyone cheered. "We want the birthday boy to sit up here by the cake."

"Yay!" Johnny cried, and scrambled to the table covered in red paper with white number sevens that they'd cut out and pasted on it.

Jenny sat opposite him. "Come and sit by me, Buck." There was a light in her eyes that touched his heart. In a very short time he'd learned to love Alex's granddaughter. Nothing thrilled him more than to play substitute daddy to her. It occurred to him then that it would be easy to do so on a permanent basis.

Alex served the pizza and drinks. His sideward glance took in her profile and incredible figure. He had to hold back from grabbing her around the waist and pulling her into his lap so he could kiss the daylights out of her.

The discussion centered on the drive to the pasture and the calves. Carson wanted to know if Jenny had seen a blue-eyed one. That question prompted another discussion about the rarity of a calf being born with eyes that color. Pretty soon it came time for the dessert. Alex took the cake out of the box. A plastic figure had been set on it inside a minicorral. The frosted wording read Happy 7th Birthday, Johnny.

The boy's smile was so wide, there was no more room for expansion. "It's a cowboy with a pony like mine!"

Alex lit the red candles. "Okay—make a wish."

He closed his eyes. "I wish Jenny and Alex could stay on the ranch forever!"

Buck stopped breathing.

Johnny blew out the candles in one go. The silence was deafening.

"Hey, sport," Carson murmured, "in the future, remember you're supposed to keep your wish a secret."

"How come?"

"It might not come true if you say it out loud."

"But I didn't want it to be a secret."

Buck watched Alex cut pieces of cake for everyone. He noticed her hands tremble as she passed the plates around. Johnny could have no idea how deeply his words had penetrated.

"Okay, sweetheart," Alex said. "Start bringing his presents over."

Jenny slipped off the bench and found one in the pile wrapped in white paper with gold ribbon. "I want you to open mine first."

With cake icing clinging to the edge of his mouth, Johnny eagerly unwrapped the gift and pulled out a T-shirt with a snake on it. "Look, mom, it says Fred's Dad."

Everyone roared with laughter, including Buck.

"I don't believe it," Tracy blurted. "You couldn't have gotten him anything more perfect!"

"Yep." Carson nodded. "That tops anything I've seen."

"It was my granddaughter's brainchild, not mine."

Everyone was still laughing as Jenny brought Johnny his next gift. "This is from Nana."

"A box of caps!" he cried, after he'd torn off the paper. "I can shoot my gun two hundred times! Thanks, Alex!"

That set everyone off again. Soon he'd opened all the presents.

Just when Buck thought the fun was over, Alex made an announcement. "I have one more surprise. Jenny— there's another bag with some gifts. Will you get them?"

Her cute face beamed as she did her grandmother's bidding. To Buck's surprise, she handed one to him. Then she pulled out the other one. "Hey—this is for me!"

"That's right."

They were wrapped in that same white paper with gold ribbon. When Buck opened his, he discovered a red T-shirt with the words Teton Valley Ranch Water Fight Champions printed on it in white.

He pinned Alex with his gaze. She'd remembered that night and had gone to the trouble to get them a prize before she'd even returned to the ranch. His heart beat unnaturally fast while Jenny tore hers open and lifted out the same T-shirt with a cry of delight.

"I love it, Nana!"

"So do I, *Nana,*" he half whispered.

She lowered her eyes. "You two deserved a prize."

"Did you hear that, sport?" Carson turned to Johnny.

"We're declaring a rematch before this weekend is over!"

"Yeah. And this time we'll win!"

"THE GUYS HAVE gone to play with the kids. Let me help you clean up."

"Thanks, Tracy, but you don't have to. It's my turn."

"I want to. Except for the time I told Johnny I loved Carson, I've never seen my son this happy. Your presence has brought a new element into Johnny's life. His cousin was here a few weeks ago and they had a wonderful time, but Johnny has changed. He loves this ranch and is going in a different direction from Cory. You don't know what this means to Carson. He so desperately wants Johnny to be happy here."

"Carson's an exceptional man. Johnny adores him."

"I keep telling him that, but deep inside he still has some demons to conquer. And then along came Jenny. I guess what I'm trying to say is that Johnny has found a new life here and really feels it's his home. He wants everyone else to love it, too."

Alex's eyes smarted. "Jenny couldn't wait to come back. She's been happier than I've seen her in several years. Her friendship with Johnny is very sweet. When your husband and his partners were inspired to do such a noble thing, they couldn't have known how deeply their goodness would affect the children. The fatherless kids of the world need more selfless men like the daddies on this dude ranch."

They stared at each other. "It's true."

She nodded. "I wish my daughter could have been the one to bring Jenny."

"Your pain must be terrible at times."

"In the beginning, yes, but time has brought healing. Jenny's my joy."

"So's my son, who has a terrible habit of running his mouth when he shouldn't. I'm trying to work on that with him. He mentioned you're...not getting married. I hope that decision has made life better for you."

"It definitely has. I didn't love Frank the way I should, and Jenny never took to him."

"Then I'm happy for you."

"Thank you." But now Alex had a new problem because Jenny liked Buck *too* much.

As for Alex's feelings for him... She looked around. "Why don't I help you take his presents and the rest of the cake to your car? Then we can go in and watch the kids until they're completely worn out and want to go home."

"That's so nice of you. Do you mind if Jenny sleeps over again tonight? Johnny begged me to ask you."

"She begged me, too. Do we have a choice?"

"Not with those two."

Once they'd taken everything out to Carson's SUV, they went back inside. Tracy gave Alex an impish look. "That giant slide looks fun. Shall we try it?"

"Why not?" She'd just seen Johnny go down it between Carson's legs, followed by Jenny between Buck's. Ross didn't seem to be around. Being a Saturday night, he probably had plans with a woman.

Alex hurried up the steps behind Tracy. The kids saw them and waved. Alex sat and pushed off. Buck was there to catch her as she reached the bottom and helped her to her feet. The contact caused a jolt of electricity to run through her.

When their eyes met, she saw the unmistakable glaze of desire in his and realized he'd been affected, too. The change in him from earlier in the day confused her.

His hand closed over hers almost possessively. "Come on," he said in a husky voice. "Let's you and I go down together this time. You first."

The kids had already gone up again. Shaking like a leaf from his touch, Alex started up the steps once more, aware of him right behind her. When they reached the top, he sat first and pulled her down in front of him, encasing her legs with his. Hunger for him licked through her veins as his strong arms slid around her waist. The feel of his well-defined chest against her back sent shivers through her.

"Ready?" he whispered the word against her neck where his lips grazed the skin.

She nodded, unable to speak.

"Do you have any idea how wonderful you smell?"

A gasp escaped her throat before he pushed off. As they flew down the chute, she realized that without a doubt she was wildly in love for the second time in her life. No longer a witless teenager who hadn't yet experienced life, she was a fully grown woman who knew exactly what she wanted. How deep the feelings of this bachelor ran for her, she didn't know. But the chemistry was there and couldn't be denied. He wanted her. *And I want him.* She couldn't blame this on widow's hormones, because she'd never been a widow, never been married and was never going to be.

At the bottom of the slide, Jenny begged Buck to

go down with her again. It was fine with Alex, who stood watching in a daze. Her mind harked back to high school. There'd been chemistry between her and Kyle and she'd let it take over.

Now here she was again twenty-four years later, in danger of making the same mistake again with a man who only had to touch her to turn her insides to liquid. Was this to be the pattern of her life? Make love with a man once every quarter of a century?

She needed to decide what she intended to do. Tonight Jenny would be sleeping over at Johnny's house again. Alex and Buck would have the whole night to themselves. Would she go home on Monday having known his possession? And then what? They'd both go their separate ways? She'd never see him again? The mere idea was enough to drive her mad.

She needed to get out of there. Get away from Buck so she could think. When he alighted once more at the bottom of the chute with Jenny, she turned to her granddaughter without looking at him. "It's getting late and we have a big day tomorrow if we're going to go camping. Tracy asked if you could sleep over again and I said yes, so I'll drive you to Johnny's house right now."

Jenny turned to Johnny. "Nana says I can stay at your house."

He'd been complaining that he didn't want to go yet, but knowing that Jenny would be sleeping over got him to agree to it.

"Come on, sweetheart." Alex took her hand and they walked out to the car.

"What about my T-shirt?"

"It's in my purse." Not looking back at the others, she drove out of the parking lot.

Twilight was turning into night. Crickets chirped in the pine-scented air. Lights twinkled between the trees and the last tinge of violet hadn't quite faded in the western sky. All of it just increased her longing to be in Buck's arms.

"Nana?"

Jenny's voice jerked her out of her thoughts. "Yes? Did you have a good time tonight?"

"It was the best! Buck's so nice. I love him." Alex had expected her to talk about Johnny, but it was Buck who was on her granddaughter's mind. "Johnny's afraid he's going to go back to Colorado. He doesn't want him to go. I don't, either."

Alex's hands tightened on the steering wheel. That was news to her. She'd gotten the impression that leaving the ranch would be the last thing he'd do. "Maybe Johnny misunderstood."

"No, he didn't. He heard him on the phone."

"Johnny shouldn't listen in on other people's conversations. I'm sure he's wrong."

"You sound cross."

She took a fortifying breath. "Do I? I'm sorry."

"Guess what? Buck has four brothers and Johnny has four uncles. That's funny."

"Because there aren't any girls?"

"Yes. Buck says I can be his little girl anytime."

Thank heaven the new house had come into view. At this point, Alex was afraid to say anything her granddaughter could misconstrue. Carson's SUV was right behind them.

She stopped the car. "Listen, sweetheart—I'm going to say good-night to you here. I need to get back to the ranch house and call Mom. She's been waiting all day to hear from me."

"Okay." Jenny undid her seat belt and leaned over to kiss her. "Good night, Nana. Johnny said he loved his party and he really likes you."

Her eyes smarted. "Thank you for telling me." She took the T-shirt out of her purse and handed it to her. "See you in the morning."

With a nod, Jenny jumped out of the car and joined the others. Alex waved before turning the car around. She drove to the ranch house in turmoil. She didn't see the truck Buck had brought to the party. Fiercely disappointed to think he might have joined Ross and headed out instead of wanting to be with her, she hurried inside the front door.

Willy waved to her from the desk as she passed him on her way to her bedroom in the rear. She did owe her parents a callback, but after what Jenny had confided to her in the car, she was too shaken to make it.

How could Buck consider going back to Colorado? After putting the past behind him, what would be the reason to change his mind? She'd believed him when he'd told her he loved his life here. Alex couldn't figure him out. As much as she wanted to believe that Johnny was wrong about what he'd heard, that little guy was smart as a whip and had the inside track on what went on around the ranch.

The news shouldn't matter to her, but it did. Everything to do with him affected her because she was painfully in love with him.

Too wired to sleep yet, she slipped out into the hall and set out for the kitchen. Buck had told her she should feel free to use it. Caffeine wouldn't help her nerves, but it was coffee she wanted. After finding a jar of the instant stuff, she made herself a cup and microwaved it.

As she started back to her room to drink it, the overhead lights went on.

"Buck—"

He stood in the doorway with his hands on his hips, all male from his powerful thighs to the contours of his hard jawline. "Willy told me you'd come in. Since you weren't in the bedroom, I hoped I'd find you in here. Why in the hell did you run away so fast?" he asked. "One minute, you were there, the next you were gone."

"It was rude of me. Forgive me."

Buck's eyes wandered over her, missing nothing. "I didn't think you had a rude bone in your body, so tell me what's going on."

"A lot of things," she answered honestly. "Too many." She drank part of her coffee before putting the mug on the counter of the island.

"Am *I* one of those things? Is that why you fled into the night?"

"I didn't flee—"

"You could have fooled me. Am I so terrifying?"

She looked away. "You already know the answer to that question."

"On the contrary. It seems to me the minute I touch you, you do a disappearing act."

Her pulse was running away with her. "You mean, the way you disappeared on me during the drive over to the herd?"

His brows furrowed. "Explain that remark."

He wanted answers. She'd give them to him. "After I showed you the pictures in my wallet, you became a different person. Standoffish. Why? The night before, I thought we were enjoying ourselves. The chemistry felt obvious. But I can only think that in the light of day with certain proof before you, the idea of being with an older woman—a *grandma*—didn't hold the same appeal."

His eyes flickered with a strange light. "You couldn't be more wrong."

As long as she was feeling this brave, she would dare to say what else was on her mind. "Is it true what Johnny told Jenny?"

"About what?" He sounded impatient.

"That you might be going back to Colorado?"

He rubbed the back of his neck, as if he needed to plan his answer carefully. "You mean, for another trip?"

"No. Permanently. It's evident Johnny was worried enough about it to voice it to my granddaughter."

Buck rubbed his lower lip with his thumb. "He must have heard me on the phone with my father a couple of weeks ago. He's had to slow down and wants me back home."

Her heart lurched. "You must be so conflicted."

"That's putting it mildly, but not for the reasons you're thinking." He walked over to the island and looped his arms around her shoulders. "Look at me, Alex." His mouth was only inches from hers.

"I *am* looking." Her voice trembled.

"How do you feel about me?"

She groaned inside. "After what happened last night, it should be clear to you."

His features hardened. "That was chemistry. According to you, I can turn it off and on at will. Let's get past the discussion of our physical attraction to each other and dig deeper to find out what's going on inside of you. Why would it matter to you if I go back to Colorado or stay here?"

"Because I know how much the ranch means to you."

His breath was warm on her lips. "It means a hell of a lot, but some things are even more important."

She could hardly swallow. "Your family has to have missed you all these years."

"I've missed them, but I'm talking about the relationship between a man and a woman. If it's right, then it trumps everything else in importance. Don't you agree?"

Alex thought she was going to faint. "Yes, although I can't speak from personal experience because my only experience was with a boy and it never turned into a relationship."

"Then it's time you found out what a real one could be like." Suddenly the room tilted because he'd picked her up in his arms. His mouth took hers in a long, hungry kiss that still didn't satisfy either of them. At the doorway, he turned out the light and carried her down the hall to Johnny's bedroom.

His rock-hard body followed her down on top of the bed. He tangled her legs with his and smoothed the hair away from her temples. In the semidarkness, his eyes were alive with desire. "I want you more than I've ever wanted a woman in my life. Everything about you appeals to me. But it goes much deeper than the physical.

"I have this impossible dream of sharing my life with

you, of having a baby with you. My mom had me at forty." She gasped. "I'm glad if that shocks you. Now you know how far my fantasy has taken me."

"Fantasy?" she whispered, out of breath.

"Yes." He covered her face in kisses. "I don't have anything to offer you and Jenny. A man needs something solid behind him." He had to be talking marriage, but hadn't said the words. The joy of it overwhelmed her. "I'm not Frank—I can't offer you the security you deserve. That takes time to build."

"If I'd wanted Frank, I would have married him."

"Be honest, Alex. You need much more than a ranch hand can deliver. While the guys and I were in the hospital, we felt it was pretty much the end of our lives. We had no expectations except to survive and try to do some good."

"You've done a lot more than that!" she cried from her soul, kissing him with abandon to convince him.

Buck was the one who eventually brought them down to earth. After relinquishing her mouth, he turned on his side, running his hand up and down her arm. "When you look at me like that, you have no idea how much I'd love to ravish you, but I'm not going to do it."

Giving her arm a squeeze, he rolled away from her and got off the bed. She hated that shuttered look hiding his eyes from her while he stood there rocking on his cowboy boots. "See you in the morning." He started for the door.

In panic, she sat up. "There you go again, Buck, distancing yourself from me. I'm not Melanie."

Her comment caught him on the raw. He turned to

her. Lines marred his handsome features. "Where did that come from?"

"She didn't wait for you to finish college because she wasn't a risk-taker. Instead, she married your brother who already had job security working in the family construction business. She was blind not to realize that you instill security by simply being who you are.

"Your old girlfriend didn't know the Buck Summerhayes I know. Otherwise she would have realized what a rarity you are. It wouldn't matter what you did for a living or how long it took. You're a survivor and a hero who takes care of everyone else and went to my granddaughter's rescue without giving it a second's thought.

"There's greatness in you. Carson recognized it when he met you. No wonder your family wants and needs you back. It's because you're a remarkable man who's true to himself."

Even from the distance, she felt his body go rigid. "That was a speech any red-blooded man would be proud of, ma'am. Good night."

*Oh, no, you don't!*

She rushed out into the hall in time to hear a door bang shut in the distance.

With her heart racing, Alex dashed down the corridor and out the rear door after him. The headlights to his truck went on. He started to back out. "Buck? Wait—" She took a flying leap to reach the door handle on the passenger side.

He slammed on the brakes. She took advantage of the moment to open the door and climb inside the cab. His expression looked like thunder. "What in the hell do you think you're doing?" He was out of breath. "Don't you know you could have gotten dragged, even killed?" The pulse at the corner of his mouth was throbbing.

"You're worth the risk."

"We've already said good-night."

"No," she fired back. "You walked out on me while I still had more to say. I think the term *slippery slope* was invented when someone tried to get up close to you and failed. This pattern you have of bolting like an unbroken stallion at the first sign you might be in danger is disconcerting to say the least. Last year I watched Hugh break one in and can see the similarity in behavior."

His expression grew as dark as a thundercloud. She'd made him angry again. The next thing she knew, he'd pulled the truck closer to the house and shut off the engine.

"Since you love this ranch so much, why don't you drive us to a favorite spot I haven't seen before? In case you're worried, I'm not tired in the least."

"That wouldn't be a good idea." His voice sounded like gravel. "We have a big day planned for tomorrow. I've got a lot of gear to get together."

"Of course." His work was never done.

Silence stretched between them. "What did you want to say?"

She took a shaky breath. "It can wait until tomorrow evening when we're at the lake and you're able to relax."

"In that case, I have things to do now." He reached across to open the door for her. His arm brushed against her in the process, turning her body to a mass of jelly. "I'll wait till I know you're safely in the house. Lock the door behind you."

"I will."

## Chapter Ten

Buck waited until Alex had gone inside.

In the bedroom, she'd sung his praises. It had reminded him of a glowing eulogy to a dead marine.

But not one word of love had come from her lips. Not one declaration that she shared his dream for a life together.

Holding her in his arms, exulting in the rapture of her kisses, he'd forgotten to be cautious and had been all kinds of a fool to have opened up to her. How could he forget it had taken Frank two years to make a dent....

Buck didn't have years. He'd been given only eight days, if you combined the two times she'd come to the ranch. After her experience with Kyle, she'd been guarding her heart all this time. To suppose or even hope she would blurt out that she was in love with Buck in such a short amount of time was ludicrous. He really was out of his mind.

He took off for the shed where they kept the camping supplies. There were tents, water toys, fishing poles, lanterns, sleeping bags and feed for the horses to load in the back of the truck. A couple of guys from the staff would drive up to the lake early with the food.

It was close to midnight when he drove back to the

ranch house and went inside. Ross caught up to him at the top of the stairs. His brows knitted together. "You look gutted. What's wrong?"

"I blew it tonight and told her how I felt."

"And?"

He sucked in his breath. "She gave me some spiel about what a great man I am."

"You are."

"Thanks, buddy," he said with a mirthless smile, "but you know damn well that kind of talk is a death sentence."

"I don't get it. I thought—"

"So did I," Buck cut him off, and then had a coughing spell. "But being on fire for each other doesn't mean she's ready for anything else. She couldn't bring herself to marry Frank, who hung in there for two years. I'm not made like him.

"I can't believe I'm saying this, but I'm glad she's flying out of here on Monday. Do me a favor tomorrow and ask Tracy to stick with her while we entertain the kids?"

Ross nodded. "What time do you figure we should get away?"

"After breakfast. I've asked Bert to get the horses saddled and ready."

"Carson checked the weather forecast. There could be light rain later in the day."

Buck frowned. "Jenny's afraid of storms. Last month our plane flew right into one over the Tetons."

"I remember. If it doesn't look good, we'll come back early."

"That's all we can do. Under other circumstances

I'd cancel the outing, but I know Jenny's got her heart set on it. She and Johnny have made all sorts of plans."

"Don't I know it."

"I'll ask a couple of the hands to bring up an extra truck for us in case we need to drive the kids back."

"Sounds like you've got everything covered."

"Except that we can't count on the weather report ever being accurate," Buck muttered.

"We'll play it by ear. Get some sleep."

"You, too."

They parted company and went to bed. For the first time in over a month, Buck wasn't fighting the urge to seek out Alex, whether she slept in the guest cabin or in the ranch house. Nothing could have cooled his blood faster than to realize his dream had no possibility of coming to fruition.

When he awakened the next morning, he looked out the window. An overcast sky greeted him and appeared as grim as his mood. He turned on the TV to the weather channel. Just as he'd feared, the earlier forecast hadn't been specific enough. A storm front would move in by evening and bring wind and heavy rainfall.

After he'd showered and shaved, he got dressed in jeans and a flannel shirt. When he was ready, he went down to the dining room. Ross was there talking to some of the guests.

While Buck ate, he phoned Carson. His friend had been outside already and was in agreement that they would have to cancel the campout portion of their outing. If they got up to the lake early to swim, they would have time to ride back home before the storm started.

The kids wouldn't like the news, but for once, their

disappointment wasn't foremost in his mind. All he could think of was that now he wouldn't have to spend a night in the rain aching for Alex who would be asleep in one of the tents only a stone's throw away from his.

Once he'd finished eating, he pulled Ross aside. "I just talked to Carson. We've decided to call off the camping-out part of the trip."

"I looked at the sky a few minutes ago. It's a good idea."

"Since the others haven't come to breakfast yet, I'm going to use this time to drive back to the shed and unload everything from the truck. It needs to be done and I'd rather do it now. I'll coordinate with the staff about just bringing lunch for us."

"Do you want help?"

They eyed each other. He could always count on Ross to know exactly what was going on with him. "Bring everyone to the barn. I'll be there to meet you and we'll head out."

There was no sign of Alex yet, which was good. He hurriedly left the dining room and headed out to the truck. Twenty minutes later, he'd finished the job and climbed back in the cab. There was a message waiting for him on his cell. His mother had phoned. On the drive over to the barn, he called her back.

As THEIR PARTY came out of the trees Jenny cried, "Secret Lake looks like a silver dollar!"

"Told you," Johnny said after they'd dismounted.

The small mountain lake with its stretch of beach was perfectly formed. With a pine forest surrounding them, the place looked enchanting and would have been an ideal spot to spend the night, if not for the impending storm.

Alex glanced at the sky for the dozenth time. It was noon. She'd been hoping for a break in the clouds, but no such luck. Thankfully, with the three men doing their best to keep the kids entertained, the children seemed to have gotten over their disappointment at not being able to camp out.

It was Alex who was still suffering over the way things had ended before she'd gotten out of Buck's truck last night. He'd been charming and friendly to her this morning. From his surface behavior you would never have known what had transpired the night before.

But Alex knew he'd retreated deep within himself. She feared it might be impossible to reach him once she nabbed some time alone with him today. So far, there'd been no opportunity for that. The men stuck together as they chaperoned the children.

Tracy stayed at Alex's side and they rode the entire way together. She found out that Tracy had been a technology specialist for the school district where Johnny had gone to school in Sandusky, Ohio.

They talked about jobs and the necessity of finding the kind of work that coincided with the kids' school day. Little by little, Alex learned about the pain Tracy and Johnny had gone through when her first husband was killed.

"Johnny changed. He retreated into his shell and had no confidence. He didn't want to play with his friends. By the time that letter from Carson arrived, I was pretty frantic. I didn't think Johnny would agree to go. If we hadn't…"

Alex understood and could hardly believe the boy her friend was describing was the same little cowboy with the shining brown eyes who was showing Jenny all the ins and outs of the ranch as if he owned the place.

In turn, Alex admitted to Tracy how her granddaughter had suffered after losing both parents. She feared that her sadness would rob her of the happy childhood she deserved.

"Buck was the first one to make her laugh since her mother's death. The night we drove to the ranch from the airport, she was scared because of the storm. He kept chatting with her and told her about Moppy the squirrel. It was like magic the way she responded—he helped her forget her fear. Then she met Johnny and they laugh all the time."

"I know. To be honest, I'm dreading you leaving to-morrow. Johnny told me again this morning he wishes you'd get a job in Jackson."

Alex almost moaned out loud. "I'm afraid Jenny had something to do with that."

"Do you know the only thing saving me is that we have a back-to-school information night on Thursday? I'm praying Johnny makes some new friends soon, but Jenny will be a hard act to follow. She's wise for her age and I think that intrigues him."

"Jenny thinks he's the funnest, funniest person on Earth."

"He has his father's personality. The first time I met Tony, my girlfriends and I were having a picnic at Lake-front State Park in Cleveland when a crew of firefighters pulled up to eat their lunch and play some football. The cutest guy in the group started flirting with me.

I secretly called him Mr. Personality. He told me after our first date he was going to marry me."

Alex smiled. "I can hear him through Johnny. That first morning he came to our cabin door, he spoke right up and said, 'Hi! I'm Johnny Lundgren. Are you Jenny?' My granddaughter was so stunned, she could only nod. Then he said, 'Do you want to have breakfast with me?'"

Both women's laughter drew the guys' attention. Alex felt Buck's gaze on her. They were setting up a table and chairs that one of the staff members had driven up with the food for their lunch. The children had run over to the water's edge and stripped down to their bathing suits to go wading.

"What's so funny?" Carson called to his wife.

"Just the kids. I'll tell you later." In an aside to Alex, she said, "Carson is so different. He was much more guarded when we first met. I had to read between the lines."

"I know what you mean. That's a trait all three of the guys seem to share," Alex murmured. "Buck was hurt long before he went to war."

"You're talking about Melanie."

"Yes."

"He got over her years ago, but unfortunately he doesn't have a lot of faith in a woman's staying power. The fear of committing again without a guarantee still looms large for him."

Alex's heart rate increased. Last night was proof of what Tracy had just confided to her. Buck was so convinced he didn't have enough to offer a woman that the thought was entrenched in him. Alex had thought about it all night and her illuminating conversation with Tracy just now had her mind spinning with an idea.

Deep in thought, she barely heard Tracy add, "Then there's Carson who suffered *after* he came home from war because he felt he'd deserted his grandfather. He's still trying to get over the guilt."

"Those poor guys. And on top of everything else, they have to cope with their disease. It isn't fair."

"No kidding."

"Food's ready. Come and get it!" Ross announced, jarring Alex back to the present. The guys were trying to hurry things up. Alex sensed they didn't trust the timing of the storm and wanted to make sure they started on their way back in plenty of time.

She and Tracy rounded up the kids. They took them behind some bushes where they could take off their wet bathing suits and get dressed. Once that was done, they all sat down to eat sloppy joes and potato chips. After finishing three of the hot beef sandwiches, Carson stood.

"As much as I wish we could stay here until tomorrow, I'm afraid we can't. As soon as everyone's through eating, we'll head back to the ranch and finish our party in the swimming pool. It's time for a water-fight rematch!"

"Yippee!" the children cried in unison.

Once Johnny and Jenny had wolfed down their cookies, Carson and Ross helped them get back on their ponies.

"The kids are really getting a workout."

"So are we," Tracy quipped. "I'm going to be sore after this."

"Tell me about it." But Alex's physical discomfort would be nothing compared to the mental agony she was suffering from.

Out of the corner of her eye, Alex watched Buck assist with the cleanup and put the camp furniture back in the truck. She mounted her mare and caught up to Tracy for the ride home. Carson led them out. Ross and Buck were bringing up the rear, or so she thought. But when she looked back, there was no sign of Buck. Ross was trailing Buck's horse behind him. She stared at him. "Where's Buck?"

"He left with Randy to get back to the ranch sooner. A call came in early this morning. His father's in the hospital. He had some minor chest pain. Nothing serious so far." A small cry escaped Alex's throat. "We told him to fly home and be with his family."

"Of course." Her concern for him sent her heart racing. He'd hidden his emotions so well, no one had suspected anything was wrong. He was a master at it. "Why did he come on the trip, Ross?"

"He didn't want to disappoint Jenny."

Alex loved him too much. Tears filled her eyes. She looked away, but not before both Ross and Tracy had seen them.

"Carson and I decided we won't tell the kids the real reason he left until we get back." He coughed. "Let them think Randy needed his help."

"That was a good idea," she said through wooden lips.

Jenny would be inconsolable when she learned she wouldn't be able to say goodbye to him before they left for California in the morning. Ditto for her.

*Oh, Buck.*

It didn't take her granddaughter long to notice Buck wasn't with them. Ross's explanation didn't take away her disappointment. After that, the subdued atmosphere among their group matched the elements. Naturally, Jenny expected to find Buck at the barn when they returned, but he wasn't there.

"Sweetheart?" Alex took her aside. "I just found out Buck's father is ill, so that's why he left the lake in the truck with Randy. He's taken a flight to Colorado to be with his family."

"In the storm?" The alarm in her voice spoke volumes.

"It's not a bad storm like the one last month. He'll be fine."

"When will he be back?"

"I don't know."

Her face crumpled before the tears came. "Then we won't see him again."

Alex knew exactly how she felt. There were no comforting words. All she could do was hug her for a long time.

"Do you want to go swimming until it rains?" Johnny could be so sweet.

"No," her granddaughter sniffed.

Tracy suggested they walk to the ranch house for some hot chocolate. Halfway there, the wind picked up and there was a noticeable drop in temperature.

A shiver ran down Alex's back. She prayed Buck's father would be all right. He *had* to be. If anything happened to him, Buck would carry around the same kind of guilt that plagued Carson.

After their hot chocolate, Tracy and Alex went into the games room with the kids to watch them play Ping-Pong. When that activity no longer appealed, they ate a meal in the dining room without much enthusiasm, and then went back to the games room to watch a movie. No one could concentrate. It had started raining but there was no lightning or thunder, for which Alex was grateful. And still no news from Buck.

By nine o'clock, Carson suggested Alex get her suitcase and come back to the house with them so the kids could get ready for bed. Tracy put an arm around her. "Plan to stay with us tonight. We have two guest bedrooms. That way when Buck phones, we'll all hear any news he has to share. In the morning, we'll drive you to the airport."

"Thank you, Tracy."

A half hour after the children went to bed in the loft, Buck phoned Carson. After he hung up, Carson turned to them. "His father's undergoing a series of tests with an important one scheduled for tomorrow. He isn't sure how long he'll have to be away from the ranch." Carson eyed her. "If he can, he'll phone you and Jenny in the morning to say goodbye. I need to let Ross know." He kissed his wife. "I'll be in the den."

Everyone was worried about Buck, but no one more so than Alex. He was in pain, not only because of what was going on with his father, but because of the way things had been left last night before he'd driven off. She felt him slipping away from her emotionally with every tick of the grandfather clock in the hallway.

Alex couldn't stand it any longer and jumped up from the loveseat. "Tracy—"

"What is it?"

"I—I need a favor," she stammered. At this point it didn't matter if she revealed what was going on inside her to Johnny's mother.

"Anything."

"I should get Jenny back in school, but I can't leave Wyoming without seeing Buck again. A phone call won't do. Last night he left the ranch upset before we could finish talking and I've been in agony ever since.

"I'd like to fly out to Colorado early in the morning and be back by evening. I still have my rental car. If you could watch Jenny for that long, you'd have my eternal gratitude and I'd make it up to you. Jenny thinks the world of you and your family and is totally comfortable with you."

"We'd love to take care of her. Johnny will be so excited when he finds out she can stay another day."

Alex smiled. "Thank you so much. I know it's a huge imposition, but if anything happens to Buck's father, I want to be there. He shouldn't be alone. But I don't want him to know I'm coming. That would put added pressure on him. I'd rather just show up."

Tracy got to her feet and walked over to her. "I'm glad someone's going to be there for him. He's usually the one helping everyone else. You've been through so much yourself. I think you're exactly what he needs."

"I hope that's true, because what you said about him earlier today definitely is. He doesn't believe that a woman will stick by him when the going gets tough. That old wound of his runs deep. I'd like to prove him wrong if he'll let me."

There was a new sweetness in Tracy's smile. "You love him."

Moisture wet her cheeks. "I do."

Now Tracy teared up. "You have no idea how much that thrills me. Buck deserves to be loved by a wonderful woman like you. Please don't worry if you can't get back to the ranch tomorrow. We're not going anywhere."

"You're an angel."

"Let's go in the den so you can make your plane reservations. Carson will give you the name of the hospital and Buck's cell-phone number."

"First, I'd better go up to the loft and run this by Jenny. If she doesn't think she can stay here on her own, then I'll take her with me."

"Go ahead. I'll tell Carson your plans."


IT WAS 10:30 A.M. when Alex arrived at Memorial Hospital in Colorado Springs. She hurried inside to get the room number for David Summerhayes. The central bank of elevators was close by. She took a lift to the third floor. There was a no admittance sign on the door to his room. Fearful of what it could mean, she went down the hall to the nursing station.

"What can you tell me about Mr. Summerhayes's condition?"

The nurse looked up from the chart. "Are you a member of the family?"

"No. A…friend."

"I'm sorry. The best I can do is direct you to the visitor lounge at the other end of the hall. Perhaps you'll see a family member there."

"Thank you."

Alex should have phoned Buck, but she'd wanted to know his father's status first so she'd be better prepared to talk to him. With her heart in her throat, she walked down the corridor where she could see a room with half a dozen people sitting at random while they waited. A TV was on, but no one seemed to be watching it. A few people looked as though they'd been up all night.

She sat for a few minutes, but soon realized that wasn't going to get her anywhere so she went back down the hall. Since she couldn't use her cell phone in the hospital, she decided to go outside and try to reach him. If that failed, she could call his parents' home and leave a message. Carson had given her the number, but she worried Buck might not like her doing that.

After pushing the button, she waited impatiently for the elevator going down. To her chagrin, it stopped at every floor. Finally, the doors opened to a full car, but some people made room for her. After she got on, she turned around to face the doors.

Across the hall, a tall, muscular guy in a crewneck sweater and jeans had just stepped onto another elevator opposite hers. The cough sounded familiar. Then he faced forward.

*"Buck—"*

His eyes swerved in her direction as her doors closed. The elevator started to descend.

*Please stop at the next floor.*

But this time it didn't. The minute the doors opened onto the main floor, she looked for the stairway sign and opened the door to go back up. Although she was still sore from yesterday's ride, she paid no heed as she dashed up the first flight.

As she rounded it to start up the second, she heard someone coming down. She lifted her head and her eyes collided with his. He slowed to a stop a few steps above her. *"Alex—"* She thought he'd paled a little. "I thought I was hallucinating just now. What are you doing here?"

"I—I came to be with you." Her voice faltered.

He rubbed his chest absently. "You're supposed to be on your way to California."

She shook her head. "Something more important came up."

There was a silence before he said, "When I couldn't get you on the phone this morning to say goodbye, I called the ranch. Tracy told me you'd left for the airport early. No wonder I couldn't reach you." He acted dazed. "Where's Red?"

Alex loved his nickname for her granddaughter. "Back at the ranch with Johnny."

"You came without her?" He sounded shaken.

"She understood I needed to see you alone. Buck—" Her voice throbbed. "Tell me about your father. The no-admittance sign on his door worried me and the nurse at the nursing station couldn't tell me anything because I'm not family."

"The sign was put there because dad has too many friends. His doctor insisted everyone stay out of the room until all the tests were done. It seems he had a severe panic attack that mimicked all the signs of a heart attack. He needs medication to get his anxiety under control. The recession hit him harder than any of us realized because he knows my brothers' families depend on the construction company being successful. But the doctor says he's going to be fine."

"Oh, Buck—that's wonderful news!" She couldn't stop the tears. "You must be so relieved."

"Relieved doesn't begin to express what I'm feeling right now," he said. "He's going to be released later today."

"Thank heaven!"

A smile curved one corner of his mouth. "We're all pretty happy. Especially my mom."

"I can only imagine. Is everyone here?"

"Not yet. They were all here yesterday. I stayed with Dad during the night. Before he fell asleep a minute ago, he told me to go back to the ranch where I belong."

Alex had trouble swallowing. "He said that?"

Buck nodded. "We did a lot of talking and came to a new understanding. For one thing, I've promised him I'll come home more often. I would introduce you to him right now, but the medication they gave him will keep him asleep for several hours."

"Are you going to your folks' house now?"

"No. I'm on my way to the airport. If I take the next flight to Denver, I can make a connecting flight to Jackson. I've left the guys in the lurch long enough."

"Buck—they understand. As long as you're here, don't you want to take another day to visit with your family?"

He shook his head. "I had my private time with Dad. Now I've got something more important to do."

"What's that?"

"You'll find out after we grab a taxi." He reached her in one step and swept her down the stairs to the main floor. They practically ran to the front exit.

"Didn't you bring any luggage?"

"No. I was in too big a hurry last night. Where's yours?"

She bit the underside of her lip. "I only planned to stay long enough to offer my support."

"So you have a return ticket for today?"

"Yes. I couldn't ask Tracy to watch Jenny any longer than that."

"Perfect. Things couldn't have worked out better."

He detained a taxi that had just dropped off an older man with a cane. "We need a ride to the airport," he called to the driver, before helping Alex into the backseat.

Once he'd shut the door, he turned to her and crushed her in his arms. He was so strong, he didn't know he was nearly suffocating her, but she didn't mind. This was where she wanted to be for the rest of her life.

"We've got a lot to talk about, but right now this is what I'm dying for." His voice shook before he kissed her with almost savage hunger. She was so consumed with happiness that the driver had to tell them they'd arrived at the terminal. Even then, several seconds elapsed before they could stand to pull apart from each other long enough to get out of the taxi.

"You blush beautifully," he whispered after he'd paid the driver. "Come on. We've got a plane to catch."

## Chapter Eleven

The seat-belt sign had just flashed on, warning them they were about to land at Jackson airport. When he wasn't kissing her, Buck hadn't been able to take his eyes off the gorgeous woman who was wearing his favorite outfit, the one he'd first seen her in.

He needed to get her alone, pronto. He was relieved when she told him she'd brought her rental car to the airport. They wouldn't have to call anyone and could take their time before they drove home.

Alex gave him the car keys before he could ask for them. He reached for her hand and clung to it all the way to the ranch entrance. But instead of taking the road to the ranch house, he turned onto a side road that wound around to the far side of the property.

"Where are we going?"

"There's something I want to show you." He squeezed her fingers. "It's my favorite spot."

When they came upon a whole hillside of quaking aspen surrounded by dark pines, he heard her gasp of wonder. "Oh, Buck—it's beautiful!" The late-afternoon sun had set the yellow leaves on fire. "If I were an artist…"

"I know what you mean." He turned off the engine

and pulled her across to him so she was half lying in his arms. "When I was telling you about my fantasy, this was part of it, with a home set right in the middle of all that color." Her neck was so delectable, he couldn't resist kissing it.

"Carson has told me repeatedly that if I want to go into business with him permanently, this parcel of land is mine."

She turned in his arms and looked up at him with her vivid, dark blue eyes. "Is that what you want to do?"

"It's what I always wanted to do, now more than ever. That's because of you and your belief in me."

"I love you, Buck. I'm so in love with you, it hurts."

"Finally she tells me." He lowered his mouth to hers. For a little while, time and place had no meaning as he absorbed those precious words into his heart. When he was halfway coherent again, he said, "I have a small nest egg, as my dad calls it. I've held on to it, waiting to use it for something worthy. If I built that house, would—"

"Yes—" She cut him off. "I'll marry you under any circumstances. Does that answer your question?"

*"Darling—"* Once again they were devouring each other. "I told my parents I'd met the woman I wanted to marry. You've brought this bachelor to his knees."

She kissed his features. "It wasn't easy."

Buck let out a harsh laugh. "What are you talking about? I was nailed the second I saw your long, shapely legs walking in front of me."

Alex raised her head. "What do you mean?"

He told her everything. "When I left the hospital, I had plans to fly directly to Sacramento and bring you and Jenny back home."

She cupped his face in her hands. "There aren't enough words to tell you how much I love you. Whether you build us a house, or we rent one in Jackson, I'm planning to get a job there to help support us for as long as it takes. Tracy put me on to an idea without her realizing it. She used to work for the school district in technology. I'm going to apply for an accounting job with the school district here in Jackson. If they don't have an opening, I'll find something else."

"Alex—" he said, his voice full of emotion. Her love was blowing him away.

"If I put my house on the market right away, we can use the money from the sale. It won't be a lot, but it will all help, because you and I are in this together for the long haul."

Her declaration humbled him, but there was still something else bothering him. "Alex?"

"What is it? You sound worried. How can you be worried about anything right now?"

"It's Jenny. She—"

"She loves you."

"I want to believe that, but she didn't want you marrying Frank."

"You're not Frank. You're Jenny's superhero. She wanted to fly to Colorado with me because she's absolutely crazy about you. When you didn't come back from the lake with us, she became a ghost of herself. If you don't believe me, ask Tracy. And there's more. When you told her you'd like her to be your little girl, she took that to heart."

Buck buried his face in her hair. "I pray to God you're right about that. I couldn't lose you now. I just couldn't."

"You'll never have to. But to help you feel better, why don't we go pick her up so you can find out for yourself and be happy."

"I *am* happy. Too happy. I'm afraid I'm going to wake up."

"Well, I can tell you this. You *are* awake and have been kissing me until my lips are swollen, my hair is a complete mess and your beard has given me a rash. While we drive home, I need the time to make myself somewhat presentable. You know Johnny. He'll take one look at us and know exactly what we've been doing. That child is positively dangerous."

Laughter pealed out of Buck. Life didn't get better than this. He wrapped his arm tightly around her shoulders. With the taste of heaven on his lips, he started the engine. It took a while for them to reach the turnoff for Carson's new house. He couldn't get enough of Alex. Before they came out of the trees, he stopped the car while they kissed as if they were making up for years of deprivation. Her passion had set him on fire.

Suddenly, there was a knock on the window. Buck was so far gone, Alex was the one who had to separate them. He raised his head and looked around. Two cute faces stared at them through the window on the front passenger side of the car. Buck lowered it.

Johnny's eyes had rounded. "Whoa, Uncle Buck!"

"Hey, sport. How's everybody?"

"Good."

"Hi, Buck."

"Hi, Red."

"Is your daddy okay?"

"He's going to be fine."

"That's good." A smile broke out on her face. "I'm glad you're back."

"We are, too." Alex opened the door so Jenny could climb in and hug her.

Johnny looked as if he was going to explode. "I've got to tell Mom and Dad! I'll be right back." He took off running, six guns and all.

Buck was glad the three of them were alone for a moment. "What have you and Johnny been doing all day?"

"We watched Moppy for a long time."

"So she finally came out of hiding?"

"Yes. Carson told us where to sit and wait."

Buck grinned. "What else did you do?"

"We looked for bad guys."

"Is that what you were doing just now?"

"Yes."

He leaned over to kiss the tip of her nose. "I hope you didn't think your nana and I were bad guys."

A giggle escaped her. "No."

"So you like me a little bit?"

"A lot."

"Well, guess what?"

"What?"

"I love you."

"I love you, too," she said back to him without missing a beat.

His heart was melting. "Do you love me enough to let me marry your nana and we'll all live at the ranch together?"

Her face lit up with joy. "I *want* you to get married."

"Then if it's all right with you, that settles everything."

"Goody!" She sounded like someone else he knew. "Now I'll have my own daddy. I've got to go tell Johnny!" She kissed his cheek, and then her nana's, before she backed out the door and raced away.

Alex leaned over to kiss his lips. "I guess you got your answer, *Daddy*."

"I guess I did."

"I think maybe we'd better drive to the house before we get caught again by the big guys because we're doing something we shouldn't be."

"Wouldn't Carson just love that—I'd never be able to live it down." After a cough, Buck started the car. When they arrived in the clearing, the whole family was outside waiting for them. He kissed one corner of her luscious mouth. "There's no rest for the wicked."

She laughed gently. The minute she got out, Alex ran over to hug Tracy and thank her for watching Jenny. Carson just stood there with a huge grin on his face. "What did I hear about a wedding?"

"It's not going to happen for a while."

Johnny frowned. "How come?"

"Because we have a lot to figure out."

"No, you don't. Dad says you can live in the downstairs of the ranch house now that we've moved out."

That kid killed him. Buck exchanged an amused glance with Carson. "We're thrilled to hear the good news about your father."

"Me, too. Thanks for everything, for keeping Jenny happy. Now it's our turn. Do you two gunslingers want to come with us? I'm going to follow Alex into town in the Jeep so we can return her rental car. While we're there, we'll grab a hamburger. How does that sound?"

"Hooray!" The kids were ecstatic.

"I'll keep Jenny with me tonight," Alex said. "There's a lot we have to discuss and we need to tell my parents." She looked down at the girl. "Your great-grandparents are going to be overjoyed."

"*Great*-grandparents?" Johnny piped up.

"That's right, sport," Carson spoke up. "You have to remember Alex is a grandmother. So her parents are Jenny's great-grandparents."

"Then they're really, really old."

Alex gave Johnny a hug. "I think they're about the same age as your Grandma and Grandpa Baretta. When they come to the wedding, you'll see for yourself."

Buck laughed. "Don't try to figure it out, Johnny. I still haven't."

*And I don't care because I'm so happy I'm going to burst.*

"Darling?"

She heard Buck's whisper from the hallway. There'd been so much excitement all evening, Jenny had barely just fallen asleep.

Alex tiptoed out of Johnny's old bedroom but didn't shut the door. Buck drew her across the hall to the master bedroom. "We need to leave this door open, too, in case she wakes up and calls out."

"Let's hope she doesn't." He gathered her in his arms and gave her a long, languorous kiss. The absence of desperation was heavenly. She'd gone after Buck today and had found him with split-second timing. The thought of him chasing her clear to California was too much to comprehend. For the first time in her life she felt complete.

"I love, love, love you, Buck Summerhayes. I only have one concern."

"What?" He drew her down on the king-size bed and stretched out beside her.

"Did you mean it when you said we wouldn't be getting married for a while? You know I'm planning to get a job right away. We'll be able to afford it, or is there something you're not telling me?"

"That's not it." He kissed her throat, and then her mouth. "I don't want you to feel rushed."

She rolled over so she was half lying on top of him. "I'm almost forty-one, and time is flying by. You wouldn't be getting cold feet all of a sudden, would you?"

"Cold feet? Woman, what you talking about?"

"You still haven't answered my question."

"I'd marry you tomorrow if it were possible."

She took a shaky breath. "Then let's do it, if not tomorrow then the next day."

He rolled her back over and stared down at her. "You're serious…"

"Yes. I want your baby. It's been my fantasy since I met you. I've given it a lot of thought and have decided Jenny needs a sibling."

"I had no idea this was going on in your mind."

"All it took was meeting the man of my dreams. As soon as I got pregnant with Christy, Kyle left the state. I never knew what it was like to have a husband who loved me and would help me raise our child. When Frank asked me to marry him, I put away any thoughts of having a baby, because he was too old to start over again on a second family."

"You'd really be willing to go through another pregnancy?"

"For you, I'd do anything. I don't know how come I'm so lucky that you came into my life. That's why I don't want to wait a couple of months for a ceremony. If we got married this week, we could be expecting a baby in that amount of time. Your mom had you at forty. Why can't I? I'm in excellent health and had no problems carrying Christy. Am I moving way too fast for you? It's just that you're going to be the most spectacular father."

He clutched her to him. "You've made me the happiest man alive. We'll see about getting a wedding license tomorrow. Carson will know of a justice of the peace."

"I'm so glad you're okay with that." She kissed him over and over again.

Buck started to laugh.

"What?" She smiled.

"If we're blessed enough to have a baby soon, be it a boy or girl, then he or she will be Jenny's aunt or uncle. But Jenny will be almost eight years older. Can you imagine Johnny having to wrap his mind around that when he's still struggling over the great-grandparent thing?"

Alex buried her face in his shoulder, trying not to laugh out loud. But that didn't stop the bed from shaking.

ALEX WAS MANNING the front desk at the ranch house when the landline phone rang. She picked up. "Teton Valley Dude Ranch."

A woman with a voice Alex didn't recognize asked to speak to Mr. Lundgren.

"I'm afraid he's out of town at the moment." Carson had gone back to Cleveland with Tracy and Johnny to visit the Baretta side of the family for a few days. "This is Alex Summerhayes." She and Buck had been married by a justice of the peace a little over three weeks ago. "May I help you?"

"My name is Kit Wentworth. My son and I are scheduled to fly in this Friday from Maine, but there's been a problem and I'm afraid we won't be able to come until Saturday. If that's impossible for you to change now, I'll certainly understand."

Alex remembered this was the third war widow who'd received a letter from the ranch. She immediately felt a connection to the woman. "I can't answer for him. If you'll give me your number, I'll have Mr. Livingston, his partner, call you back as soon as possible." He'd be taking care of this family.

"Thank you very much."

"You're welcome."

After hanging up, she tried reaching Ross on his cell phone. She got his voice mail and left a detailed message. Buck had taken some guests down the Snake to shoot the rapids and wouldn't be back for another hour.

It was almost time to check on the kids, who'd been swimming in the pool. To her relief, Willy breezed into the foyer. "Hi, Alex."

"Hi, yourself. I'm glad you're here. I'll see you later." She had something important she had to do before she got Jenny.

Alex rushed to the back of the ranch house and pulled

a home pregnancy test out of the dresser drawer. For the past few days, she'd been sleepier than usual and remembered she'd felt that way before she found out she was pregnant with Christy.

This was her third day of testing. If an obstetrician knew what she was doing, he'd tell her she'd put way too much pressure on herself and was bound to be disappointed. She promised herself that if she got another negative reading, she'd let a week go by before trying it again.

Fearful of the same result, she waited a few minutes, and then looked at it, bracing herself.

*Pregnant.*

No. She didn't believe it. But there it was. The instructions said the result was 99% accurate.

A new kind of happiness permeated her body.

Where was her husband? She had to tell him! He'd go crazy when he found out he was going to be a father. While her mind spun with all the changes that would be taking place in their lives, it dawned on her she needed to check on the children.

She ran out of the bedroom and down the hall to the back door, almost colliding with Buck. "Oh—you're back!"

"Whoa, darling—" He caught her in his arms. "What's the big hurry?"

"The kids are still in the pool."

"They'll be fine." He kissed her soundly. "Let me wash my hands and then I'll go with you."

Uh-oh. "You can't go in our bathroom. Use Jenny's."

"Why?" He coughed.

"Just because."

"Just because you told me not to, I'm going in."

"No, Buck. Wait—" She wanted to plan something special for tonight to give him the news, but he was gone in a flash.

She started down the hall after him.

There was no sound. Maybe he hadn't seen the test, but she'd been in such a hurry, she'd left it in plain sight.

When she walked into the bedroom, her husband was just coming out of the bathroom. He reached her in two long strides and drew her into his arms. For a full minute he just rocked her. His quiet sobs of joy told her that he knew what it was like to feel complete. This was only the beginning.

\* \* \* \* \*

*Watch for the final story in the*
DADDY DUDE RANCH *series,*
*HER WYOMING HERO, coming October 2013,*
*only from Harlequin American Romance!*

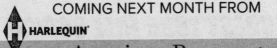

# REQUEST YOUR FREE BOOKS!
## 2 FREE NOVELS PLUS 2 FREE GIFTS!

### ♦ HARLEQUIN

*American ★ Romance*®

## LOVE, HOME & HAPPINESS

**YES!** Please send me 2 FREE Harlequin® American Romance® novels and my 2 FREE gifts (gifts are worth about $10). After receiving them, if I don't wish to receive any more books, I can return the shipping statement marked "cancel." If I don't cancel, I will receive 4 brand-new novels every month and be billed just $4.74 per book in the U.S. or $5.24 per book in Canada. That's a savings of at least 14% off the cover price! It's quite a bargain! Shipping and handling is just 50¢ per book in the U.S. and 75¢ per book in Canada.* I understand that accepting the 2 free books and gifts places me under no obligation to buy anything. I can always return a shipment and cancel at any time. Even if I never buy another book, the two free books and gifts are mine to keep forever.

154/354 HDN F4YN

| | |
|---|---|
| Name | (PLEASE PRINT) |

| | |
|---|---|
| Address | Apt. # |

| | | |
|---|---|---|
| City | State/Prov. | Zip/Postal Code |

Signature (if under 18, a parent or guardian must sign)

### Mail to the **Harlequin**® Reader Service:
**IN U.S.A.:** P.O. Box 1867, Buffalo, NY 14240-1867
**IN CANADA:** P.O. Box 609, Fort Erie, Ontario L2A 5X3

### Want to try two free books from another line?
### Call 1-800-873-8635 or visit www.ReaderService.com.

\* Terms and prices subject to change without notice. Prices do not include applicable taxes. Sales tax applicable in N.Y. Canadian residents will be charged applicable taxes. Offer not valid in Quebec. This offer is limited to one order per household. Not valid for current subscribers to Harlequin American Romance books. All orders subject to credit approval. Credit or debit balances in a customer's account(s) may be offset by any other outstanding balance owed by or to the customer. Please allow 4 to 6 weeks for delivery. Offer available while quantities last.

**Your Privacy**—The Harlequin® Reader Service is committed to protecting your privacy. Our Privacy Policy is available online at www.ReaderService.com or upon request from the Harlequin Reader Service.

We make a portion of our mailing list available to reputable third parties that offer products we believe may interest you. If you prefer that we not exchange your name with third parties, or if you wish to clarify or modify your communication preferences, please visit us at www.ReaderService.com/consumerchoice or write to us at Harlequin Reader Service Preference Service, P.O. Box 9062, Buffalo, NY 14269. Include your complete name and address.

HAR13R

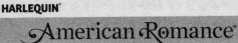
A sixth sense told Conway he was being watched. He opened his eyes beneath the cowboy hat covering his face. Two pairs of small athletic shoes stood side by side next to the sofa.

"Is he dead?"

"Poke him and see," whispered a second voice.

Conway shifted on the couch and groaned.

"He's alive."

"Maybe he's sick."

"Look under his hat."

"You look."

Conway's chest shook with laughter. Small fingers lifted the brim of his hat and suddenly Conway's gaze clashed with the boys'. They shrieked and jumped back.

He pointed to one kid. "What's your name?"

"Javier."

Conway moved his finger to the other boy.

"I'm Miguel. Who are you?"

"Conway Cash."

Javier whispered in his brother's ear, then Miguel asked, "Why are you sleeping on our couch?"

"Your mom wasn't feeling well, so I stayed the night."

"Javi…Mig…. Where are you guys?" Isi's sluggish voice rang out a moment before she appeared in the hallway.

"Mom, Conway Cash slept on our couch."

"It was nice of Mr. Conway to stay, but I'm fine now." Isi sent him a time-to-leave look.

Conway stood and handed her a piece of paper. "Your sitter left this for you last night. She wanted you to read it first thing in the morning."

While Isi read the note, Conway said, "I'd really like to make it up to you for what happened last night. Is there anything I can—"

Isi glanced up from the note, a stunned expression on her face.

"What's wrong?" he asked.

"Nicole quit. She's moving to Tucson to live with her father."

"Maybe your mother could help out with the boys."

"I told you a long time ago that I don't have any family. It's just me and the boys." She paused. "You offered to help. Would you watch the boys until I find a replacement sitter?"

Babysit? Him? "I don't think that's a good idea."

"It would be for two or three days at the most."

"I don't know anything about kids."

"Never mind." Her shoulders sagged.

Oh, hell. How hard could it be to watch a couple of four-year-olds? "Okay, I'll watch them."

She flashed him a bright smile. "You'll need to be here by noon on Monday."

"See you then." Right now, Conway couldn't escape fast enough.

*Find out if Conway survives his new babysitting duties in*
**TWINS UNDER THE CHRISTMAS TREE**
*by Marin Thomas*
*Available October 1, 2013, only from*
*Harlequin® American Romance®.*

# American Romance®

## A Holiday for Healing and New Beginnings

Jackson Stone will always be grateful to the Lamberts, who took him in when he was just a kid. But since the accident that killed his foster brother, Brock, he stays away from the family at Coffee Creek Ranch. Especially now that Brock's former fiancée, Winnie Hays, is back in town with her little boy. The simmering attraction between them may surprise Winnie, but Jackson fell for her at first sight years ago. Can this Christmas be a time of healing and a new beginning for both of them?

## *Big Sky Christmas*

# by C.J. CARMICHAEL

Available October 1, 2013, only from
Harlequin® American Romance®.

HARLEQUIN®

# American Romance®

## A rancher comes to her rescue.

At the magnificent Wyoming dude ranch run by
Ross Livingston and two fellow ex-marines, families
of fallen soldiers find hope and healing. When lovely
widow Kit Wentworth and her son arrive, Ross
immediately finds himself drawn to them. Soon he's
able to bring young Andy out of his shell—and touch
Kit's heart as no other man has.

## *Her Wyoming Hero*

## by REBECCA WINTERS

Available October 1, 2013, only from
Harlequin® American Romance®.

## GROWING UP FEMALE

"Mother, I'm pregnant with a baby girl."
"What is she doing?"
"She is singing."
"Why is she singing?"
"Because she's unafraid."

To her mother, to the generations of mothers who came before her, Beatrix Palmer was a success. Before she had even gained a college diploma, she had won a husband. But then Beatrix lost the husband to her best friend, and, after that, the daughter he had implanted while fantasizing about the best friend.

Now Beatrix must do the only thing a self-respecting mother can do. She must search for her runaway daughter and her absent husband. But her quest becomes a discovery of herself as she hopscotches across oceans and through history to find traces of her daughter and pieces of herself. And finally, Beatrix discovers more than the daughter she lost and the mother she fled. She finds herself and the freedom from that feminine fear which has been handed down from one generation to another since the beginning of time.

"Kept me laughing with a tear in one eye all the way through . . . moved me deeply"—Leslie Fiedler

# Her Mothers

## E. M. Broner

A BERKLEY MEDALLION BOOK
published by
BERKLEY PUBLISHING CORPORATION

The section "The Sheller" was published in slightly altered form in *New Letters*, Winter 1974.

The sections "Looking for Mothers: Biological," "Primer: Ten Ways to Lose Daughters," "Peopleography," "Where Do Daughters Go When They Go Out?" were published in *Moving Out*, Volume 4, Number 2.

The section "Foremothers" was published in slightly altered form in *Elima*, Volume 2, Number 3, Spring 1975.

The sections "Remnants (1) and Remnants (2)" were published in *Shdemot, Digest of the Kibbutz Movement*, Volume 1, Number 3, Spring, 1975.

THANKS TO THE OSSABAW ISLAND PROJECT FOR BOTH ATTENDING TO HER AND GRANTING HER PRIVACY.

Grateful acknowledgment is made for permission to reprint from Bertolt Brecht's *The Caucasian Chalk Circle*, translated by Eric and Maja Bentley in *Parables for the Theater*, University of Minnesota Press, Minneapolis © copyright 1948 by Eric Bentley.

*"A woman writing thinks back through her mothers."*
—Virginia Woolf
*A Room of One's Own*

Her Special Mothers

MARCIA FREEDMAN, MEMBER OF KNESSET, ISRAEL
JULIE JENSEN
VIRGINIA KELLEY
RUTH KROLL

# Looking for Friends

## A Girl Should Have a Girl

A.
"I'm pregnant, mother."
"Have a girl."
"Why?"
"A girl should have a girl."

B.
"Mother, I'm pregnant with a girl."
"How old is she?"
"Seventeen years old."
"Then you're pregnant with me."

A 1944 maroon cardboard cover, not padded like the navy cloth cover of the year before. The war has come, and, with it, austerity in the yearbook.

"Wasn't it *fun*!" someone has written in her yearbook.
Another writes, "Your French class pal."
She does not remember the green ink of "Wasn't it *fun*!", the round, good-girl penmanship of her French-classmate, or "Michael Schwartz" in brown ink. She does remember

3

her French teacher in purple ink who has written, *"A ma chère . . ."* The pencils have blurred, the ink faded with the people: "The swellest kid ever! Oh you gorgeous kid!" He was obviously not looking at her.

"One of my oldest friends," she has not seen since.

Whom does she know? She studies each page of twenty-five head shots per page, twenty pages of five hundred faces, another short page of an additional sixteen heads, braided, fluffed, cropped, in ROTC cap, plus eleven dark names without pictures, without study hall listing, majors, clubs, mottoes. It is a game book of 516 mounted heads, eleven faceless beings.

"Losers. I know all the losers."

Even the winners were losers.

There is the head of Shirley Panush. It is wide-eyed and intelligent. Now it hides those wide eyes and its 172 IQ in Rabbi Panush's attic room. Shirley was voted "The One to Make Hay With" by the Zionist Organization of America. There she lies on straw in the attic, her room too hot in the summer, drafty in winter. She had been kissed enduringly in high school and could endure it from no one else since.

There is a dark print of the head of Janice. Janice, however, was swarthy, though Jewish, and she did marry a Dark, a Black, and her parents sat *shivah*. But the Black left swarthy Janice, for she was a nag. But her parents will not renew acquaintanceship, for she has been tainted. And what has been mourned cannot be reborn.

There is the head of Pauline, some acne on the forehead, attributed to irregular menstruation. That was not all that was irregular in her life, parents, diet, place of abode. Once Pauline wanted to be an architect. She decorated the doors of her Murphy-bed closet with pictures of Frank Lloyd Wright.

Now Pauline lives with the owner of a liquor store in a flat above the store.

The eyes, forehead, hair, chin of Lois Goldman, lover of chemistry and daughter of a Romanian pharmacist. The Romanian pharmacist left his business to Lois's brother, for a girl cannot carry on the family trade or the family name. The brother has fulfilled his father's expectations. The business is

4

success, issuing few prescriptions but making money on a
liquor license.

Lois Goldman married a doctor who cannot administer to
her. She has lost forever her family name.

Beatrix searches that book of years. A girl with dark pitted
skin and oversized teeth is listed as being on the Swimming
Team. Beatrix remembers her. In Beatrix's constantly
revised list of Best Friends, Swimming Team had a low
number. Another low number is a girl with one undeveloped
eye. Under her name is no list of accomplishments. She's
a nonswimmer, even. Beatrix knew her well, had played
dolls, Monopoly, Michigan Rummy for long hours on the
girl's front porch. Beatrix left her for a girl friend with two
eyes.

Roz's head fills the oval, Roz, Commercial, overweight,
kinky-haired, who walked home from school each day with
her. A blondie with big earrings and a big smile has inscribed
a herself, "To my honey." She's Norma, everyone's
honey. A fat-faced boy with the beginnings of a moustache is
gazing at Beatrix. He had a crush on her. She was not
flattered.

Her own face comes upon her: a fox from the woods, Jack
from his box, a car swerving at her. She does not dimple like
Shirley Panush. Her hair is not neat as Inez Muller's. She
does not have lifted eyebrows and an amused smile like
Marcia S. Liebowitz. She is not blonde, blue-eyed, frilly-
bloused like Razel Schiller, who can only manage a General
curriculum and belongs to Girl Reserves.

Beatrix has half her face in shadow. Her lipstick is 1940s
purplish red. Her hair is newly washed and shapeless. To this
day, her hair would be frowned on by neat Girl Reserves or
Home Ec Club.

Her eyebrows are painfully plucked, not by her own hand,
but by the hand of the beauty parlor. She had not the courage
to pull out those thick hairs from the heavy brows. The blouse
she wears has a peter pan collar, is made of soft rayon
material, white, with capped sleeves. She is not exactly
frowning, but she is more than serious. Grim perhaps. Or
grave. There is a vein visible in her forehead. The lines from

5

nose to mouth are deeply shadowed. Her face is smooth, a little puffy, seventeen. What is she looking at? Her eyes bore into something. Her hair is ruffled as if by sudden wind. It is the most peculiar, self-conscious picture among all those 516, amidst all that mounted game. Maybe she deserved to walk home with overweight Roz.

Even the ugly girls look nice, a large flower in the hair, light eyes catching the cameraman's flashbulb. But only she among all of those intelligent faces, only she—*not* like IQ'ed Shirley, mechanically gifted Pauline, athletic Janice, scientific Lois—only she among the girls in College Prep glasses, with reflective faces, she, a nonsinger in the Spring Festival, a noneditor of the Yearbook, non-Spanish Club, non-Latin Club, never having spoken in the Speaker's Bureau, only she of the strange wild hair, throbbing vein in the forehead, intense, almost angry eyes, puffy eyebrows, jersey blouse stretched over breasts so flat the bra cups folded inward like craters on their cones, only she is still known.

It is for her, Beatrix Palmer, that BOB'S BICYCLE AND REPAIR SHOP can be proud they advertised in the Yearbook, next to LLOYD'S FURS, THE DAIRY BAR, BATES LUGGAGE, GROSSBERG'S GROCERY, THE ROMANIAN PHARMACY (of Lois Goldman's Romanian father), MEN'S HABERDASHERY (of Janice's dashing father), and Mr. Aishikin, who wrote: "V . . . —FOR TOTAL VICTORY."

C.
"I'm pregnant with a girl, mother."
"What is she doing?"
"She's going to a reunion."

Which she did do twenty-five years later. Beatrix was the only one with a date, her assistant book editor. Beatrix was also the only one at the reunion whose child was unaccounted for, whose husband had disappeared years before.

The assistant book editor held her arm like a sling, up the carpeted stairs of the nightclub. He yawned. He disturbed the three-master of a hanky riding on his jacket pocket to wipe his face, his hands against this press of people. He has accompanied her to the reunion for she is on the program to talk up her book.

Sarcastic Cynthia is ahead of Beatrix, her shorter husband two steps up, and Cynthia a step ahead. She has also moved ahead in other ways. Cynthia has moved East while Beatrix has stayed a rung down in the Midwest. She does not recognize Beatrix. Or she recognizes her and is annoyed. Bea's name is on the program. The program, moreover, is printed on thick stock to make up for wartime deprivation. Cynthia is holding the thick name of Beatrix Palmer.

Perhaps Cynthia is shy and has nothing to say. Perhaps Cynthia is ashamed. She is ashamed about her undergraduate major which began as English but, by Junior Year, became Beatrix's husband.

That year Beatrix lost her husband, her friend Cynthia, and, for irregular attendance, her semester's credit. Beatrix did gain, that same year; she gained about thirty pounds, a daughter, implanted while the husband was dreaming of Cynthia.

The husband is on the West Coast now, no one knows where. The daughter is traveling eastward, no one knows wherefor, whereto.

In Senior Year, Cynthia raised her goals, from classmate to graduate student to her instructor. There he is ahead of her, but still the same height. And, for all her villainies, Cynthia looks wonderful. She exercises every morning, doing The Elbow Touch, The Wrist Pushes, Small Arm Circles, Forward Arm Crosses, Arm Curl, Arm Pulls, Four-Count Toe Touch, Tummies Aweigh. She does her facial exercises: the Buccinator, Caninus, Mentalis, angulare, orbitale. She dyes her hair carefully, strand testing it beforehand, making sure it is one shade lighter than her hand used to be, for her face, twenty-five years later, is also one shade paler. She can wear trim skirts, even though she menstruates, for Cynthia, unlike clumsy Beatrix, can insert Tampax. Cynthia is determined, an engineering sort, and the tampon rests in the vagina, held in place by constricting muscles. Cynthia is also a connoisseur. She tastes tea. She knows that it belongs to the camellia family, is grown on tropical and subtropical estates, and comes from India, Ceylon, and Indonesia.

7

Why, then, is Cynthia looking dour? Why does she seem bored? Perhaps she thought her name should have been listed in that class catalogue. The Program was full. One Most Likely to Succeed from twenty-five years ago was listed, as well as One Who Did Succeed. They were two different names, both of men. One Most Likely succeeded in being the first to die, of leukemia, the summer after graduation. One Who Did Succeed employs twelve oral surgeons in a dental complex managed by his sister, who has had banking experience.

About whom is Cynthia speaking so loudly? About the four best friends of Beatrix.

"Shirley is a hermit," says Cynthia, now recognizing Beatrix. "Is that right?"

Beatrix looks at her date. He is sensitive to the requirements of the escort and envelops her in soft-voweled, consonanted conversation.

Cynthia has dieted, culturally informed, and sun-lamp tanned herself for this reunion. She is not to be put off.

"Where's Janice?" she asks Beatrix. Explanatorily to her husband, "The only one of that group that did anything. . . ."

The husband frowns. He's not a bad sort.

Is Cynthia saying that Beatrix did nothing of interest?

"She married a Black man," Cynthia tells her Full Professor. "Her Hadassah mother must have died."

Actually, the mother did die, and the father and Janice's younger brother, too, all from diseases, but Janice's family blamed her for having weakened their defenses.

Lois Goldman arrives with doctor. She gives Beatrix a shy smile, for she has known her, and Cynthia a large one, for she has not known her very well.

"That's another," Cynthia checks. "What 'd do, Lois? What ever did you do after graduation?"

"I've been a wife and mother," Lois begins. Cynthia has turned away.

"What's that all about?" Cynthia's husband asks softly.

They meet again in the Ladies. Overweight Roz is there, jolly, not kinky Jewish but wigged. Norma Honey is there, still small, still bosomy. She measures her four feet ten inches against Roz's five feet ten inches. Marcia S. Liebowitz is in Ladies, her amused graduation picture no longer so arch. She has suffered from Bell's Palsy and one side of her smile has slipped. Razel Schiller of blue eyes and frilled blouse has not attended and is not inquired after.

Cynthia and Lois are waiting, each first in line for the two toilets.

"Where's Pauline?" Cynthia asks Lois.

"She's not doing anything much," says Lois.

"Nor was she when I knew her," says Cynthia.

A strange thing is happening to Beatrix. Women ignore her. She has been in Book Review sections and on Morning Shows but the women do not see her. She, waiting for the booths, is a threat to each inside the booth. She is a reminder of high honor-point averages, of hands lifted eagerly in class, of mind gone to small matter.

Being ignored is, to Beatrix, worse than being dealt with rudely. Beatrix feels as if she will topple backward, like a cardboard Jackie Kennedy doll her daughter had Before Assassination, whose feet kept bending and who would stiffly, slowly fall. Beatrix Palmer feels the room is too close. Her face dissolves, nose sinking into its own cavity, eyes and mouth stretching to meet each other, neck flesh melting into tendons.

" 'Fess up," says jolly Roz from her booth. "Who has The Migraine? Who has The Change?"

Cynthia flaps her hands dry, not waiting for the warm air flow.

The enemies are still enemies and the friends have drifted.

THE PROGRAM

  I.  Introduction of Emcee

 II.  Emcee introduces Faculty of 1944

    (1)  Chemistry

        (Bald, even in 1944, an enemy of Romanian Lois's, and, in addition to being anti-Romanian and anti-woman, he has been consistently anti-Semitic in an all-Jewish school.)

9

    (2)  Shorthand
        (An enemy of College Prep.)
    (3)  French
        *(A ma chère Beatrix.)*
    (4)  Math
        (Jewish Math, the only Jewish teacher in the high
        school and solemn with the responsibility of it. He
        also teaches Hebrew on Sunday.)
III.  Orchestra
   (1)  Miller Medley
   (2)  Ink Spots Spot
IV.  Our Authoress. . . .

Beatrix is introduced. The emcee gives her a generous, long introduction. Her former classmates fidget. It is Auditorium again. The emcee cuts his introduction. Beatrix comes forward carrying note cards. The emcee groans. The classmates laugh. The emcee is someone with the same last initial—P—who had shared the same alphabetical study hall, someone Beatrix has not seen since last marking. He grabs Beatrix by her 3 x 5's.

"Why should she speak when she's so beautiful?" P asks.

He rips her 3 x 5's. Band crescendoes, applause for fleeing Bea. People are still ascending the stairs as she and her date go against the current. People are registering at the desk of Judy and Johnny, high school sweethearts, winners of First Married.

Up the stairs puffs the boy who once had a crush on Beatrix, the boy with a premature moustache in those hairless days. Now he has no moustache but has grown full sideburns.

He tells Judy and Johnny, high school sweethearts, "I sat up all night memorizing the names and faces, especially of the guys. I know all the guys' names. No use memorizing girls. They change their names."

Beatrix has changed her name back to her high school one.


D.
"Mother, I'm having a baby girl."
"May she be a doll, a living doll."

10

# The Living Doll

She plays on the floor beside her grandfather. He wrinkles his nose at her. She brings him the doll. He kisses the doll's nose and lifts dolly to kiss mommy's nose.

"Sweet cheeks," he calls her.

The grandfather cries, real tears, when his little grand girl is broken like a dolly, when her nose is broken. He sighs and cries. He never again enjoys seeing her. There is a slight hump remaining, a fault in Lena's doll face.

E.

"Mother, I'm pregnant and I don't want her."

"Go to an abortionist or a psychiatrist."

"Which?"

"They're the same. They're different."

"How the same? How different?"

"They both look into your womb. The abortionist sees the fetus there, the psychiatrist your mind."

F.

"Mother, I feel ill. What's happening?"

"You're being born."


## THE PHYSICIAN'S BOOK

We are all in that obstetrician's book. We are born into the book with a case number, an admitted-into-hospital name. We already have an address and a date of admission, a period of gestation, the diseases from which we suffer, our father's full name (his name precedes the mother's), our other's name secondarily. They are both living. But the grandmother, Lena Gurnev, oh she is dead, although her husband David Gurnev lives.

The child is recorded, July 5, stillborn, legitimate, male, white, died on the same day. No cause of death is filled in. In proper order the doctor signs his signature, the nurse hers, the father his. No mother's signature.

11

How is the child disposed of on that same July 5? "Under-taker" is written, in a slightly European pen stroke, instead of the usual, "Home."

The male Palmer heir died, the eldest heir. Beatrix was conceived into the obstetrician's book and taken "Home" instead of to the "Undertakers" although only a female.

Mother Palmer does not err again. No more stillborns. No more white females. She brings home two more male Palmers.

G.
"Mother, I'm pregnant with a girl."
"What is she doing?"
"She's crying."

The daughter of Beatrix Palmer fell in love with a four-year-old when she, Lena, was three. Lena, named for her missing great-grandmother, had brown sausage curls and a print dress that said "I love you." She had a cloth doll whose matching print dress loved *her*. Everyone loved Lena, her mother, her grandmother, her grandfather, her dress, her doll, everyone but the four-year-old across the hall who loved his orange tractor shovel that was a model of his father's real tractor shovel.

Lena would await Howie's attention, holding her doll out to him. He, gruff as his construction-worker father, would knock the doll to the ground and run his orange tractor shovel over it.

Lena wept for hours whenever she left him. In her sleep, in the white lamb decal crib, she called his name. He, across the hall of the apartment building, slept soundlessly.

AT THE STUDY

Beatrix is at her study. Across a pitted old aluminum table are notes for her text on American women of the nineteenth century. She is reading *The Writings of Margaret Fuller, Love Letters of Margaret Fuller, The Roman Years of Margaret Fuller*.

She is at her study. She is reading *Louisa May Alcott, Miss Alcott of Concord, Louisa May Alcott: Her Life, Letters and Journals*. She is reading *The Journal of Charlotte L. Forten*. She is reading *Selected Poems and Letters of Emily Dickinson*.

She is reading. She is reading *Rosa Luxemburg Speaks*, in a crimson cover. She thinks of a title for a book, *Red Rosa*, but it sounds like a fairy tale to go with *Snow White*. She is reading J. P. Nettl's biography of Rosa.

Beatrix Palmer would know only heroic women. She would be a heroine.

She is at her study with documents scotch-taped onto the wall: the proclamation of the American Shakers, "Equality of the sexes, in all departments of life."

She is studying. Paper frames bend with their old photographs. Her mother, with then dark (though dyed) hair; the mother's cheek in her palm, the mother's face animated, her own responding, her hair dark then also (not dyed then also), stacked glasses, saucers, the candles, the bit of photo of Einstein. (How her family would have loved its own Einstein, perhaps Baby Palmer stillborn that July 5.) There is another photo of long, rich, frizzy dark hair, the eyes averted, the face somber, the hair a curtain of night over that face.

Another photo. The dark-haired girl smiling, her hands on her belly. She is standing alone. No men are framed in the room, aside from a card in purplish ink signed: "Thos. Wentworth Higginson, Cambridge, Mass., March 21, 1884," aside from a postage stamp of Thoreau designed by Leonard Baskin, sent to her and canceled, hence canceled Thoreau. All other men have been canceled.

She is at her study. The globe turns lopsidedly, the globe is dusty, once that dark-haired girl's, seldom used since to see the world since the dark-haired girl saw the world. The globe lurches—it is the dark-haired girl's birthday. She is in a purple land between pink INDIA and yellow CHINA. Before that, cards arrived from blue SOUTH PACIFIC, from Auckland with the nipple mark for the seaport of North Island, from yellow JAVA on the INDIAN OCEAN. The mother never knew of such oceans or seas, Tasman, Coral, South China, Timor. She never knew of Micronesia and Melanesia.

13

She never knew the map of her daughter's head, those blood-shot rivers in the eyes, the tongues her daughter spoke in anger, the ears where no sound intruded, where nothing vibrated, the chest where all sounds vibrated and drummed back messages of hatred.

There were blue shadows between the tight veins of Lena's forehead, greenish on her chin, the cheeks would flush pink, and the hollows under her eyes would be yellowish green as if healing bruises.

H.

"Mother, I'm pregnant with a girl."

"What's it doing?"

"It's menstruating."

A rare close moment between them. The daughter coming down the stairs, her forehead bumpy, her chin picked.

"No breakfast. It'll make me sick."

The mother argues. She never learns. The mother will never learn. She will always argue and drive opponent and proponent from her.

But the girl is suddenly weary and weepy.

"It's something gross," says the little girl. "I can't tell you."

She tells her.

"Maybe it's the barbecue sauce with the chicken. It ran through my stomach to my underwear."

The mother begins to feel air currents under her armpits, on the soles of her feet; she feels tickles in the air, up the throat, in the nostrils. She tries, she succeeds, in not laughing.

Lena, however, begins to weep.

"I have a dread disease," says Lena.

The daughter is right. She does have a dread disease and, by the mother's calculations, made on the basis of her own mother and grandmother, that little girl will have a dread disease for forty years. No scientist will prevent the sting, the paleness, the headache, listlessness, the kneading stomach, the burn in the small of the back, the itchiness, nervousness,

14

but each scientist will practice the sin of incuriosity, and so her daughter will flow, pale red, reddish brown, deep-staining crimson, for forty years.

I.

"Mother, I have a surprise."

"What is it?"

"I'm pregnant with a baby girl."

"That's no surprise."

What will she, twentieth-century mother, say to her daughter?

She looks into history.

There are her mothers! Hello, Margaret Fuller, hello, my mother. She is one of Beatrix's historical mothers.

"MARGARET?"

Raucous male laughter at an American Studies Conference.

"A horse face," says a goat-bearded professor. "Do you know how she held her audience's attention at her Conversations? She froze them to their chairs in horror."

"Uglier than Emily?" asks a twittering, fringe-haired professor of Criticism.

"Emily?"

"The poetess."

"Uglier."

"Uglier than Elizabeth Peabody?" asks a young assistant professor, who *would be* a goat-bearded American Studies scholar or a fringe-haired critic.

"Taller, thinner, more solemn, but uglier," says the American Studies scholar, expert in Margaret Fuller.

Beatrix Palmer reads a paper: "The Easily Intimidated Ralph Waldo Emerson and His Intimidator, Margaret Fuller."

No one questions her substantially. They like to gossip.

"Was there any actual marriage certificate issued?"

They are speaking of Margaret Fuller and the Marchese Ossoli.

No one asks about Margaret's "History of the Roman

15

Revolution," written from primary sources, with Margaret as a participant.

"Did Thoreau find the bodies?"

Thoreau, not intimidated like Emerson, rushed to Fire Island upon hearing that the boat Margaret Fuller had sailed on from Italy had capsized. He found neither Margaret nor the Marchese nor the "History of the Roman Revolution," but he found her Roman son, a baby, still warm but drowned.

They bypass Beatrix Palmer at the podium.

"Was she embraced by the Roman sun?" asks the twitterer, "and given a Roman son?"

His hand to his mouth, his cough of self-appreciation/deprecation.

But what if Beatrix Palmer were the mother of Margaret Fuller? Margaret and her decade-younger lover Angelo and little Angelino are sailing home. Margaret writes to Mrs. Fuller:

"When I think of you, beloved mother, of brothers and sister and many friends, I wish to come." (Joseph Jay Deiss, *The Roman Years of Margaret Fuller*, Thomas Y. Crowell, 1969, p. 302.)

(In Beatrix's family there are two brothers and no sister. Could Lena return to them? There was once that stillborn brother of Beatrix's, Lena's stillborn uncle.)

If Beatrix were Mrs. Fuller in that small New England town, awaiting her scandalous daughter, would she hope that they be shipwrecked off Fire Island and washed away?

Mrs. Fuller is not ashamed. She does not dread the ship's arrival. She stays at the Manchester, New Hampshire, home of her son and writes to that troublesome daughter:

"If we could know when you would arrive, we would be at the Depot to conduct you to our house, but all the drivers know where my son lives—at the corner of Chestnut and Central Streets. May the great God preserve you and conduct you in safety to your home." (Deiss, p. 313.)

The great God did neither.

Would Beatrix address Lena thus?

16

J.

"Mother, I'm going to have a baby girl."

"When?"

"When I become pregnant."

"Who will make you pregnant?"

"My lovers."

"Who are they?"

"A chick and a dude."

"WHO ARE THEY?"

"I haven't met them yet."

The night after the Reunion her assistant editor takes her to a blue film. It is in the way of business. Her company is letting go of trade editors and fiction writers to expand the text division. They are thinking of expanding *The Pioneers* further into text. The young assistant editor is currently editing a history of the skin flick.

"The porno film is an historical reality," he explains humorlessly, "and, must, therefore, be studied."

He is working from Brigitte Bardot and her towel, through *I Am Curious (Yellow)*, Warhol's *The Couch*, quickie nudies, the transvestite Cockettes. It will be academic—all but the book jacket.

The party is academic. When the flick begins, in living color, a heated argument develops on the couch between a Labor Zionist and a New Left universalist. Pillows and boos are hurled until the professors retire into the dining room and farther yet, to the punch bowl, for argumentation.

Beatrix Palmer is sitting on the rug, her back against the love seat. Her assistant editor is helping to set up equipment, to get the focus sharp, the sound clear before he returns to Beatrix, tripping over cords and legs on the way. He slips down against the love seat, his finger sliding under her arm and down her ribs. He would mount her but so would the host's German shepherd. Perhaps it is the porno affecting the shepherd, or all those reclining figures. He even mounts a standing pants leg or two.

Two women in black fright wigs appear, one considerably older than the other. Both women seem to be Cleopatra types.

17

They wear Pharaoh headdresses and snake bracelets. CU on one writhing woman, camera dollies in, woman is fondling her own breasts, shaking them, catching them, concentric circles, counterclockwise. Her hair is still wig black, her eyes are closed, camera dolly on down, black patch of hair covered by more black, the back of the head of the older Cleopatra, Our Lady of the Dike. ECU, this time, extreme close-up, of public pubic hair, labia, clitoris. Hand-held camera stops dolly action. CU on licked lady, mouth opened, eyes rolling, much as her breasts had rolled before. Enter the Hero, in furs—that is, a fur robe, not a fur coat, and a Viking hat—Hollywood Viking, a fur yarmulke with two horns attached. The ladies in the audience laugh and feel tender. He is a boychik, maybe sixteen, seventeen.

Up bolt both Cleopatras, down goes Hero. CU on erection. The camera becomes confused tracing the paths of each raven-haired seductress. There is Technicolor red, red tongues that look as if they have been eating candy hearts or cinnamon balls. The two red tongues meet on the erected tower. Hold. Slow motion following upwards the flicking tongues.

It is a brief film. Black hair, red tongues, brown Viking fur, grayish skin.

Beatrix is upset by the film. She can do nothing about the excitement. With her assistant editor it would be like Sweet Sixteen Viking. She is nervous and bad tempered. The editor takes her home. He cannot argue with her or be impatient. She is one of the better moneymakers of his publishing house.


K.

"Mother, I'm going to have a baby."

"Who will the baby be?"


"A Rani looking at Herself in a Mirror, a Rani with the Newborn Parasvanatha."

"How will I recognize her?"

"Her eyes will be edged in black. The iris will be blue. Her skin will be brown."

"Is that all?"

"Her earrings will be red stones in silver hoops, and she will be giving birth to a Hindu deity."

The mother is Western; in fact, Midwestern. Beatrix's mother is European. Beatrix's mother's mother, Lena Gurnev, is Sephardic. Lena is Eastern.

Lena says: "Steadfast a lamp burns sheltered from the wind; such is the likeness of the Yogi's mind."

This is the Bhagavad Gita.

Or Lena might say: "Betwixt me and Thee there lingers an 'it is' that torments me. Ah . . . take this 'I' from between us."

Lena has learned this from Hallàj.

Or Lena writes:

" 'Who is Me?'

" 'The Buddha who lives at my name and address.'

" 'Have you found him in the midst of the Ten Fetters, innumerable Defilements, Three Fires, and the Illusion of Self?'

" 'Not yet, but I am looking.'

" 'Who is looking?'

" 'The Buddha.' "

When the mother tries to speak to Lena, Lena's hands cover her ears.

Her mouth says: "The most important thing is Silence. In the Silence, wisdom speaks, and they whose hearts are open understand her."

Who are those people Lena is seeing, those Eastern people?

The mother is an archivist, a keeper of journals of Western women. Beatrix, for her first book, taped the voices of pioneers, women who went to Staten Island.

Beatrix had received a small anthropology grant to work on the oral history of the dying-off immigrants who came to the New World before and after the First World War. She and a photographer girl friend went into apartments, flats, private dwellings, old folks' homes, and hospitals with tape recorder and camera.

19

At first they interviewed the old men and the old women. It was difficult not to interview each of a pair. Sometimes an old sister or brother would chime in. Gradually, out of the trappings of a patriarchal society, Beatrix and her friend discovered that it was a matriarchy that put the costume of dark suit, skullcap, and beard on their men. They prayed for sons, but it was the women who held the families together when they were separated by the war—the women and children in Russia, Poland, Germany, Latvia, the men in New York, Chicago, Detroit, Canada. It was the women who invented ways to feed the family once they were reunited. Their book became one of pioneering women.

At first the old people were nervous at the sight of the "machine" and of the uncovered camera with its case dangling. Beatrix would not turn on the machine until the women were at ease, until they themselves said, "Put that into your machine. Why talk for nothing?"

They spoke and the photographer worked with high-speed film, with shots of old eyes lit in memory; pursed, animated mouths; gesturing, stiff hands.

Beatrix learned of their entrance into The Island, of the statue that greeted them with a poem by a Jewess. She learned that the Statue of Liberty was a Jewish landlady.

The book of transcribed and edited tapes with its accompanying photographs was called *The Pioneers*. It outsold the Museum of Modern Art's *The Family of Man* in Jewish circles.

Beatrix was invited to give readings from it to Jewish Senior Citizens Clubs; the members pursued her afterward with their autobiographies. Dances were choreographed from the lives of the book by everyone, from the American Ballet Company to Habonim Youth Groups. Her friend received royalties from the photographs, which were printed on rich paper and sold separately.

They had been under contract for some years to complete *The Remnants*, a book about the survivors of the Holocaust who came to the New World before or after the Second World War. The stories seemed more repetitiously tragic, and Beatrix and her friend were desultory in their work habits. The

20

ook dragged and was yet unedited and the photographs were
ot of the same quality as those in *The Pioneers*.

L.
"Mother, I'm pregnant. Who am I?"
"Your own mother."

M.
"Mother, I'm pregnant with a girl."
"Where is she?"
"At a restaurant."
"What is she doing there?"
"Misbehaving."
"What are you doing?"
"Slapping her hand."

Looking for Friends (1): Romanian Lois

Three years ago Beatrix Palmer was dined at Topinka's by
er visiting executive editor. He wanted to expand *The
Pioneers* into a sociological text for ethnic studies classes and
e was concerned with the slow progress of *The Remnants*.
Beatrix and her friend had already used up the advance.

Romanian Lois and her daughters were at Topinka's. They
vere lunching. They were waiting to have dessert with Lois's
usband, whose office was in the Medical Building across the
treet.

Lois did not recognize Beatrix, for Beatrix had spent part
f her advance on appearance. Not only were her eyebrows
lifferent but her hairline was reshaped by electrolysis, her
air recolored a reddish brown (the black tints had turned
eddish in the sun anyway). Beatrix bought clothing in the
xpensive shopping mall in the Medical Building.

The puffiness of high school had left her face. Her face had
ot become haggard but that which made her face babyish
nd vulnerable and, perhaps, petulant, had left her.

Her eyes concentrate on Lois's table. She is distracted
rom her editor's discussion of paperback rights. The vein in

Beatrix's forehead throbs at Lois. The lines from her nose to her mouth, though shaded with white underbase, are there, though faint. Her expression is not quite grim, more grave.

For Lois is slapping her youngest's hand, lifting the hand which dangles between her fingers and slap, slap, slapping the back of it. There is now visible a tomato juice stain on the tablecloth. Beatrix, at first, mistakes it for blood.

It is an earlier scene. At Lois's house. Her Romanian mother is slapping Lois's hand at the table, in front of dinner guest Beatrix Palmer, in front of the silently chewing older brother and the frowning father. Had Lois grabbed for food at the table? Had she spoken out of turn? Those claps, those thunderous slaps obliterated the cause.

The father rises, agitated with the disturbance at the table. The mother's hand is on her forehead. The brother's spoon is moving to and from his mouth, carrying, resupplying his dessert. Lois sits quite still. Beatrix asks to be excused.

Beatrix goes to the bathroom but cannot vomit. She returns to find the brother's napkin across his plate, Lois and her mother clearing the table, and the father feeding bits of chicken to the canary.

"Here, cannibal," he jokes, feeding bird to bird.

Beatrix's dessert, a torte, has been refrigerated for her. She is not asked to help with the dishes, for she is a guest, although the mother is not fond of her and is reluctant to have her at their table.

The brother has a date. His mother smooths his hair, touches his collar, kisses him. He tweaks her. The father nods proudly from his armchair in the living room.

"Good night, sir," calls Lois's brother.

(Beatrix is thrilled. A Jewish boy talking like that!)

Upstairs both girls rummage through the older brother's dresser. They find a variety of heroes, Trojans, Ramses among them, as well as Dr. Long's *Sane Sex Life and Sex Living*. The girls sleep together in Lois's single bed, their backs together, each masturbating herself. Bea dreams of the older brother. He is feeding her chicken. She becomes his cannibal, chewing his meat. She is happy the next morning that older brother is sleeping late.

"He came home in the wee hours," tiptoes in and whispers Lois's mother.

Sometimes Beatrix loves this family. More often she is terrified by it.

Lois wishes to speak to her father. She wishes to get into the high school Chemistry Club, whose faculty adviser is bald Mr. Haddock. Lois told Mr. Haddock that she had read all of her father's volumes on Luther Burbank and all of the chemistry books at home and at the pharmacy. But the adviser will not let her into Chemistry Club. It is traditionally all boys, he explains to her, as is Chess, as are the Hi Y's. Mr. Haddock tells Lois to join the Home Ec Club and learn her kitchen chemistry there. Lois weeps before her father. He turns his tie inside out and wipes her eyes with the lining. Lois's father bends Lois into his lap. The mother comes in to see, drying her hands.

"Sarah Heartburn," says the mother.

She takes the heavy 78 rpms of *Romanian Rhapsody* out of the cabinet and stacks the records on the spindle. The machine is noisy, the records old and scratchy. Lois's father asks the buried head on his shoulder to dance. The mother is watching. Lois is persuaded to dance with her courtly father.

"I rather thought I was your partner," says the mother.

N.
"Mother, I'm pregnant with a baby girl."
"What does she want to know?"
"Will her mother be her friend?"
"No, her enemy."
"And her father?"
"He will court her but he will destroy her."
"She wants to know how."
"He will dance with her and hold her close in order not to see her. He will sing to her in order not to hear her."

O.
"Mother, I'm pregnant with a daughter."
"What's she doing?"
"She's dating her best friend's lover."

Looking for Friends (2): Shirley and
the Ritual Slaughterer

P.

"Mother, I'm pregnant with a baby girl, and she wants to
kill someone."

"A best friend or a casual acquaintance?"

"A best friend."

"That's easier. You see each other more often and can take
better aim."

"Genja," said her father.

"Let me!" The aunt pushed into Shirley's room with the
food tray.

So how did it go from Genja to Shirley in one person? The
same way it went, in one family, from Muny to Charley,
Paltiel to Benny, Nuny to Anna, Marcus to Max, as they
became name-changers and tried to become natives in the
New World.

Beatrix was native-born and Shirley foreign. In high
school Shirley became the native and Beatrix the foreigner.

What changed Beatrix's citizenship from New World to
Old? What changed her grading, in that judgmental time,
from Jumbo Egg to Small?

Beatrix erred in choice of friends; for instance, Beryl
Boumberg, a German boy. Beryl was a mime, but the class
shifted uncomfortably when he simpered across the stage. He
painted his face clown white, his lips red, but the class saw
only the lipstick. His wrists were mobile—fish flops, dying
butterflies, a sustained parting gesture. The class saw no
athletic throw of the arm and also, that he was no club man.
He was, though, club-footed. And he was a grade lower than
Beatrix, thus precipitating her downgrading.

Beatrix erred mannerisms. Although American, she was a
peasant, a *mouzhik*. She ate soup noisily, her soup spoon
shoveling toward her, instead of lifting away from her. In a
restaurant nothing on the menu looked familiar. She had no
idea what to do with the multiplicity of spoons and forks, like
weapons laid down in a truce. Her voice was loud when it
should have been hesitant, shy when it should have lifted.

24

Beatrix's ways were unbecoming; that is, it was apparent to those of higher aims that she was becoming nothing to which they aspired. Their aspirations were to be the non-professional wives of professional men, the dependent wives of independent businessmen.

What was unbecoming about Beatrix? Her hair, makeup, dress, gestures.

Her hair was uncontrollable. Her eyebrows grew together. A sense of the hirsute prevailed—from legs, armpits (where sweat collected and which no amount of Arrid could dry), upper lip, that wild hair. She began to shave here and there, the way she polished shoes, streaking her legs, cutting painfully under her arms. She plucked eyebrows until the tender skin puffed red and they became like an epicanthus fold. She bleached her upper lip. But everything was to distract from, to counteract what was there. And what was there was Mediterranean, although Bea's ancestors were once from the steppes of Russia (Lena Gurnev had, far back, been from the steps of the Inquisition).

Beatrix's lipstick was dark purple although her skin and eyes were pale. It was a threatening mouth whether or not she used it to threaten.

Her skirts hung; her small waist and fleshy hips were unfittable in teen-age clothing. Her blouses were girlish; her sweaters extra large. Her blouses were tight across the broad shoulders and under her arms; she floated inside the extra-large sweaters like a fetus. Her shoes were sloppy saddle. If she used Esquire White over the white section, it smeared onto the blue. If she brightened the blue with Shoe Blue, it ran into the damp white.

Her voice was unmodulated. Her hands either fluttered or jerked in excitement, narrowly missing the eyes of people with whom she was intensely conversing.

In contrast, Shirley Panush was Nordic blonde, her hair controlled, her makeup slight, dress fitted, gestures royal.

"Cheer up your room a little," Shirley's father said. "Use color."

Shirley wanted no color, fought off the painter while he was doing the rest of the house.

25

"Be reasonable, Genja," said her father. "We can't have him back again just for your room."

Shirley chose red. Her father said that was too dark. Why not a sunny yellow, a sky blue?

"White," said Shirley, in those days of dark green.

"That's all?" asked the father.

That was all. But her aunt *would* bring in pretty pillows, a quilted spread. Shirley threw them out of her attic room window.

"You can't have a bare bed," said her aunt.

"Bring me black sailcloth," said Shirley.

They did, hurriedly. She made a spread on her aunt's old treadle machine, which the aunt and the father had dragged up to the attic for Shirley.

"Why lie in black?" asked Shirley's father. "It's like mourning."

"So it is," said Shirley.

Soon she would begin to scream. They would have to wipe her with cold water and hold ice cubes in washcloths against her face. They didn't argue.

Once she brought them pleasure, pure pleasure. She made up for the loss of her mother and of their country, she was so agreeable, so pleasant.

It was a time of fire and color. These high school children held hands through newsreels of burning vessels, oil slick on the ocean from sunken submarines, the conflagration of London, flaming ships in Pearl Harbor. It was a confusion of flares, bombs, explosions, an amusement park of war for those waiting children who necked and petted and let Kate Smith love America for them.

Shirley Panush's father left Germany, the large synagogue where he officiated, and his wife's remains.

Bolts of material had arrived in their community, containing the stamped, identical Stars of David. The rabbi asked the women of his congregation to be proud, to embroider yet more stars for the altar, for the holiday tablecloths. But his wife did not care for that regular, repetitive pattern. She would pin it on sometimes, sometimes not, even though it was to be sewn on all clothing. Her nature was more brilliant than regular, as was her appearance.

26

Where her family was cool and deliberate in speech, her German sounded Italianate. They were cool in coloring, but she was all the primary shades with her blue-black hair, naturally red lips and cheeks, tawny yellow eyes. Her daughter, Genja, had green eyes, apricot skin, pinkish-purple veins when she flushed. She was of secondary colors.

The mother was a linguist and pianist but the mechanics of living were not always clear to her.

"Mother, my baby girl is a linguist and a pianist."

"Tell her that is not important."

"What is?"

"Whom she marries."

"That's all?"

"No, also if she can find her way back home."

Frau Panush called everything a machine.

"Turn off the machine," could be the radio, iron, phonograph, the light switch.

If she went to pay a visit, she would wander in the wrong direction and have to phone home "on a machine" to ask her husband, the rabbi, where she was and where he was.

One day on the streets Frau Panush told an SS man, "Officer, I am lost."

"Where are you going, Frau?" he asked gallantly.

She told him the locale of their house and that it was near their synagogue.

She did not return, charged with failure to wear the armband, intent to disguise her identity, and accosting an official of the state.

"Mother, I'm pregnant with a baby girl and she's a *rebbetzin*."

"Then she's nobody."

"But she's in danger."

"Then she'll die."

"She's married to a rabbi."

"He will live."

Rabbis survived if no one else. Religious organizations paid handsomely for them. Out came Genja, her father, her father's sister. But the rabbi was less than he had been. American synagogues want American rabbis, but they do not care if the one who officiates over the slaughtering of their meat has an accent. Rabbi Panush became a ritual slaughterer and also a *melamed*, tutoring slow Bar Mitzvah pupils in Hebrew.

"Mother, I'm pregnant with a baby girl."
"What is she?"
"The daughter of a *melamed*, a teacher."
"Then she will learn nothing."
"The daughter of a ritual slaughterer."
"Then she will be ritually slaughtered."

Rabbi Panush was strict, even with his slow pupils, teaching the *aleph beth* with the edge of the ruler. But Shirley was gay. She sang with the melodic voice of her mother, giggled like a Viennese, flirted like a Hungarian, was as ambitious as an American.

"Mother, my baby girl has a girl friend."
"Tell her it's impossible."

Shirley had her mother's artistic nature. She took the few art courses taught in high school, all by Miss Rose Cogley, B.S., M.E., and she won the Sunkist Oranges Poster Contest. The prize was a trip to Florida for Shirley, her father, and Miss Rose Cogley, B.S., M.E. The old aunt sulked at home and refused to put on lights while the family was out of town. She fretted in dusk and went to bed as soon as darkness fell. She cleaned in light. Shirley returned from Florida with her hair blonder and her skin tanner.

"Mother, I'm pregnant with a baby girl."
"What's her problem?"
"She has a blonde girl friend."
"Tell her never to stand next to her."

Children crowded the rabbi's front porch until Beatrix,

Lois, Janice, and shy Pauline were crowded off onto the stairs. They sat there watching, coveting.

The old aunt never invited the children inside but watched from behind the living-room drapes.

"Mother, my baby girl has good taste."

"What does she want to do?"

"Select the drapes."

"Tell her the one who selects the drapes darkens or lightens the house."

The drapes were selected by the aunt—climbing, waving, stretching rubber-plant leaves. All of the furniture in the *rebbe*'s house was selected by the aunt for practicality, frugality, and sentimentality.

When a boy on the porch smoked, the aunt would knock against the window, her mouth pressed against the pane, a fish mouth, not clearly heard, but calling, "You'll set the porch on fire."

Everything else was on fire. There were fire wardens in London, saboteurs in France. There was the RAF being shot down in flames. There was Jimmy Cagney parachuting behind enemy lines in *16 Rue Madeleine*. There was Gregory Peck, leading his fellow patriotic Russians in the forest, a tiny band against the Nazis.

"Mother, I am pregnant with a baby girl and she is worried."

"Why?"

"The boys are fighting."

"But what are the women doing?"

"They're dancing."

The girls were in a chorus line, like Rita Hayworth waiting for Gene Kelly to discover her.

It was too much excitement, that combination of war and death. Love had to come along, had to be a little like war, like death, like being blitzed together in London—yet distant, for these children were but spectators. So they bombed into each other, exploding, leaving shrapnel of themselves.

29

"Mother, I'm pregnant with a baby girl and she's speaking."

"I'm listening with my stethoscope."

"She says her girl friend's brother has *not* been drafted."

"Then he must give an explanation."

"But her girl friend has also *not* been drafted."

"She need never explain."


The brother had a bum knee.

All the men at home had to give explanations, even movie stars on and off screen.

"Why are you out of the army, buddy?" a screen comrade asks Gene Kelly early in the film.

"Enlisted and wounded right off," says Gene Kelly.

He is then free to entertain the troops and to discover Rita Hayworth in the chorus line.

One late afternoon, Romanian Lois's brother arrived—the one with the bum knee—but he could still drive his father's car. He was sent to bring home bad girl Lois. Lois had not cleaned her bedroom before going to school and she was going to clean it now before the day was over.


"Mother, my baby girl has gone to school."

"Did she make her bed?"

"My baby girl has gone to work."

"Did she make her bed?"

"My baby girl has gone out into the world."

"Not if she neglected to make her bed."

"Hello, kid," said Lois's brother to Beatrix Palmer.

Bea blushed. *Sane Sex Life and Sex Living* before her.

"Hello, kid," says Lois's brother to Shirley Panush.

He then sat on the porch and smoked nonchalantly. When the aunt knocked at him, forming her soundless words from the other side of the window, Lois's brother went to his car, took a lap robe from the back seat, fastened it against the window, leaned the porch chair there, and continued to smoke. When he left to drive Lois home, Shirley was invited to accompany.

30

"Mother, I'm pregnant with a baby girl and she's dreaming."

"Don't let her tell anyone."

"Her dreams are betrayed!"

"She told someone."


The children still gathered on the porch but Shirley was not among them. Rabbi Panush would ask Lois where her brother was. The crazy aunt would shake her finger at Lois from behind the glass.

"I used to know where he was," Lois said to Beatrix.

"Where was he?" asked Beatrix.

"Sleeping with my mother," said Lois.

"You don't mean it!"

"I don't mean it."

Beatrix didn't ask her again.

They all went to a ZOA hayride. Some of them had dates. Beatrix did not. The girls watched Shirley disappear into the straw while kissing Lois's brother. She stayed under until Beatrix began to scream, afraid Shirley was choking to death. The couple sat up. Beatrix thought they looked terrible with glazed eyes and smeared faces.


Like dog paws in their laps, like a bus window opened on a windy day, so the abruptness and shock of Senior Prom.


"Mother, I'm pregnant with a baby girl."

"Does she have a date for New Year's Eve?"

"No."

"Does she have a date for the Senior Prom?"

"No."

"Then tell her not to be born."


Distraction. Shirley Panush passed out in American Lit. At first she laid her head down on the desk. She tried to raise her hand to be excused. Excusing her was complicated. A request had to be submitted to the office, but Shirley felt too ill to go alone. A message was returned from the office that someone would have to accompany Shirley. Miss Richardman, the American Lit teacher with the bobbed hair who taught "Thanatopsis" as a contemporary American poem, refused to jeopardize the health of her students. Shirley could be contagious. Miss Richardman herself could not take time out to deliver Shirley to the office, for American Lit had so much material to cover in so little time. Shirley fell from her seat.

The nurse told Miss Richardman that when she phoned Shirley's house the next day the old aunt hung up on her. The nurse tried again, alarmed at Miss Richardman's suggestion of contagion.

The father's tired voice had said, "No, not contagious, certainly not contagious. More like a hemorrhaging."

"A hemorrhaging?" asked the nurse.

"More like appendix," said the father.


"Mother, I'm pregnant with a baby girl and she is crying."

"Why?"

"Because she is pregnant and her lover is not."

"How does she know?"

"Only she is hemorrhaging."


The girls *had* to speak to each other. About the Prom.

"Is Sarcastic Cynthia going?" Beatrix asks.

"Yes, she's going."

Beatrix doesn't want to know with whom.

"Is Roz going?" Lois asks.

"Yes, she's going."

Lois wants to know with whom.

"Her cousin in the Eleventh Grade."

"She has no pride."

"She had to go. Her mother bought her a dress."

"Did you see it?"

"No."

"Didn't she want to show it to you?"

"Yes."

"Is Shirley Glazer going? Razel Schiller in General? Marcia S. Liebowitz? She's not going?"

"She's going."

"Norma Honey's going."

"Norma's always going."

"Who's she going with?"

"The son of Lloyd's Furs."

"Who's Marcia going with?"

"A Bob's Bicycle boy."

Lois's brother enters the kitchen.

"Hello, kid," he says to Beatrix. "Hello, sport."

Beatrix has Noxema on her pimple.

"I have the tickets already," he tells her. "Want to go?"

Lois is mad at her but Beatrix wants to go.

Cynthia comes over to say hello to Beatrix. She is also very pleasant to Lois's brother.

Beatrix is not a good dancer. The brother holds her close so she won't fall. He bends her into the HiLi position, pressing his lips to her forehead, his stomach against hers. When they straighten up, Beatrix's back is sore.

He puts his hand on the bare back of her borrowed formal.

("A borrowed formal and my borrowed brother," said Lois. "It's disgusting.")

"Does it hurt?" he asks.

His voice is very deep. Maybe he has a slight Romanian accent. He is sympathetically rubbing Beatrix's back.

"Better?"

"A little," whispers Beatrix.

They dance and he blows into her ear.

"Like that?" he asks.

"No," whispers Beatrix.

"Why not?" blowing into the other.

"It tickles."

"Then you like it," he says, "a little."

After the dance he buys hamburgers. The pickle and tomato slip out of the bun onto Beatrix's lap, for she is squeezing the bun too hard. He takes her for a drive and parks under the street light.

"We'll be in shadow that way," says Lois's brother.

He also says that the hamburgers didn't satisfy him; he's

33

still hungry. Could he nibble—on her cupcakes? See the cherry on each top? He knows everything. He's been reading Dr. Long also.

Beatrix looks down at her bra. He has pulled it away from her cupcakes. His nails are carefully filed. He has a golden watchband. He has a white shirt and cuff links. But he is Lois's brother. He is Shirley's love. His hands cup around the cupcakes. Beatrix sees her chest heaving. His hands rise and fall. She begins to sob.

"Take it easy, kid," he tells her.

She begins to perspire, onto his white cuffs, dripping from his cuff links, wetting his wrist under the watchband.

He tries to kiss her but her lips are trembling. She closes her eyes and feels her face dampening with tears, her nose running.

"What a mess!" he says.

He moves the car. She is driving down Main with her bra hanging under her breasts. The bra flaps like an empty egg carton.

"Jesus Christ!" he says.

He reaches into the back seat at the next traffic light for his lap robe.

"Do something with yourself," he says, throwing the robe at her.

By the time she does something with herself they are in front of her house. He walks her to the steps and lets her climb alone. The living-room lights are on. Her parents are waiting up for their Prom girl.

The door opens.

"Miss America!" says her mother.

He drives off.

Lois calls the next day.

"He didn't come home in the wee hours," she says.

In careful detail Beatrix tells Lois about the HiLi, the back rub, blowing into the ear, nibbling at her cupcakes. Beatrix is giggly and breathless. Lois is attentive and quiet. Beatrix knows what she is doing. She is neither giggly nor breathless when she hangs up, and Lois is not quiet. Lois is not quiet to Shirley whom she visits that afternoon in the hospital. Shirley

34

begins to scream. Shirley's father is phoned. Shirley's father forbids Lois's brother or Lois or any of the girls to see Shirley because they overly excite her.

Shirley's aunt will keep them away. When they come to the hospital, she is crocheting outside of the door. She calls, "Nurse! Nurse!" down the corridor. When Shirley is released from the hospital, Lois's brother visits her at home. He comes up the porch stairs, and the old aunt, behind the window, pulls the shade down on him.

Shirley waits for him to visit. One night she runs out of the house. Her aunt had dozed off, but the father hears the front door opening and rushes after her.

He is chasing her, he, the *melamed*, and she, the poor learner. He must teach her the holy way, the holy tongue, and he must beat her with the ruler on her shoulder, on her head, on her heart until she learns.

"You're killing your mama all over again," says the rabbi.

He is the ruler. There is a double welt on Shirley's cheek.

"Thank God she isn't alive," says the rabbi.

"She was right," says Genja. Her voice is cool. "She was right to choose to go out in the daytime."

The rabbi pauses. What is her logic?

"To choose to leave off her armband."

The ritual slaughterer waits.

"To choose to see an SS man."

The rabbi begins to raise his arm, as he would the knife against the throat of beef, of chicken.

"To speak with him, to choose to leave you, to choose rather to die than to live with you."

His face is ashen.

"I make the same choice," says his daughter.

The ruler has fallen. Left on the ground. The rabbi takes Genja home.


"Mama, I'm pregnant with a baby girl."

"How is she?"

"She's dying in the womb."

"Why?"

35

"Her lover has left her."
"She's so young. Tell her to live."
"No, there's nothing else to live for."


Looking for Friends (3): Black Janice

Q.
"Mother, I'm pregnant with a baby girl."
"What color?"
"She doesn't know."

"Mother, I'm pregnant with a baby girl."
"How is she spending her time?"
"Visiting with girl friends."
"What are they doing?"
"Loving each other."
"How?"
"They talk, they console, they caress, they kiss."
"Is your baby rich or poor?"
"Poor."
"Only the rich can afford such a friendship."

"Mother, I'm pregnant with a baby girl."
"What is she doing?"
"Enjoying herself."
"With what?"
"With the war. With race riots."
"Tell her she'll never have so much fun again."

My Spanish teacher joined the Navy and was torpedoed and killed. In 1942 we had the race riots.

On Janice's porch there is a new glider. There are also hooks above us for a porch swing. This was taken down, to my regret, and replaced by the tame glider. I told my parents about Janice's swing, rusting in the garage. They warned me never to ask for it. We have old kitchen chairs on our porch which my parents take in every night so the paint won't peel.

The action in a glider is like floating on a rubber tube in

Walled Lake. There are no surprises. But, as Janice and I talk and glide and slide from side to side, we soon enter the house and go into her bedroom. We masturbate ourselves or each other, depending on how late it is in the day. Broad daylight, we do ourselves. Dusk, each other. One day we forgot to lock the bedroom door. Janice's mother entered. It was dim in the room but she could see our bodies squirming under the cover. I was Dirty Bea, not allowed back in the house again. Janice's mother threatened to tell my parents while I sobbed and put my panties on. It was more humiliating than when I was caught stealing *Peggy Goes to London* from S. S. Kresge's.

And yet, yet I had the impression that Janice's mother could not understand *why* I wanted to *touch* Janice.

"One thing makes a riot," Janice's father said to his wife, his daughter, and his son (not in order of favor but of chronology). "Strangers."

In her house Janice was the stranger, the daughter of a dainty mother but built like her muscular father. From a family of light skin and hazel eyes, she had a wide nose, full lips, skin that tanned blackish brown in the summer, fading slightly in the winter. Her mother never accepted Janice's size. She would return from shopping with sample-size dresses for Janice, too short, too high waisted, with tiny calico prints that emboldened Janice's already broad face.

Janice's father laughed. Her younger brother, much like Janice in appearance, also laughed.

"She looks like Baby Snooks," said her father.

"Why, daddy?" mocked the younger brother, a big-mouthed, ugly Fanny Brice with her baby radio voice.

Janice stretch her mouth between her fingers at her brother.

"Look at her! Now she looks like Joe E. Brown," said her brother.

Janice's body was like her flat, wide face. Her nipples were wide and flat, her breasts and stomach flat. A poor appendectomy left lobes of flesh like an ear listening at her side. Her thighs rubbed when she walked. If she wore corduroy pants, they squeaked.

Her mother, looking past Janice, always saw Cinderella's

foot for the sample slipper, a wisp of a waist for that Deanna Durbin dirndl, slender white hands to give the manicurist each week.

To the brother, honors accrued: captain of the Jewish Center Swimming Team, captain of the Junior High Basketball and Track. If he were in High, he'd be several lettermen, just as his sister before him had captained Girls' Soft Ball, Girls' Stick Hockey, and was Lead of Synchronized Swimming.

Janice, at Synchronized Swimming demonstrations, was weightless on water, executing the most beautiful butterfly stroke, back stroke, breast stroke. She was the Center in the Center of the Flower routine, while the other swimmers were merely petals. She was the Sea Horse in the Dance of the Sea Horse and Swan Princess in a nautical version of Swan Lake. She would arch, dive, flip, leap while her parents attended the meets at the damp, bluish-green chlorinated pool. Her mother sighed at Janice's dripping short black hair, at her shape in the tank suit, and, after the meet, at Janice's lumbrous, sullen walk.

At the time of the riots Janice was making up Biology in summer school.

One morning the class watched while the National Guard encamped on the high school grounds. The class was having Biology class break and Janice had been batting balls over the fence into the encampment. The young guardsmen gathered along the fence.

"Yeah, Blackie!" they called. "Sock it, nigger."

"Blackie" to Janice who still attended the Sholem Aleichem Yiddishkeit Institute.

"Mama, I'm pregnant with a baby girl and she wants to be other people."

"Who does she want to be?"

"Razel Schiller and Norma Honey."

"Why?"

"They unfurl Razel Schiller's frilly blouse. They call after Norma Honey, 'Look at those big earrings shake!' "

"But those are insults!"

"She envies their being insulted."

A guardsman, one of the older members of the company, threw a hard ball over the fence straight at Janice's head. She saw it coming, could have ducked but caught it bare-handed and made off with it.

"Whoo-ee!" yelled the guardsmen. "She got one of your balls! Good thing you didn't throw the other!"

Janice took the ball to a corner of the field. In the soft dirt around the roots of a black ash she buried it and sat there nursing her hand. A young guardsman, leaning against the tree on the other side, watched Janice paw the earth with one hand, bury the ball, tap down the ground.

Janice looked up and saw him watching her. He went back to writing to his little sisters, messages on the back of Ford Assembly Line postcards. Janice returned to Biology.

The next morning, during Biology break, the class crowded at the Good Humor truck or threw a softball around. Janice walked to the black ash and had her Creamsicle there. Her hand was in her book.

"How is it?" the young guardsman asked.

Janice took her hand out of the book and showed him. The index finger was in a light metal splint, the bone chipped.

"How long?"

"A month," she said. "No sports."

"Not even swimming?"

"Yes, I can swim."

"That's good. It's hot."

The others were wandering into the building. Norma waved good-bye. Razel Schiller stayed there. She wasn't even registered for summer school.

The guardsmen called, "Come back for night school!"

"I'm off tonight," the young guardsman told Janice.

Janice said nothing. She felt like the bark of the tree, stiff, encased.

"You want to come by?"

"I'll see if I can."

"Ask them."

Which she did not, could not, even though the boy was all

her mother would have had her be: slender, delicate-featured, soft-spoken, blond, shy, even a homebody writing to those sisters.

She walked by the field after dinner, nervously, not knowing where to look for him. The guardsmen lined up against the fence—but he was waving to her from the corner so she could avoid the encampment. Her walk became exaggeratedly casual and athletic, while he glided next to her, stepping softly, looking down at the sidewalk. At the next corner she, watching him, stumbled. He took her hand.

Then her walk became less lumbrous and his more affirmative. They walked past the Eagle Dairy and he asked her what she wanted. She was afraid to eat. He had a double-dip orange pineapple and gave her licks. They walked to the movie house and looked at the stills, but she couldn't be gone that late, movie-late, in the middle of the week.

"Study hard in the school year and you can stay up longer in the summer," said her dad when she told him she was going to a friend's.

"Which one?"

"Beatrix Palmer."

"Your mother said she's a bad influence on you."

"Maybe Shirley's—just two blocks away!"

"That girl's doing something with all those guys on the porch, even if her father's a rabbi."

"Pauline in the apartment around the corner."

"Nobody's ever home at Pauline's. She's always alone."

"I'll ring the bell and tell her through the intercom to come out."

"What'll you do? Stand on that main street in front of the door? You're asking for trouble."

"We'll go to the Viennese bakery for éclairs."

"You don't need the extra weight."

"I'll just walk. It's a nice night to walk."

"It's a rotten night to walk, hot and humid."

She went down the stairs and out, lying no more.

Janice and the guardsman walked home, a short walk but a long time. He told her about Ironwood, mostly farms and farmers drinking, and the boring little high school he went to. He had no plans. Maybe he'd go into regular service. Did he

40

think about the war? He laughed. We think about the crops, he said. He liked to swim, to ride his old horse. He liked, best of all, his pigs.

"Smartest animals in the world," he said, "smarter than any dumb old dog. They can be watchdogs, I mean it. They'll squeal and warn you about strangers coming."

"You mean watch *pigs*."

They squealed. They laughed. They were a barnyard of noise. And, not thinking, she told him how to get to her house, and there they were. On the glider, not reading his newspaper, staring at Janice holding hands with, shame of shames, not even a regular soldier, that farmer National Guardsman, in that wrinkled uniform—was Janice's father.

The father rose and shook the newspaper at the boy. Jan and the boy thought the father was squawking, that it was part of the farm game. They laughed until the farmer came down the porch steps, rolled the newspaper, and slammed the guardsman with it. The boy walked off, not looking back.

"Mama, I'm pregnant with a baby girl and she's grieving."

"Why?"

"Her love is leaving."

"He'll come back."

"No. They never come back. They never look back."

I was not allowed to see Janice at her home. In school she became irritable, sarcastic, and did small violent acts. What began as playful slaps on the back, became cuffings of the ear, a slugging match with Norma Honey, a tripping of Marcia S. Liebowitz on the way home from school, goosing and hooting at fat Roz, spitting at Razel Schiller and calling her "bitch." Janice phoned at eleven that night to apologize, but Razel's parents would not disturb Razel, gone to bed, and Janice did not apologize in person or by phone again.

"Mama, I'm pregnant with a baby girl and she hates."

"Whom?"

"Every girl she knows."

"That's because she's not allowed to hate boys."

41

College. Janice hitches into town without phoning her parents, staying at one girl's house or another's. She complains about the food at State, creamed *drek* on toast. Lois and I, enrolled at City, eat at home.

Janice's parents begin calling around. Janice has not returned to State, and Student Affairs has sent an inquiry. Janice's father phones shy Pauline, who stutters when he accuses her of withholding information. He calls Romanian Lois, but Lois's mother intercepts and will not allow him to speak to Lois. He phones Rabbi Panush's house. The maiden aunt hangs up. Then he phones me.

Janice's father says to me, "You should know where Janice is. My wife tells me you were so—so *friendly* with Janice."

I tell him, "Janice should have left home a long time ago."

He is silent. Perhaps he will apologize.

"I wish," he says, "I wish you a miserable marriage and crippled offspring." Which became somewhat prophetic.


"Mama, I'm p. with a baby g. and she's run away from home."

"You have two choices."

"What are they?"

"Hire a detective or don't hire a detective."


Which Janice's family did, and which I did not do years later.

The detective agency, after a month, found Janice on the South Side of Chicago, living with one soldier after another. She met them while helping out at the USO.


"Mama, I'm p. with a baby g."

"Who is she?"

"A niece and a daughter."

"Who are her uncles?"

"An optometrist and a dentist."

"Who is her father?"

"A haberdasher."

"Who is her mother?"

"Nobody."

42

Janice's father consulted with his brother, the optometrist, and his brother, the dentist.

"Drive her to work with you," they advised the haberdasher. "Let her do something there, keep books, keep busy."

"Mama, I'm pregnant with a b.g. and her father wants to keep her. '

"What does he want to keep her?"

"Busy."

"In the meantime," said the uncles, "we'll look around—a nice predental from the University, an optometry student from Chicago. She was in Chicago. They'll have something to talk about."

"Mama, I'm p. with a b.g. and she can't solve her problems."

"She's not supposed to."

The uncles said, "We'll find somebody to solve her problems. It's a case of high spirits which, unless controlled, could blacken her name."

Janice did not phone us upon her return. A couple of years later she phoned me—from Los Angeles. Her mother had written Janice that I was getting married. She wanted to know what shower gifts I received. She, although married before me, had received no shower gifts, no wedding presents. I sent her my silver pitcher and creamer, still in their plastic wrapping.

I apologize for doing that, member of my family who gifted me. I apologize, Harold, my ex-, for not having told you. I received no thank-you note from Janice.

Janice worked simple ledgers for her father. She worked in hats, ties, shirts, handkerchiefs, underwear, socks, wallets, suspenders, belts, sweaters, pajamas, bathrobes, and cloth slippers. She worked in his shop which, three years before, was in the riot area.

She was paid generously and bought expensively for herself. The parents approved. Her younger brother invited her to track meets. She was pleasant to the customers, respectful to her parents, distant from her friends.

"Mother, I'm pregnant with a baby girl and you will be proud of her."

"Why?"

"She is pleasant to the customers, respectful to her parents, distant from her friends."

"An ideal daughter."

One Friday before three o'clock, Janice went out with the deposit and did not return. Stock was also missing, the father discovered when he did inventory. The same detective agency found Janice in Colorado with a Black man, a good customer of the haberdashery, whom Janice had outfitted in accessories. They were married. His family was willing for an annulment, as was hers. But Janice and her husband moved farther yet, to California. Janice's father wearied of the chase.

She sent letters home in a year or two. They were returned unopened. She sent a package of photographs of her children. It was returned. She phoned and her parents hung up. Once the brother answered and said, "Haven't you done enough damage?"

She let her little sweet-voiced daughter phone. The parents, on the other end of the line, were shocked and silent, then softly hung up.

The brother was injured at a sports meet, suffered a concussion, hemorrhaged, and died. Janice's aunt phoned Janice. She called home.

"Mama?" she asked. "Daddy?"

"Come," they begged. "Leave that man. Leave his children."

She came, spent a week in mourning, thinking it over. Thinking over the comfortable house, her room still unoccupied, the polite but stiff greeting from her uncles, her father's chain of haberdasheries.

"Take my husband into the business," she said, "and I'll return."

"There is no husband," they said.

In the mornings Janice's mother brought her hot chocolate in bed. Her father shared the newspaper with her and listened to her political opinions. She had become a Communist and a Unitarian but he commented on neither.

The phone rang at the end of the week of mourning. The father handled the receiver nervously.

"It's for you," he said.

"Mama?" asked her daughter.

She returned to the West Coast, wearing a new wardrobe and dissatisfied. Within five years both parents died. The uncles handled the estate, a few thousand for Janice, the rest divided up among the Midwestern family, a Jewish Old Folks Home, and a room donated to Bethel Hospital.

Janice's young daughter was accepted into Talented Children's Art Classes, Saturday morning at the museum. The son had perfect pitch for the piano and was a perfect pitcher, besides, said his daddy, in Little League. Janice coached the Girl's Swimming, and her husband the Little League, but they found neither peace nor happiness, for Janice nagged while her husband dragged. He left her for no other woman, faithful indeed to both wife and children, but he left for a quiet room, some Sunday fishing, a little joy.

"Mama, I'm pregnant with a baby girl."

"What does she want to know?"

"Will she be happy in marriage?"

"Let her stay in the womb, for once she is out of it, she could marry a baby boy who would crouch in *her* womb and refuse ever to leave."

Looking for Friends (4): The House That Pauline Built

R.

"Mother, I am pregnant with a baby girl."

"Then tell her there are no alternatives."

That last year of high school, Beatrix could no nothing to please Pauline. Cause and effect were not connective. Why

45

did Pauline stop talking to her for the month of November? Why did she suddenly wait for her in the cold after school to begin talking again? Why did Pauline not respond to her apartment bell? Beatrix was sure the intercom was on and that she heard Pauline breathing when she identified herself.

She would beg, "Press the buzzer, Pauline. Let's go to the Chinese restaurant." No sound. "We can go to the Viennese bakery for chocolate éclairs." A click and the static of communication would cease.

Before every school event Pauline became depressed: a football event, the French Brunch, Christmas vacation, the Prom, Senior Skip Day, Graduation.

Beatrix, the good girl, attended what she could, miserably. Pauline missed all, miserably. Beatrix went to the football game and pinned a large school badge to her plaid skirt. She cheered, leapt, smiled, and walked home alone, except for the peanut shells a sloe-eyed former New Yorker had tossed into her hair. She sat on the bleacher step, and he, above her, kept leaning over. When Beatrix returned home her mother laughed shrilly at the outsized football medallion and asked Beatrix what that growth was on her hip. She asked it several times in front of Beatrix's father and some aunts and uncles who were visiting. Bea went up to her room where she saw the peanut shells in her uncontrollable hair, realized why the sloe-eyed New Yorker was leaning so close to her, and loosed uncontrollable tears.

Ah, they were all a crowd of shrieky, teary girls who abused their parents! Except for silent Pauline who abused no one but sipped water from a cloudy glass, clicked it slightly against the ceramic plate, and tapped the white dish with her fork, staring ahead, tap tap blindly, in that Chinese-American restaurant.

Beatrix looked for her at the French Brunch, held at the French teacher's house. Tea and croissants had been prepared by the French teacher's old French mother.

There, too, the girls cliqued up. Sarcastic Cynthia went with Rose Anne Epstein, who was going to go to Smith. Marcia S. Liebowitz had a girl friend. The French teacher patted the seat next to her for Beatrix, "*ma chère*, my little partner.'' It was wallflower time again, but Beatrix, at least, had tried to climb the wall.

Pauline, although A in Grammar and Style, could not be graded on Oral, for she refused to speak when called upon. She refused to attend when notified of French Club meetings, although she had paid dues for the whole semester.

"Mama, I'm pregnant with a b. girl and I'm selecting her name.''

"Name her after someone deceased.''

"Then she will start out partially dead.''

Pauline was named for her grandfather, Palti, a bad-tempered grocery store owner. Palti disliked his two sons for monopolizing his wife's attention. In spite, he died before Passover, leaving his small wife to fill all those Passover orders and his two young sons to deliver them.

The wife squinted when she read the Yiddish paper. The sons wore thick glasses when still young. Palti found offense in this and accused them of being scholars in order not to support him in his older years. Eventually, the older son stayed with the mother but left the grocery store. The younger stayed with the store but left the mother to marry.

"Mother, I'm p. with a b.g. and she's married.''

"To whom?''

"To a man who visits his mother.''

"The mother and son—what is it they do together?''

"They confide, kiss, caress, dine, settle accounts, and whisper.''

"Whisper? Then the b.g. can sue for divorce on grounds of adultery.''

S.
Pauline's father married a flit, a girl given to permanents which burned and frizzed her hair, to flutterings of the hands, and wrinkling of the nose. She would not help out at the grocery.

"Mama, I'm pregnant with a b.g. and she wants to grow up to sell.''

"To sell what?"

"Housecoats, budget dresses, and lingerie."

"On or off her body?"

The husband worked at the grocery with his mother and his wife went to work for Daisy's, a chain of cheap clothing shops. She worked in a Polish neighborhood where Daisy rented its lower level to a beauty shop. The customers emerged from the salon with Polish braided hair in fantastic twists, glazed and decorated like Easter bread.

"Mama, I'm p. with a b.g. and she wants to work when she becomes pregnant."

"And then?"

"She wants to work afterward."

"And then?"

"She wants to work while the child is growing up."

"And then?"

"She doesn't want to come home after that."

After Pauline's birth, her mother frequently took the bus to Daisy's to show Pauline off to the other saleswomen, to her former customers, and the beauty shop operators. Soon Pauline was provided with a playpen in the back room, while her mother sold lingerie, dark prints, and pastel formals at Daisy's for thirty cents an hour.

"Mama, I'm p. with a b.g. and she put her baby into a playpen."

"And then?"

"And then into a Murphy bed."

"And then?"

"Into a restaurant."

"And then?"

"Into the closet."

Beatrix visited Pauline in her small, dark apartment. Pauline's apartment faced the alley. The front of the building was on a busy bus route. Next door to the apartment building was the Viennese bakery. Across the busy street was Chinese-American cuisine.

Pauline's father moved back home with his mother and brother.

Beatrix went down the corridor to Pauline's apartment. The door would be blocked by the Murphy bed. Pauline would have to lift the bed to let Beatrix in. Her mother slept in the back bedroom. The doors of the closet that housed the Murphy were decorated with photographs: white cottages with shutters, antebellum houses, brick houses in rolling hills, and, last year in high school, Frank Lloyd Wright houses. With Chanukah money Pauline subscribed to *Architectural Forum*.

"Mama, I'm p. with a b.g. and she wants to be an architect."

"What does she want to do?"

"Design houses."

"Impossible. She has to be a housewife, not a designer of houses."

Pauline's mother moved. She moved in with the owner of the liquor store, a block down from Daisy's. She lived above the liquor store but she continued to rent the dark, little apartment for Pauline. Pauline stayed in the living room on the Murphy, although the bedroom was not being used. The mother did store some old clothes there which took up much of the dresser and closet space.

Pauline's mother would come by with her key, leave a few dollars in the kitchenette or leave a shopping bag with specials at A & P, apple butter, jars of lime-flavored pears, pickled beets, Ann Page breads.

Pauline ate, most often, in the Chinese-American cuisine near the bus stop. Beatrix, waiting for a bus, would see Pauline sitting at a starched white tablecloth, which she did not have to worry about staining, did not have to clear of dishes. Beatrix would see the red-jacketed boys nodding and smiling and whispering themselves back into the kitchen so that Pauline, unlike Beatrix, did not get stomach cramps from table dispute, from family accusations. There sat Pauline in the picture window, twirling her water glass thoughtfully, an elbow on the table, a fist at her chin, three other chairs around the table pushed in.

Pauline's mother left notes in the apartment for her daughter:

"Did you remember to wash your greasy hair this week?"

"Do your clothes have to go to the cleaners? Smell the armpits."

"Did you clean your hairbrush yet? I noticed that it was full of hair and looked as if it had fallen under the bed."

Sometimes Beatrix agreed with Pauline's mother. When Pauline slept over—not often—Beatrix would ask Pauline to shower. Pauline would think about it. Usually she would not shower.

She had strange motivations for her decisions. In Pauline's apartment there was no shower, only a tan tub standing on its legs, in a tan bathroom. It was a toy bulldog of a tub on bowlegs, staring while Pauline read on the toilet. The senior year in high school Pauline painted her bathroom lavender and the bulldog black. It was not much better. If anything, the black bulldog was more ominous than the tan had been, and Pauline became constipated.

Pauline's father visited Pauline once in a while. He was relieved not to see his wife there. When any of the girls were visiting—Lois, Janice, Shirley, or Beatrix—Pauline's father would lecture them on sex.

"Watch out for men," he told Beatrix. "They want only one thing from a girl. When they get it, they're through. They go on to the next girl for the same thing."

"Mother, I'm p. with a b.g., and she's being lectured."
"By whom?"
"The father of her girl friend."
"About what does he lecture her?"
"About her erogenous zones."
"What information is he giving her?"
"He touches her erogenous zones and says, 'These are your Maginot Lines, the weakness in your defense.'"

50

"Tell her not to worry. He's an old soldier who talks and doesn't shoot."

Graduation. Beatrix unhappily wearing, under her black robe, the graduation dress selected by her mother. Beatrix had gone with Pauline down to Daisy's and had purchased a turquoise rayon, skin-tight dress with a maroon parrot perched on one hip and nestling one breast. Pauline's mother had been generous with her time while Beatrix tried on dresses.

At first Mrs. Palmer laughed shrilly and asked Beatrix, "What have you there, a costume?"

Then Mrs. Palmer was incensed that Pauline's mother had sold that dress to Beatrix. She insisted on being driven to Daisy's for a refund. It was not the policy of the store to refund. You could get credit for another purchase, but Beatrix's mother told the manager of Daisy's that she would report this shop to the Better Business Bureau for selling unfitting and ill-fitting merchandise to a young girl.

Said Beatrix's mother to Pauline's mother, "Don't treat her as you do your own daughter."

The money was refunded. Beatrix's mother, who knew Beatrix's size better than anyone, bought a tasteful, long-sleeved blue frock with rounded collar and softly falling pleats. Beatrix wore it for years. It wore well but all of her life Beatrix remembered the parrot's beak under her breast. She had reason to remember this, for when Pauline came to graduation and removed her robe, it was Pauline who was the parrot. She parroted in that dress, her hair washed and rinsed and as golden as Shirley Panush's hair (Shirley was given a diploma *in absentia*). Senior boys reached for the bird of her, for her feathery-soft hair. Pauline smiled, her back to them, her head slowly turning, like Betty Grable in her picture to the fighting troops.

At the end of June Beatrix, pressing Pauline's buzzer for minutes, was interrupted by the super.

"Moved out," said the fat woman.

Beatrix looked then at the name plate, blank as an empty eye socket. She did find Pauline at Daisy's. Pauline was distant and affronted on the telephone.

The other girls, less close to Pauline, could now be closer. Beatrix was given reports. Janice, in from State on one of her secret weekends, told Beatrix that Pauline had become puffy and stuffy and was promoted to Head Sales and Bookkeeper of the Daisy branch. Her mother worked under her. Pauline was living with her mother and with the owner of the liquor store.

The girls were silent.

Janice phoned Beatrix on her next trip into the city.

"Pauline fired her mother!" said Janice. "Oh, if we could all do that!"

Pauline allowed Beatrix to lunch with her and Janice a month later at a delicatessen. It was a Chinese-modern delicatessen. Pauline, with her knowledge of Louis Sullivan and Frank Lloyd Wright, of Form Follows Function, looked around at the pagodas, with prices of corned-beef sandwiches lettered on them, with slanty-eyed girls shouldering tilted parasols—club-sandwich prices on the parasols. On another mural, Tea Drinking Ceremony, BEVERAGES was lettered in oriental-style script.

It was Sunday afternoon.

"Where are you going now?"

Janice was hitching back to State. Beatrix was sneaking home. It was forbidden for her to see Pauline, after the business with the dress. (It was also forbidden, by Janice's mother, for Janice to see Beatrix.)

"Where are *you* going now?"

"I'm dropping in on my mother," said Pauline.

"I thought you lived with her," Janice said.

"No. She's back at the old apartment."

"Where are you?" Janice asked.

"With the owner of the liquor store," said Pauline.

We lined up at the cashier's.

"First a Chinese restaurant," said Pauline, "then a Chinese delicatessen. That's my life, from crazy to crazier."


Looking for Beatrix

T.

"Mother, I'm pregnant with a girl. What will she be?"

52

"What she was."

"What if she doesn't want to be what she was?"

"Then she will change, slightly."

"Beatrix," asked her father, his head in her crib, "what will we do to free Sacco and Vanzetti?"

This was the first of unsolvable problems put to her.

"Beatrix," asked her father, interrupting her Ninth Grade Social Studies homework. "They're killing our people. What will we do?"

He was reading the Belsen Black Book.

Beatrix wrote a report for Ninth Grade Social Studies: "The Nazis and their Death Camps." The teacher pointed out Beatrix's misspellings and disbelieved her information. The class was informed that this was an example of historical bias and racial exaggeration. The teacher was a Southerner, Miss Sample, whose specialty was The War Between the States and The Failure of Reconstruction.

Beatrix, news editor of the McAfee Intermediate Bulletin, incorporated her information into her column, "Bea's Bonnet." The principal censored the paper and refused to let the issue come out. Beatrix stormed home. Her parents averted their eyes. They held each other's hands.

"The principal must have a reason," said her mother, said her father.

"Beatrix," asked her father when she was in high, "what will we do about your middle brother who has an acne'ed back? What will happen to your youngest brother who is stunted in growth and stutters?"

The middle brother's back inexplicably healed, but the younger brother neither gained in growth nor in speaking facility. Beatrix investigated and discovered an elementary school, slightly farther from their neighborhood school, with students less competitive and faculty less oppressive.

"You are jealous of him," said her father. "You want to send him away so that he should not get better marks than you at your old school."

"You already count him a failure," said her mother, "so you send him with the other failures."

The youngest brother learned to control the stuttering by

53

never speaking. Although normal height was eventually gained, he thought he was short for he humped in and out of places, shrank before others, slunk, shadowed in day, retreated at night.

"Beatrix," asked her father, "what will you do about the British?" Beatrix was doing Government homework for City. "They are preventing our people from escaping to Palestine. They are another extermination camp."

When Beatrix's father cried, Beatrix became his mother. His eyes wet her blouse collar, her heart. She had access to City's ditto machine, on which she had been sending out "City to the Service"—a newsletter to City students fighting the war.

Beatrix poured her wrath into purple ditto until her parents received visits from City Journalism Department and the Army Information Service about the anti-British propaganda Beatrix was disseminating. Her parents made Beatrix promise she would discontinue publication.

"Beatrix," asked her father, wringing his hands, "what will we do about anti-Semitism in the land?"

Beatrix was still living in her old room, without Gene Kelly, without Gregory Peck, without Harold Steiner, with Baby Lena.

"Where?" asked Beatrix.

"California," said her father, "in the congressional campaign."

Beatrix left Baby Lena with her grandparents and traveled out to Los Angeles to campaign against R. M. Nixon, Republican candidate for Congress. He was waging an anti-Semitic campaign against Helen Gahagan Douglas. Helen Gahagan Douglas was not a Semite but she *was* a congresswoman *married* to a Semite. She was accused in leaflets and pamphlets and speechlets of following the Communist and Yiddish party line. Her voting record paralleled the CP line, and her husband, Melvin Douglas, followed the Yiddish Theater line.

When Congressman Nixon was elected, Beatrix's parents worried that he would take vengeance on his opponent, Beatrix. When he became Vice-President, her parents urged Beatrix to unlist her phone. When he became President they waited for the pogrom. Not that it didn't come—but no one came to take Beatrix to jail, or the pale, or an internment camp.

The girls knew about Beatrix's mouth. They knew that fearful and trembling, she was yet a dragon slayer. It was Janice who urged Beatrix who lectured the haberdasher father. Hence the father's curse upon Beatrix.

Maybe a curse has a life of its own, a force that enters our lives. We fight that curse, always expecting to be defeated by it. Bea, the Dragon Slayer, knew that when her love asked for her hand in marriage, one day he would release that hand, that when Sarcastic Cynthia asked to be introduced to Harold, Harold would, in turn, introduce himself into Cynthia. For the Dragon Slayer, every adventure presumes a battleground, a dragon, the possibilities of being slain, of slaying, or of running from the field in defeat, garments sullied, eyes glaring, blood from superficial wounds speckling the tall grass.

U.

"Mother, I'm pregnant with a baby girl."

"What's happening?"

"She's being aborted."

"Tell her not to take it seriously. She'll get used to it."

V.

"Mother, I'm pregnant with an abortion."

"Tell her we are all abortions—and more."

"What more?"

"Intrusions, conditions . . ."

"She doesn't want to listen to you."

"That's why she's an abortion."

It was an abortive year for Beatrix. Her husband had left her, unsettling her. A publishing house that had an option on her proposed cookbook, *Cooking Without Fear*, let the option drop. When the firm became infirm and Beatrix was generally unhoused from home and publishing house, she determined that everything that could be developed, completed, concluded would be so.

She finished her degree in Anthropology. She began preparing Lena for adulthood. She completed the cookbook, using Lena's ominous drawings of vegetables: cabbages with growths inside, translucent leaves over humped shadows, tomatoes dripping juice like blood, spears of carrots, pregnant zucchini with puffy features.

"M., I'm p. with a b.g. and she wants to do everything."
"She'll need help."
"Her helper won't let her do everything by herself. He wants to do more and be more."
"Then he needs help."

"M., I'm p. with a b.g. and she wants to be a writer."
"That's penis envy."
"But she wants to write cookbooks."
"Then that's an acceptable degree of penis envy."
"But her doctor wants to write cookbooks with her."
"That's womb envy."

Beatrix was deep into treatment, substituting doctor for father-lover-editor. Her doctor, in turn, was pleased that Beatrix, although invading the male domain of publishing—indicating penis envy by her need to exhibit herself—was yet working on a womanly subject. He enjoyed the topic, how Beatrix conquered her fear of the kitchen. That fear, he explained in a Foreword to the book, was instilled by her own mother's reluctance to share the role of homemaker.

"M., I'm p. with a b.g. and she's afraid of the kitchen."
"It's your fault."
"Why is it my fault?"
"If life is mundane, the kitchen is woman's sole domain."

"M., I'm p. with a b.g., and she wants to learn to cook."
"Don't let her."
"She wants to prepare breakfast."
"Then she'll have to carry it upstairs on a tray."
"She wants to bake a birthday cake."

"Then she'll have to carry it into the dining room for the guests, with its candles blazing."

"She wants to roast the Thanksgiving turkey."

"Then she can carve her future on its carcass."

"She is not allowed to carve the turkey. The man must carve. She enjoys serving the meal."

"Good, then she's prepared to be a servant."

The doctor allowed himself a smoke of a Freudian cigar while devising topics for the revised cookbook: Your Mother-in-Law Is Coming for a Visit; Your Former Husband Comes for Brunch and a Visit with his Child: What to Serve? Your Mother Is Coming to Console You. The last has sub-topics: Mother Brings Something That Doesn't Go With the Meal and Insists on Filling the Company Up With What She Brings Before the Meal Is Served, or, You're into an Organic Bag and Your Mother Calls It *Milchiks*.

The doctor was a playful man who rode a bicycle in good weather during the ten-minute grace period between patients. He thought the book would be therapeutic for his other patients. He invited them, as well as therapist and analyst friends, to write comments, forewords, afterwords. He promised that this group book would be group authored. When he insisted upon being listed as chief editor, Beatrix quit therapy.

"M., I'm p. with a b.g. and she's in therapy."

"What does her therapist do?"

"He plays eagles."

"How is that game played?"

"He throws her the baseball bat; she catches it. He places his hand higher than hers on the bat. They hand-climb up the bat, alternating hands until his cupped hand grabs the curved handle of the bat. He perches there, the eagle."

"He's grabbing the end of his penis. He's masturbating. Throw away that bat. What does she need that dirty thing for?"

Beatrix dropped the idea for the book, dropped her doctor, kept her fear of cooking and her daughter, bore her relationships with mother and father, and began a new book.

She called it, tentatively, *Unafraid Women*, women who both cooked and lived without fear. She had to go back a long way to find them, about a hundred years for some of them.

W.

"M., I'm p. with a b.g. and she can't find her mother."

"When did she last have her mother's address?"

"A hundred years ago."

Beatrix finds Mothers Margaret, Louisa, Emily, Charlotte, and other mother superiors in this convent of her search.

"M., I'm p. with a b.g. and she is looking for her mothers."

"What is Mother Margaret Fuller doing?"

"Mother Margaret is there, her mouth opened in Conversations. She is planning the Roman revolution."

"What is Mother Louisa May Alcott doing?"

"Mother Louisa is piquing her father. He is opposed to corporal punishment but he must whip little Louisa for her disobedience. Mother Louisa is also writing herself to death to support her father."

"What is Mother Emily Dickinson doing?"

"Mother Emily Dickinson is falling in love through the mails. She is also writing seventeen hundred seventy-five poems and publishing seven."

"What is Mother Charlotte Forten doing?"

"Mulatto Mother Charlotte says, 'Unless it be about slavery, it has slight interest for me.' "

Beatrix is taking years with *Unafraid Women*. She is afraid of them.

X.

"Mother, I'm pregnant with a baby girl."

"What is she doing?"

"Remembering."

In such a state of being unloved, untreated or mistreated, unpublished, unheard, Beatrix discovers that her friends are all in town at the same time. Even Shirley Panush spoke to her on the phone about a reunion.

They take pictures. The girl friends stand clustered around an oak, their faces in shade. Shirley is seated on a park bench. The photo captures her crutches leaning against the bench, for Shirley cannot walk without help. Her legs have given way to varicose veins, swollen ankles, trick knees, and thrombosis. The blood clot travels and must constantly be dissolved and her blood thinned out before it reaches Shirley's heart, lungs, or brain.

In the photo, Janice, the athlete, has indistinct features. She has tanned herself dark in California and the photo is contrasty. Janice is darker than her brown husband. Although her features are unclear, one can discern a scowl, but perhaps Janice is squinting at the sunlight.

Lois is lovelier than she was in the Yearbook, that crimson book with its cheap cardboard, wartime cover. Romanian Lois is less Romanian, more slender, her shape controlled, her hair flowing. As is the hair of her daughter who wears white dresses and whose straightened hair is blowing in the slight breeze.

Y.

"M., I'm p. with a b.g. and she has kinky hair."

"Straighten it."

"And she has crooked teeth."

"Put braces on them."

"A projection on her nose."

"Smooth it."

"Acne'ed skin."

"Treat it."

"Fallen arches."

"Fit them."

"Turned-in toes."

"Correct them."

"Then what should I do with my b.g.?"

"Sell her."

Lois has a hand on each girl's shoulder.

Beatrix is somber and armored. She holds Lena like a

59

lance, the sword hand of her mother. Lena's features are hidden under Lena's brown hair. She has been crying because she wanted to play with Howie, her four-year-old neighbor. Instead, she had to come into the sunlight for the photo.

The photographer is Pauline who will not allow herself to be shot, she says. She has quickly taken over the reunion. She has ordered the girls around as if they were in her shop at Daisy's. She has told them what positions to assume, where to stand, when to smile, how to place the children. Pauline is The Boss.

"M., I'm p. with a b.g. and she wants to be the boss."
"Of what?"
"She doesn't care, just boss."
"That's because she has never been in charge of herself."

Z.
"Mother, I am pregnant with a baby girl and she has stopped growing."
"Why?"
"She is finished."

Beatrix is alone in the room at Hillel House. The phonograph is playing and Beatrix practices dance steps. She is a self-conscious dancer still, from those Prom days, but she is now a woman with fleshy hips, small waist, full calves. Her shoulders are wider than Joan Crawford's. Her breasts are large-nippled, pointy, and small.

She dances, puts the tone arm on automatic, and repeats the dance on the 78 rpm. From a couch turned away from her rises a young man.

"Not again," he says and turns off the record.

Beatrix is about to give combat. The young man changes his mind, replays the record, and offers to dance with Beatrix. She refuses. He will not accept refusal. He holds her close. She stumbles as she did at the Senior Prom. His thighs guide her. He dances slowly, both hands on her waist, swaying her, preparing her, lifting her slightly. She is gradually subdued. Her eyes close. When lifted she soars and is surprised to be returned to Hillel carpeting. She opens her eyes. He, eye level, is smiling. Laughing at her? She becomes defensive and stops dancing. His hair is curly. So are his lashes. His eyes are laughing hazel.

Beatrix will not date. It is against her Socialist principles. Nor will she wear dresses or skirts anymore. She has explained it to her professors. She must wear slacks until the day when men's legs are also remarked upon. She must wear flannel shirts until the day when men, in addressing her, look at her eyes and not the eyes of her breasts. Her professors are startled at this outpouring and agree that she be given permission to wear slacks. It is practical in this cold climate. Madame Bosse disagrees. She will not allow slacks into French. Beatrix drops French.

Beatrix wears no makeup. She pickets fraternities, barbershops, the campus restaurant and bar because they discriminate racially. Beatrix is an EVD Socialist—Eugene V. Debs Socialist Study Group, although her father calls it BVD. The EVD'ers have formed a campus cooperative and several couples have moved in, as well as four singles—Beatrix and three male EVD'ers. Sometimes guests visit and Bea finds her room occupied. She is annoyed. Are *they* Socialists? On those nights she sleeps home.

Her room now, in fact, is occupied by a capitalistic couple. Beatrix is wandering through Hillel House, looking for a place to study.

If Beatrix returns to the home of her parents, she will, for no reason, begin screaming at her mother. She will, for that reason, be excused from the dinner table by her father. She will cause her stuttering brother more speech difficulty, and her acne'ed brother will become self-conscious. Yet Beatrix's parents want Bea to stay home, are suspicious of the co-op, sure it will be her downfall, the shame of the name. The only way for Beatrix not to shame the name is to marry and change it.

This Hillel boy is different because he is in English studies, and that is a non-Jewish, nonreformist field, as well as nonpreprofessional. He is *not* prelaw, predental, premed, preed. He *is* lighthearted, dresses with style, and is very pretty, which confuses Beatrix, with her emphasis on mental prowess rather than bourgeois appearance.

Who are Beatrix's friends besides Pauline at Daisy's, Shirley in her attic, Lois studying Chemistry for Early El—where there is no need for Chemistry—and Janice eloped to California? Besides—in later life—Mothers Margaret, Louisa, Emily, Charlotte, Rosa Luxemburg, Eleanor Roosevelt, Anaïs Nin, Kate Chopin, Mary Ann Evans, Frances Perkins? Who are her friends—in later life—besides the psychiatrist who will attend her and offend her, besides Lena and Lena's four-year-old love Howie and all those they will meet? Who are, who will be, her friends?

She is best friends with Bert. He disappeared soon after she met him. Perhaps he starved. When she knew him at EVD's, he had no money for food, no place to bathe. (There was only cold water at EVD.) Beatrix's mother fed him occasionally but would not let him use a towel.

"M., I'm p. with a b.g. and she wants to bring home a friend."

"Who's her friend?"

"He's a deeply pitted, emaciated Irishman."

"He can't come here."

"He's IWW, he's bitter, he's humorous."

"He can't come here."

"He's her guardian."

"That's all right but he can't come here."

"Who is allowed here?"

"Those who already have a home, who have eaten and bathed beforehand."

Bert is the guardian of Beatrix in that co-op. And Beatrix and Bert are also friends with Norman and Norman's duck walk and the large pimple on Norman's nose, because Norman will be a worker's lawyer. Bert, Beatrix, and Norman also love Charles, the Black elevator operator.

"M., I'm pregnant with a b.g. and she has a friend who is Black."

"What does he do?"

"He is the elevator operator on campus."

"That's all right."

"He is working for his tuition."

"Then that's not all right."

Black Charles is majoring in drama. He takes Beatrix to the People's Theater where he performs in *Stevedore* and in William Saroyan's *Hello Out There*!

Beatrix talks for hours in her room at the co-op with IWW Bert, pre-worker's lawyer Norman, actor Charles. They tuck her in at night, each kissing her forehead (Norman), cheek (Charles), hand (Bert).

And yet, in this her life, her parents cannot accept her and Beatrix cannot accept herself. It is Harold who accepts her, Harold with his rich speaking voice, slight body, spiral hair. He accepts the fact that she stumbles when she dances yet dances, that she screams at her parents, teases her brothers, and yet returns home, that she would make the land more civilized but lives in the hovel of the co-op. He accepts the fact that she is a virgin yet three men kiss her good night every night.

He accepts her slacks, her face pale without makeup (for she would attract no one by artifice), and that she weeps when he kisses her at the end of an evening. She closes her door on him, yet opens it to others for she knows that he would kiss the forehead, the cheek, the hand—he says, until she is damp between her thighs and that he will then kiss his way up or down them.

And so Beatrix and Harold marry. It is a proper marriage with a hall, two rabbis from her and his parents' respective synagogues, and with a catered dinner. After the dinner there is a sweet table. To the sweet table she is allowed to invite her EVDs, Bert, Norman, and Charles, as well as any of her old high school friends. She sends invitations to Shirley, Janice, Pauline, and Lois. Janice's invitation is returned with the hand on the envelope pointing to: Whereabouts Unknown. The other three girls do not respond in the special, stamped enclosed envelope for responding.

63

Harold will not move into the Debs co-op. He says that he has nothing against it but its lack of privacy, filth, bedbugs, and nosy people.

Harold and Beatrix, without income, become children again in her parents' house, using a bedroom and forcing the acne'ed and stuttering brothers to combine into one room so that the young couple can have a bed- and study room. Harold moves in with the pictures of Gene Kelly, Gregory Peck, and Eugene V. Debs.

It is not long before Harold and Beatrix are looking for more privacy from the family and from each other. They even visit the co-op but Bert has left the city to organize in the field, Norman as been busily studying for the bar, and Charles, the Black in drama, has dropped out of City because the Drama Department theater has been turned into a library for the returning World War II vets. There is no place for Charles to act on campus.

Cynthia, from Advanced French, begins to invite Beatrix and Harold to her house. She is an only child and it is quiet there. They talk, take classes together, and attend films, this troika of friends. Cynthia switches out of French to major in English. Beatrix and Cynthia love each other.

One afternoon Beatrix cannot find Harold. He is not under the Big Clock in Main, where he had promised to meet her. He is not at the drugstore across from City, at the library in the theater. He isn't at Hillel. She walks to the co-op. It is cold, a draggy winter. Spring is late. Beatrix's shoes become wet and her hands stiff. She knocks on Norman's door. The room is quiet, the door locked. Charles's room is empty. She tries the door of her old single. The shades are down. The bed is full. She cannot make out the figures clearly but she knows them. Harold's curls are growing out of Cynthia's groin.

# Historical Mothers

## Looking for Mothers

"Mother, I'm pregnant with a book."
"Hard or soft cover?"

Beatrix sits at her desk. A book falls from her nineteenth-century shelf, the spine bouncing on her little toe. She is in pain. So are her authors: Margaret, Louisa, Emily, Miss Forten of Philadelphia and Sea Island. There are other mothers hovering on other shelves: Red Rosa Luxemburg, Mother Doris Lessing, Mother Anaïs Nin.

Beatrix is notating and recording, for they are each other's mothers and daughters. Why didn't Turgenev write *Mothers and Daughters* rather than *Fathers and Sons*? Why didn't D. H. Lawrence write *Daughters and Lovers* instead of *Sons and Lovers*?

## Looking for Mothers (1): Mother Emily

What did Beatrix learn from her mother Emily? She learned valuable mathematical data. In fifty-six years of life

Emily wrote 1,775 poems. During her lifetime, she published seven. That means Emily had 1,768 unpublished poems. That also means that if Emily wrote poetry every year of her life from birth on, she would have written thirty-one and some poems each year. Since that premise is illogical, Emily probably started writing at eighteen or nineteen, and then she would have written about forty-eight poems a year. That means she would have written a poem every week in the year but four, or a little less than one-seventh of a poem a day.

"Mother, I'm giving birth to a poetess."
"Tell her there's no such thing."

From her Mother Emily, Beatrix learns to work and to sustain. But from fluttery, stuttery Emily, Beatrix has to learn not to flutter and to let her youngest brother do the stuttering. Emily fluttered to her correspondents. She made her diminutive self more diminutive, her own meaning demeaning.

Two of Mother Emily's loves were Reverends, who maintained their reverential distance. Each she probably met once. Reverend Charles Wadsworth she addressed, in her correspondence, as "Master," and she was his "Daisy." Reverend Thomas Wentworth Higginson she called "Preceptor," and she was "Your Scholar," "Your Gnome."

LOOKING FOR MOTHERS (1A): MOTHER EMILY
IS ASKED QUESTIONS. SHE ANSWERS ELUSIVELY

Mother Emily's voice, through the scrawly handwriting, is either throaty or babyish. Perhaps she lisps. Consciously.

Thomas Wentworth Higginson is puzzling over a letter with handwriting like fossil bird tracks, with little punctuation, mostly dashes. The letter is unsigned, but, on a separate card, within a smaller envelope, signed in pencil, is the signature—"Emily Dickinson from Amherst."

Mr. Higginson finds therein four poems and a letter.

Mother Emily's voice is throaty, unsure—carefully unsure—with this correct gentleman:

Mother Emily: "Mr. Higginson—Are you too deeply

occupied to say if my verse is alive?'' (Emily Dickinson, *Selected Poems and Letters of Emily Dickinson*, ed. Robert N. Linscott, Doubleday, 1959, p. 5.)

Mrs. Higginson is sitting in a wheelchair where she sat herself some years ago in order not to have to move anywhere. Reverend Higginson tells Mary Higginson of the letter, this curious letter with the fossil bird tracks, little punctuation but dashes, unsigned with the enclosed, penciled card.

"Well, well," says Mary Higginson.

Mother Emily: "The mind is so near itself it cannot see distinctly, . . ." (*Poems and Letters*, p. 5.)

Reverend Higginson thinks that is very sensible.

"Humph!" says Mary Higginson.

Mother Emily (plaintively): "And I have none to ask." (*Poems and Letters*, p. 5.)

Reverend Higginson thinks that is touching.

"Mother, I'm pregnant with a baby girl and she's writing a letter."

"What is she writing?"

"She is begging for advice but she is being modest, maidenly, and retreating."

"Then she is manipulating her correspondent."

Mother Emily: "I inclose my name, asking you, if you please, sir, to tell me what is true." (*Poems and Letters*, p. 5.)

Mr. Higginson is flattered to be called upon for the truth. He immediately replies with the truth. He receives another letter. Mary Higginson, adjusting her lap robe, is incurious.

Reverend Higginson informs Mary (he informs her of everything always and asks her advice on every occasion, and he immediately marries someone else named Mary when she dies) that he really knows nothing about Miss Dickinson, but he knows everything about Miss Dickinson.

"Nonsense!" says Mary Higginson.

Reverend Higginson tells Mary that he does not know why Emily refuses to leave her house in Amherst, why she refuses even to try to publish, why she will not visit him.

"Perhaps she is wise," says Mary.

But, says Reverend Higginson, he has questioned Miss Dickinson and knows every aspect of her life.

Reverend Higginson: "I asked her what she looked like."

Mother Emily: "I had no portrait now, but am small, like the wren; and my hair is bold, like the chestnut bur; and my eyes, like sherry in the glass, that the guest leaves. Would this do just as well?" (*Poems and Letters*, p. 9.)

"Mother, I'm pregnant with a b.g. and she is asked for her portrait."

"What does she send?"

"A poetical, verbal description."

"Then she is indescribably homely."

Mother Emily: "You asked how old I was." As old as my verse.

"Mother, I'm pregnant with a baby girl and she's asked how old she is."

"What does she reply?"

"She's a poet, as old as her verse."

"Then she's not young."

Emily is thirty-two.

Reverend Higginson: "What did she read?"

Mother Emily: "You inquire my books . . . I went to school, but in your manner of the phrase had no education." (*Poems and Letters*, p. 7.)

"Mother, I'm pregnant with a baby girl and she's been asked about her education."

"What does she reply?"

"That she had none."

"Then she is educated."

Emily went to Amherst Acacemy, for two years and spent an additional year at Mount Holyoke Female Seminary.

Reverend Higginson: "Who were her companions?"

Mother Emily: "You ask of my companions. Hills, sir

and the sundown, and a dog, large as myself, that my father
bought me. They are better than beings because they know,
but do not tell." (*Poems and Letters*, p. 7.)

"Mother, I'm p. with a b.g. and she's asked about her
companions."
"What does she reply?"
"Nature and animals are her companions."
"Then she has many male friends and goes to parties."

The house was full of young men, music, and small cele-
brations.
Reverend Higginson: "I asked about her family."
Mother Emily: "I have a brother and sister; my mother
does not care for thought, and father, too busy with his briefs
to notice what we do." (*Poems and Letters*, p. 7.)

"Mother, I'm p. with a b.g. and she's asked about her
family."
"What does she reply?"
"That they are all distant from her and her father does not
notice her."
"Then she is close to her family, attended by her sister and
her brother and dominated by her father."
Reverend Higginson: "I gently probed her sense of
worth."
Mother Emily: "I could not weigh myself, myself. My
size felt small to me." (*Poems and Letters*, p. 8.)

"Mother, I'm p. with a b.g. and she's asked her worth."
"What does she reply?"
"That she's of little worth."
"That's because her correspondent is afraid of worthy
women."
"No, mother, he loves worthy women. He has many
friends amongst them."
"Then they must not attain greater worth than he."

Reverend Higginson: "I asked what made her write her
poetry."

71

Mother Emily: "Because I am afraid. . . .Will you be my preceptor, Mr. Higginson?" (*Poems and Letters*, pp. 7, 9.)

"Mother, I'm p. with a b.g. and she's asked why she writes poetry."

"What does she reply?"

"She says that she writes because she's afraid, and will her correspondent teach her?"

"That means she's written many poems and needs no instruction."

When Mother Emily had written this letter to her preceptor, she had penned more than one poem. In 1858 she wrote fifty-two poems, copied them over in ink, and sewed them into booklets. By the year of her letter to Reverend Higginson, 1862, she had written another 356 poems.

Mary Higginson is wheeling angrily, round and round in her chair. Her husband is dozing, sitting upright.

"Why do the insane always cling to you?" she, a dervish, asks. "Why are you the rock moss adheres to? Why are you the wall climbers entwine? Why are you the last stop, end of the line?"

She peers into the reverend's face. He is smiling faintly.

"Is he dreaming of her?" she brakes her chair. "What's happened to reality? What's happened to his sense of duty, my God, his Christian duty?"

A woman, a wild, uncorrectable, unmet woman is the danger to Christianity and to duty, while Mary, Virgin Mary, tart-tongued and contrary, is confined and refined and no threat at all.

Beatrix, choose carefully, for we can pick and choose not only our mothers but among their qualities!

Beatrix will forget this after Harold leaves. She will speak to men in her high, nervous Mother Emily voice. She has been trained to speak in this fashion. Her normally rich, low voice will be used for friends from the Eugene V. Debs Socialist Study Group, for Bert of the pockmarks, Norm of the duck waddle, Charles in the elevator. She will ask all other men, helplessly, to help her with math or to help her hang something on the wall or to help her fix her plumbing.

72

Poor Beatrix, even a woman's plumbing isn't so hard to fix.

Mother Emily, what else have you to teach Beatrix? Obliqueness and crispness. Parallel pain.

Mother Emily: "I never lost as much but twice,/And that was in the sod." (Thomas H. Johnson, ed., *The Poems of Emily Dickinson*, Harvard University Press, 1955, I:38.)

Beatrix too has a double loss, Harold and Lena, burying the memory of the former, keeping alive that of the latter.

Mother Emily: "To fight aloud is very brave—/But *gallanter*, I know/Who charge within the bosom/The Cavalry of Wo—" (*Poems of Emily Dickinson*, I:90.)

Beatrix can transcend this with the best of the Transcendentalists. Her own hardships become her book, *The Pioneers*. She will handle disappointment and bravely throw the ingredients of *Cooking Without Fear* into the garbage can, into the wastebasket of wasted effort. She will be brave enough to deal with *Unafraid Women*.

Beatrix will have to learn, beyond Emily's tutelage, how not to please.She will have to try to prop herself up on her elbows and not sag. She will have to learn how not to greet or to retreat. But not yet. She may never learn all that.

With Mother Emily, Beatrix learns physical passion. Not from Harold when she was that child bride.

"Please *me,* honey," he would say. "Please me." Groaning. "Please. Oooh. Please."

Little Beatrix Bride was not content but did not know enough to be displeased or to ask Harold for pleasure.

How did Mother Emily know pleasure?

Mother Emily: "Come slowly—Eden!" (How did she know the pleasure of slow entrance?) "Lips unused to Thee—/Bashful—sip thy Jessamines—/As the fainting Bee—/Reaching late his flower,/Round her chamber hums—/Counts his nectars—Enters—/And is lost in Balms." (*Poems of Emily Dickinson*, I:148.)

Only one way Mother Emily could have known all that.

"Mother, I'm pregnant with a baby girl and she's masturbating."

"Good. It's the only pleasure she'll know."

73

What exactly did Beatrix miss the most? Meeting Harold after class under the Big Clock? Whispering with him between the rooms of her parents and that of her younger brothers? Or did she miss the stopper in her cork, the stopping of the draft in the chimney? It is as if all orifices remained open. Certainly her eyes took years to close, years to sleep, for she was vigilant against villainy long after the villain had departed.

## Looking for Mothers (2): Mother Margaret

"Mother, I am pregnant with a baby girl."
"Have only a pretty girl. Don't have an ugly daughter."

Beatrix, undress. Look into the mirror. It is not obscene to be privately seen.

What do you like? Can't you say even to yourself? Then, what do you hate about your appearance?

Hair. All that hair, I hate. Hair on upper lip—faintly there—long stiff hairs on chin, wild hair on my head, even when shaped, quickly becomes shapeless, waves, curls, no hairline, just intruding tendrils. Mediterranean hair. Hate my pube hair, bushy, curly forest—primeval forest. People look at the top of my head and know what's down below. They don't know that I have a white hair in the patch.

My accordion-pleated naval I hate, my navel accordion pleated because of Lena. Stretch marks on the sides of my hips—one on each hip—like white stripes down uniforms—I hate those—those are from Lena.

Do you hate Lena?

Oh, no. That's now allowed!

Turn around.

I hate the back, my hairy anus, even that! My big hips. My stomach muscles have sagged. There is that protrusion under the accordion navel, over the black pube.

My breasts I hate—too small, nipples too large. The nipple on the r.s. larger than the nipple on the l.s. Beauty marks on the breasts, especially on the r.s., not so beautiful. Blue veins around the brown nipples; one stiff black hair on the nipple of the r.s.

Thighs, hate thighs. Loose. I'll be my mother again. Never will I be able to wear a bikini or a topless, or sun in Nice. Never can I wear hip huggers, for my hips cannot easily be hugged. Rubbing thighs. Black-and-blue mark on the back of my r. leg.

Legs too full, shoulders too wide, neck too long. Eyes are becoming smaller, elbows wrinkled.

Well, now, is there anything you *don't* hate?

I *don't* hate my shoulders, my full mouth, my winged brows, my dimpled knees, my rather aristocratic, narrow feet, my graduated toes.

My shoulders are Joan Crawford-wide. My curly hair is Jane Russell's *Outlaw*-ish hair. My mouth is good. My arms are long and no longer skinny. My eyebrows are clean. They never grew back after that frantic high school plucking.

Ah, I see something else I hate. My womb, my womb. I hate my womb.

You mean, you can actually *see* it?

Yes, when I sit down, between the walls of my vagina, like a nestling, like the ugly naked red head of a turkey buzzard, this featherless, blood-red womb protrudes.

Then it's all bad?

No, no. The effect is not bad. My back is not white and soft like Pauline's Betty Grable back. My hair is not gentile-straight like Lois's Romanian hair, my skin is not creamy like Shirley's used to be before she went up into her attic. I am not graceful like Janice in the water. I have freckles on my shoulders. But the effect is of a tall, slender woman.

So, you like it?

No, I hate it.

## LOOKING FOR MOTHERS (2A): MOTHER MARGARET DRESSES

She spends an hour each morning dressing, brushing her long, light hair, putting a single, large, fresh flower into it. She is the eldest child, medium sized, with a proud walk. One thinks that she is tall.

"Mother, I'm pregnant."

"Have an eldest daughter."

"Why?"

"Then you don't need a father, then you don't need a mother."

Margaret's breasts developed early and they press against the bones of corsets and convention, against the soft silk across her bosom.

They are plain women, my Mothers Emily, Margaret, and Louisa May: Emily with her long face and staring eyes; bald Louisa May who lost her rich auburn hair in illness, who lost her teeth, at least in my copy of the encyclopedia; plainest of them, Mother Margaret, whom Ralph Waldo Emerson described: "Her appearance had nothing prepossessing. Her extreme plainness—a trick of incessantly opening and shutting her eyelids, the nasal tone of her voice—all repelled." (Ralph Waldo Emerson, William Henry Channing, James Freeman Clarke, eds., *Memoirs of Margaret Fuller Ossoli*, Phillips, Sampson and Company, 1852, I:202.)

Ugly Emerson, hypochondriac, effeminate Higginson, short, egocentric Mr. James Nathan (known only because he corresponded with Margaret Fuller), undersized, long-nosed Thoreau! A mother can have a homely boy, and he can still be a joy. A mother can have an eccentric son, and he is the center of her heart.

But, says Mother Margaret: "When all things are blossoming, it seems so strange not to blossom too. I hate not to be beautiful, when all around is so." (Mason Wade, *Margaret Fuller, Whetstone of Genius*, Viking Press, 1940, p. 80.)

"Mother, I'm pregnant with a baby girl and she wants information."

"What does she want to know?"

"What does it mean when men say, 'Up against the wall, MF?' "

"It means, Margaret Fuller."

"But why?"

"They're afraid of her."

"Mother, I'm pregnant with a baby girl ard she's not beautiful."

"Then let her be the eldest and the support of her family."

"Mother, I'm pregnant with a baby girl and she wants some information."

"What does she want to know?"

"How can she learn to be independent and strong?"

"Let her always be short of money and the head of her family."

Mothers Louisa May and Margaret were always short of money and heads of their families.

All these Big Mothers write letters. Mother Emily and Mother Margaret do, and they write foolish letters.

The quill slides in the finger. The pen is smooth. The fingertips touch the paper. Then pen is put to the mouth, to Emily's flat chest, to Margaret's full chest. Margaret touches her breastbone. She wishes on it. Mother Emily is thirty-two. Mother Margaret is thirty-five. Each writes to a gentleman, and each calls him her guardian, although that gentleman is the same age or a year younger than Little Ms. Emily and Ms. MF.

They bring themselves to their gentlemen. Little Ms. Emily has all those packets and baskets and tiskets and taskets of poems, but she asks for advice on the writing of poems. Ms. Margaret has brought a whole curriculum vitae with her, but implores Mr. Nathan to protect her.

Why didn't you hear about MF? You were too busy learning about Emerson and Thoreau.

MF has brought work experience with her, hard to come by for a little lady in the 1840s. She has edited *The Dial*. She has been literary editor for Horace Greeley's *Tribune*. She held Conversations for intelligent women in Boston, charging twenty dollars for ten lectures. She traveled westward by covered wagon to Oregon and back and wrote a travel book on her adventures. Needing to research it, she was the first woman allowed into the Harvard Library. She wrote the feminist tract, *Woman in the Nineteenth Century*.

But when little Mr. James Nathan visits her, she forgets her vital curriculum, for her blood stirs with something elemental.

What has Beatrix to learn from Mother MF? That women make double entries, afraid of their heads and too full of heart.

Little Mr. James Nathan is thirty-four. He has gone from Germany to New York. He is a businessman. That is his experience. He is slight and blue-eyed and that is also his experience. He is Jewish, which is quite an experience, both for Mr. Nathan and for Margaret's biographers.

Biographer Mason Wade is impressed that Margaret knew a member of the Jewish species: "One of the many presentiments of Margaret's mystical period was that some day she would know intimately a member of the Jewish race." (Wade, p. 162.) "Intimate." Oh, come off it, masonic Wade.

Mr. Jewish Nathan was "A personification of all the romance of the East." (Wade, p. 163.) He was also, like his fellow Jews, "clever."

Beatrix is jolted into reality. She also "intimately" knew a Jew but he was not the personification of "all the romance of the East." Harold was more the personification of the Jewish northwest section of her city.

Everyone is surprised by Mr. Nathan. Mr. Joseph Jay Deiss (*The Roman Years of Margaret Fuller*, Thomas Y. Crowell, 1969, p. 21) writes: "To her surprise he revealed himself as a Jew."

Mr. Deiss, was it a quick peak? Was he smooth as a doorknob? Top of a mushroom? Did Jewish Nathan unzip before there were zippers, or pull out of his drawers?

Poor Mother MF, this attraction to a Jew was the first step in her downfall, leading to enslavement by Mediterranean types, to pregnancy with or without marriage, and certainly to death by drowning with a certain young Italian and their certain young offspring

LOOKING FOR MOTHERS (2B): MOTHER MARGARET WRITES LETTERS

My Mother, What are you writing? Why are you doing this to me?

Mother Margaret writes to Jewish Nathan: "You must protect me. Are you equal to this?" (Margaret Fuller, *Love Letters of Margaret Fuller*, *1845-1846*, D. Appleton, 1903, Letter X.)

"Mother, I'm giving birth to a baby girl and she must be protected."

"From herself?"

"Yes."

"From him?"

"Yes."

"From them?"

"Yes."

"There is no total protection. There is only submission, conception, contraception."

MF: "I know little about the mystery of life, and far less in myself than in others." (*Love Letters*, XI.)

"Mother, I'm pregnant with a baby girl."

"What does she know?"

"Little about the mysteries of life and far less in herself than in others."

"Then she chooses not to know what other baby girls have chosen not to know."

"What should she do?"

"Choose to know."

Beatrix is crying. She has mottoes from Mother Margaret on her boards: bulletin, sleeping, ironing.

"AS MEN BECOME AWARE THAT FEW MEN HAVE HAD A FAIR CHANCE, THEY ARE INCLINED TO SAY THAT NO WOMEN HAVE HAD A FAIR CHANCE." (Perry Miller, ed., *Margaret Fuller, American Romantic*, Doubleday Anchor, 1963, p. 143.)

"THE FRENCH REVOLUTION AT LEAST CALLED HER 'CITOYENNE' RATHER THAN SUBJECT, SO THAT ALTHOUGH SHE MAY HAVE BEEN GUIL-LOTINED, AT LEAST IT WAS AS A CITIZEN AND NOT

SUBJECT." (Miller, pp. 143-44.)

Writes breast-heaving Mother Margaret: "Lead me not into temptation and deliver me from Evil." (*Love Letters*, VII.)

"Mother, I'm giving birth to a baby girl and she is praying."

"For what is she praying?"

"She is praying not to be led into temptation and to be delivered from evil and presumptuous sin."

"She is praying to be tempted, to be evil and to sin."

Mother Margaret is kissing the scented envelope before she sends it off: "Are you my guardian to domesticate me in the body and attach it more firmly to the earth? . . . Choose for me a good soil and a sunny place, that may be a green shelter to the weary and bear fruit." (*Love Letters*, IX.)

"Mother, I'm giving birth to a baby girl."

"What does she want from life?"

"To be as the good soil, a shelter, and to bear fruit."

"Then she wants nothing from life."

Only the year before, my Mother Margaret wrote that, instead of frailty, thy name is woman, "FRAILTY, THY NAME IS MAN." (Miller, p. 138.)

Only the year before, my Mother Margaret wrote: "KNOW THAT THERE EXISTS IN THE MINDS OF MEN A TONE OF FEELING TOWARD WOMAN AS TOWARD SLAVES." (Miller, p. 147.)

Beatrix ponders on what to do when one's mother fails her daughter, returns her favorite dress to the shop, laughs at the peanut shells in her daughter's wild hair? Still, that daughter has slept on her mother's breast on long rides.

My Mother Margaret writes to Mr. Nathan (né James Gotendorf): "I cannot do other than love and most deeply trust you, and will drink the bitter part of the cup with patience." (*Love Letters*, X.)

"Mama, I'm giving birth to a baby girl."

"What is she?"

"Patient."

"Then leave her in the hospital."

My Mother Margaret, as all women, would forget her accomplishments and her past. She must be nothing before a lover. She has forgotten her pleas for the Indians, for prisoners, for the rights of women. Standing eye level to Mr. Nathan, she has no rights. Therefore, she must bow. "I feel today as if we might bury this ugly dwarf-changeling of the past, and hide its grave with flowers." (*Love Letters*, X.)

"Mama, I'm pregnant with a baby girl."

"What does she want to do?"

"Hide her past."

"And then?"

"Bury the future."

My Mother Margaret is religious.

"Mother, I'm pregnant with a baby girl and she's religious."

"Has she been a minister, a priest, a monk, a rabbi?"

"No."

"Is she at the pulpit? Does she open the Holy Ark? Does she marry and bury others? Does she minister final unction? Absolution? Does she wear a tallith and make a minion? Does she carry the Torah around the synagogue? Does she hold the chalice of holy wine for the congregation? Does she sit on the listening side of confession?"

"No."

"Then she's not religious. She's stupid."

And yet my Mother Margaret has written: "Women are . . . the easy victims both of priestcraft and self-delusion; but this would not be, if the intellect was developed in proportion to other powers." (Miller, p. 169.)

One day my poor vain Mother Margaret received a poem from "S." She copies this poem out in a fair hand to make Mr. Nathan jealous and to show him how others have addressed her. No poet, Mr. Nathan instead gifted her with a puppy.

Friend "S" wrote to my Mother Margaret in 1844: "Thou are the Wind, the Wanderer of the Air,/The Searcher of the Earth." (*Love Letters*, XII.)

"Mother, I'm pregnant with a baby girl."

"What do they call her?"

"Wind, the Wanderer of the Air,/The Searcher of the Earth."

"Then she has no name and they will forget her."

As Beatrix reads these letters she is afraid. She thinks of her affairs, humiliations she submitted to, forgiveness she always requested, the effort to give him pleasure, his withdrawing, Bea left quivering.

Mother Margaret writes to the puppy-giver, "I shall expect you to-morrow, but I wish it were to-day. Twenty-four hours are a great many." (*Love Letters*, XIII.)

"Mama, I'm pregnant with a baby girl and she's waiting."

"For what?"

"For him to come."

"Then tell her not to be born."

"She's waiting for them to come."

"Then tell her not to be born."

"She's waiting to come."

"How many times?"

"Mother, I'm pregnant with a baby girl and she's coming."

"Ah, the little beauty. How many times?"

"Many times. She wants to know who else is coming."

"Tell her Mother Margaret is coming, Mother Louisa is coming, Mother Emily is coming, Mother Rosa is coming, Mother Doris is coming, Mother Charlotte . . . ."

"Then she has many friends."

Mother Margaret: "My feeling with you was so delightful. It was a feeling of childhood." (*Love Letters*, XV.)

"Mama, I'm pregnant with a baby girl."

"How does she feel?"

"Childish."

"Tell her not to, for there are those who would have her act as an adult until she becomes one, and then make her regress."

Beatrix never tacked up photographs of men after Harold had ripped down Gene Kelly and Gregory Peck from her closet door. (Eugene V. Debs fell off unaided.) Now Beatrix is tacking up Emily. Emily's hair is parted in the middle, covering conches of ears so that they hear no stirring of tendrils, no waves of wavy hair.

Beatrix has Olivettied two portraits of Margaret Fuller. Portrait One: A book opened in her lap, perhaps her own book of western travels. Her large eyes abstracted, hair more decorative than Emily's. Her dress has a dark ribbon and white collar under her full neck. White cuffs balloon from her wrists. Portrait Two: Similar pose to Portrait One, but Margaret is in Rome and the journey has tired her. Her hands are held in maidenly fashion in her lap, except that she is no maiden. A shawl warms her in the chill Roman winter. Her breasts are fuller, her neckline lower. What has her face given up from Portrait One?—innocence, romanticism. With experience in Portrait Two comes a compressing of the lips, a thinning of that full face, eyes less dreamy, waist expanded. She has traveled to where she would go in Portrait One. She will never be able to return from experience.

Why does Bea treasure these unattractive portraits of unattractive women? Why is Mary Ann Evans there or Rosa Luxemburg, Rosa wearing a great bird in her hat at a Socialist rally? She has a photograph of Doris Lessing, with Mother Doris's gray hairs unplucked, thicker than the black, all tucked into a bun. She has a portrait of Mother Anaïs Nin talking animatedly to women students. Why does Bea frame these photographs, these engraving copies from paintings? Because the women are not looking at or thinking about men.

Beatrix is tempted to cheat. There are many heroes: soldiers, governors, statesmen, sportsmen, movie men, stablemen. Their portraits are lovelier than Margaret's. Even the heroes and the lover of Margaret are lovelier than Margaret. Bea would tack up Margaret's two Giuseppes and one Giovanni, but she must resist. Once she surrounds herself with photographs of men, she will begin looking at the shiny surface. She will run her finger over the face. She will bend to kiss it. Then she will have to run out of her house looking for a hero.

Giuseppe Mazzini, founder of the Roman Republic, is looking at Beatrix. He has a wide-browed face, a straight nose, large dark eyes. Romantic Giuseppe Garibaldi, commander in chief of the Roman forces, is standing in red cape and plumed hat. And Giovanni, a decade younger than Margaret, this Marchese Giovanni Ossoli, is sitting worriedly. He has short dark hair, a moustache, a worried brow. He is worried about being disinherited while he is creating a new heir. He is Margaret's lover.

Resist handsome images. Resist creating heroes. Resist doing their TV makeup, hand tinting their photographs, blackening their hair, whitening their reputations. This is no task for women. Let men seat themselves at the mirrors of their dressing tables. Let them switch on the thousand watts around the mirror to see Before and create After.

Mother Margaret, you have helped Beatrix. On Bea's refrigerator, next to the wheat germ recipe are MF's words that women will attain "REAL HEALTH AND VIGOR, WHICH NEED NO AID FROM ROUGE OR CANDLELIGHT TO BRAVE THE LIGHT OF THE WORLD." (Wade, p. 70.) Natural women will appear among unnatural men.

But who is Mother Margaret? She is truth to women. She is lies to men. What has she said to Beatrix? "I believe that at present women are the best helpers of one another." (Miller, p. 186.) And she knows sadly that: "Now there is no woman, only an overgrown child." (Miller, p. 188.)

And Bea meets the overgrown child, Childe Margaret, when she reads her love letters. We must learn how to read the love letters that women write. We must learn that they are lies.

84

Mother Margaret: "I like to be quite still and have you the actor and the voice. . . . You have life enough for both . . . I wish . . . to see you now and borrow courage from your eyes." (*Love Letters*, XVII.)

"Mother, I'm giving birth to a baby girl."
"Ah, soon she will have the gift of life."
"Oh no. He will have life enough for both of them."
"Soon she will have speech."
"Oh no. He will speak for the both of them."
"Soon she will be independent."
"Oh no. She wants to borrow."
"Borrow what?"
"Borrow courage."

ACH! thinks Beatrix. What is happening to Margaret's vision?

"Mother, I'm pregnant with a baby girl and she is sighted."
"What can she see?"
"The boy playing in the corner vacant lot, the grocer boy, the newspaper boy, the delivery boy, the class president—a boy, the head of the debating team—a boy, the head of the speaker's bureau—a boy . . ."
"Then she's a blind girl."

Beatrix is holding a man in her arms. He is weeping. He has given a sermon and the audience was inattentive. He spoke to his class and they shuffled their feet. He called to a passing bus and the driver drove on. Bea is stroking his head. His teeth are uneven, perhaps there is more than one set of them in his mouth. She asks him to open his mouth. The teeth are crooked and brown. There is only one set. They are, although tall, crooked and brown, his baby teeth. She feels motherly toward her love.

So does Mother Margaret: "I thought of you with that foolish tenderness women must have towards men that really confide in them. It makes us feel like mothers." (*Love Letters*, XIX.)

85

"Mother, I'm giving birth to a baby girl."

"What does she want to do with her life?"

"Be a mother."

"And then what?"

"A grandmother."

"No more?"

"A great-grandmother."

"And what else?"

"Nothing else."

How many cradles did Beatrix rock? Lena's, of course. But larger ones.

"I can't sleep!" cried the Pimpled Poet.

They were in a motel. She put a quarter into the vibrator and rocked the Pimpled Poet.

"My poems were rejected!" he sobbed.

The more he cried, the tighter she held him. He drank all of her liquids. Her lips became parched, her nipples sore, her womb juiceless. Still he drank, the drunkard.

Mother Margaret has a request: "Your heart, your precious heart (I am determined to be absolutely frank), that I did long for." (*Love Letters*, XIX.)

"Mother, I'm pregnant with a baby girl."

"What does she long for?"

"His heart."

"What will she do with it?"

"She will tear it apart and swallow it in slippery chunks the size of oysters."

Beatrix is walking by streetlight. There is a long shadow ahead of her. She was walking on the head of the shadow. Once it walked beside her but she had hurt it, and now she carefully paces behind. Why doesn't she hop on a bus and go home? The buses have stopped running. Why doesn't she call a cab? She never carries extra cash. The boy must carry the money. The girl must be spent on. How long does she walk? About two hours. Ah, then they are walking in the direction of her home? No, away from it. What will she do? She will walk until she collapses. What will the shadow do? Shadows never tire. They only shorten and lengthen.

Perhaps Mr. Nathan cannot take such passionate letters. She writes but her elbow is at his windpipe.

"Touch," says her cleavage. "Touch," say the parted lips. "Touch," say her restless hands in her lap.

Mr. Nathan touches.

"Don't touch!" says Mother Margaret.

She is mortified. Mr. Nathan, né Gotendorf, thinks she is "a dame."

"Mother, I'm pregnant with a baby girl."
"Whom does she love?"
"A Jew."
"Tell it to change its name."

Beatrix has loved Jews and non-Jews, capped and decapped. They both cause pain and discomfort.

Mother Margaret: "My Beloved Friend . . . Saturday, 19th April, 1845 . . . Pain is very keen with me. I cannot help fearing it. . . .Yet . . . I submit and say: when and how much Thou wilt." (*Love Letters*, XX.)

"Mother, I'm pregnant with a baby girl."
"What is she feeling?"
"Pain."
"That's good preparation."

Once Beatrix loved a musician. He entreated her to attend all of his performances. He questioned her about them afterward. He begged her to attend while he practiced. He asked her preferences as to his techniques, the passage played this way or another. He asked her to listen to the performances of rival musicians and to compare them to his. It took up all of her time. Beatrix was very flattered.

Mother Margaret: "I keep your guitar by this window; if only I could play upon it." (*Love Letters*, XXI.)

"Mother, I'm pregnant with a baby girl."
"What does she want to play?"
"She wants to play upon his guitar."
"As he will play upon her organ."

Once Beatrix loved a psychiatrist. He took his temperature every day: "Now I am feeling a trifle sad. Now I am feeling rather glad. I am elated. I have slipped to plateau. I am at rejection." It took all of Bea's time. She was very flattered.

"Mama, I'm giving birth to a baby girl."
"Is she happy?"
"As happy as he."
"Then she feels nothing."

Once Beatrix loved a doctor. He told her all about herself: when her eyes were dilated and menstruation was coming, when her cheeks were flushed and a cold was coming, when her breath quickened and she was coming. He talked constantly. It took up all of Bea's time. She was very flattered.

"Mother, I'm giving birth to a baby girl, and I've chosen the obstetrician."
"Who is he?"
"Mother, the obstetrician has told me of a good pediatrician."
"What's his name?"
"The pediatrician has chosen a good gynecologist for my vaginal infection."
"I'm glad to hear of him."
"For my postpartum blues they've picked a good psychiatrist."
"His name?"
"In case anything goes wrong, they've chosen a mortician."
"Whose firm?"
"The Kaufman Brothers. And the rabbi came to see me, and the president of the synagogue."
"Who are those men?"
"They are all insurance salesmen."

Once Beatrix entered a literary contest. It was while she was nursing Lena and doing graduate work. She needed the money. She had many uses for it: a fan for her airless bedroom, dishes to replace her cracked ones, driving lessons, baby-sitting money. Her story was very good. Her friend, the Pimpled Poet, was also entering the contest. He had many uses for the money: skin treatment, insurance for his car, a necessary trip to inspire more poetry. Which would he choose? Beatrix asked him. He looked at her. "Skin treatment?" he questioned. He had chosen correctly. Beatrix did not enter the writing contest. They both lost.

One day Beatrix was weary. She had to rest her head on someone's shoulder. She had no telephone then because she was afraid of telephone curses. She went to a phone booth outside of a supermarket. All the shoppers parking saw her. All the shoppers pushing their carts through the doors saw her. She phoned the Pimpled Poet, the Shadow, the Musician, the Doctor, the Psychiatrist, the Preacher and told them she was weary and had to rest her head on someone's shoulder. They were all otherwise occupied that evening.

Mother Margaret: "My head is heavy, let me lean it on your shoulder, and you divine these deep things." (*Love Letters*, XXII.)


"Mama, I'm pregnant with a baby girl and she's leaning on her lover's shoulder."

"Why?"

"Because only he can divine deep things."

"Then either she is shallow or he's a carp."


Mother Margaret: "Said Beethoven . . . 'there is the god-like in man!' There is also the angel-like in woman." (*Love Letters*, XXIV.)


"Mama, I'm pregnant with a baby angel."

"Good. That puts her one down from God."


Mother Margaret: "I wish much I were strong, that I might be a fit companion for you." (*Love Letters*, XXVI.)


"Mother, I'm pregnant with a baby girl."

"What does she want to be?"

"A companion."

Beatrix was audience to her musician friend, but she never applauded loudly enough. She was nurse to her doctor friend, but she did not seem to sense his needs. She was patient with her psychiatrist friend, but he had more adoring patients. She listened to readings by her poet friend, but someone else taped him. She was congregation to her minister friend, but he, by his calling, belonged to the world. She trailed her shadowy friend, but in total darkness he disappeared. She reflected each one.

Mother Margaret: "I open my thoughts to the loved soul who has brought me so much sunlight . . . I know you ask nothing of your moon except a pure reflection in a serene sky." (*Love Letters*, XXVII.)


"Mother, I'm giving birth to a baby girl."
"What does she want to be?"
"A moon, a reflecting moon."
"Not a sun?"
"No, that's for a baby son."


"Beatrix, you have a baby daughter."
Beatrix stuck out a black tongue and mourned. She had had a daughter by twilight. Her doctor wanted no trouble from her.

At his desk, Beatrix had explained:
"I want to help out in this birth."
"Certainly."
"I don't want to be overmedicated. I want to be aware of what's happening. I want to participate."
"Certainly, certainly, certainly."

He, therefore, prescribed twilight so that she would be overmedicated, not aware of what was happening, not help out or participate. It was, after all, his delivery.

"But I asked for other medication!" cried Beatrix.
"Did you?" Surprised. "I thought you were someone else."

Put their feet in the stirrups, all the riders look alike.

In the bed with Beatrix lay another, a profane, screaming, nightmarish woman, a dybbuk who entered Beatrix, scratched her face, bit through her tongue until it blackened with dried blood.

Lena was born in twilight, her hair wet and matted, her head misshapen from the long hours of travail.

When Lena was born in twilight, Beatrix put away the following:

1. *Boxing gloves*. No blue rubber boxing gloves tied to carriage. Pink rattle tied to carriage. No fighting, no punching, rather taming. Soft leather fitted gloves later on, garden gloves in middle age. No feel of gymnasium. No ropes. No coming fighting from a corner. The idea is to corner.

2. *Balls*. No football, soccer, volley. Later, men will accuse Lena of trying to steal their balls, of shifting their goals, foul play, netting them—when all they wanted was to put balls over the goalposts, over the nets, into the basket, into the bleachers. All they wanted was her to cheer for their tennis in summer, football in fall, ice hockey in winter, baseball in spring.

3. *Trains, schooners, buses*. Lena would not be a railroad woman. She will not aspire to Lionel trains, to skipper a schooner, unleash a Greyhound. By land, sea, or air, she will have to be taken there.

4. *Microphone*. Lena will never announce, denounce, pronounce, renounce. She will not announce news, denounce dictators, issue pronouncements, renounce a throne to marry a commoner.

5. *Plumber's snake, tool chest, handsaw, tire wrench, jack*. Lena can use the plunger, even the screwdriver sparingly. She can use the small silver soldering iron to make cuff links for her love. When she gets a flat tire, she can smile at passing cars on the interstate highway until one stops and a brawny, handsome stranger emerges, walking slowly toward Lena to fix her flat.

6. *Superman pajamas*. No quick changing for Lena, rather careful training to match cosmetics with garments, phosphorescence for evening, delicacy for morn. No bursts of energy, no walking through walls. Lena's greatest fear was to be stuck against a wall as wallflower. No bullet-proof chest. Lena's chest hurt constantly from one reproof or another.

91

7. *Maps*. Why should she find her way? Let her stay close to home.

When Beatrix bore Lena in twilight, Beatrix's parents came at visiting hours. Harold had gone and was not heard from. Husband? asked the registrar. Beatrix had hesitated. The nurses tittered. Girls know you can't give birth without a husband. Lena later found that out and went looking to complete the form.

When Lena was borne in twilight, Beatrix's parents bought Beatrix the housecoat and perfume from the Gift Shoppe downstairs. They bought the layette and sent her flowers with Best Wishes.

When Beatrix, herself, was borne at twilight, her mother cried that she was no male heir, that the heir, born July 5 in the Obstetrician's Book, had gone to the Undertakers. Beatrix was the replacement. She would undertake to replace the male heir.

Beatrix's grandfather mourned his wife, Lena Gurnev.

"Name her Lena," he told Beatrix's mother and father. "Let her replace her grandmother."

But Beatrix's father also had a replacement, his late father Benjamin. Beatrix replaced a grandfather and a dead baby brother. Beatrix became a replacement for the males in her family.

When Beatrix's baby was born in twilight, Beatrix's mother had put Harold's clothes and books into the garage to mold.

"Don't name her after a man," said Beatrix's mother.

Beatrix's baby became her own great-grandmother, aged at birth, gestures feeble, her cry tinny, a dribbler, needing nursing and old wives' tales. When Lena was older, her skin smooth, head shapen, hair flowing and not matted, a shapely woman, then she became a baby.

"Mother, I'm pregnant with a baby girl."

"Of what religion?"

"Bahai."

"What?"

"Mormon."

"What?"

"Protestant."
"What?"
"Buddhist."
"What?"
"Muslim."
"What?"
"Parsi or Hindu."
"What?"
"Catholic."
"What?"
"Jewish."
"At last!"

Among the things that Beatrix gave away when Lena was born at twilight was the circumcision board. She was to be held in no Elijah's Chair by no godfather. She would not be fed whiskey and the tip of her uncovered. She would not have to sob as she was admitted to the race. No one would sign her Circumcision Book as witness. When Lena was born her genitals went unsnipped, unadmitted, unwitnessed. No one cheered her and she sucked no cloth dipped in schnapps to pacify her.

Mother Margaret is not feeling well. She writes to Mr. Nathan dolefully: "I have been very ill; last night the pain in my neck became so violent, that I could not lie still. . . .I went crying into town this morning, and nerves all ajar and the pain worse . . . it was a sort of *tic douloureux.*" (*Love Letters*, XXVII.) Why couldn't Mr. Nathan still that *tic*? Warm it, hold it, silence it?

"Mother, I'm pregnant with a baby girl."
"How does she feel?"
"She has a migraine."
"So will she always."

Later Mother Margaret will chronicle the Roman revolution, though that chronicle be washed ashore at Fire Island as Mother Margaret is washed ashore, along with her marchese and her still warm sonny. Mother Margaret's most important book, from primary sources, is never found, although friend Thoreau searched the beaches. He only found the still-warm body of the son.

There is a stone at Fire Island commemorating Mother Margaret. There is a stone in Beatrix's heart. She is an orphan.

Never mind the other letters. Do not learn your alphabet, women. Do not pen your letters.

MF: "Monday evening, 19th May. . . . You have so much more energy and spirit for the fight! I must try not to throw down the poor little silk glove again in defiance of the steel gauntlet." (*Love Letters*, XXX.)

"Mother, I'm pregnant with a baby girl."
"Is she ready for the fight?"
"She accepts no challenges."

From Mother Margaret, Beatrix learns to accept challenge. Never mind that Mother Margaret writes, Friday evening, May 23, about her letters: "Perhaps you had better destroy them . . . as they are so intimately personal." (*Love Letters*, XXXII.)

"Mother, I'm pregnant with a baby girl."
"How does she occupy herself?"
"Writing intimate love letters."
"He will never destroy them but will ask her to buy them back."

Which is why one must not "know intimately a member of the Jewish race."

Or a Pimpled Poet. Beatrix wrote long letters to the poet. He wrote couplets and quatrains in reply. Later she found her letters incorporated into poems and stories. One of his stories bore her name as a character and described her lovemaking habits. She did not object. She was flattered.

Above Bea's typewriter, against the built-in bookcase, Bea has tacked, from her Mother Margaret: "LET ME USE,

THEN, THE SLOW PEN.'' Mother Margaret, too, is a slow writer. Bea knows that it is all right to take care and pains with a book. It's her inheritance.

Looking for Mothers (3): Mother Louisa

"Mother, my baby girl's father is a writer."
"Then she must be a book so he will read her."
"My baby girl's father is a dreamer."
"Then he has stolen away with her dreams."
"My baby girl's father is a wanderer."
"Then she will stay close to home."
"My baby girl's father is a spendthrift."
"That's all right. She will pay the bills."

What has Beatrix to learn from Mother Louisa? She studies a title page. Nineteen books by Louisa. And Beatrix is struggling with her third.

Beatrix is critical, as one must be with one's mother. The title page is deceptive, full of gaiety and romance. That is the fiction of Louisa's life. There is little gaiety to writing nineteen novels, to writing one's self to death. Mother Lousia's books are bouquets, *Under the Lilacs, Flower Fables, Garlands for Girls, Rose in Bloom*, yet no one threw, bought, or brought flowers to her. She does not escape to the circus, as in *Under the Lilacs*. Mother Louisa's escape, at the age of thirty, occurs when she joins the circus of the Civil War as a hospital nurse. She then escapes from the hospital and returns home with typhoid pneumonia. She has been gone six weeks.

"Mother, I'm pregnant with a baby girl and she's going into the world."
"I'll give her six weeks. That'll show her the world."

They all make an escape, one way or other, in their thirties, all those Big Mothers. Mother Emily, out of her back door, inside of an envelope inside of another envelope. Mother

Margaret abroad. Mother Louisa to Washington, D.C., Mother Charlotte to Sea Island in her late twenties, to marriage at forty.

"Mother, I'm pregnant with a baby girl and she wants to make her mark in the world."
"Tell her to be thirty and a spinster."

When did Louisa start becoming happy? At twelve, for at twelve Louisa writes in the diary that she kept in Concord: "Life is pleasanter than it used to be, and I don't care about dying anymore. . . .I had a pleasant time with my mind, for it was happy." (Ednah D. Cheney, ed., *Louisa May Alcott: Her Life, Letters, and Journals*, The Abbotsford Publishing Company, 1966, p. 40.)

"Mother, I'm pregnant with a baby girl and she's happy."
"How do you know?"
"She doesn't think about dying anymore."

Also at twelve, Lena went to an Abraham Lincoln costume and birthday party. Lena went as Ann Rutledge. She had uncovered her mother's white wedding dress. She found a white plastic flower. The children said Lena lay on the floor through the whole party, not speaking, eyes closed, holding the stiff flower.

Like Mothers Emily and Margaret, Louisa May is not beautiful. It helps Beatrix to look into her full-length bathroom mirror. Mother Louisa is six feet tall and ungainly.

"Mother, I'm pregnant with a baby girl and she's six feet tall."
"Then let her grow four feet of chestnut hair."

Which Louisa did and which she later lost to fever—all four feet of it.

Despite all of those books for little women and old-fashioned girls, despite garlands for the girls and *Lulu's Library*, did Louisa May like girls? No. Girls could not run races, jump from roofs, or be six feet tall.

Mother Louisa: "I have a fellow feeling for lads and always owed Fate a grudge because I wasn't a lord of creation instead of a lady." (Louisa May Alcott, *Hospital Sketches*, Sagamore Press, 1957, p. 15.)

"Mother, I'm pregnant with a baby girl and she has a fellow feeling for the lads."

"She can't. She's not a fellow."

Did Lena want to be a laddie instead of a lady? Beatrix could not know. She had, by bearing Lena in twilight, eliminated names. Lena could not be (unless appended to):

 Aaronson, Adamson, or Airman
 Bronson or Berman
 Clarkson
 Donaldson
 Edelson or Earlman
 Fegelson or Fineman
 Gerson or Gittleman or Goodman
 Harbison or Haldeman
 Isaacson
 Jacobson or Gherman
 Lewisohn or Lehman
 Morrison or Masserman
 Nathanson or Nieman
 Olson or Operman
 Peterson or Packman
 Robertson or Rackman
 Swainson or Sachman
 Tilson or Tallman
 Ullman
 Williamson or Wineman
 Youngman or Ziegman
Lena became Lena Gurnev Palmer-Steiner.

To what does Mother Louisa owe her success? To whom, answers Earl Schenck Miers: "To know Louisa May Alcott

. . . one must know also the father whose compassionate, indestructible nature was the warm kiss shining in her eyes.'' (*Hospital Sketches*, p. 12.)

Forget you, Earl Schenck Miers. That is a greater fiction than the nineteen titles on the title page. Men become characters because women have built their character.

Who made Bronson Alcott? Who were his mothers?

Little Fat Elizabeth Peabody was his mother, applauding his teaching techniques in his Temple School. His head was the temple, his brains the fount. Earnest Miss Peabody published transcripts of his techniques in ''Record of a School.'' Bronson also notated his admirable practices in ''Observations on the Principles and Methods of Infant Instruction.'' Except that he had not provided for his family during that time, or paid the bills. The constables closed the school, took away the bust of Plato.

Little Louisa stamped her foot at them, ''Go away, bad man, you are making my father unhappy.'' (*Hospital Sketches*, p. 13.)

An employer insulted Beatrix's father about his age.

Little Beatrix stamped her foot. ''Go away, bad man, you are making my father unhappy.''

A woman insulted Beatrix's father on his size.

Little Beatrix stamped her foot. ''Go away, bad woman, you are making my father unhappy.''

A neighbor insulted Beatrix's father on his income.

Little Beatrix stamped her foot. ''Go away, bad man, you are making my father unhappy.''

A close friend insulted Beatrix's father on his daughter.

Both Beatrix and her father remained silent.

In the beginning, created Bronson Alcott Fruitlands, and moved his family to that spare commune.

Little Louisa writes in her journal, at ten: ''More people coming to live with us. I wish we could be together and no one else. I don't see who is to clothe and feed us all, when we are so poor now. I was very dismal.'' (Marjorie Worthington, *Miss Alcott of Concord*, Doubleday, 1958, p. 13.)

Fruitlands decays, and the creator, Bronson Alcott, takes to bed with nervous breakdown.

Marmee Alcott nurses him to health.

Marmee Alcott stamps her foot at disaster and says: "Go away, bad event. You are making my husband unhappy."

Then it came to pass that Louisa May's daddy wanted to travel. He wanted to take his carpetbag to England and his good and worthy friend, Ralph Waldo Emerson, paid for the voyage. His good and worthy family, however, was left to its own devices.

When the bills became too great, Marmee went to work in Boston. When Marmee's health broke down, Louisa wrote. She wrote until she wrote herself to death. All the bills were paid.

"Mother, I'm pregnant with a baby girl and she wants to please her father. What should she do?"

"Tell her to be born on his birthday and to die the day after he does. That way, he'll have been taken care of."

Louisa obliged, being born on Bronson's thirty-third birthday in 1832. In 1887, Louisa was fifty-five and ailing and her father was eighty-eight and ailing. She visited him, but it was storming and she had forgotten her warm fur cloak. She died of penumonia but not until the day after her father's death. She was laid to rest across the foot of her father's grave.

Up yours, Earl Schenck Miers of Edison, New Jersey. Miss Peabody, Mrs. Alcott, and Miss Alcott made up the character Bronson by applauding, nursing, and supporting him.

He was the guest conductor to a well rehearsed orchestra. He was the rooster who crowed long after sunrise, when the chickens had already laid the eggs.

Looking for Mothers (4): What Did Fathers Do for Their Daughters?

What did Timothy Fuller do for his daughter Margaret? He let her help with her sick mother. He let her educate her four younger brothers and her sister. He allowed her to work five to eight hours a day helping him write a history of America.

For his daughter he died, allowing her to become head of the household. He allowed her to support her sick mother and four younger brothers and her sister.

What did Bronson Alcott do for his daughter Louisa? He was an eccentric who made her concentric.

Mother Louisa: "I wish we could be just a *real* family, like everyone else." (Worthington, p. 15.)

Bronson let his daughter Louisa forgive him over and over. If someone errs, someone else forebears.

One winter day Bronson Alcott was given ten dollars in cash to purchase a warm shawl for his wife, who sorely needed one. He walked into town with the money tucked into his pocket. He passed a bookstore and forgot about the shawl. When he proudly returned with his books, the family was indignant. How contrite was Bronson! How ashamed! He was immediately forgiven.

Bronson Alcott went off to seek his fortune—westward or through New England. Sometimes he wore a white, pocketless tunic so that he would not be tempted to carry worldly goods. Louisa worked, earning two dollars a week doing washing. Marmee worked, sisters worked. Four months later Bronson returns, one dollar earned. How contrite was Bronson! How ashamed! He was immediately forgiven.

Louisa May defined a philosopher as "A man up in a balloon who required at least three women to hold the ropes that would keep him on the ground." (Worthington, p. 56.)

From Bronson, daughter Louisa also learns total despair. Here is Bronson Alcott's suicide note in his *Journals*, after the failure of Fruitlands: "Shall I say . . . that I was not made by this world, not for it—wherefore am I placed on it if I was found unfit? And the world . . . bruised him with an iron hammer, as the bricklayer breaks an old brick to fill up a crevice." (Worthington, p. 39.)

Bronson took to bed to starve himself to death. Marmee daily left him a cup of tea. He daily refused. One day, the cup was emptied. He reached out for Marmee's hand.

How old was Mother Louisa when she looked into the river and thought of drowning herself? She stared down at the mill dam, at the running water below. Louisa was twenty-six. Her hair was thick and brown, her breasts full. No one loosened her hair. No one cupped his hands over her breasts. But, for practical Louisa, death is the final unemployment.

"There is work for me," she says and scurries away. (Worthington, p. 97.)

What artifacts did Miss Beatrix leave, typed on an electric typewriter? What last message to parents, Lena, to faraway Harold?

She was using a borrowed electric portable and was unfamiliar with electric machines. Her final note was unreadable. Words were broken in the middle or scurried to catch onto other words. The machine quadruple spaced the lines or typed lines one atop the other.

After the pills, Bea's head dropped onto the keyboard. Her hands pressed the whole alphabet. The borrowed machine buzzed. The keys pressed into Bea's face. She awoke, downed coffee, tea, and stimulants all night.

"There is work for me," said Bea.

She had to be home in case a letter arrived from Lena. Perhaps Lena, like Louisa, had gone to nurse in a hospital and had contracted a dangerous disease. Bea did not know with what Lena could have been in contact or contracted, for Lena had not contacted Bea for six weeks, six months, eighteen months.

Bea had to remain at home in case her father contacted her by phone. She now had a phone to curse or to hear curses.

"What shall we do to save Lena?" he would cry.

Bea would make a fiction. It was good writing practice.

"Lena is learning about life," she comforted. "Lena will soon come home."

"And Harold, too?" her father would ask hopefully.

Bea would hang up. To comfort someone else is to discomfort one's self.

Which is what Beatrix was not willing to do. She was not willing to learn: to spend money carefully; to drive; to fix whatever was falling, slipping, leaking, creaking, drooping, dripping, or sparking; to control Lena; to play cards; to read maps or to find her way.

Since Lena cannot find her way either, no wonder Beatrix and Lena have found different ways.

Mother Louisa *was* willing to discomfort herself. She was

101

willing to shovel snow, carry water, blacken a clergyman's boots, split kindling, make fires (all for four dollars for seven weeks' employment with that dastardly, shiny-booted clergyman), do sewing, teach children, take in washing, or write a book.

Mother Louisa: "I love luxury but freedom and independence, better." (Worthington, p. 85.)

And Mother Louisa learns that though not a boy, she can go to war like a laddie, though not a son, she can "come out right and prove that though an *Alcott* I *can* support myself." (Worthington, p. 83.)

Eventually, Louisa makes a good financial investment, *Little Women*. Women are of some use, after all, especially if they are "little."

Louisa has done research for *Little Women*, internal and external. In research, Louisa has had a two-week romance in Paris with a Pole twelve years her junior. In research, Mother Margaret has had a romance in Rome with an Italian a decade her junior. What should Bea learn? To research.

Bea had a young friend. She led him by the hand. Sometimes he would pull back, but Bea would say, "It won't hurt." She softened love for her young friend. He was the virgin and she the de-virginizer. He was of smooth skin; the flesh of her upper arms was already loosening from the bone. He was blond and seldom shaved. Her legs prickled when the hair grew back.

With each young man, Bea aged. Her hair stiffened. The accordion navel, when squeezed, became a toothless mouth, gums, a devouring stomach. It frightened her lovers who thought they might never extricate from that hag of her mouth. Her face loosened its grip like the stomach.

Bea went for advice to a WW. a Wise Woman, Anne Marie.

"Anne Marie," said Bea, "Is it true what Mother Louisa has written in her column 'Happy Women?' "

"What is it she has written?" asked Anne Marie.

"She wrote that for 'All the busy, useful, independent spinsters I know . . . liberty is a better husband than love to many of us.' " (Worthington, p. 191.)

Anne Marie listened. Her face was wizened. She has had a

busy, useful, independent spinsterhood. She opens her mouth to speak. It is a navel mouth.

"Men are the spice of life," said Anne Marie, "so handsome to look upon, thrilling to hear, decorative in the home with their shaving and pomading."

Anne Marie's eyes turned tawny in memory.

"But," she asked, "can we afford to keep them, afford not to work so they can be industrious, afford to let our muscles sag so that they can be strong, afford to age so they can stay young, afford to let them go outdoors while we peer out through curtains and blink in unfamiliar sunlight?"

## MUSICAL HISTORICAL

While Beatrix is researching for *Unafraid Women*, she discovers that a Mrs. Gildersleeve, in 1863, asks Louisa May Alcott for a literary contribution. Mrs. Gildersleeve is writing an anthology called *Heroic Women*.

Bea startles! A hundred years ago? And she, Beatrix Palmer, is struggling with such an anthology yet. She must do something different. Perhaps her heroic women, her unafraid females will sing instead of talk. She'll write, Life Is a Musical, a Musical Historical.

Mother Margaret will stride on stage, singing in a rich voice of Transcendentalism or of the Roman revolution.

Little Ms. Emily will sing a throaty bluesy to Higgy. From her letters Bea will excerpt:

> The sailor cannot see the north,
> but knows the needle can.
> The hand you stretch me in the dark
> I put mine in.

And she will add the refrain:

> Will you be my preceptor, Mr. Higginson?
> Your friend, E. Dickinson.

Miss Quadroon Forten will be a natural—a Motown song,

Black blues infinitely better than white blues. Miss Forten will quote from a letter of her grandfather's. Perhaps she'll have an operatic voice, like Shirley Verrett's:

> Did the God who made the white man and the black
> Cast away His work and turn His back?

Beatrix, who cannot carry a tune, sings everything to "Three Blind Mice."

She has an inspiration for the book: *Singing Mothers*.

Beatrix stops. She turns off the tape. She puts down her pen.

Beatrix once belonged to the PTA of Lena's elementary school. The mothers sang at each meeting, dressed in navy and white, and billed themselves in the PTA announcement as: "The Mother Singers." When the school turned Black, they were mother others and stopped using that title.

It is all wrong. Beatrix has wasted another year of her life. Her women must speak, must not choose to please with each note. Mother Mary Ann Evans did not sing. Mother Rosa listened to music but she did not warble a tune. Let Lotte Lenya sing in her whiskey voice for all of them.

Rest, mothers.

## HAVE CHILD/WILL WRITE CHILDREN'S BOOK

Bea has another idea. She will send to Little Golden, to Red or Green Fairy, to *Jack and Jill* or Simon and Schuster the stories she wrote for Lena. In each story, Little Lena does something remarkable.

"Do you like them, Lena?" asked Beatrix.

"I hate them," says Little Lena.

"Why?"

"You took my name from me."

Each publishing house kept them not two weeks.

"These are private family stories," wrote the children's editors.

It is no comfort, no provisions in the cupboard, to have

unpublished children's books, cookbook, musical historical. But, on some things, you can't count.

Once Bea's mother told Bea's father, "There will always be anti-Semitism."

"Yes," said Bea's father, "but don't count on it."

On misfortune, also, one cannot count. When one has adjusted to self-pity, a certain squint of the eye, a discouraged limp, then fortune befalls one. It may seem as abrupt as acorns falling from an oak, unless one has spent years watching the growth of the oak.

Fortune befell Beatrix Palmer, who, nevertheless, had been preparing for it, blowing birthday candles to it, wishing on stars to it, stamping it into her palm when white horses paraded by.

This was *The Pioneers*, a book quickly conceived, lightly pursued. She spent no more than a few visits with each of the interviewees. She always came away, if not with stories, then with goodies: crocheted flowered shawls that they had given to her for listening to them, embroidered tablecloths, sachets, decorated towels. Whatever their hands were not too arthritic to do, they gave to her. From one woman she received bottlecaps covered in purple and white thread, crocheted into a hot plate. They gave her aprons made for Senior Citizens Bazaars, cosmetic bags for curlers, sewn over gallon plastic milk bottles. Whatever they could do, they did for her. Whatever they could say, they said for her. She was being rewarded while she was working on it. For that she received royalties for several years. She could live modestly. Who needed more than five thousand a year? And she earned extra giving lectures to Senior Citizens groups, reviewing interview-type books for book pages. She became a consultant on geriatrics, even a panelist. Once on a panel of geriatricians and psychiatrists, she found herself opposite her former psychiatrist. He was effusive to her. She listened impassively to his remarks and frequently, thoughtfully contradicted them. His cigar went out.

Success is a group. Once she had royalties, she received grants. Once she had grants, she was admitted to Mac-Dowells, Wurlitzers, and other writers' colonies.

Her life changed. Her parents' phone calls were respectful.

Her father asked literary advice on letters to his friends. Her mother whispered at the beginning of each phone conversation, "Am I disturbing you?"

Bea begins to lose fears. She can change a typewriter ribbon without rushing her portable down to the typewriter store each time it types palely. She can insert new blades into her razor.

Orifices are less threatening. Until now, Bea was afraid of all orifices except anal, as her former psychiatrist, fellow panelist would have informed her. Her nose would become solidified walls of mucus, dry and unbreathing. When she ripped at the mucus, the walls bled. The nasal passages were unusually genteel then, sensitive without their coating, afraid of odors. Bea would apply deodorant everywhere—to bathroom odors, cooking odors, underarm and vaginal odors. Bea's ears would become blocked with wax. She would then be hard of hearing and was afraid that people were talking about her behind closed doors, behind her closed ears. She went to her ENT man who vacuumed out the wax. Then every whisper pierced her. Her urethra stung when she urinated, until she applied medication. Her vaginal walls clung together. Harold had said he had to pry her open.

Only her anus was open, generous, a playground slide.

With fortune, Bea's heart, hand, ENT, vagina walls opened. She bestowed love, generosity, attention, and the clasp of her womb on those who needed one or all from her.

It is the final generosity to embrace one's mother.


Looking for Mothers (5): Biological

"I love you," Beatrix one day told her mother.

Her mother commenced a series of statements: "It's about time," "So it's finally paying off," "What took you so long?" but choked them back. Bea's mother, instead, burst into tears.

Bea almost ran from the room, especially when her father rushed in and accused, "Haven't you done enough to your mother?"

But her mother waved him off and he left, looking amazed at the cannibalistic scene behind him: the mother chewing Bea's hair, her ears (without their wax), nibbling her nose (no more sinus trouble), kissing the lips with Hungarian Mira's nonallergenic lipstick, her neck, with anti-crepey neck on it, her shoulders. Bea's mother did "*Miesele, Meisele,*" little mouse, little mice, to each finger, tickling up Bea's inner arm.

Bea was in her mother's oven—baked, basted, fluffed, stuffed. Bea's insides began to drip like a Thanksgiving turkey. Her eyes glazed over as if newly basted. Her arms felt like well done drumsticks, separating at the joints. Bea lay on the plate at her mother's feet.

*The teeth of Bea's mother:* Widely spaced. Threads were broken off between them, the tongue poked pink behind the white bars. They chewed carefully. The teeth of Bea's mother were a picket fence, tombstones, outposts. It was more heartbreaking when the teeth of Bea's mother had silver fillings than when her hair turned from brown to silver.

*The hands of Bea's mother:* Slightly bent, slightly chapped, slightly burned, slightly cut. When Bea's mother could no longer move the wedding ring over the knuckle, Bea wept.

*The eyes of Bea's mother:* Nothing abrupt, gradual coloration. Not summer blue skies, not warm twinkly eyes. These were thoughtful gray, twilight or dawn. No climate changed them. If they looked upon Bea, she suddenly became Birthday Bea or Tidy Bea, starched, bathed Bea, patent-leather-shoes Bea, Bea with sausage curls. If the eyes of Bea's mother shifted away from Bea, she was Bad Girl Bea. She had stolen from S. S. Kreśge's. She had shaken the dusting mop into her mother's clothes closet, rather than opening the door on the cold air of the back porch.

*The mouth of Bea's mother:* Kid gloves, soft underwear. It was less a moving of the lips and a speaking of words, but the brushing of the lips against her. The lips of Bea's mother were European-shy. They did not believe in kissing a child's mouth. They kissed the forehead, the top of the head, the fingers, arms, knees. They bit the *tuchas*, but it was incestu-

107

ous, it was spreading germs, to kiss a child's mouth. Unless there was a drowning. The lips also did not kiss animals or kiss anyone who did kiss animals.

Bea's mother asked her granddaughter Lena, "Did you kiss the cat?"

"Yes," said Lena.

"Then you can't kiss me," said the lips of Bea's mother.

One day Lena said, "No. I didn't kiss the cat."

Her grandmother allowed Lena to kiss her.

"I fooled you!" cried Lena. "I did kiss the cat!"

Bea's mother turned pale and rushed to the bathroom to brush her teeth, scrub with a washcloth at her lips, her cheeks, her forehead.

*The feet of Bea's mother*: In slippers, heelless slippers, or lace-up shoes. They used to be in shoes with little heels and in shoes with buckles, but now the feet of Bea's mother like to be blanketed, swaddled, put into buntings, laced and attached firmly to the ankles.

*The breasts of Bea's Mother*: Great bulges of dough with chocolate-chip nipples, saddlebags, pouches.

"Mother, I am pregnant with a baby girl."

"Has she told you that she loves you?"

"She is ashamed to tell me."

"When she tells you, press the words between the leaves of your Unabridged, iron them between sheets of wax paper, trace them, let them be as the rubbings of stone, rare historical marker."

Bea says farewell to her parents. She is going to an island, the island of one of her mothers—Charlotte Forten of Philadelphia. Miss Forten sailed to Sea Island, off the coast of South Carolina and Georgia, in 1862 and stayed until 1864. Bea wants to celebrate the Centennial of her mother's visit.

"Must you go?" ask the lips of Bea's mother, drop the eyes of Bea's mother, cross the laced feet of Bea's mother, fold the hands of Bea's mother, click the teeth of Bea's mother, heave the breasts of Bea's mother.

We cannot stare into the features of our mothers for too

long. It makes it difficult for us to leave, and we must leave our biological, our biodegradable mothers.

Looking for Mothers (6): Charlotte Forten

Bea had written:

Dear Owner, Caretaker, Scion, Real Estate Agent of Sea Island:
   I am researching Charlotte Forten's stay on your island. She lived there from 1862 to 1864. Could I come down and look at the butterflies, trees, flowers, and skies that she described?

Beatrix Palmer

The letter was hastily typed. The alphabet suffered from her nervous touch: H's became N's, P's were O's—all tails wagged away, L's, S's were urgently, darkly pressed. It was the letter of an erratic.
The reply began:

Dear Typist, Historian, Writer or Real Estate Buyer:
   I have no information on Miss Charlotte Forten, but come right ahead, little lady.

Beatrix stiffened. How did he know she was a "little lady"? Had he peeked at the size of her bra cup? Her vaginal opening? She was normal otherwise.

If it is convenient with you, we will send our ferryman over to the Hilton to ferry you across.

Jack Ferguson (Col.)

Harold Steiner had been gone for seventeen and a half years. Lena had been gone for one year. Beatrix Palmer was afraid to inform her parents of her departure. They felt her job was to be right at home, waiting for Lena. They asked her daily, the past year, if she had heard from Lena. They were to ask another 730 times.

"The row was delightful. It was just at sunset—a grand Southern sunset; and the gorgeous clouds of crimson and gold were reflected in the waters below, which were smooth and calm as a mirror." (Ray Allen Billington, ed., *The Journal of Charlotte L. Forten*, Dryden Press, 1953, p. 128.)

Charlotte Forten was correct, as she was, also, in her description of the ride to the house:

"As we drove homeward I notice that the trees are just beginning to turn; some beautiful scarlet berries were growing along the roadside; and everywhere the beautiful live oak with its moss drapery. The palmettos disappoint me much. Most of them have a very jagged appearance, and are yet stiff and ungraceful. The country is very level. . . .There are plenty of woods." (*Journal*, p. 129.)

Beatrix's ferryman was not what she had anticipated. Perhaps she expected a furtive, hunched, graybeard to row her across Styx. Perhaps she expected to forget her past as she was taken to Sea Island.

Her boatman had long, light hair, Southern-blue eyes, was tall and slender. He was silent on the ride over from the mainland and when he spoke, she had trouble understanding his South Carolina accent. As she approached the island, her past *did* recede.

"Never saw anything more beautiful than these trees. It is strange that we do not hear of them at the North. They are the first objects that attract one's attention here. They are large, noble trees with glossy green leaves. Their great beauty consists in the long bearded moss with which every branch is heavily draped. The moss is singularly beautiful, and gives a solemn almost funereal aspect to the trees." (*Journal*, p. 129.)

"Is Jack Ferguson, Colonel, here?" Beatrix Palmer asked.

"No'm, he ain't," said her ferryman.

"Is he on the island?"

"No'm, he ain't."

He lifted her luggage—her suitcase, typewriter, ream of cheap paper, carbon, paper clips, eraser, pencils, ball-points, all the costuming of the writer.

All the separate parts of her profession nestled against him. The paper did not fly from him like gulls at the dock, like the white egrets in the rookery they passed. The paper clips did not click against him, the carbon rub, the erasers erase. He carried her profession into the mansion.

"Who lives here?" she asked.

"You and me," he said.

There were sounds in the kitchen. An ornate wooden door swung open. Cooks and servants, black and white, came to greet her in silence.

"Do they live here?" she asked her ferryman.

"They don't live in Main House," he told her. "They live in Middle House."

"Do you know of Charlotte Forten?" she asked him.

He was carrying her luggage up the staircase to her bedroom.

"Is she coming, too?" he asked.

"Yes," said Beatrix Palmer.

He deposited her belongings and went down to the hall to his own room.

She unpacked until the dinner cord was pulled. She unpacked and hung her dresses in the walk-in closet. She unpacked and folded her sweaters and underwear into the 1920 dressers with their hand-painted roses. She unpacked and spread lipsticks, matching rouges, eye shadows, musk perfume, nail clippers, photo of Lena across the dressing table.

She descends for dinner, casually dressed. Not her ferryman. He is wearing good slacks, a Mexican shirt, a soft leather jacket. His hair is freshly washed.

There are two places set for dinner at the massive oak table in the baronial dining hall. She is seated at one end, he at the other. He is seated at the head, she at the foot.

What does the head say to the feet?

"Did you have a nice day?"

"Yes, thank you."

"Did you get yourself settled?"

111

"Not quite."

"It takes some doing."

"Yes."

"Colonel Ferguson said you were a historian?"

"Sort of."

"You're doing a history of the island?"

"Part of."

"Seems funny to find a woman Yankee historian working on a Southern coastal island. I never saw one of those before."

"I've never seen a ferryman seated at the head of the table, wearing soft hair and a soft leather jacket."

He smiled. She smiled. The head and the feet would get along.

"What are you looking for down here?" he asked her.

"Ghosts," she said.

"You'll find those aplenty!" he laughed. "More ghosts than egrets, and there's an egret rookery up the road."

"What do the ghosts do?" she asked.

"Different things to different people."

After the meal he escorted Beatrix into the living room. They poured coffee into Wedgwood cups from the silver coffee urn. He made the fire, lighting pitch pine as kindling for the oak logs.

Beatrix reclined, persuaded by the soft couch.

"I have a little Scotch," he said. "Want to come to my room for it, or want me to bring down a glass?"

"Bring down the Scotch," said Lady Beatrix.

They drank. The logs crackled.

"What kind of ghosts?" Bea asked.

"The kind you deserve," he said.

As the fire died and the room cooled, they were less amicable.

He kicked ashes over the last of the sparks and placed the fire screen before the logs.

"Shall I escort you to your room?" he asked.

"No," she said. "I'll sit here a bit longer."

"I might not hear if you call," he said. "I can't always make out a Yankee voice."

He ascended, taking off his jacket as he climbed the long

112

stairway to the upper balcony. From her position on the couch she could watch him down the corridor to his room. She had not wanted to be alone, but she did not want to be coerced into company. After all, she had just come from the mainland.

The fire died. She heard rattling at the patio door, upstairs footsteps, pots in the kitchen. She heard laughter from girls and deeper-voiced men. The laughter blew in like a radio turned up with the station drifting.

Next to her a pillow suddenly dented and the air chilled. She sat clutching the arm of the couch.

"Hallo!" she called. What was his name?

Doors opened, all of the doors of the house seemed to open to hear her. His door also opened and she saw his shadow down the stairs. The dent in the pillow next to her released and the pillow puffed again. The cold air dissolved.

"I'll take you," he said.

He gave her his arm up the stairs. He opened her bedroom door and led her into the room. He turned down her covers for her. He crawled under them, for her. She was too chilled to undress but lay next to him in her jeans and shirt.

"That won't do," he said.

His fingers were warm against the cold ash of her skin.

Politely, he gave her his arm, around her back. He gave her his leg, she on top, his legs around her. He was her fiddler crab; he was a pointed, drill shell. They moved like crustaceans all night under the quilt, until dawn. The tree shadows branched onto her typewriter, onto her desk. The chair in front of her desk began to move. They awoke.

"Thank you," he said politely and went down the hall to his room.

She saw him at breakfast and not again for the day. Beatrix took her first walk in the woods, carrying *The Journal of Charlotte L. Forten*.

"Was there ever a lovelier road than that through which part of my way to school lies? . . .It is lined with woods on both sides. On the one tall stately pines, on the other noble live oaks with their graceful moss drapery. And the road is carpeted with those brown odorous pine leaves . . . sauntering along, listening to the birds and breathing the soft deli-

113

cious air. Of the last part of the walk, through sun and sand, the less said the better." (*Journal*, p. 133.)

Bea spent her days walking in the woods, on the white sandy beach, looking at the sky and the Southern coastal birds: the brown immature egrets, the white mature ones, the big blues—heron, ibis. She avoided the island grazers, the wild ponies, feral pigs, some donkeys. She listened for deer, the raindrop-soft sound of them. She did everything she never did in real life. Perhaps that is why the unreal life entered her bedroom through the walk-in closet, the rose-decorated bedsteads and dressers, the orange-tiled bathroom floor, the double windows looking out on the river. The spider-crab shell on her tall dresser wiggled its legs. The clam shell, still attached by a bit of membrane, although opened out, began to clap open and shut. An island tiger-eye shell righted its self and snail-paced its way across the glassed top.

Her collected thoughts are like her shells: red-veined slippers, Florida Ceriths, sand dollars, white and red-ribbed scallops, jingle shells, eared-arks, moon shells, pen shells. Her thoughts jingled, ribbed, rubbed. She will come, in time, in two years' time, to know these shells intimately. Now time antecedes and predicts.

Beatrix listens and hears what Mother Charlotte heard. It is November 30, 1862, and her students are shout-singing, led by Prince. They sing a mother song:


Old mother, old mother, where hab you been
When de gospel been flourishin . . .

My mother's gone to glory, and I want to git dere too
Till dis warfare's over . . .

I wonder where my mudder gone,
Sing oh graveyard!

Graveyard ought to know me
Sing Jerusalem!
Oh carry my mudder in de graveyard.
Sing etc.

114

Oh grass grow in de graveyard
Sing etc.
Lay my body in de graveyard
Graveyard ought to know me
Sing Jerusalem!

(*Journal*, pp. 141, 142.)

Charlotte is not a mother's daughter. She is a father's daughter, as are Mothers Margaret, Emily, Louisa May.

"Mother, I'm pregnant with a baby girl."
"You'll carry it nine months; he'll carry it the rest."
"Who?"
"Her father."

Charlotte's grandfather, James Forten, was her mother. Her uncle, Robert Purvis, was her mother. Her father, Robert Bridges Forten, was her mother.

Grandfather James Forten preceded the Abolitionist movement by a generation and shaped the views of William Lloyd Garrison. Her uncle Robert Purvis was called Father of the Underground Railroad. Her father, Robert Bridges Forten, was an antislavery lecturer, a fighter of the segregated school system of Philadelphia, and died in the Forty-Third United States Colored Regiment during the Civil War.

Charlotte was made pregnant by her grandfather, her uncle, and her father. She was the bearer of the dream. Margaret Fuller's father Timothy impregnated Mother Margaret with *his* dream of writing an historical text. Louisa May was impregnated by her handsome father Bronson, who dreamed that his books would have widespread publication.

According to Editor Ray Allen Billington, Charlotte was a "delicate young woman of sixteen" in 1854 when she left Philadelphia for Salem, Massachusetts, and commenced her journal. She was also "a person of color." Oh, off it, Editor Billington!

And yet, they *were* all delicate young women, all of my mothers. Margaret Fuller had migraines. Louisa had terrible aches in her joints. Charlotte would begin teaching and would suffer relapses in Salem, with her white students, and on Sea

115

Island, with her Black students. The cause was clear, the symptoms also: energy, ambition, dreams equal migraines, joint pains, bodily weakness. My mothers were not trained to run the race, and, when a few of them did, their chests ached, their legs stiffened, they panted long before the finish line.

Charlotte began her journal (they were all journalists—my daily mothers, Margaret, Louisa May, Charlotte): "A wish to record the passing events of my life, which, even if quite unimportant to others, naturally possess great interest to myself. . . .Besides this, it will doubtless enable me to judge correctly of the growth and improvement of my mind from year to year." (*Journal*, p. 33.)

It is Salem, May 1854. She is going on Sweet Sixteen.

She has been denied entrance to two ice cream saloons with her friends. She has watched, behind the curtains of her grandfather's house in Philadelphia, the capture and manacling of fugitive slaves. She has had to separate herself from others on the omnibus and train. Her friends are not admitted to concerts, though they have tickets. Her friends are turned away from museums. She is Sweet Sixteen.

They were once all Sweet Sixteen, all of my mothers. *The Mother of Bea at Sweet Sixteen*: She had taken off her Russian schoolgirl uniform. She engaged in smuggling to support her family, dressing as a Ukrainian peasant, suppressing her Russian and Yiddish. Her family smuggled itself across the border to Poland and, from there, sailed to the Promised Land. The promise was a job in a laundry. The oil goes from her skin. Her face is either flushed or dried. Her wavy, soft black hair is matted or frizzled in the heat. She falls in love with an educated man. She smuggles herself into his life. She has no time to read a book. She is Sweet Sixteen.

Bea is Sweet Thirty-Eight.

When Bea was Sweet Sixteen her friends gave her a compact with a large mirror and leather case. The initial on it is F. Why F?

"We could not find B or P," said Shirley, Janice, Lois, and Pauline.

Her parents give her a Sweet Sixteen party. It is not a surprise party. She has been informed that the relatives are invited and her friends are not.

Her grandmother gives her a green leather jacket. Bea is ashamed to wear it. It is too boyish. She returns it to the department store and her grandmother cries. When Bea is thirty-eight she finds that same-style green leather jacket in the same department store. She buys it and never takes it off, but her grandmother never knew for she died soon after Bea's Sweet Sixteen.

An aunt and uncle gift Bea with *Twentieth Century American Writers*. The paper is thick. The smell is not moldy or like shelving paper or drawer-liner or notebook paper. The smell of the book is of rich wood. The photographs of the authors are unbearded or of youngish women. Bea enters the book and never leaves it. She decides at Sweet Sixteen to lie between its pages.

Charlotte Forten is Sweet Sixteen.

"I wonder that every colored person is not a misanthrope. Surely we have something to make us hate mankind. I have met girls in the schoolroom—they have been thoroughly kind and cordial to me—perhaps the next day met them on the street—they feared to recognize me . . . Oh! It is hard to go through life meeting contempt with contempt, hatred with hatred, fearing with too good reason to love and trust hardly anyone whose skin is white." (*Journal*, p. 4.)

It is May 25, 1854, when Charlotte is almost Sweet Sixteen.

"Another fugitive from bondage has been arrested, a poor man, who for two short months had trod the soil and breathed the air of the 'Old Bay State,' was arrested like a criminal in the streets of her capital . . . all this to prevent a man, whom God has created in his own image, from regaining that freedom with which he, in common with every other human being, is involved." (*Journal*, p. 34.)

Mother Louisa is watching this scene. Mother Louisa is Sweet Twenty-Three.

Mother Margaret is not watching. She had been active in the Roman revolution of 1848. She had recorded its betrayal and defeat. She set sail to America, suffered shipwreck and death on July 19, 1850. Mother Margaret has not been watching for four years.

Mother Emily is Sweet Twenty-Four. She is afraid to

watch. Perhaps she is afraid to watch because she has weak eyes; perhaps, because she has other weaknesses. Mother Emily has now pursued her studies and is safely home. She will leave her home in nine years, 1863, while Mother Charlotte is on Sea Island. She will leave her home either for her weak eyes or for her faltering courage.

Mother Emily: "I was ill since September and since April in Boston for a physician's care. He does not let me go, yet I work in my prison and make guests for myself." (*Poems and Letters*, p. 13.)

Lena is Sweet Sixteen. Beatrix Palmer bakes a cake. She ices a pink "16" on the frosting of the double-chocolate cake. Beatrix puts the cake carefully into the refrigerator to allow the frosting time to harden. Beatrix tiptoes upstairs with Birthday Breakfast—French toast, 100 percent pure maple syrup, wedges of pink grapefruit that she had cinnamoned and heated. Beatrix knocks. Her hands are occupied, but she pushes open the bedroom door of the Birthday Girl.

The room is a mess. It is usually thus. The bed sheet rises in waves. The covers are ruffled like sand at the beach. Drifts of clothing, picked up and discarded, are strewn about. The bathroom is empty. The closet has also been emptied—of clothing. Lena will not be a captive, a fugitive slave. She has made her escape to Canada through the underground railway of freaky friends. The cake hardens in the refrigerator.

Charlotte Forten's father is in town, for "the excitement in Boston is very great. The trial of the poor man takes place on Monday . . . there seems nothing too bad for these Northern tools of slavery to do." It is Saturday, May 27, 1854, in Charlotte's Journal (*Journal*, p. 35.)

Also in town is the Reverend Thomas Wentworth Higginson, who will later encounter Charlotte on Sea Island. Bronson Alcott, Louisa's daddy, is in town. They are plotting the rescue of the fugitive slave.

Charlotte, on Wednesday, May 31, walks "past the Court House, which is now lawlessly converted to a prison . . . I believe in 'resistance to tyrants' and would fight for liberty until death."

Charlotte's daddy has failed to rouse opinion. Louisa's daddy has failed to rescue the fugitive. Mary Higginson's husband has also been unsuccessful in carrying off the fugitive slave.

On Friday, June 2, Charlotte writes: "Our worst fears are realized; the decision was against . . . and he has been sent back to a bondage a thousand times worse than death . . . I can write no more. A cloud seems hanging over me, over all our persecuted race which nothing can dispel." (*Journal*, p. 37.)

Charlotte is Sweet Sixteen.

Janice is Sweet Sixteen. Her parents rent the back room of Lully's Restaurant. The invitations, table decorations, and Sweet Sixteen dress are color coordinated. The table favors are red lollipops and red carnations. The invitations are Valentine's red and white. The cake is white frosting with red maraschino cherries. Sweet Sixteen Janice has a red sequined formal with a white cloth peony between her breasts. Her breasts are smaller than the peony. Her hips are larger than the dress. The side seams have split at the waist. Beatrix is not invited. It is to be remembered that she did not conduct herself in a ladylike fashion.

Pauline is Sweet Sixteen. The girls fill her Murphy bed with presents. Her mother has gone out to buy day-old A & P Ann Page cake.

Romanian Lois is Sweet Sixteen. She is sent to the beauty parlor. Her nails are manicured. When she returns, her father gallantly kisses her hand, her shaped nails, her clipped cuticles. Lois's brother drives around picking up the girls. They are invited for dessert with the family, and they are all returned to their own homes within two hours.

Beatrix Palmer is sitting on a piece of driftwood. She has walked in the woods until she came upon this lake. Beatrix Palmer reads her Mother Charlotte's journal. Her hand is falling asleep, her elbow hurts from being crooked with the book.

Charlotte Forten is not interested in anything unless it be about slavery. She quotes the words of her grandfather:

119

"Resolved, That we will never separate ourselves voluntarily from the slave population of this country; they are our brethren by the ties of consanguinity, suffering and wrong." (*Journal*, p. 9.)

Charlotte Forten, long before the event, is preparing herself with indignation. She will sail to Port Royal, South Carolina. She will be ferried across to St. Helena's, the first schoolteacher of runaway slaves.

Beatrix Palmer is also preparing herself with indignation. She has been studying the faded writing framed and hung in the living room of Main House.

"1812," Beatrix reads. "Four lots."

Each column adds up to about $12,200. The page adds to approximately $48,000. She reads that Old Rose, age seventy-five, is only $20; Peg, thirty-eight, is $500; but Nelly, seven, and Betty, five, are $200 and $175 respectively. She reads that Cato, fifteen, is $350; Sarah, nineteen, is $400. Under Sarah's name, Stephen, five months, is only $50. In these lots relationships are not noted or known. Is Stephen, five months, a relative of Sarah, nineteen? If separated, will they long for each other, that Stephen and Sarah? Jacob, seventeen, is $400. Betty, fifteen, is $300; Tabby, two, is $125. Are Betty, fifteen, and Tabby, two, related? Was Betty a thirteen-year-old mother? Mary, two, is $125; Grace, four, is $175; and little Bob, five, is also $175. Sambo, forty-five, is $425, Black Sambo is.

Beatrix glances around as she reads those names. Is someone watching her? The names are blurred as if someone's hand passes between her vision and the frame. She looks closely. The four lots, each containing forty names, blur, tilt in their frame. Beatrix leaves Main House.

Beatrix, sitting at the shore, is lonely. She walks back again toward Main House. She walks through the woods. Woodpeckers loosen twigs. She hears, in the palmettos, rooting feral pigs.

It is dusk. Sounds reverberate; the pigs shake the palmettos. Donkeys and ponies and wild cattle thrash through the underbrush. Birds rattle leaves. Beatrix pauses to look at a rusted water tank that has fallen over on its side. Snakes begin to glide out of the water tower. Beatrix runs along the cattle path. She trips on a root and sprawls. Her hands are muddied as is *The Journal of Charlotte L. Forten*.

Beatrix returns to Main House, through the Servants' Entrance. The kitchen workers greet her. She shows them her muddy shoes, muddy hands and knees of jeans. She shows them, also, the soiled pages of Charlotte Forten.

They wipe her hands, brush the caked mud from her jeans, give her an old kitchen knife with which to lift off the mud that is stuck into her heels. They dampen the pages of the *Journal* and blot them with a kitchen linen towel.

If Beatrix hastens, she can bathe before dinner. Beatrix carries her shoes up the stairway, not to muddy the carpeting. She hurries into her unlocked bedroom, through to her unlocked bathroom. Water is pouring into her tub. Soaking off the mud from his hands, knees, and body is her lover.

The next day, Beatrix Palmer reads of Mother Charlotte's first school day for her runaway slaves:

Nov. 5, 1862, Wednesday: "Had my first regular teaching expedition and to you and you only friend will I acknowledge that it was *not* a very pleasant one. Part of my scholars are very tiny—unusually restless." (*Journal*, p. 131.)

On Friday, November 7, Mother Charlotte wrote: "the mocking birds were singing . . . I think 'my babies' were rather more manageable to-day, but they were certainly troublesome enough." (*Journal*, p. 132.)

Charlotte's delicate body tires. Her spirit wearies. She constantly admonishes herself: "Let me not forget that I came not here for friendly sympathy or for anything else but to work." (*Journal*, p. 147.)

All of her mothers examine and reexamine their motives.

"Mother, I'm pregnant with a baby girl."
"What is she doing?"
"Reexamining herself."
"Oohh, what pleasure!"

On her Sweet Sixteenth, Mother Charlotte wrote, Thursday, August 17, 1854: "My birthday.—How much I feel to-day my own utter insignificance! It is true the years of my life are but few. But have I improved them as I should have done? No! I feel grieved and ashamed." (*Journal*, p. 47.)

Three years later, Thursday, June 15, 1857, my mother Charlotte wrote: "Have been undergoing a thorough self-examination. The result is a mingled feeling of sorrow, shame and self-contempt. . . .Not only am I without beauty and talent, without the accomplishment which nearly everyone of my age, whom I know, possess, but I am not even *intelligent* . . . entirely owning to my own want of energy, perseverance and application." (*Journal*, p. 106.)

That is Sweet Nineteen and still of little worth.

Looking for Mothers (7): Daughters and Birthdays

Louisa May writes to her father on her birthday. She is in her chilly little garret in Boston. It is November 29, 1856. Louisa May's birthday is also her father's birthday. She is his birthday present.

Mother Louisa: "Dearest Father—Your little parcel was very welcome to me as I sat alone in my room, with the snow falling . . . outside and a few tears in (for birthdays are dismal times to me); and the fine letter, the pretty gift and most of all, the loving thought so kindly taken for your old absent daughter, made the cold, dark day as warm and bright as summer to me."

(During this correspondence, Mother Charlotte is Sweet Twenty-Two.)

Mother Louisa: "I will tell you a little about my doings, stupid as they will seem after your own grand proceedings . . . . I love to see your name first among the lecturers, to hear it kindly spoken of in the papers and inquired about by good people . . . at last filling the place you are so fitted for, and which you have waited for so long and patiently." (Worthington, pp. 82-83.)

"Mother, I'm pregnant with a baby girl."
"What is she doing?"

"She is praising her father."

"How is she praising him?"

"She is longing to see him first among lecturers, kindly poken of and inquired about."

"She is not praising him. She is writing his obituary."

"Why?"

"So she can live."

In this birthday letter, Ms. Louisa has told her father that hough an Alcott, she will support herself. She also tells him, 'I can't do much with my hands; so I will make a battering-am of my head and make a way through this rough-and-umble world." (Worthington, pp. 82-83.)

Ms. Forten also makes a battering ram of her head and goes o St. Helena's.

Mother Charlotte, October 28, 1862, Tuesday A.M.: "Our hip rode gently along over a smooth sea leaving a path of ilver behind it . . . have passed Edisto and several other slands and can now see Hilton Head." (*Journal*, p. 125.)

"Mother, I'm pregnant with a baby girl."

"What's she doing?"

"She's making a battering ram of her head."

"That's better than what he's doing."

"What's he doing?"

"He's making a battering ram of his prick."

Beatrix is ashamed. It is this sensual life that leads her to xploit her own body, to exploit even her mothers. It is the rees, the clinging moss, the shush of pine needles underfoot, he soft air, those clean sheets, that boat ride in bed every ight.

Beatrix is weeping. She is darkening in shadow, she is eddening by fire. In the living room she mourns Little Billy, welve, $325; Little Lucky, twenty-two, Nanny, sixty, $250; Old Granny, seventy-five, with one leg, a bargain at $25.

What would Mother Charlotte think about Beatrix's being on Sea Island?

Mother Charlotte: "It's another white making time out of his crime."

123

Mother Charlotte: "It's another Jew writing history on our misery."

John Davis, thirty-four, is $500. Lolly, twenty-four, is $400. Big Tom, forty-five, is $420. Buck, forty, is $350.

Beatrix Palmer: "You cannot be your mother; you cannot be your heroine; you cannot be another's color."

Beatrix is largely alone. Not Charlotte.

Charlotte meets Harry, who learns quickly to hold a pen correctly and to write.

"I must inquire," says Charlotte of her first adult student, "if there are not more of the grown people who would like to take lessons at night." (*Journal*, p. 133.)

Unlike Beatrix, who is idling, Charlotte is useful. She sews for old people on St. Helena's. She makes a warm, red jacket for an old woman. She hears an old man tell what a happy year this has been, "nobody to whip me nor dribe me and plenty to eat." (*Journal*, p. 132.)

My Mother Charlotte speaks to Old Harriet and to Bella.

Old Harriet tells Mother Charlotte: "Three of [her] children have been sold . . . [because] master's son killed somebody in a duel and was obliged to 'pay money.'"

Bella "is rather a querulous body . . . One by one her children at a tender age have been dragged from her to work in the cotton fields. . . . She has had to see her children cruelly beaten." (*Journal*, p. 143.)

Beatrix wanders in the forest, but Charlotte visited Harriet Tubman one Saturday, January 31, 1863: "She is a wonderful woman—a real heroine. Has helped off a large number of slaves, after taking her own freedom. She told us she used to hide them in the woods during the day and go around to get provisions for them. Once she had with her a man named Joe for whom a reward of $1,500 was offered. Frequently in different places she found handbills exactly describing him, but at last they reached in safety the Suspension Bridge under the Falls and found themselves in Canada. . . . Joe had been very silent . . . moody. . . . But when she said, 'Now we are in Can[ada],' he sprang to his feet with a great shout and sang and clapped . . . in joy. How exciting it was to hear her tell the story. And to hear her sing the very scraps of jubilant hymns that he sang." (*Journal*, p. 161.)

124

# Looking for Mothers (8): Come Home Where You Belong

"Mother, I'm p. with a b.g. and she is leaving home."

"Her father will ask her to return."

"But she is getting her schooling."

"Her father will ask her to return."

"But she has gone forth to do her life's work."

"Her father will ask her to return home where she belongs."

Beatrix receives mail. Her ferryman has been to the mainland and back. He carries her letter in his leather pouch. She is the only one on Sea Island to hear from the mainland. Her father wrote:

The weather is not good. Your mother's health is as good as can be expected, although the weather keeps her housebound. She slipped on the ice on the way to the supermarket and twisted her ankle. When that repaired, she fell from a chair while hanging the kitchen curtains and bruised her ribs. Have a restful vacation. . . .

Louisa May's daddy wanted her back, too. Margaret Fuller's daddy died and couldn't have her back. Emily's daddy lived until Emily was forty-four and he had his baby with him all of that time.

"His heart was pure and terrible," wrote Emily of Lover Father, "and I think no other like it exists." (*Poems and Letters*, p. v.)

Twice during Mother Charlotte Forten's schooling did Father Forten write to Salem demanding that she return home. He had sent her to Salem in order *not* to send her to the segregated schools of Philadelphia, but his baby has been gone from him too long. He wants her back. He wants her back, Wednesday, September 27, 1864. He wants her back Friday, March 16, 1865. Each time her teachers intercede for her.

There are other fathers. Thomas Wentworth Higginson is not a father, but he is so viewed by Ms. Emily and Ms. Charlotte.

On Tuesday, August 1, 1854, Ms. Charlotte sees Mr. Higginson for the very first time: "Mr. Garrison gave an interesting account of the rise and progress of the anti-slavery movement in Great Britain. I had not seen Mr. Higginson before. He is very fine looking, and has one of the deepest, richest voices that I have ever heard." (*Journal*, p. 46.)

She sees him again, New Year's Day, 1863 on Sea Island. "I found myself being presented to Col. Higginson, whereat I was so much overwhelmed, that I had no reply to make to the very kind and courteous speech with which he met me. I believe I mumbled something and grinned like a simpleton." (*Journal*, p. 154.)

Should Beatrix make something of this? Something of Hig's "deep, rich voice," something of his "kind and courteous speech?" Should she turn this into historical fiction? Should she turn this shy friendship into passionate romance? *The Colonel and the Mulatto*. Think of the cover illustration: she is dressed in white, although she is brown. He is bending her backward, as in the Old HiLi dance at Beatrix's Prom. A river sparkles behind them. He is dressed in his colonel's uniform. Her lips are parted; her eyes closed.

What is Charlotte thinking? "Col. H. is a perfectly delightful person in private—So genial, so witty, so kind. . . . My heart was full when I looked at him. I longed to say, 'I thank you, I thank you' . . . and yet I *c'ld not*. . . . Words always fail me when I want them most." (*Journal*, p. 156.)

Why not a little historical distortion, projection, projecting itself from paperback to Celluloid, projecting Beatrix from poverty to income?

Beatrix squirms. She is not the only night rider in her bedstead/bedsteed. Charlotte rides horseback with her colonels, long, sensual rides. She hears that she is "more than" liked by a certain soldier. "But I *know* it is not so . . . .Although he is very good and liberal he is still an *American* and w'ld of course never be so insane as to love one of the proscribed races." (*Journal*, p. 187.)

It is again dusk. Beatrix trots down the path, so does a boar after her. A kitchen woman's white dog was gored by him yesterday. Beatrix has been warned, also, to stay clear of the marshes. The house lost a large pig there last week, when, during a heavy rainstorm, the alligator of the marsh caught hold of the pig's leg and pulled it under.

"The screams haunted me for three or four days," said one of the kitchen people.

"What does the alligator do with the meat?" asked Beatrix.

"Hides it on shore till it ripens."

As Beatrix trots back and enters through the gates of the estate, over the metal grating that keeps cattle out, she sees a light on in a tabby hut—an old slave hut made of limestone and oyster shells and whitewashed. Through the window she sees her lover, wiping his hands on a paint rag, looking at a small canvas on an easel. She pauses, then decides not to interrupt.

That night she is alone at the fire. She goes alone to the patio to bring in more firewood. Her lover is not there. She has had to dine alone. She has moved from the foot of the long table to the head of the table. The women bring in her shrimp dish, made from shrimp caught off the island—then close the heavy wooden kitchen door behind them. She hears her own utensils on the table. She hears her teeth against the fork. She hears her spoon against her dessert dishes, lifting the figs that have been picked from the fig tree behind Main House. She moves to the living room.

She will not go hunting for him, not at head or foot, not studio or stairs or bed. There are footsteps again. Either it is he or it isn't. She won't hunt. She hears other sounds: pistol shots, whip cracks, moaning, sobbing, laughter. Beatrix decides that Charlotte's *Journal* is breathing out loud, that women are describing the slave owners beating the slave children, the separation from families. Beatrix does not cower before fiction or fact.

The fire has burned a hole through the middle of the logs. There is a wooden ring around the flame. The finger of flame is consuming the ring. The ring crashes inward. It thunders outdoors. There is laughter and weeping. There is the crash of silver and gold. Pieces of eight shoot into the flame. Lightning shoots through the living room. Beatrix looks up. On the balcony, stories above, stands her lover. He is slowly beckoning, his arms outstretched to her, his index finger crooked,

127

his third finger tickling at her. The cushion next to Beatrix is not dented. Cold air does not appear. All is still.

"Ben!" someone screams.

Patio scrapings, horse's hooves, revelers, clattering dishes, clinking treasure.

"BEN!"

Only the shadow of the hand of Ben, over the balcony, reaching, reaching down to Beatrix. Beatrix does not scream. Or the shadow would enter her mouth. She closes all her orifices. She lets the mucus dry up inside her nasal passages, closes off scent. She lets her ears wax over. She lets her womb walls cling to each other in terror. The shadow rubs her back, chucks her chin, passes over her hair. Her hair resolutely clings to Beatrix's head. Her chin presses down to her neck. The storm is over. The night has passed in a second. It is dawn, and the kitchen workers are banging the screen door. The tree branches are scraping fingernails at the window. Beatrix goes into the kitchen, stiff-legged.

"Help me pack," she asks the women.

They ascend with her. Her clothes are strewn around her room. (It is Lena's Sweet Sixteen.) The bathtub water is flooding onto the orange-red tile floor, over the carpeting. The chair is sliding in the water to and from her desk. Only some of her notes are dry. The women put her clothes through the washing machine and dryer in the Laundry Room. Beatrix puts her damp notes into the sun to dry.

Everyone is tired of the Civil War. Higginson is ill and must go North. Emily Dickinson is writing worried letters to him. Mary Higginson is writing worried letters to him. Charlotte Forten is ill and must go up North. Beatrix is becoming ill and must go up North.

It had been so brave. They had all been brave. Louisa May had joined up and fought the war as a nurse in the Washington military hospital in 1862. She had tended the victims of the bloody battle of Fredericksburg. The women are their fathers' laddies. Louisa May was proud of her brave white soldiers. Charlotte Forten was proud of her brave Black soldiers in Col. Higginson's Black Army Regiment. But everyone is tired.

"Ghosts of my mothers!" cries Beatrix.

She is packed and ready to leave Sea Island. She pauses at the patio where the voices originated the night before.

"Ghosts of my mothers!"

They are laid to rest, those motherly ghosts. They are too tired to sew any more warm red jackets, to teach adults how to hold a pen, to tend the wounded, to sew packets of poems, to hold conversations, write observations. Their fingertips are callused—poor, toothless, hairless Louisa May; their full breasts have dried—poor Margaret; their migraines and joint pains have disappeared—poor Charlotte; their sore eyes and sore nerves are soothed—poor Emily.

Beatrix must leave them. She must go past them, to prehistorical mothers, to foremothers, to the opening of caves of herself.

"Enter me, ghosts of my mothers!" she whispers in this Southern land.

They are tired. A yellow butterfly drifts by. A black-and-white, zebra-striped butterfly loops by. Two Monarch butterflies mate. They couple with double sets of wings, on the patio stones. They hold tight, leaping together onto the glass top of the wrought-iron table. They leap again upward, the reverse of autumn leaves, attaching themselves to the oak tree. The oak has leaves of butterflies. The grass has ribbons of snakes. The palmettos have spots of hogs. The ghosts have folded themselves, like seldom used underwear, old gloves, button boxes, back into drawers.

A limping Black man appears for Beatrix's luggage. His name is Jimbo.

"Where is Ben?" asks Beatrix.

"Ain't no Ben," says Jimbo.

"The other one, the one who brought me here," says Beatrix.

"I'se the one brung you from the mainland," says Jimbo.

"The ferryman," says Beatrix.

Jimbo does not understand Yankee dialect.

"Do you often see Colonel Jack Ferguson?" she asks.

"Not often," says Jimbo.

The motorboat rocks. They are in the wake of another motorboat. Jimbo is sprayed.

"Since he's not been on this earth for these many years."

"He invited me down," says Beatrix.

Fishermen in a passing boat have caught a seagull in their net. It is a brown, immature gull.

"What you doin' with him?" calls Jimbo.

"Fish feed," says one of the fishermen.

The fisherman twists the gull's wing. The gull snaps at him with loud clacking beak. The wing is broken, hanging only from one tendon. The gull tries to fly, falls, swims, spinning in the water.

"Colonel Jack Benjamin Ferguson?" asked Jimbo.

"Yes," says Beatrix.

"He must've called you from his grave, then," cackles Jimbo. "Maybe he's mad that I didn't weed the mound this month."

"Nobody by that name comes down?"

"Nephews of the late Colonel, they come down. They got title to the island for their lifetime."

"Does one of them paint?"

"Sure they does," says Jimbo, "they paints the woods red, they paints the deer, the hogs, the birds a bright red."

Beatrix is confused.

"Sometimes they paints people red," says Jimbo. "Once there was a duel on the island and two people painted each other red. One was Colonel Jack Benjamin Ferguson, a red hole through his ear."

Beatrix begins to cry hysterically. Jimbo has to pilot. He cannot pat her shoulders.

"Ma'am," he calls behind him. The words come broken through the wind. "Sometimes they comes back, all the folks of the island—Black Bart, the pirates, the parties, the duelers. The chairs are filled with them. I always sit on their laps or step on their toes. It's like dancing with the days past."

Beatrix has been waltzing with her mothers. She has been walking on the shoes of her fathers.

## LOOKING FOR BEATRIX'S MOTHER

Beatrix rushed across the water, through the air, by air terminal bus, by taxi, to her mother.

"Forgive me, mother," she said, "for everything I have done to you."

"I know exactly what you did," said her mother, and listed: (1) You had your father sign your report cards; (2) When you told about your day, about your night, you looked at your father; (3) When you spoke of foreign affairs, money affairs, travel affairs you looked at your father. . . ."

The mother was still listing when Beatrix left the house.

Mother Emily Dickinson had written to Higginson, when the latter inquired after her family: "I never had a mother." The mother outlived the long-lived father.


Looking for Friends Again

"Hello, I'm phoning an old friend. This is Beatrix Palmer."

"Who is this?"

"Beatrix Palmer."

"Who do you want?"

"Lois Goldman—the doctor's wife—I knew her in school. . . ."

"The mizus not at home."

"Can I leave a message?"

"Don't seem to be no pencil around."


"Hello, I'm phoning an old friend. This is Beatrix, Beatrix Palmer."

"Who's the old friend?"

"Janice."

Long pause. "My niece? She's been out West for years. Afraid I can't help you."


"Hello, I'm phoning an old friend. This is Beatrix Palmer."

Pause. "Hello."

"Pauline?"

"Yes."

"What are you doing, Pauline?"

Pause.

"What are you doing these days, Pauline?"

"Same as in *those* days."

She does not speak again. Beatrix prattles, slows, stops. She has offended once more.

"Hello, I'm phoning an old friend. This is Beatrix Palmer."

It is an old woman who answers. "Who? Who?"

Beatrix repeats. No one is on the line. A moment later, a man's German-accented voice.

"What is it you wish, please?"

"This is Beatrix Palmer, an old friend."

"Yes. What is it you wish, please?"

"I wish to speak to Shirley."

There is whispering, a conference.

"Hold the phone a little, please."

The conference moves away from the phone.

The father is panting on his return.

"She is unable to come to the phone. She remembers you. Very well. We all remember you. Call again, please. Perhaps she will be able to come to the phone."

"Hello, I'm phoning an old friend. This is Beatrix Palmer."

"Which partner do you wish to speak to, please?"

"Norman. Labor Law."

Norman of the Eugene V. Debs co-op does not remember Beatrix Palmer at first, does not want to remember the co-op.

Suddenly Norman remembers.

"Bert is dead, you know. Frozen to death downtown on some park bench years ago."

"What happened to Charles?"

Black Charles, the drama major and elevator operator, had traveled up to the top floor.

"Head of Harlem Theater. See him, my wife and I, when we fly to New York to do theater."

"Yes," says Beatrix.

"My best to your husband," says Norman. "Did you call,

Beatrix, for business? Did you need a solicitor, a counselor?" When Beatrix said she did not, he repeated best to Harold and rang off.

Best to that marriage that froze to death downtown years ago.

"Hello, I'm phoning a friend. This is Beatrix Palmer."

"Who is your friend?"

"The photographer."

"The photographeress?"

"The woman photographer of your firm."

"She's not here now. She's off taking pictures of Southern coastal trees."

"Why?"

"She's doing a book for Time-Life. She's doing a book for Friends of the Earth. She's doing a book for *Reader's Digest*."

"But she's supposed to be doing a book with me. *Remnants*. What does she know about Southern coastal trees?"

"What does she know about remnants?"

"Hello, mother, I'm phoning to see how you are."

"Why the sudden concern?"

"Hello, Bob's Bicycle Shop, are you still in business?"

"Sure, we're still in business."

"I want to fix my bicycle."

"We don't fix. We just sell new."

"Hello, Lloyd's Furs. Are you still in business?"

"Sure we're still in business."

"I'm calling about storaging a fur."

"Not if you didn't buy it here. We only storage what we sell."

"Hello, Bates Luggage. Are you still in business?"

"We're expanded."

"I need some lightweight luggage."

133

"That's no problem."

"I need some low-priced, lightweight luggage."

"That's a problem."

Good-bye, Marcia S. Liebowitz, French Teacher, Jewish Math, Shorthand, Bald Chemistry, Shirley Panush, Romanian Lois, Black Janice, Pauline. Good-bye, Bob's Bicycle and Repair Shop, Lloyd's Furs, The Dairy Bar, Bates Luggage. Screw you, Sarcastic Cynthia, Fat Roz, One-Eyed Susan, Norma Honey, Razel Schiller. Good-bye Judy and Johnny, high school sweethearts.

"Mother, I'm pregnant with a baby girl and she's looking for a friend."

"Tell her when she phones, her friend will be on the West Coast, will be affronted at being found, will be hiding in the attic, will be at the beauty parlor. Tell her not to look for a friend."

# Foremothers

## Looking for Past Mothers, Way-Past Mothers

If there is one grant, there are two. If there are Wurlitzer and Ossabaw, then there are also MacDowell and Yaddo. If all the writing colonies are full, there is a travel grant overseas. She is to work on *Remnants*. She goes to Israel, the land of the immigrant and the pioneer.

Her father phones. "Keep an eye out for Lena on the way," he says.

## Four Are the Matriarchs: The First Matriarch

"Mother, I'm pregnant with a baby girl."
"May she be the mother of heroes."

She journeyed to the South for there was a famine in the land. Avram watched the shepherds moving past. They turned to look into her dark eyes, at her black skin, her black hair. They stared at the folds of cloth around her belly and hips.

Avram shouted, "You are seeking to entice!"

She had been leading the goats, now a dwindling herd. She had put up the tent she brought to her marriage bed. She had also brought her dowry of two striped robes and her neck beads. She milked the goat. She cooked the last of the kid meat.

Avram suffered from thirst, from fear. She, like a camel, did not seem to have his hunger or his need for water.

"Tell them," he commanded, "that you're my sister, not my wife."

She was asked. The shepherds asked. The soldiers asked. Other than that she spoke seldom, laughed never—was to laugh, later, *once*.

She told the soldiers, "We are traveling into Egypt together, my brother and I. We have no water. We have cooked our last kid."

They took their pleasure with her while Avram sat outside of the tent, drinking their water, eating their provisions. Then the soldiers brought her to the Great House. They pulled aside her garments from her body. Despite famine, the flesh curved. Despite thirst, the shoulder and buttocks meat was juicy. She was given to Pharaoh, who had her while Avram sat outside of the Great House counting his newly gained sheep, oxen, asses, camels.

This time, for the first time, the King of the World plagued Egypt, plagued the shepherds with loss of sheep, the soldiers with loss of battle, the Great House with loss of riches, the Pharaoh with loss of pleasure.

Avram sat by the crossroads, counting his flock.

Pharaoh came out of the Great House: "What have you done to me here! Why did you not tell me that she is your wife? Why did you say, 'She is my sister?' and so I took her to me as wife. But now, here is your wife, take her and go." ("In the Beginning, An English Rendition of the Book of Genesis," Everett Fox, translated from the German of Martin Buber and Franz Rosenzweig, in *Response* 14, Summer 1973, p. 36.)

Once again she traveled with Avram up from Egypt, only

the journey was in stages and slower for they were rich in cattle and precious metal.

The nomadic years passed. Maybe because of the great journey in the desert, or the early famine, or the time she was had by shepherds and soldiers, by princes and pharaoh, Sarai in no way thickened, never bore fruit. All life around her fattened—the camel, the oxen, the she-goat. Trees bore fruit—the date, the fig—but she remained bony. Her walk did not fill the striped cloth of her robe. Her neck beads and hand beads were the larger on the scrawny neck, the veined wrist.

Avram saw her stirring behind the veils in her section of the tent. Her hand would crack bowls of nuts for his callers, but the tent was silent of children.

"You are truly sister," he said to her, lifting the curtain between them, "not wife, for you have borne me no seed."

Sarai, Contentious One, frighted and gave unto Avram her she-servant, an Egyptress—much as Sarai herself had been given away in an earlier day. Sarai could not look upon Hagar, not when Hagar came behind the curtains to prepare the meals, not, afterward, when Hagar's belly stretched and smoothed over. The eye of the belly stared at Sarai, the evil eye of the belly, until Sarai beat the woman upon her face and neck. When Sarai lifted a stool to plunge into the eye of the belly, Hagar fled. Hagar returned from flight for there was no other tribe that would have her thus.

The son of Hagar became thirteen. The master of Hagar was ninety-nine, and, on a day, the foreskins of the son and the father were cut with a sharp stone. On a day, three men appeared before the tent of Avram. They were given the hospitality of the nomad—young oxen, meal cakes, cream, and milk.

The men would have none of provision until they had asked, "Where is your wife?"

Avram lifted the curtains of the women's section of his tent. His wife was grinding meal. She was grinding her gums. She smiled, a wrinkled smile, at the strangers.

They went in upon her, upon her old bones and desert-dry

139

skin. She, courtesan again, as in those desert-bright days of the Pharaoh, laughed within herself.

The three men left. (Some claim it was one man.) The sun was too bright. Avram was ninety-nine, Sarai was ninety—and the three men in the hot sun melted into one imperious man who shouted across the desert, "This set time next year, your wife has a son."

Her name would no longer be Contentious, but Sara, Princess, the mother of tribes. She bled for a month after the visitors left. She bled on the sand, over the carpets, into her garments. When she ceased to bleed, Avram entered upon her in one terrible painful night. He came in, unwrapped his body, took in hand his old familiar rod as if it were his walking stick, and ground it into her.

She, who had little flesh left, neither teeth nor hair, bore with green seed, and it came to pass within that time of bearing, that Sara's face smoothed, her hair grew in fuller, her lips reddened.

When the child was born, Sara was satisfied. She gave suckle to the baby. She laughed behind the curtain of the women's section, and the curtain stirred with her laughter. When Yitzhak was weaned, her breasts shriveled again, her lips paled, and flesh withered. Then she noticed Hagar. Then she noticed the thirteen-year-old son of Hagar, the circumcised Yishmael—"Heard by Elohim."

Sara was, as truly she spoke, not merely the wife of Avram. She was wife and sister-daughter of his father, but of a different mother. She was doubly jealous of Hagar—an Egyptress acquired while Sara was with the Pharaoh. This stranger, neither sister nor wife, had filled her womb. The God of the World had—when Sara was with the Pharaoh—stricken every womb in Egypt. No head came through, no shoulders shouldered their way out. It was because the sister and the wife of Avram was in the bed of the Pharaoh. When Pharaoh returned Sara to her brother-husband, so the wombs of Egypt filled. But this Egyptian womb had been filled and had given birth to the favorite of Avram, to the son hearkened to by Elohim.

Hagar was merry. Yishmael was joyful. Yitzhak, the

140

baby, stared at the blue sky, at the desert bugs upon his fist, stared at the stripes on his rug.

Sara did not speak to Hagar. She spoke unto Avram—with the voice of his long-ago sister, the daughter of his father, the daughter of his mother, the voice of his past and his present.

Sara said, "Your future is with me in my tent. With my son. Kill Hagar. Kill her child."

Avram ceased patting the dark head of Yishmael. He ceased attending to Hagar. Sara waited. She kept her son hidden from Avram until a servant came unto Hagar, unto Yishmael and said, "You have been in the desert before. Go again."

Yishmael turned to go into the tent of Avram, but a sharp spear stayed his way. With spears they were driven from the tents, from the oasis. At the edge of spears they were sent into the desert.

The desert was cruel, mountainous. There was shade only from small trees. No water, no provisions were provided them. Hagar told Yishmael to crouch in the shade of the one tree, while she wandered looking for any of her tribe, looking for water. She found a well. She filled the goatskin with water and hurried back to give Yishmael drink.

Yishmael and Hagar lived in the desert, became huntsmen and bowmen. He remained with his mother, taking unto himself a wife she brought him from Egypt, another Egyptress.

Sara remained in the city of tents. She rested upon her couch and appointed another as handmaiden.

She was the First Matriarch.


Looking for Lena

"I saw her," said a warty woman with one long dark braid, carrying her basket of leeks on the Jerusalem bus.

"Where?"

"Right here."

"When?"

"Just now."

The bus driver asked the passenger to remove her basket of vegetables from the aisle of the bus. The woman refused. The driver stopped suddenly in the middle of the road and would not drive farther. The woman pulled long leeks from her basket and whipped the driver across his head and neck with the leeks. He continued his route.

"I know her," said a *sheitl'ed* lady. "I will never forget her."

"Why?"

"She was right here, against the Kotel."

We were standing at the Western Wall.

"What did she do?"

"She banged her head against these warm stones. She wept until mucus flowed into her mouth."

"Are you sure it was she?"

"No one has ever wept like that before."

"That's the girl," said a student at Haifa University.

"How do you know?"

"Because of what she did."

"What did she do?"

"She took the bus from the foot of Mount Carmel to the very top, to the university. Then she climbed out of the bus. I followed her. She ascended the steps of the new buildings, until the highest point of the campus. She climbed the steps of an unfinished building, taller than any of the others."

"And then?"

"She shouted, 'Higher. I want to climb higher!' "

"Did she climb down?"

"No. When I left with the last bus down the mountain, she was still sitting on the top step of that incomplete building."

"I know her," said the florist in Tel Aviv. "She bought so many flowers from me."

"Did you ask her why?"

"She said they were to decorate a grave."

"Diid you ask her whose?"

"She said the person was not yet deceased."

142

"Everything is to learn about," said Naomi.

Beatrix is shivering. Tel Aviv is cooling in the evening. Naomi rises and closes the door to her porch. They had dined among Naomi's plants, listening to the Sea of the Median, and to caged birds on a neighbor's porch.

Beatrix had lectured on *The Pioneers* at Tel Aviv University. Naomi, a Senior Lecturer in Biology, took Beatrix home for Turkish coffee and for a biology lesson.

They lie on Naomi's stiff Arab rugs. Naomi was not the instigator, originator, vilifier, seductress. They had showered, taking turns. They had dressed in long towels and spread the towels under them, against the itchy rugs. They had wiped a water spot from each other's limbs, from a nipple, a lower lip. They had mopped a poorly dried forehead. Their fingers on each other were stiffer than the hidden straw in the rugs. Their fingers made knobs of nipple and clitoris. It was not tickling. It was a rubbing, a mortar-and-pestling. They each knew what to do.

Beatrix lay her head on one of Naomi's breasts and then on the other. It was a fount, a spring, like this city of their lovemaking. There was the *tel* of Naomi's bosom; there were the springs of Naomi's nipples, armpits, juices of the belly, sweat from the back of the legs, sand of the oasis, salt of Naomi's sea.

Afterward they did not ask:

"Do you love me?"

"Did you have other lovers?"

"How did you lose your virginity?"

Virginity is neither valuable nor valueless between women.

"Do unto another as you would have her do unto you," and they lay back after the *mitzvah*, after following the Golden Rule.

"Tell me your story," said Beatrix to Biological Naomi.

"I am here," said Naomi, "because my father wanted to be here."

"Where is your father?"

"Not here. There."

There in the Diaspora in America, Naomi was trained to return to the Land. There, a descendant, she was taught to ascend the Judaean Hills.

"I was raised in the movement," said Naomi.

Naomi's eyes are hazel, her hair thick brown, her lips full and warm red, her cheeks high-colored. There are no men for Naomi in Israel. Men have been depleted by the wars. Yet Naomi stays.

"Why do you stay, Naomi?"

"It was my destination. There is nowhere else after one's destination."

Naomi's father is an official in the Labor-Zionist movement. Independence Day is not the fourth of July; it is Israeli Independence from British colonialist rule. Elections are watched closely, not to Congress but to Knesset. Naomi knew about gun-running when she was three years old. She knew about Israel Bonds, cash-running, shortly afterward.

When Naomi finished high school, she moved into a Labor-Zionist co-op. Her father came to speak to the group, the Bayit, the House, on their Tuesday night cafés. He spoke on Israeli-Arab relations, on Israeli poetry, on the British and French change from Neutralism to Arabism. After her father's seminars, the Bayit would serve felafels, humus, and other Israeli-Arabic dishes. The whole co-op went as a group to Israel. There they split. Some went into democratic-socialistic kibbutzim. Naomi came to the city, where she tried to start a city kibbutz, an *irbutz*, with a young Israeli. When he was killed in the War of '67, she enrolled at Tel Aviv University, became a biologist and a Lesbian Zionist.

We lie in the dark, Naomi and I. We are holding hands. She has a large ring on one finger. Her hands are big and the ring is not too obtrusive for those hands.

"Are your parents alive?"

"Oh yes."

"What are they doing?"

"My dad is dreaming."

"And your mother?"

"She sleeps without dreaming."

"Of what is your dad dreaming?"

144

"Of his return to the Land."

"Is he proud of you?"

"No. He disinherited me."

"Why?"

"For leaving him to come here."

Beatrix sleeps on her towel, on the striped Arab rug. The colors are not color-fast and the stripes have bled through, becoming another, paler rug on the bare floor.


## Four Are the Matriarchs: The Second Matriarch

Avram called for the eldest servant of his household.

"Swear!" said Avram.

The servant put his hand on Avram's testicles and swore by them that he would help Avram to carry on his seed.

Avram did not search out a sister for Yitzhak. But, among the people of Avram, the servant found Avram's niece, first cousin to Yitzhak.

To the niece gave the elderly servant "a golden nose-ring a half-coin in weight, and two bracelets for her arms, ten goldpieces in weight." ("In the Beginning," p. 60.) He himself put the ring on her nose, slipped the bracelets up her dark arm.

"Take her and go," said her brother Lavan and her father Betuel, for they knew that within the camel bag of the old servant were gifts for them. And the servant also brought out jewels for the brother and mother of Rivka.

Yitzhak was forty years of age when he beheld Rivka. Her face was veiled but he brought her into the tent of Sara, his mother, where he unveiled her face and her body, and Rivka comforted him on the death of his mother.

Although the servant's hand had rested upon the testicles of the father-in-law that the seed of the house of Avram continue and the tents multiply, yet was Rivka "a hardened-root." ("In the Beginning," p. 66.)

Her cousin, Yitzhak, is forty, the pampered son of old parents ("thy son, thine only son, whom thou lovest, even

Yitzhak''). His mother is gone and this hardened root lies within her tent, heeding not the admonition of her brother Lavan, "Our sister, be thou the mother of thousands of ten thousands."

Yitzhak prayed, not Rivka, Yitzhak who besought the Lord as his father had done in Sara's old age. Rivka conceived, but her time was not happy, no laughter as with her mother-in-law. The movement within her belly was painful. She cried out but Yitzhak heard her not. She would put her hand on her belly, hoping to warm and calm a dissatisfied limb, to hold a knee, elbow, foot, or head. All within her was knobs. The boys came out embattled, one with fine baby fuzz, kicking off the clinging hand of the second.

That which Yitzhak loved did Rivka despise. Yitzhak, once under the knife himself, loved only danger and those who sought it. Rivka, alone in this land but for her nurse, never again to see her family from the Aramean Field, sought quiet and companionship.

Her quiet son, her favorite, carried within him cunning, while the one who roamed had within him trust. Thus did the twins exchange themselves in part.

Yitzhak was sixty, and, like his father Avram, a dissembler. When the famine came Yitzhak went to Gerar, as Avram had done before him. Yitzhak enticed the King of the Phistines with a view of Rivka, for Yitzhak was sixty and Rivka yet young. The King let Yitzhak sojourn in Gerar.

And Yitzhak said unto Rivka, "You will tell the people of the place that you are my sister."

Although aging, Yitzhak was ever fearful of being harmed. He had faced death once in a glinting knife and ever after he squinted at it. He did not now want to be killed for a fair wife.

And it came to pass that the King of the Philistines craved Rivka and went to her. He found there Yitzhak fondling Rivka's breasts, touching her thigh, kissing her body.

The King had been about to commit mortal sin, lying with the wife of a guest, thinking the wife his guest's sister.

Yitzhak fared well with "sheep-herds and oxen-herds and many working-cattle." ("In the Beginning," p. 68.) His cousin-wife, like his own mother, like his father's sister-wife, would love one son, would revenge herself upon spoiled Yitzhak. She had been taken from the Aramean Field, from her mother and father and brother Lavan; she had been scorned and called a hardened root; she had been called his sister before the king, to entice the king during a famine. She would make her son her lover. She would husband her son, train him in cunning, help him to steal the blessings, the land and the love of his father from her eldest born. She would create enmity between Yaakov and Esav. She would warn Yaakov to flee for "your brother comforts himself on your account, to kill you." ("In the Beginning," p. 73.) She would send him, my only son, my son, to the land of Lavan my brother until "your brother's anger has turned away from you and he has forgotten what you did to him." But it was she, Rivka, who had kindled the anger, fed it, quenched it only when it threatened to destroy her child.

Rivka dissembled. As Sara had attacked the women in her household, so Rivka attacked her daughters-in-law, the wives of her eldest son, Esav.

Rivka approached the bedside of Yitzhak. She had made him broth. She spoon-fed him while he held shakily unto her feeding hand. He was not only blind and senile; he was obedient.

"I loathe my life because of the daughters of Het," said Rivka. ("In the Beginning," p. 74.)

A drop of broth spilled on Yitzhak and burned his chest.

"If Yaakov should take himself a wife from the daughters of Het, like these, from the daughter of the land, what then shall life be to me?" ("In the Beginning," p. 74.) She wiped his chin.

So it was Yitzhak who ordered Yaakov to travel forth into the land of his mother, to the household of her birth, to the incestuous bed. There, among blood-cousins, he must take a wife.

Esav, the elder, saw that his wives, the two women of Canaan, were hated by his mother and were evil unto his father. Esav saw that, like his uncle Yishmael, he was the stranger.

147

Yaakov, the younger, traveled from Beer-Sheva to the Aramean Field, to the tent of his uncle Lavan. Thereafter he became the husband of two sisters, both nieces of his mother. They were to be the Third and Fourth Matriarchs.

Esav, the bitter, Esav, the fool, tried once again to please. He wed no woman of Canaan, no Hittite, but a daughter of a son of Avram, his cousin. But *she* did not become a matriarch.


## Remnants (1)

Bea is working on *Remnants*, without her photographer. She is interviewing and documenting survivors of the Holocaust. She finds them everywhere. They drive taxis, dangerously turning around from the front seat to tell her their stories. They lunch on the old train, built during the Turkish rule, offer her cucumbers, yogurt, fresh Israeli bread, and their stories. Their arms are blue-tattooed, this special breed, this stamp of people, these middle-aged, aged, bald, these men with thick, graying hair on their heads, Brillo-like hair springy on their chests, these women who push crazily on buses, charging seats, disturbing the conductor. These survivors are still elbowing their way to air on the cattle cars; they are still filling their starving stomachs.

She sees the women in the Turkish baths. They are eating cheese-filled pastry. They are lying voluptuously naked on the carpets or sunning on the roof. They are bare-armed, bare-legged, bare-thighed, bare-breasted, but they are tattooed. They are dressed in numbers.

Her German florist and his wife are tattooed. The fishman at Super Sol's is numbered. The Polish bakery lady is not only tattooed but her face is half burned off. Neighbors across the street from her rented Jerusalem apartment rest tattooed arms on the railings of their balconies and watch their children playing soccer in the street.

She sees them at all the memorial places, looking into mirrors, at Yad Vashem, the Memorial to the Holocaust, at Holocaustal museums, watching Holocaustal films. Their children come, their grandchildren, their cousins in the Diaspora.

"It can never be seen enough," they explain.

Not everyone tattooed is marked as Superior Product, Grade A Beef. Not everyone is Blue Ribbon, but they are remnants, streamers from other lands, banners of another time, these streaming ribbons of people crossing the Mediterranean. No one led them out. No one divided the sea for them. In fact, the world was unified in preventing their departure.

One red-haired fifty-year-old, the treasurer of his village, and his widowed sister tell Beatrix their tale. In their twenties, some twenty-five years ago, they sailed to Palestine on a coal boat. The British turned them back. They were fleeing the Nazis, who had already killed their parents and their younger sister. But the British turned them back. They tried for five months to land, for five months not to be returned to Poland. Black with coal dust, coughing, their eyes streaming, they finally landed.

The sister holds up a photograph of her family. She is in uniform. They are the Socialist Youth Group. There she is, under her heavy chins, her thinning hair, twenty-five years ago, soft, round face, light eyes. Her brother, wearing a worker's cap, is next to her. The youngest sister poses in Youth Group uniform, with her hair braided on top of her head, her hands braided in her lap.

"She was *lakachet*," taken, says the sister, and wipes her eyes. She fits her thumb on her sister's face and leaves her print on it.

She sees other numbers. An Air Force security agent and his young daughter sit next to her on the train from Haifa to Jerusalem. They are going for the Maccabee Games. Air Force security kisses and pets the young daughter who has his own face.

"If you want to keep your daughter," he advises Beatrix, "give her everything she wants and don't bind her wrists, and you will keep her forever."

But he is afraid he will not keep his fourteen-year-old forever. She has blood clots in her legs. After the soccer

149

games, they will go to the Western Wall to pray for the success of her leg operation.

The child sleeps on his shoulder. He encircles her head with his tattooed arm.

They are circus people. The Tattooed People. The Experimented-On People. Still, they live.


Bearers of the Dream (2)

In Haifa Beatrix visits a singer. She is small and half of her height is her black hair. She walks on platform dude shoes. She struts. Her voice struts. Her voice is a platformed voice, thrown higher than she is.

The singer talks about her throat problems, her tight vocal cords, the chest that is too resonant. She talks about theater problems. Eighteen-year-olds are getting all the singing jobs. Tall girls are hired first; short girls last. She talks and eats. She is staying away from milk products, however. They clog the throat.

"Tell me your story, Rina," says Beatrix. "Are your parents alive?"

"My father is alive," says Rina.

"Your mother is dead?"

"My mother was always dead, but she is not dead."

"What are your parents doing?"

"My father is dreaming."

"Of what is he dreaming?"

"Of singing."

"Does he sing?"

"He always sang. He played guitar, banjo, mandolin. He sang on the radio, played the banjo in family bars. We sang, when I was a baby and he not yet middle-aged, at the openings of auto dealerships. We did Chevrolet openings together. We did the new gas stations. He sang on the Yiddish Hour. We tap-danced Saturday afternoons at a downtown movie house. We were a team, my father and I, like Shirley Temple and Jack Haley, Shirley Temple and Bojangles Robinson, Shirley Temple and George Murphy."

150

"What did your mother say?"

"She didn't notice."

"What did your father teach you?"

"To sing and to go home afterward, not to go on the road. A single girl always comes home."

"What did you do?"

"I came here, where I can go home every night. It's a small country and it chaperones me."

"Is your father proud that you are doing what he taught you to do?"

"No. He has disinherited me."

"Why?"

"Because I am doing what *he* wanted to do."

"That's all?"

"And because I, a single girl, did not return to his house at night."


## Four Are the Matriarchs: The Third and Fourth Matriarchs

What do I learn from my mothers? Sister against sister, woman betrays woman. The man is the seed and the woman the gourd, filled with seed and rattling or dried and to be discarded.

Beatrix learns what is praiseworthy. Avram is praised for offering up his son, his only son, but he offered up both of his sons, both of his only sons, one to the desert and one to the slaughtering place on the mountaintop. How is it that later both boys, brothers despite their mothers, bury their father Avram together? "Yitzhak and Yishmael, his sons, buried him in the caves of Machpelah." ("In the Beginning," p. 64.)

Mother, you made a contest of the womb. You named your children as prizes. And when you tired, you sent your maid-servants to bear for you. You dissemble, mother. You make fools of your men.

Lea, older mother with weak eyes, with squinting, suspicious face, with graying hair, unable to find her own love, found another's, her younger sister's.

There was a plenitude of wombs for Yaakov, two wives, two maidservants. First he came into Lea. All night he rent her. All night he reared and pawed the earth. He did not know his mare. In the morning on his rug slept the head of that old gray mare, her face relaxed, her mouth crookedly open, a faint snore issuing. Her eyes, not clearly open in daylight, peered white beneath the nonclosing lids, like moon still visible in the morning sky. It was as if Lea watched him while she slept.

Lavan did not overly punish his son-in-law. Only for a week, a bride week, did he have to saddle and bridle her. Within seven days he would have Rahel, the one he had first kissed at the well. It was for Rahel that he had lifted up his voice and wept. (The old servant, another time, at the same place, had met the maiden Rivka at the well and had wept his thanksgiving. They are all wells, our mothers; wells of our generations. It is for them that the Old Testament, the Old Testicle, is written.)

For seven nights did Yaakov come in upon Lea. Did he dream, all that time, he was with Rahel? Or did he see the pretty maid Zilpa crouching in the corner of the tent? Did he dream of her soft flesh, for we dream of someone when we make love, either the person we are loving or the person we would like to.

Lavan not only gave Rahel unto Yaakov, but also her maid Bilha. Yaakov loved Rahel that bridal week until the tent stakes shook. Lavan was shrewd. With four women, Yaakov would work those extra seven years and not notice. With one daughter, Rahel, Yaakov would have turned swiftly back to Yitzhak and Beer-Sheva, the land of Seven Wells.

The women are bearers or hardened roots. For weak eyes, God, the Majestic Plural, compensated with strong womb. For Rahel's pretty face and fair form, God compensated with spontaneous abortions.

Lea held each of her sons before Yaakov. Why did he continue to come in upon her tent if she displeased him? Perhaps he came on her in anger. He would go into that tent, slap her, stripe her face like the rugs under her, hurl her down. And she would be so grateful, for she had that blurry vision, those bad, squinty eyes, and he dangled every year another son. She called those sons: Son's Sight, Hearing, Joining, Giving Thanks, and said, "Indeed, now will my husband love me." ("In the Beginning," p. 79.)

It was an animal pen in that tent, crawling, squalling babies. In Rahel's tent it was cool and quiet; yet Rahel wept.

Like her husband's grandmother, Sara, Rahel gave up her serving maid, Bilha, to bear for her. The child would be raised as hers when Bilha would have borne across the knees of Rahel. Rahel thanked God for Bilha's son and called him Judge, for God had judged and had heard the voice of Rahel.

The women contested. Bilha bore again; Rahel named the child Contester. Lea gave her maid Zilpa unto Yaakov. Zilpa bore. Lea went into the tent of Rahel with the umbilical cord dangling from the unwashed infant and told Rahel, "I call him Fortune," for God had made her fortunate.

And the sisters quarreled and bore through their maids. Yet once again Lea went into the tent of Rahel and held up another son and said his name was Bliss for he was her bliss.

Yaakov walked between babies in all the tents and there was no thought of any other thing.

The eldest son of Lea finds a magic root to make Lea full-bellied again. Son's Sight brings the mandrake for his mother but Rahel pulls at Lea's hair, begging for the mandrake.

Lea screams, "Is it too little that you have taken away my husband,/must you also take away the mandrakes of my son?" ("In the Beginning," p. 80.)

She intercepts Yaakov, coming home tired from the field. He must lie that night with her. He does. He cares no longer whose womb he is filling, so long as it is warm and tight-fitting.

Lea bears "Hire," for she has hired Yaakov for the night. Yet another night Lea rocks with Yaakov and bears a sixth son. She rushes to the tent of Rahel and holds him up, Prized One.

She also bears a daughter, Dina.

Lea's tent is full.

"How many children have you, Lea?"

"Six."

"But I see seven here."

"Six are my sons. We do not count daughters as our children."

So it is to this day in the tents of all Bedouin.

What is happening to Rahel? She bleeds irregularly. She grows listless and has nothing to add to the prophecy that her children shall cover the earth as the stars in the sky, as the tents in the oasis. And her tent flaps open to admit another baby, other nephews. They all look like Yaakov.

Then it comes to pass that Rahel, too, bears a son.

"God has removed my disgrace!"

She calls him: "May He add to me another son." ("In the Beginning," p. 81.)

When they flee from her father Lavan, it is Rahel, the one who could not steal the mandrake roots, who steals the totems of her father. Perhaps Rahel thinks these totems will impregnate her, that this tribal god of Lavan will do for her what it took Him too long to do. Lavan comes looking for them, as Yaakov moves his tribe back to Beer-Sheva. Rahel hides the totems. Lavan looks into her tent. She tells her father that she is menstruating and cannot rise to bid him enter, for menstruating women are as camel dung, only not so useful. Her father would be cursed by his totems if he entered the tent of a bleeding woman.

Yaakov comes to Shekhem, which is on the west bank of the Jordan. He drives his household and cattle as far as Beth-Lecham, the House of Bread.

Rahel has been traveling on camel, and it is her time. She has been bumped. The sun has been merciless upon her head. Her bearing goes hard for her.

She is bearing, dying, and cursing her son with the name Son-of-My-Woe, but Yaakov takes him from the tomb of Rahel's womb and calls him Son-of-the-Right-Hand. Rahel cries, or sighs. The womb shudders closed. She is buried on that spot.

Yaakov puts a standing marker there where she has died and goes to his tribe to count out his sons, twelve, and his years and his father's years. When Yaakov goes from that place of Rahel's Tomb, Lea stays at the marker yet a moment longer, a faint smile upon her face.

The sons of Yaakov, twelve in number, what happens to them? They are named: Despoiler, Warrior, Ruler, Sailor, Toiler, Viper, Goader, Farmer, Seeder, Soothsayer, Devourer, Divider. The daughter, Dina, what is to happen to her? She will not be Rich Man, Poor Man, Beggar Man, Thief, Doctor, Lawyer, Merchant, Chief. She will be raped and then not mentioned again.

Mothers, what have you taught me? When we sing at the Passover table "Who Knows One?" One is the Lord in Heaven and on Earth. We come to Four are the Matriarchs. We come to Nine are the Months of Childbearing. Mothers, you have taught me that a woman is as good as her womb. If she bears, her sons will place a standing marker where she has died. And if she is barren, she is not part of the Old Testicle.

Mothers! Sara! Rivka! Lea! Rahel! You have taught your daughters that women fight for the penis of a man. The winner will be honored with burial in the Cave of Machpelah or under a standing marker on the road to Bethlehem.

Who named *you* my mothers? Who named *this* a matriarchy?


Remnants (2)

Beatrix completes her research on *Remnants*, for, as Yossef told his brothers: "God sent me out before you/to prepare you as a remnant on earth,/to keep you alive for a great deliverance." ("In the Beginning," p. 126.)

Their great deliverance is to be alive, is to be working extra time on *Shabbat* to supplement the income, is to send sons into the army to be killed.

But they are alive. Beatrix sees them in the green hills of Judaea, walking among the twisted, ancient olive trees. They are alive in development towns, working under the hot sun.

They are alive on the boulevards of Tel Aviv. They climb Mount Carmel in Haifa. They are alive inland and in port cities, on mountains, in deserts.


## Bearers of the Dream (3)

In the artist's village of Ein Hod she meets Ilana, a Russian potter. Ilana has a rounded belly, a rounded bottom, handles of arms.

"Tell me your story, Ilana," says Beatrix.

They have returned from a concert in the stone amphitheater of Ein Hod. Wild dogs had rushed across the stage while the chamber group bowed. A donkey with a scarred nose had walked this distance from an Arab village nearby and had brayed. A scorpion is crawling across the stage.

Ilana and Beatrix shiver in the night air, but yet it is warmer in Ein Hod than in Jerusalem, Tel Aviv, or Haifa. The days are sweltering. Beatrix cannot bear her clothes upon her body. Ilana works naked in the pot shop. The women sweat while the clay dries.

"I am the daughter of collectors," says Ilana. "My parents came from Leningrad with a shipload of furniture and with a large library. My father is a man of culture."

"And your mother?"

"My mother is paralyzed. She gave birth and saw it was a girl and never spoke again. She walks slowly with a cane. She writes her requests shakily. She sleeps separately."

"What did you do in your father's house?"

"I admired the samovars, the art books on the Hermitage. I admired our piano, our phonograph, our sheet music. He is an importer. I fingered the materials he brought from France, the lace from Belgium, the Indian silk. I went to Bezalel Art School to make more objects for his collection."

"Then he is pleased with you, Ilana, that you are a potter?"

"No. He has disinherited me. Cousins inherit the sheet music and piano. An aunt inherits the Belgian lace. The

156

samovar belongs to my mother. The paintings are bequeathed to the Israel Museum. The empty apartment will go to a nephew.''

"Why did he disinherit you?"

"Because I would not stay home and be part of the collection.''

## Bearers of the Dream (4)

Beatrix visits Rut'y. Rut'y has a car and will drive Beatrix to the airport at Lod when her research is complete. She is a social worker in the Ministry of Absorption.

Beatrix and Rut'y have coffee and onion soup at a Jerusalem restaurant.

"Tell me your story, Rut'y," says Beatrix.

"My father was a labor organizer."

"And your mother?"

"She was organized by my father. She was carefully placed in the kitchen where she met the plants that needed watering, the flour and sugar and shortening that needed baking, the neighbors that needed gossiping.''

"What was your life like at home?"

"I went with my father to strike meetings. I went with him, as a child, to women's prisons, where he helped to bring reforms. I went with him to the Arab communities, where he brought the Israeli Arabs into the labor movement.''

"And then what did you do?"

"I went to Hebrew University to study sociology."

"Then your father is proud, for you are working with the new immigrants.''

"No. My father is cross. He has disinherited me."

"Why is this?"

"Because I am not there for him when he returns from the rallies.''

"But your mother is."

"Yes, but her head is in the oven, or over the flower pots, or peering in a neighbor's door.''

"Your father is disappointed in you?"

"Fathers are always disappointed in us. We bear the dreams they have already shed."

Beatrix marked her tapes, paid her rentals on the apartment in Jerusalem, the hotel in Haifa, the sublet villa in Ein Hod.

Then she searched out her own remnants. She looked for a brown-haired girl in the branches of olive trees, in the towers of minarets, in the citadel of the YMCA, in the bunk beds of youth hostels, the sulphur baths of Tiberias, the shops and bazaars in the markets of the Old City and of Jaffa. She looked for her in the sunset over the Mediterranan and in the sunrise on Mount Carmel. She listened for her call when shepherds passed with their goats on their way to the Judaean Hills. She took a bus into the Sinai and slept in the sand, hoping the girl would be at Eilat or Sharm es Sheikh. She climbed Mount Sinai at 2 A.M., arriving on the summit at six, for sunrise. She thought if Moses received the tablets there, she might receive some word of her remnant, her commandment. But when the sun rose, she fell asleep on the ground in exhaustion. Her guide had to return from the rest of the group that had already descended in order to lead her back down the mountain.

Beatrix looked among Russian-speaking cafés of Tel Aviv, Roman and German cafés, cafés of the young, actors' cafés, cafés of the intelligentsia, the journalists' cafés. She looked in abandoned Arab villages and in development towns.

She returned to Rut'y, the woman in the Ministry of Absorption.

"Absorb me, Rut'y," she pleaded.

"I cannot," said Rut'y. "You are already absorbed in something else."

Rut'y took Beatrix to the airport at Lod. No terrorists had landed during this month to machine-gun tourists. No women had boarded planes, during her visit, with hand grenades stuffed into their brassieres. Yet Beatrix was terrorized.

What if all messages from the brown-haired girl went undelivered or undeciphered? What if clues dropped were undetected? What if the brown-haired girl was in the Midwest while Beatrix was traveling in the Mideast?

"Mother, I am pregnant with a baby girl and she has left me."

"Then you must spend the rest of your life looking for her."

# Looking for
# Daughters

# Primer: Ten Ways to Lose Daughters

## I. Talk Too Much

"Listen to me," says Beatrix.

She wants ears uncovered, eyes attentive, mouth closed. She wants no squirming, no plucking at clothes, no twisting of fingers. Beatrix speaks without pagination, inserting marginalia, notation, documentation. She bolsters her arguments. She stuffs in data. She fills out with fact.

Lena is weeping.

"I have said nothing to offend you," says Beatrix.

"Shut up," says Lena.

## II. Compare

When Lena was at puberty, when she started the forty years of walking through her menstrual desert, her skin erupted.

"*I* always had good skin," said Beatrix.

"Shut up," said Lena.

### III. Be Helpful

In the Ninth Grade Lena was up all night writing a report. It was dawn. The first class would be in two hours.

"Let me help you," said Beatrix.

"No," said Lena.

"I wrote a book. I can help you write a report."

"Shut up," said Lena.

### IV. Have Historical Perspective

The girls in her class are invited to a pajama party. Lena is not. Her friends have made the Honor Roll. Lena has not. They have new holiday clothes. Not Lena. They all have fathers. Lena has none.

"It's only of importance at this stage of your life," says Beatrix in a kindly voice.

"Shut up! Shut up! Shut up!" says Lena.

### V. Be Silent

From oration, exhortation, explanation, divination, Beatrix went to an offended silence. She decided not to return accusations with refutations, opposition with a reasonable proposition. Beatrix answered ire, rage, fury, wrath, insolence, meanness, unworthiness, vengefulness, irrationality, anguish, defiance, grief with paragraphs of silence, pages of quiet. Days would go by and the only sounds in the House of Palmer would be in the kitchen or bathroom.

One day Beatrix went into Lena's bathroom. Lena was sitting on the covered toilet, crying into a thick towel.

"Lena," said Beatrix in a kindly voice.

"Shut up," said Lena.

### VI. Have Goals for Your Daughter

Lena graduated *cum laude* from Junior High. Beatrix kissed the mouth she had allowed to wear lipstick. She kissed each eyelid she had allowed to wear eye shadow. She kissed the right wrist for which she had bought a watch.

"From high school," said Beatrix, "you'll be *magna, summa, supra, dea*—."

"Shut up," said Lena.

## VII. Be Organized

Lena is going on a trip with her class.

"Did you take a face cloth, a hand towel, portable toothbrush with its small tube of toothpaste, Arrid, Noxema, Selsan shampoo, nail clipper, nail file, Cutex Oily Polish Remover Pads, Junior-Size Kotex, clean sanitary belt, address book, notebook, sharpened pencil?"

Lena is going for a four-day weekend.

"Shut up," said Lena.

## VIII. Teach Politeness

"Did you shake hands? Did you ask about their kids? Did you write Thank You notes? Did you offer to carry their packages? Did you say, 'I'm sorry?' Did you apologize? Did you excuse yourself? Did you say, 'Pardon me?' Did you say, 'Would you repeat that, please?'?"

"Shut up," said Lena.

## IX. Teach Caution

"Did you double-date? Did you carry bus fare? Did you keep your pants on? Did you stay away from the park and dark side streets? Did you let him know what kind of girl you are? Did you make sure he met your mother?"

Lena is silent.

"I'm speaking," said Beatrix.

"Shut up," said Lena.

## X. Be Energetic

"Here are your vitamins, this for your cold, here's for night blindness, this for the white spots on your fingernails. Do you have lunch money? Did you get your research from the library? How much time will you have for homework tonight? Are you prepared for the Friday test in Algebra II? Have you worked on Group Project for History? Did you get to the cleaners? Did you take your run-down heels to the shoemaker? Did you practice for Piano? Have you checked out Swimming at the Center?''

Lena is silent

"Did you hear me?" asked Beatrix.

"Never again," said Lena.


## Looking for Daughter—In Purses

She searches in her purse. She searches for the *right* purse. One is a red, drawstring Indian bag. Another is an oilcloth traveling bag. A third is a cheapy bag. Fourth is a classy leather bag. Fifth is an antique bag.

The mirrors are falling out of the red, drawstring Indian bag. She bought it at World Bazaar. The mirrors are falling out and the white beads are loosening from the white thread design. Several rows of mirrors are intact.

Bea sees herself in the horizontal row of tiny mirrors, a bit of an eye, an arch of brow; next row, the nose; two rows down, the mouth. Above, near the missing drawstring of the drawstring bag, Bea sees bits of her black hair reflected. She is faceted like *The Fly*. Vincent Price would recognize her. She sees a broken mirror of world. As the mirrors loosen from their embroidered pockets, Beatrix also sees what's behind the mirror: the red cloth of the purse, red behind eyelid, sun coming up, bloodshot red of eye, gouged-out eye, empty socket of eye where mirror has fallen like a tear.

In this purse she has no clue to daughter. She has a black bobby pin, although she cannot remember when she last used bobby pins. She used to pin her hair up, but the heavy uncontrollable hair would begin to creep out of pins, barrettes, and nets. With her hair up, her cheeks fattened and her eyes narrowed. As the hair avoided its holders, her face would be restored to her. She stopped putting up her hair and tried to curl ringlets above her ears. They stuck out like springs or slipped horns.

In the purse Beatrix has a key to an office. The purse also once had a binding, that time when she took it to Buffalo—looking for daughter.

She looks into her large, oilcloth traveling bag. It is black-and-white polka-dotted, with double handles. The zipper is ripping from the binding, for she had overloaded the purse when she went to California—looking for daughter. Bea overloads everything, plugs, her arms with laundry that falls on the stairs as she mounts them, books to be returned to the library, books that are lost between car and library return box.

In the black-and-white shiny purse is a health card to a clinic, a phosphorescent green pencil that says GLOW and Cixon 250-2. She has these clues if only she could read them.

The plastic partition of the traveling bag is torn. The bottom of the bag is full of gleaming black beetles of pins. Now she knows where all pins go, to the bottom of purses. She finds a black wide-toothed comb for which she's been searching. It's the only comb that does not tear her hair and that can fit into her five purses. Between its wide teeth lint lodges. She finds a nickel, a dime, two pennies, and an Israeli *lira*. She is surprised to find the two pennies in her purse for she has always saved pennies for Lena and still automatically puts them into a large coffee can in case, when Lena is found, she is penniless.

Beatrix finds a poem on green ditto paper, a poem someone pressed into her hand when she gave a lecture. The poet is anonymous for the poem continues and is signed on page two and she has lost page two. She has marked the green ditto ink in red pen. She sees that she objected to "leaking heavens," "the sneer of the mouth and mind," "snakings of the soul." She has no idea what this poem is about or how it can lead to Lena's whereabouts.

She picks up that cheapy bag, light-green cloth with garish orange beads. The bag has a white fringe at its base like a lampshade. She bought it on sale and thought to send it to Lena in case Lena wrote. Then she became insecure about her purchase. Lena would object to the color, the excess of beads, the gaudily beaded flower and peacock design, and would have one more excuse not to return home. Beatrix uses the purse and is ashamed of it, yet she finds it more practical than her other bags for it has a simple zipper, closed compartments, and shoulder straps.

From this cheapy bag she takes out her wallet. The plastic of the photograph insert is discolored. It is blackened like a disease across Lena's baby forehead. The eyes are worried in the mother's arms. The bonnet is too small. She has rims of fat showing through the gauzy white pinafore. Bea is holding her and leaning back with the weight. Bea's earring hangs crookedly. Her blouse is unevenly buttoned. Bea is plump after childbirth. The mirror of this wallet is a shiny aluminum paper. It is scarred. Bea sees her scarred face in it.

She has a photograph of Lena wearing a Girl Scout cap. Lena is fourteen and joyously smiling. Behind Lena lurks a shy friend, hidden by Lena's rich brown hair and Girl Scout cap. Between the baby and the Girl Scout is a four-year-old in plaid dress with white collar and cuffs, with a red ribbon on the back of her head and small bits of bow sticking up like terrier's ears. Lena has bangs. She is smiling. But the photographer used a flash and her face is flattened, and the smile is faded. Lena is fifteen and is holding Beatrix's hand against a tree trunk. The tree divides and separates their heads. Their hair is foliage. They are holding hands tightly but not looking at each other.

"LENA!" screams Beatrix.

Her window is slightly open to let in air. It is early Spring and her call sails like a kite. A child outside brakes his bike and looks up at her window.

Beatrix has one classic bag, purchased with her royalties. It is a Judith Leiber Inc. bag. It is to be admired as sculpture, standing on the dresser on its accordion base. It has elegant thin straps. There is gold trimming on the lovely clasp and on the rims of inside compartments. The name of the designer is in golden script. But it is too small to carry supplies.

And then there is a French bag, an antique. It has tiny golden beads, tiny white beads on a golden satin background, with pale pink and darker pink and golden buds with green embroidered leaves edging the purse. Inside, it is rich golden satin. Lena bought it for her, out of Lena's allowance, one summer in London.

Beatrix Palmer had been given an advance by *Commen-*

*tary* to cover her expenses while she researched: The Jew in London: (a) Immigrant Jewish-British Literature; (b) The Jew in Parliament; (c) The Jew in Society. She wrote half of (a), never completed (b), and did not know how to contact society for (c).

But it was a summer for Bea and Lena like the golden satin lining of her embroidered purse. Sunsets came gradually, from cool yellow to golden. The coverlets on their twin beds were white satin. French windows opened above a garden with rose trellises and English cherubs riding tricycles. Birds sang while Lena nestled on Beatrix's lap. There was no time to write an article.

There was time to locate Lena's lost pocketbook at the Lost and Found on Baker Street. They found no pocketbook there but many Chamberlain umbrellas and bought one. There was time to teach Lena to read chapters, books, series with the Narnia adventures. There was time to cut hair, to buy Lena a matching Scottish skirt and tam, with a dolly also in Black Watch.

There was time for Portobello Road where Lena found Bea's purse. She bought it for her mother out of her allowance, borrowing ahead until the Fall.

Inside of the antique purse is a flowered paper napkin on which is written the telephone number of a French couple whom she met at a party and who invited her and Lena to visit them in Nice. There is nothing else within the purse. But when Beatrix thinks of her French beaded bag, of the old woman in a French garret, eyes fading, laboriously stringing those hundreds of beads, Bea feels a great sense of responsibility to the bag, to the allowance of Lena, to her child's love for her on the day of Bea's summer birthday in London.

"Mother, I am pregnant with a baby girl and she has left me."

"Search for her."

"Where should I be searching?"

"Look for the father."

# Looking for
# Fathers

## Looking for Fathers

If you're a daughter, where do you look for your father?

You used to look in crockery and glassware. In the moustache cup you hunted for his moustache. In the drinking glass next to his bedstead, you found his teeth drinking the water. The jaws are slightly ajar, the teeth smiling.

They toast you. "*L'haim*," say your father's teeth.

If you are at the beach, you look for your father in his bathing suit. If he has changed in the tall grass, or under a beach towel, to avoid paying for the shower room, you may catch a glimpse of clams without their shell, of unkosher, unscaly seafood, scallops maybe. Or, if it is like meat, more like pork.

You used to be able to find your father at the furnace, carrying out ashes. That was before gas and oil heat. You can still sometimes find your father pulling down the garage door, after he has parked the car there for protection in winter.

If you listen for your father at night, he is sending out a code with staccato snores. If someone in the family has died, your father is crying. If you creep into his bedroom to look, there are no tears on his face.

When your father comes home from work at five, you rush into his arms. When your mother comes home from work at five, you nod at her. It will take her an hour and a half to get dinner on the table.


Looking for Fathers (1): Off to Buffalo

"Mother, I'm pregnant with a baby girl and I want to know what she's learned."

"To shuffle."

"Where?"

"Off to Buffalo."


Beatrix receives an announcement. Annual Buffalo film festival. Her coordinator on *The Pioneers* has sent it to Bea, with a name encircled and an arrow pointing to a face.

That face is obscured by a camera, as are all the faces on the announcement. The filmmakers have probosces, tubular organs of lenses, attached sucking snouts, as they focus on each other or on the reader of the announcement. Jonas Mekas has his thin, pale face and his thin, pale hair obscured by the camera. Stan Brakhage has gray earlocks, puffy cheeks, and binocular eyes, with a lens snout over his full, petulant face. Stan Vanderbeek's beard is cropped by the camera. Bruce Baillie's light eyes do not show nor does Ed Emshwiller's smile.

"If he's there, she's there," said her mother, about Bea's husband and daughter.

"It's a hundred percent sure she's found him," said her father.

Changes occur in one's life, not in the search or in the pain, but in physical accomplishment. Beatrix had learned to dive in elementary school, to bike in Junior High, to type in High, and now in middle age, to drive.

Beatrix leaves for Buffalo. It is a four-hour trip. It takes Beatrix six and a half.

174

Her father phoned before she went.

"Give him my regards," said her father. "Tell him I bear no hard feelings."

Being a parent means being once removed from the experience of one's children.

Her program had listed: HAROLD STEINER, the name and face her photographer coauthor had encircled. Showing: Birth, Sunrise, Stillness.

What did he know about birth, running away before the time? Sunrise? He grumbled each morning because he had stayed up half the night. Stillness? He paced like a formerly free-roving creature, now caged. While driving or riding, at his desk, in classroom, on the bed, he moved, tapped his foot, shifted his seat, drummed his hands, jerked his head, climbed over her and under her.

It could not be the same Harold Steiner.

Beatrix stops in Canada for coffee. She nervously takes out her wallet in the dining booth and, into her coat, counts out her money. Has she enough? Did she take too much? Should it have been in Travelers Checks? In larger denominations? Smaller? The pleasant waitress serves her coffee and adds toast without charge. She gives Beatrix change in American silver. Beatrix is drawing and loosening the drawstring of her Indian bag until she breaks the string and has to carry the purse out to her car like a grocery bag, holding it by the bottom. She sets the purse on its haunches in the front seat and it falls over. Photos slip out of the plastic case. The girl in the plaid dress curtsies and her bow wobbles. The baby in Bea's arms struggles to climb down. The Girl Scout flings off her cap. The teen-ager holding hands with her mother against the trunk of the oak, wrenches loose. Lena wobbles on her fat knees, walks proudly with her bow on her head, boyishly without her Girl Scout cap and bangs her mother's arm against the bar of the tree in her hurry to flee. Where did they all run to? Here, there, everywhere.

Here is Buffalo.

Beatrix turns the wrong way off the expressway and goes deeper downtown, along the street of businesses, cleaning plants, diners—Red Barns, White Towers, a delicatessen—churches, churches.

She stops in front of a pawnshop to ask directions. People, waiting on the curb before that grille of closed pawnshop, wave her back in the opposite direction. She makes a U-turn and drives away from the business district to the grassier area of the university.

The conferees register at the same motel. She registered while her suitcase rested like a poodle beside her legs, her purse spilling out the contents of its red stomach.

Beatrix wanted to ask the desk clerk if she could examine the register to look for the signature of Harold Steiner. She would, if she remembered mystery films with James Dunn and Glenda Farrell, palm a five-dollar bill. The skinny, pimply, voice-crackling clerk would, at first, refuse, then he would see that handkerchief corner of green and would say, spinning around the hotel log, "Oh, certainly!" Perhaps with inflation the price had gone up and was now ten dollars to look at someone's signature, or two tens, or maybe not even in American dollars. It wasn't worth it.

Because she had arrived two and a half hours later than she had anticipated, the first event on the schedule was already in session in the auditorium of the U, across the street from the motel. She washed, cleaned her nails, put water up her nostrils, astringent on her skin, Lady Esther on her hands, foot powder inside of her shoes, Murine in her eyes, and went across the street.

*Billy the Kid* is on. It's not *The Outlaw* with Jane Russell and the late Audie Murphy, late war hero, late alcoholic in a shoot-'em-up. It's not Southwestern deserts and mountains; it's not cowboys and Indians. Somewhere in the Northwest the camera is walking through the woods. The camera bearer is crackling twigs with his feet, is looking into rock pools. The camera bearer makes love. There is a body without a head. The camera bearer squeezes her breasts. She is astride the camera bearer. Her stomach is working and the tape recorder of the camera bearer picks up the sobs of the headless woman, her sighs.

Beatrix is the voyeur. All of the probosces of the filmmakers rape the woman. They poke into her vagina, into her opened yelling mouth, linger on her nipple, up her thigh; the

176

filmed subject climbs in bed with the camera. There is no private moment. There is nowhere a drawer, a closet door, a closed window, drapes, a shaded lamp. All bulbs are nakedly shining: tips of penises, tips of nipples, faucets dripping.

There is a break for dinner. All the conferees join together in the same dining hall. Beatrix has pinned her Festival of Filmmakers badge—green and white—onto her sweater, but she forgot to magic-marker her name on the paper that slipped into the badge. Beatrix, wearing her blank-name badge, is looking around for a table to seat herself and for the table that seats Harold Steiner and Lena Gurnev Palmer-Steiner.

Beatrix sees Jonas Mekas sitting quietly, speaking Hungarian with his brother. She sees handsome women filmmakers sitting together. Their work is not being shown. Only women are being shown, women lovers and mothers, typecast. She hears Stan Brakhage talking. His voice goes into the soup and climbs out, nestles in the mashed potatoes, rolls on the brussels sprouts. His voice eats her dessert.

She had walked from table to table. One table of men ignored her although there was one empty seat at the table. If she sat in it, their conversation would boredly include her or rudely exclude her. She wants to sit with the women. One is tall and has dark hair pulled back in a pony tail. The other is short and has ear-length curly gray hair. They smile and nod to her but continue deep in conversation. Beatrix would never insert herself without knocking, ringing, phoning, apologizing, writing ahead.

She sits at a table with one other person. He is alone, head down, fingering his fork. He is not wearing a badge. He is startled that she has seated herself and he half-rises to touch the back of her chair.

"How do you do?" he says.

He studies his empty plate again. He scratches inside of his wrist. His eyes are hazel. He is bald. He wears a torn sweater and boots.

"Excuse me," he says, "I'm preoccupied."

So is Beatrix, searching the tables. Will Lena be with Dada? Will her hair be long, as in her high school photo?

Short, as under her Girl Scout cap? With a ribbon, as when she was four? With a bonnet too small for her fat cheeks and big head?

"What did you say?" said Beatrix. "I'm a bit preoccupied. You'll have to excuse me."

Immediately her table partner falls in love with her, a love that will last unswervingly for the whole weekend conference.

Stan Vanderbeek passes. His golden hair is held back with an elasticized band. He wears a white turtleneck.

"Hello, Barney!" he says.

"Yes," says Barney, Beatrix's table partner.

Ed Emshwiller passes. He has carried a camera to dinner.

"Barney!" he calls.

"Right," says Barney.

"Do you know Harold Steiner?" Beatrix asks. "No," says Barney. "Do you?"

"I don't know," says Beatrix.

Barney cups his hands around his mouth.

"HAROLD STEINER! HAARROOOOLD STEII-NER!"

Everyone is silent. A gentleman rises from one of the white-clothed tables and makes his way to Barney's. He is slender, of middle years. He is not bald like Barney, not blond pony-tailed like Stan Vanderbeek, not gray-bearded and camera-carrying like Ed Emshwiller, not puffy-faced and booming-voiced like Stan Brakhage.

"Hello?" he questions Barney.

"Harold Steiner?"

Beatrix has said nothing. She would like to unpyramid the napkin and put it on her hair and be a white-haired old lady sitting sedately there. She would like to raise the forks and look out between the bars of the tines.

"This is—" Barney looks at her empty name card. "Miss Film Festival."

"How do you do?" says Harold Steiner.

Harold Steiner is the right age, probably the correct weight and accurate height. She cannot see his eyes. They were, in the announcement, peering into a camera. Now they're blinking behind sunglasses.

"Yes," says Beatrix. "Thank you."

Barney is frowning. He had planned to neither comfort nor discomfort his seat partner.

"Just checking, Harold Steiner," says Barney. "Keep that in mind. We've got our eye on you."

"Fuck off!" says Harold Steiner.

Perhaps that is a clue. That angry voice sounds right. Bea cranes to see his table, his companions. A young woman is next to his emptied chair. Half of Harold Steiner's age. Beatrix stands up. Barney's hand covers hers.

"Anybody else we want me hollering for?" he asks.

The young head at Harold's table turns its profile. Does the nose have a slight hump? The eye she sees in the frieze is following Harold Steiner back to his chair.

"No, thank you," says Beatrix. "Would you excuse me a moment?"

"No," says Barney. "I would not."

"Then," says Beatrix, "I will have to cry, pee, wash up at this table."

"Help yourself," says Barney.

He is holding on to both of her hands now. She cannot leave.

"I am Harold Steiner," says Barney.

Beatrix is shaking. Her soup spoon, pea spoon, fruit compote spoon spill: broth, summer green peas, and canned colorless grapes.

The festival resumes. A California filmmaker shows films, and, afterward, is insulted in the question-and-answer period by a New York filmmaker. A New York filmmaker shows electronic films and is insulted by an Oregon filmmaker. A Florida filmmaker shows beach and surf and is attacked by an Arizona filmmaker, who is into deserts. Barney sits alone in the last row of the auditorium, picking at his sleeve. A Boston filmmaker shows experimental, hand-painted films and his *raison* is questioned by a Colorado filmmaker who has just shown his family in films. Barney, in the last row, rises and paces.

Beatrix is sitting on an end seat, closer to the middle of the auditorium. She had wanted to be where she could survey the crowd ahead of her, behind her.

Harold Steiner had changed after dinner. He is without the sunglasses. Beatrix leaves the auditorium during one of the Q's & A's. She has diarrhea.

Barney is standing outside of LADIES. He is more than standing; he is standing on his head.

"I needed that," he tells her. "Everything else was on its head tonight."

He takes her hand and leads her away from the conferees, who will be at the motel bar discussing, cussing, consulting, insulting each other.

He takes her to the elevator, up to six, onto his bed, and elevates her further yet, like the torso in the film, breasts grabbed, sobbing, stomach muscles pulling in, releasing. Beatrix has no head. She has no legs. She is a torso and under her the ground is rolling.

"Go home," kisses Barney later. "I like to sleep alone."

Beatrix has left her key at the desk. A message awaits her.

"Is there something I can do for you?" HAROLD STEINER.

It is lettered, not scripted, nondescript, and she does not recognize it.

Beatrix is calm. Perhaps any man can do it for her. Does she need *one* man to do it to her? You meet a man in a taxi. He offers you a stick of gum. You tell him, "Never mind the preliminaries. Do you like to be on top or below?" A bus driver engages you in conversation. You admire the way he turns corners. "Drive to my house," you tell him. "Let the passengers wait."

A waiter serves you gracefully. The plate slides before you. His hands are slender. You rise and take his arm. "I'm not hungry yet," you say.

A student is studying in the library. He is at the table near you. His hair curls on his neck. He looks up and blinks, his eyes tired from the book. "Come rest your eyes," you say, and press his head into your breast.

Beatrix sleeps soundly.

At breakfast Barney is sitting at a table with the two handsome women filmmakers. Beatrix hesitates. He smiles; they smile at her. She has been invited, formally, as to a baby

shower, a wedding, an anniversary, a New Year's Eve party.
She can now sit with them.

"Harold Steiner," one of the women is saying.

"What?" asks Beatrix.

"His films are on this morning."

### BIRTH

The camera bearer's hands are birthing the baby. They pull
the baby from the womb. Everyone in the womb room
exclaims. Blankets are rushed over. Pan over mother's
sweating, exhausted face.

"Are you happy?" asks the voice of the camera bearer, the
hands holding the mike up to her.

The woman smiles into the mike. The baby cries into the
mike. The guests exclaim around the mike.

(Applause of audience. Next film.)

### SUNRISE

The sun is coming up slowly. A young woman is seated in
a chair. She is naked. Her baby is sleeping. The camera
focuses ECU on hardening breasts. The baby stirs. The
breasts lactate. One white drop falls over the curve of the
breast, rolls down her ribs past her hip to her thigh.

(Muffled applause.)

### STILLNESS

CU on sleeping baby. Fists closed, fists opened. Head
turns slightly. CU on baby's blanket, white like egg whites,
puffing with breath of baby. CU on butterfly against window
—long-distance lens—on trees outside, walk to windowpane. Kettle boils on stove. Birthing, lactating young mother
stares out of window while steam from kettle mists the room.
Young mother wipes windowpane. A clear circle. A butterfly
whirring within the circle.

Harold Steiner goes on stage for Q & A. He is without
sunglasses. He *is* with birthing, lactating young mother, now

181

fully clothed and carrying the child. They all bow.

"Why did you make this domestic scene?" asks one of the women filmmakers. "It's a clichéd topic."

"Are you telling me," says (not asks) Harold Steiner, "that the birth of my child, my nursing wife, are clichés? Clearly, madam—or is it miss—you have had no child-bearing experience, or, if you had, it is in your dim past and you cannot bear its being recalled."

Lena is not here. If this is Harold Steiner, it is not Beatrix's Harold Steiner. The half-his-age woman is neither Beatrix's daughter nor her ex-daughter.

Barney is smiling.

"Anybody else I can call for you?" he asks.

She calls for him at night and he answers the call. He fills her ears with his fingers, his tongue. He fills her eyes with his poking nose. He fills her mouth with everything that probes—all his digits. And, she discovers also, the next day, his films are very good.

They are not of lactating mothers, riding torsos, butterflies pressed against panes, childhood, electronics. They are shots that move slowly, dreamlike, so that one would want to recline while viewing. As one watches carefully—the way he makes love—the leg steps forward, the other; then, a hand swings toward you; the eyes meet yours. It is mesmerizing. That night, when Barney takes her upstairs, she tries to stand on her head. She fails. She hurts the back of her neck. But she *has* tried to stand on her head. He returns to his somnambulist world when the conference concludes and she to her night-marish one.


Peopleography

In loss, people are titled. I know a woman who is divorced. She is entitled to divorcee. I know a woman who has outlived her husband. She bears the title of widow. I know a woman who has survived the deaths of her parents. She is an orphan. But what am I, a mother without child? To what am I entitled? To grief. I am aggrieved. To sorrow. I am sad.

182

*Sad: sated, satisfied, surfeited.* . . . 3a. afflicted with . . . grief . . . 4b. a dull somber color or shade—sad brown and black.

I am not satisfied, despite definition. I am not *sated*; I do not find this loss overappetizing. There *has* been a *surfeit* of sighing. My hair, between beauty parlor appointments, is "a sad brown."

I know of a woman who is legally separated from husband and child. Each day she counts her features, takes her pulse, shakes her sleeping foot. She can bear no further losses.

I know of a woman who is legally married to a roaming man. She sleeps with toy chimpanzees, poodles, rabbits, and bears. She puts her head on their soft bellies, encircles them with her arm. She places them between her legs. Each day she counts her animals. She can bear no further losses.

I know of a slaughterhouse. I would place people into the stocks. I have a list for my cattle truck to pick up.

*The Fathers*: Lois's, Janice's, Pauline's, Shirley's, and Lena's. The Fathers of Rina, Ilana, and Rut'y. Lavan, the father of Lea and Rahel.

*Husbands*: Lois'' medical husband in his Medical Building office, wearing his white lab-and-butcher coat; Pauline's liquor-store owner and nonhusband; Harold Steiner, wherever he is, whoever he is, whose ever he is.

*Mothers*: Who cannibalize their daughters, contest their sisters, molest their sons.

Them would I send screaming down the shoot. On their heads, between the eyes, would my hammer descend. Against their necks would I, the ritual slaughterer, draw my blade.


Looking for Fathers (2): The Conference

Bea is offered two hundred and fifty dollars to participate in a panel at State U—where Janice had eaten creamed *drek* on toast. The subject is "Literature of the Immigrant." Bea will represent The Oral Tradition.

Bea is sent the list of copanelists. There is the name of

Professor Harold Stone: *Stone*, an English professor, an anglicized *Stein*. Harold, if she remembers him from those years ago, could anglicize, even uncircumcise himself to fit into English Departments.

She drives slowly to State, unhappy on interstate highways for speed freezes her and expressways slow her. She perspires when she arrives, perspires in the winter chill. She, a panelist, is given a suite with color TV, besides her two-hundred-and-fifty honorarium.

A cocktail party precedes the conference. This is State U beloved by State Legislature. It has no urban problems, no urban courses. It has no Blacks, no Communists. So it is well provided for in yearly legislative budgets. State U can afford martinis in unlimited supply. Beatrix has one. Beatrix has two. Beatrix has unlimited supply. Beatrix has three and is in somebody's lap. The lapel above the lap bears his name: Professor Harold Stone, Indiana U.

Indiana U to you, Prof. Stone.

She can see well enough to realize it is not her Harold Steiner. It is an old man, this Prof. Harold Stone, as old as Dr. Long of *Sane Sex Life and Sex Living*, as old as Pauline's late grocery store father or Lois's late Romanian pharmacist father.

"Well, this is very pleasant," says a deep, rich, not old voice. It has timbre. He must have sung in church.

He hugs her to him. He rocks her in his arms. She decides to stay in that cradle.

She sits next to him on the panel. His topic is Henry Roth, and Roth's sleeper, *Call It Sleep*. Bea does not listen to the criticism. Rather she and the audience are taken with his anecdotal, nonscholarly speech. He knows Henry Roth. He knows everybody. He knows Meyer Levin who tried to get a second edition published of *Call It Sleep*, after the book failed during the Depression. He isn't even Jewish and he knows all those immigrants.

Beatrix is less oral about the oral history of the immigrants. She speaks softly, forgetting the mike, until the back rows of the conference shout: "Louder!" Prof. Stone readjusts her throat mike and holds her shaking hands under the table while Bea's voice and thoughts firm.

184

They have dinner together with the other panelists. Prof. Stone regales them with tales of his family and with reminiscences from his book, *Love and Other Affairs*.

Bea studies his face. His nose is arched; his cheekbones are high. His eyes are not faded blue. His hair is not wispy white. His hands are not age-spotted, arthritic, or shaking. He is the handsomest man in the room.

"Will you excuse me, my dear?" he asks her.

Bea is disappointed. He must circulate to greet his colleagues and former colleagues; his former students and lifelong friends, his admirers, his publishers. It is a cotillion and he is gracefully weaving in and out.

She goes to the bar. A man with turquoise belt buckle, turquoise ring, black straight hair pulled back with a leather thong, is popping shots of whiskey into his mouth like oysters.

"What is your specialty?" she asks him.

His eyes are turquoise. His smile is greenish.

"Want me to show you?" he asks.

She, the member of the panel, becomes haughty.

"I'm an American Indian from Wounded Knee," he says. "I'm here to buy guns and to fuck women."

She wanders away and is introduced to a Black Lit specialist who is angry that his specialty was not included in immigrant literature. His suit is elegant, more formal than any panelist's. His shirt is silky, his tie an amazement of colors. He talks about his wife in law school, his daughters taking ballet.

"Why are you here?" Bea asks him.

"I'm here to make contacts for my people," he says, "and to fuck me some women."

She is introduced to an Egyptian novelist. He speaks English beautifully, as well as French and Russian, besides his native Arabic.

"Why are you here?" Bea asks him.

"I demand equal time with the immigrant Jews," he says. "There are many Arab-Americans writing also, and they are not represented."

"Then that's why you're here!"

"That, and to fuck some women."

She is introduced to a magazine publisher. He is an angry young Jew. His magazine is angry, young, and Jewish.

"Why have you come?" asks Bea.

"Because I represent the Jew as Eternal Immigrant," says the publisher, "and because I want to fuck some women."

She searches for Professor Harold Stone. He is searching for her. He gives her his arm and escorts her away from the Indian, the Black, the Arab, the Jew.

"Why have you come to this conference?" Bea asks her aged, charming friend.

"To reacquaint myself with old friends," he says, "and to fuck some women."

Beatrix has her monthly, her cycle, her bad time, her period, her exclamation and question marks, her curse, her ovulation, her menstruation.

Professor Stone is horrified. He releases her arm.

"There are certain taboos that are signposts to mankind," he says. "Incest is one. Menstruation is the other."

He gags. His lips become white and his firm hands shaky. His blue eyes milk over.

"Blood," he says bloodlessly.

She is at the back of the cave. She is Rahel sitting on the totem of her father Lavan, and he will not enter his daughter's tent because of her filth. She is every chicken cut open, every entrail, liver, and heart lifted, leaving dark blood spots. She is the Blood Woman, Blood Worm, Blood Blister, Vampire. She sucks blood from the neck of sleeping boys; she sucks her own napkins when she is finished with them.

She is moony and loony. She is a trap and the penis could be snapped off inside. She has bear teeth in her womb, claws in the vagina, tusks in her Fallopians.

She is an accident, a murder. She is the body thrown from the car, or under the wheels of a train. She is assault, rape, wound. She is Homer's Strife, striding through battlefields. She is the Norse Hel, at the mouth of the underworld.

Her womb snaps, cracks, barks, whispers, whines, gasps, gags, snores, curses. Her womb says secret words that no one can define. Her womb is the Rosetta Stone. Its writing is cuneiform. Its walls are papyrus.

The tool he uses is the stylus. Prof. Stone takes his tool in his hand, upstairs. Color returns to his lips, firmness to his hands, a light to his eyes.

In the same building at State U as the one housing The Conference on Immigrant Literature is a Conference on Abortion and a Counterconference on Friends of the Unborn.

Women who anticipate the unborn are picketing the abortionists, psychologists, penologists, environmentalists of the Conference on Abortion. They push their bloated stomachs at Beatrix. They try to hand her pamphlets. The cover of the throwaway is lurid, a fetus expelled. "They Have Souls. They Have Hearts. You Have A Heart, Too." Beatrix shakes her head. She has no heart. The picketers spit upon her.


Looking for Fathers (3): Hillel House

Her publishers are sending Beatrix out to the West Coast for Jewish Book Fair. She will speak on the paperback of *The Pioneers* and on the new hardback, *The Remnants*.

Her artwork for *Remnants* was a problem. Her photographs with Instamatic were instant but trivial. She wrote to her interviewees asking for other photos. They went to studios that posed them: women with the fingers of one hand touching a cheek, the other hand covering up a tattooed wrist. Men standing, one hand on the back of a chair, to show how much taller they are than the chair.

The women were Israeli beauty-parlored, hennaed, backcombed, and sprayed. Their lips looked as if they had been pressed onto a handkerchief and removed from the reality of face. In the lighting of the photograph the lips were the same shade as the hair, flattening the effect of nose, cheeks, brow. Their eyes were penciled, also their brows. Some wore false lashes and falsies. She recognized no one from their photos. Each received a Thank You note and a small check for the photo from the publishing house.

A cartoonist was then hired to do Steinberg-ish line drawings. But the Holocaust cannot be caricatured. Then Chaim Kupferman, from an Israeli kibbutz, was asked for permission to use his concentration camp series. Rico Lebrun was approached. It became a search for barbed-wire art. The book became more abstract and the voice sepulchral, prophetic, beyond the one face, that set of gestures.

Beatrix will be preparing her audience for *Remnants* by playing them tapes of the interviews.

*Unafraid Women* is postponed but the publishers have taken an option on Beatrix's proposed anthology, *Mothers and Daughters*. Beatrix has submitted a list of stories, excerpts from novels, and synopses from films dealing with that relationship. Now Beatrix is looking for one of those characters of that special relationship, from San Diego up to San Francisco, looking for Lena Gurnev Palmer-Steiner.

Beatrix is worn, her hair and skin dry from too much sun too quickly absorbed. She has spoken at the San Diego Conservative Synagogue, at the Brandeis Summer Camp, the Emma Goldman Jewish Landschaft Hall, the Los Angeles YM & YWHA, the reform temple in San Francisco.

The elevator of her hotel is filled with Retired Principals. They are definite, corseted women who crowd Beatrix at the Information Desk, the newsstand, and into the cafeteria. When she wants to sit alone, they seat themselves in her booth and then ignore her. The cafeteria has taken on a special character, like a Teachers' Lunchroom. Beatrix, over chicken salad, is back at McAfee Intermediate or is posing for Yearbook in High. She is ignored and begins to worry about promotion and self-promotion. She worries about grades, report cards, honor points among the critics. It makes her nervous to rise and leave her dishes on the table. The women glance at her plate to see if she's cleaned everything off. Beatrix wonders if she should carry soiled silverware and plates away on an aluminum tray.

She lies down on the textured spread of her hotel-room bed, which proceeds to spread its mottled pattern over her arms and neck. Beatrix reads the literary gossip column of the *San Francisco Chronicle*. Despite thirteen speeches in two weeks, Bea is not gossiped about. She has failed to be promoted. Who is gossiped about is HAROLD STONE: ex-restaurateur, ex-educator, ex-promoter of prize fights, rock concerts, and poetry readings. He is into something new, porno-promo, working out of his own film company,

Hillel House. They are shooting in Mill Valley. Beatrix goes on location to locate her ex-husband.

She ferries across the Bay in a boat that is hours off schedule. A woman stands next to her on the pier waiting, wearing a long skirt and carrying a basket of eggs. She never moves, never tires. On the boat ride the woman stands at the prow, the wind billowing her skirt, scrambling her hair, her basket steady under her arm.

Bea has been wearing a pantsuit and carrying an overnight case. She has been restless during the wait, sitting on the dock, asking the time every fifteen minutes. During the boat ride, Bea goes into the rest room to change pantsuit for folksy smart, reappearing in a Pakistani purple skirt, Yemenite silver coin earrings. She stands next to the solid figure of the woman with the eggs. Bea picks up and puts down her overnight case. She stands at the prow, walks to the stern, and passes Alcatraz and other rocks without thinking about them.

The boat docks near an amusement hall full of nickelodeons, pianolas, animated wooden figures engaged in running trains or in training animals. Ticket booths of mechanical fortunetellers move their eyes, heads, arms but deliver vague fortunes to Beatrix.

It is near the amusement palace that she finds Harold Stone and the Hillel House crew. They are surrounded by signs: "HEALTH HAZARD."

"THIS IS AN EXPERIMENT CONDUCTED BY THE DEPARTMENT OF HEALTH, EDUCATION AND WELFARE."

His cast is standing or sitting in a series of booths.

"Harold!" calls Beatrix.

"Shh!" someone tells her.

"HAAROOOOLD!" says Beatrix.

Harold turns.

"No thanks," he says. "You're too old."

Beatrix advances on him. There is no possible way for them to recognize each other from over twenty years ago. How could Harold recognize her when he knew that Eugene V. Debber in slacks, size 44 men's shirts, no makeup, uncontrolled hair, puffy brows, someone given to shrieking at her mother or tearing into him? The woman confronting him is no

189

crybaby. She must be somebody's Old Lady, wearing careful hair and Pakistani purple. She's wearing dude shoes, rings on each finger, bells and coins on her ears.

"Get her off the set," says Harold.

"What's happened to you, Harold?" Beatrix asks in astonishment.

Nothing, except age, disease, baldness, and corpulence. His head is a doorknob. His features are squeezed together. His chin reverberates after each phrase. He is wearing a vest over no shirt. His stomach is lifted by his pants belt until it is riding high on his chest. Harold is wearing leather cowboy boots.

"Where is Lena?" she asks.

"Will somebody do something about this personage," says Harold.

"LENA GURNEV PALMER-STEINER," says Beatrix. "Where is she?"

"What's she doing? Calling for her Pomeranian?"

"LEENA!" shouts Beatrix. "Where are you?"

She is becoming frantic. She is sure that in the cast of young men and women she has seen Lena. She runs around to the other side of the set where the booths are open. They are outhouses. It is a row of toilets. The name of the film is posted: WC ON THE WC.

In each booth someone is active. In one, a camera is filming a young boy urinating, a boy about twelve. In the next, a man is defecating and grunting. He holds a mike against his mouth. In the third, a spread-legged girl is busy with urination, defecation, and constipation. In the fourth, a man is urinating between a girl's legs. In the fifth, a man is urinating into a girl's mouth. In the sixth—.

Beatrix backs away, aghast. In this pose Harold recognizes her.

"Beatrix," he says. "Baby. . . .My wife," he tells everyone. "My child bride, from whom I had a child. I never saw the child, didn't, in fact, see much of that child bride." His cast has gathered around him.

Beatrix, however, was right. She did see someone else whom she knew. Someone in orange wig, someone lined up to use the "facilities." Lena slips away.

"Let's go to the chow wagon, honey," Harold tells Beatrix.

They go, instead, to an ice cream parlor in this quaint town, an ice cream parlor with homemade ice cream, homemade rough wooden booths.

Harold is chatty. His voice becomes an English major's:

"It's a new subject. Water Closet on the West Coast. Hasn't been dealt with visually. Got the idea from Documenta 4 at Kassel, Germany, when they showed German artists into these trips, cutting pieces off their penises, slashing themselves—the body is the canvas. They defecated into each other's mouths. The body is the receptacle. I hated it, Beatrix. I loved it. Very Swiftian, scatological. I am trying to bring the satirical methodology of the eighteenth century to this hypocritical age. . . . ."

Beatrix, giver of thirteen recent speeches, is speechless.

"Know how I got into it?" asked Harold. "From instinct. From honoring my past. What did I love the most from the past?"

Beatrix is looking at her coffee. There is no cream in this quaint place. There is that ersatz vegetable milk that oils on the surface of the coffee. She is drinking chicken-soup coffee.

Clearly, she was not what he loved best from the past.

"My job as a movie usher," said Harold. "In High I ushered at the Linwood La Salle. I wore a uniform the color of your skirt and carried a flashlight. I poked into balconies with it, at the sides of the theater, the back rows, up girls' legs, into people's eyes. That was power. To cast a little light into the Midwest darkness."

He is consciously overstating. His eyes are also shifting. He wants to go back to his set, and she has unsettled him.

"Where is Lena?" asks Beatrix.

"I don't know any Lena," says Harold. "Honest, Bea. I never knew a Lena."

"Maybe she changed her name," says Beatrix forlornly.

"For God's sake," says Harold. He waves for the restaurant check.

"My daughter," says Beatrix. "She left home a while ago, a year—maybe three."

"Why would I know where your daughter is?"

"She's *your* daughter!"

"No," says Harold. "What you don't have isn't yours. She isn't your daughter, either."

He holds her by the elbow, releases the elbow to pay the overpriced bill.

"It's a Brechtian concept," says Harold, "as exemplified in *The Caucasian Chalk Circle*. There's a rather crude translation by Bentley:

> what there is shall go to those who are good for it,
> . . . the children to the motherly . . .
> The carts to good drivers . . .

Were you motherly, Beatrix? Or a good driver?"

While Harold is holding forth, off the set goes Lena, wearing her orange wig, her spangled Liza Minelli glasses. She is cheap *Cabaret*. As mother tracks, she backs off. As mother searches, she disperses.


## Where Do Daughters Go When They Go Out?

Into the receiving blanket of the world.

> Lena Gurnev Palmer-Steiner
> Went to the East, went to the West
> Looked for the very ones
> That she loved best.

She found: a talking live oak. The tree spirit inside of the knot called her into the forest. Its gnarled mouth spoke. Toothless gums opened. Woodpeckered freckles flashed at her. The Spanish moss made it hoary and the old face of the tree said,

"Lena Gurnev Palmer-Steiner, go out of the woods to the sea."

She goes to the sea, ankle-deep, she the embryo reentering

the brine. Her legs goose-pimple. Her knees freeze. Her thighs sigh. Her cunt grunts.

Arms of waves beckon, further out. Fingers of waves clutch at her. Her nipples shrivel. It's high tide. She's thrown back on shore.

She goes into the sky. She floats wispily across the moon. She indulges in clouds, sparkles through stars.

Lena Gurnev Palmer-Steiner, descend! She is a balloonist, an ascensionist.

On land her mother pulls the umbilical cord. The balloon of Lena Gurnev Palmer-Steiner floats to earth.


Looking for Fathers (4)

Can one follow father? Into the front seat of the auto, putting your head on his shoulder. Onto the dance floor, arm on his. At a restaurant, eating by candlelight across from him.

You and father retire, carrying lanterns to light the stairway. You pause on the landing to kiss good night.

"Good night, my father."

"Good night, beloved daughter."

You enter your separate rooms, turn down the covers, plump the pillows, remove lounging garments, and recline. You cannot sleep. You rise from your bed and tiptoe on thick carpeting to his room. He is awaiting you.


Looking for Fathers (5)

She looks for fathers: behind doors, inside of offices, through revolving, department-store entrances.

She looks for fathers up escalators, down elevators.

She looks for fathers from the dental chair, for they will drill into her.

She looks for fathers breaking up cement, drilling next to her.

She looks for fathers in uniform, whistling and directing the traffic of her.

She looks for fathers with reflecting shields, operating on her.

She looks for fathers behind desks, remonstrating her.

She looks for fathers filling out forms, informing her.

She looks for grandmothers.

She folds her writing into their laps and they envelop her.

She opens her beak in their kitchenette and they cut her meat into bite-sized pieces, blow into her soup spoon to cool the broth, mash the carrots with butter to slide it down her gullet.

She puts her mouth against their ear. They hear all she has never uttered.

She puts her mouth against their breasts. The milk of the grandmothers flows again.

She puts her ear against their mouths and they fill her hungry ear with the words of lovers.

Lena Gurnev Palmer-Steiner, come home.

# Beatrix at
# Home

Beatrix at Home

"Mother, I am pregnant with a baby girl and she criticizes me."

"What does she criticize?"

"She criticizes me for dyeing my hair, shaving under my arms and on my legs, for trimming my pubic hair, for putting on Mitchum super-dry deodorant, for clipping my cuticles, reshaping my hairline, piercing my earlobes, pedicuring my feet, polishing my nails, exercising my ankles by stepping on and off thick books."

"She criticizes you because she will be doing that, too."

Beatrix has returned home. She is reading the local press.

WOMAN'S BODY BELONGS TO MAN, SAYS MINISTER.
"The abortion reform bill is wrong," the Rev. Charles Williams, president of the . . . Baptist Ministers Conference said Monday, "because it sanctions killing and because it leaves the decision to doctors, most of whom don't believe in God, and to women whose bodies don't really belong to themselves.

"No woman's body belongs to her," he told a press conference sponsored by antiabortionists. "I don't know who told them a dream like that. My wife belongs to me. She belonged to her daddy until she belonged to me."

Buttressing his statements from the baby-blue-bound, gilt-edged Bible . . . Williams read, "In sorrow thou shalt bring forth children."

Some of that is true.

## Weighty Bea

Bea has gained weight. She will soon develop thick ankles, high blood pressure, lethargic habits. She will have to buy her clothing at the Big Girls Shoppe.

She goes on a diet with Pound Watchers.

For Breakfast: 1 egg or hard cheese and 1 slice bread

For Lunch: fish or lean meat and 1 slice bread

For Dinner: lean meat, broiled fish, and fresh vegetable salad.

Bea must not despair. Pound Watchers will not leave her cupboards bare. It is all compensations. For no husband, husbanding ways. For no children, childish habits. For no lover, self-love.

Pound Watchers carefully arranged for her snack.

Snack Bowl at Night: slices of green pepper, cucumber, celery, shredded red cabbage.

"Nosh to your heart's delight!"

## Bea Gives Thanks

Beatrix makes a Thanksgiving turkey. She tapes the menu onto her refrigerator so she won't forget any of the side dishes.

She is serving:
  Turkey
  Chestnut stuffing
  Cranberries and orange slivers
  Candied kumquats
  Onions and white sauce
  Sweet potatoes in glazed apples
  Eggplant salad
  Carrot torte
  Pumpkin and pecan pies
Her parents are invited to eat at an aunt's.
Beatrix eats alone.


## Muscley Bea

If she cannot do it for herself, Exercise Ed will do it for her.

There he is on the cover of her exercise book, crouching as if doing the *kazatzki*. If she does her knee bends, she, too, will be a cossack.

"Hi girls!" says Exercise Ed. "Let's exercise!"

If she lies on her back, lifts her knee, and touches it over the other leg to the floor, if she reverses this process with the other leg, at least fifteen times a day, says Exercise Ed, "Watch those hips shape up!"

There is a double knee over.

"The waistline will benefit a good deal from this one, too," promises Ed.

"Ed, do you promise?"

"Bea, I solemnly promise."

She can do the "Sitting Bounces," which Ed calls "a fun exercise." Bea can do the Scissors Legs and "snip the hips away." Bea can do arm exercises, tummies aweigh, and bust exercises, but, warns Exercise Ed, "They work best when you're SMILING!"

Bea will exercise and exercise but she will never look muscular like Exercise Ed.

## The Faces of Bea

Bea readily admits that she is ignorant about her facial muscles. She never knew, as Fanny Face-Saving tells her, that "every muscle of the face is there to do its job." Bea never knew that "every muscle of the face has a beginning and an ending."

Bea is ready. Bea is set. Bea will go:

First her forehead and scalp muscles have a beginning and an ending, then her eyelids, upper lip and mouth, cheeks, nose, chin, and throat. All, all working for Bea.

Each scalp raise will lower her age. Time will freeze with every eye squeeze. She will firm the skin of the chin. She will smooth every facial groove.

Bea does this one-half hour every day. She becomes flushed, easily tired, and bad-tempered.

## Tinting Bea

Bea does not want to be her age. Bea does not want to be her color. Bea does not want to be her shape.

Bea's hair wants to be gray every two weeks but Bea must combat colorlessness with various hues, Natural Auburn, Natural Brown, Natural Black.

Bea readies the operation:
    rubber gloves
    plastic shoulder cape and towel
    scissors
    newspaper covering sink
    cold cream to wipe off streaking on the face
    a clock
    a book to read during the 25 minutes or the additional 20
        minutes to make sure the stubborn gray is pene-
        trated.

The directions begin with a warning: "to do so may cause blindness."

You are promised that your new hair color will leave your hair extra shiny, extra manageable.

It has taken Bea the whole morning. She will have to do it again soon.


## Bea and TV

One Sunday, August 26, Bea reads the listing of TV movies for the day.

At noon on Sunday she can see *Student Prince* (1954) with Ann Blythe and Edmond Purdom (voice by Mario Lanza) or *Ride Beyond Vengeance* (1966) or *Stopover Tokyo* (1956) with Robert Wagner and Joan Collins.

At 1:00 P.M. she can see *My Six Loves* (1962) with Debbie Reynolds and Cliff Robertson.

At 2:00 P.M. she has vast choice: *Jennifer* (1935) with Howard Duff and Ida Lupino; *Kenya, Country of Treasure; Heart of the Golden West* (1942) with Roy Rogers and Gabby Hayes; *They Won't Believe Me* (1947) with Robert Young and Susan Hayward.

At 4:00 P.M., Bea can watch *Three Brave Men* (1957) with Ray Milland and Nina Foch.

At 6:00 P.M., *We Joined the Navy* (1962) is playing.

At 7:30 P.M. is *Twist of Fate* (1954) with Ginger Rogers and Jacques Bergerac.

At 8:00 P.M. is *That Certain Woman* (1956) with Bette Davis and Henry Fonda.

At 11:45 P.M. is *Three Bites of an Apple* (1967) with Tammy Grimes.

At midnight: *Danger Has Two Faces* (1966) or *The Last Adventure*.

Beatrix need not watch a movie. She has other choices open to her.

She can see "The Partridge Family" on Channel 5. She can see "Eleven Year Itch" at 8 P.M. where "Danny learns the vagaries of the female heart."

If Bea wishes to rise early or if she cannot sleep the night through, she can see "Agriculture USA" at 6:22 A.M. on Channel 5. Eight minutes later, at 6:30, on the same channel, she can see "Agriculture Today."

At 7 A.M. is "Fantasy Funhouse" or "Gilligan's Island," or "Pebbles and Bam Bam." "Lassie" is still around at that hour.

At 11 there is "Wrestling" on Channel 56. at 12:30 there is again wrestling. At 1 there is "Golf for Swingers" or "I Love Lucy." There is more wrestling on Channel 12.

At 1:30 is "Roller Derby." At 3 there is wrestling or, if she wishes, "I Love Lucy" repeats yet once more at 6 P.M.

Bea can go through the whole day without a movie. But if she wants to see a film that night on TV, she can see *Dark Victory* (1939) with Bette Davis and George Brent. Bette Davis has an unnamable disease, and before she passes on (we should also not name our ending) she selects a worthy wife to service George Brent.

Tomorrow night Beatrix can watch another film with Bette Davis, Mr. George Brent, and Mary Astor. Both women service handsome, moustached George. He is reported missing in an airplane crash in the jungles of the Amazon.

"Give me something to live for! His child!" cries Bette to pregnant Mary.

It is *The Great Lie*.

Or Beatrix can watch other films in which Joan Leslie services James Craig (1948), Gloria Grahame services Rory Calhoun (1957), Claire Trevor services Robert Ryan (1951), and, in that same good year, June Allyson services Van Johnson in *Too Young to Kiss*.

Diet, darling Beatrix. Have your recreation. Everything in moderation. But don't deprive yourself.

From Embryo to Out You Go

*Embryein* (gr.), to swell inside. Compare to *sauerkraut; qairu* (Goth.), thorn; *veru*, spit; *bryein*, to swell.

202

That sauerkraut is swelling inside. Each leaf is added, each thick, veined sheet; the sauerkraut of the brain is growing. The cabbage of the head and belly are layering. The *thorn* of the body is pricking. The *spit* is gathering in the sewer.

*Fetus*—see *feminine*. Feminine is *female* (ME variant influenced by male, diminutive). *Dhei*, to suck reduced form *dhe-mna*, in Latin *femina*. Suffix reduced form *dhe-to* in Latin *fetus* . . . *dhe-kundo* in Latin *fecundus*, fruitful . . . fertile, lucky, happy (*felicity*). *Delu* (OE), nipple; *tila* (OHG), feminine breast. Also see *fellatio*.

If an ''unhatched young vertebrate,'' an ''embryo,'' soaks in that female brine, is to be nourished by the *delu* and the *tila*, and all of life is pickled and floating and will be suckled by that originator, that fruitful, happy, lucky originator, no wonder then that men, not feminine, must hate us. We are the conception, the water jar, the nourishment, the expelling from the Garden of Eden.

How could they not hate us? There is little for them to do if we are conception, reproduction, resurrection. They must hate our breast. Why else do they grab it? They must hate our urine. Why else do they jab it?

They grow too big to slip back in through the slits of nipple, the eye of the navel, the mouth of the womb.

So they punish us at birth and give us pain and punish us in life and give us pain.

## Periodical Bea

For no good reason on this earth, Bea still fertilizes.

Being an imprecise person, Bea cannot possibly follow exact tampon directions. She cannot make decisions between:

a. placing one foot on the toilet or chair, or
b. sitting on the toilet seat with knees apart, or

c. squatting slightly with legs apart
whichever seems most natural and comfortable for yo

None did, none was. Poking with that cardboard Toots
Roll between bladder, rectum, vagina, hoping, as in som
dime-store game, to fit rolling object into right hole, sl
invariably ended up leaving in the cardboard and pulling o
the cotton. Or she would end up with bloody fingers and th
tampon floating inaccurately in a sea of blood.

Those careful explanations of what to do with graspi
thumb and forefinger, aiming directly at the small of t
back, removing the forefinger to free the withdrawal cord, .
of that required an engineering student, a mechanical geniu
or someone less shy about poking into cavities like a den
assistant.

Bea sidles up to the drugstore counter, trying to avoid t
gray-haired man behind the cash register, trying not to sta
near the male customers in line. She has selected her napki
her dinner napkin, her breakfast napkin, her man-siz
napkin, not folded next to her plate, not folded under h
chin, not folded in her lap, her neat napkin folded betwe
her legs.

She can have Stayfree and run, like the black-hai
beauty in gossamer dress, through green fields. In gossam
dress? Nowhere under that transparent material can B
make out belts, pins, metal tips, wads of cotton batting.

Bea, all of her life, has failed the menstrual ads. They we
so discreet, they whispered. She would never, if she heed
them, be inconvenienced by bleeding, backaches, nause
bad circulation in feet and hands, twitching of leg muscl
chills, or cracked lips. The girls in the Land of Magaz
Menstruation, the girls with periods in the periodicals le
immediately into the water, wearing tight swimsuits or,
short, crisp, white, swinging tennis skirts, there they w
out on the court!

Bea was taking mincing steps from bed to bathroom, b
to teakettle. Not those girls who won blue ribbons at ho
meets, who attended balls gowned in Modess.

At the store she bought boxes, daintily marked like har
kerchief or stationery boxes. Soon all sanitary produ

204

would be sold in stationery stores. On each napkin would be the wearer's initials. Have them monogrammed for your best friend!

She carries these boxes home proudly, not in the old brown paper bag. Her Stayfree goddess trips through a blur of green. On each box, flora, fleurs-de-lis, green mint leaves, Kotex-blue roses. The boxes vie for euphemism and fantasy. Tear along the perforated edge for a visual experience of napkins backed in green or pink. Smell them. They are perfumed. Wear them as edgings on cashmere sweaters. Wear them as earmuffs in cold weather.

Bea wonders if she is normal, if she has ever really menstruated in her life. Perhaps it is all psychology and if she were less neurotic, she, too, could roll in dewy flowers, jump hurdles with her stallion, or dive from the highest board.

The Orphan

Beatrix has bursitis. Beatrix has dandruffitis. Beatrix has colitis.

Factory smokestacks have entered her lungs. She is developing emphysema. Soot has settled on her skin. She has burnings and itchings. She never leaves the house in winter. Her ankles swell.

Nevertheless, Beatrix Palmer is regal. She is receiving royalties from *The Pioneers, Remnants, Mothers and Daughters*. She is given her third advance for *Unafraid Women*.

Her parents have passed away into the unmentionable place where Bette Davis goes when she goes out.

Beatrix is tired. When parents go, you are not only orphaned, you are stepped up a generation. She wants to retire.

Good-bye, French teacher, *ma chère*, who has suffered from an unmentionable disease. Good-bye, Bald Chemistry, now bald all over. Jewish Math is hanging on, working out problems.

Romanian Lois has jumped out of the window of the

Medical Building. Her two daughters are sent to boarding school. Her husband marries the daughter of the doctor in the next suite.

Janice has reunited with her husband. He is fading. He is becoming a white man.

Shirley descends from the attic and takes over the kitchen. She flushes out her old aunt, hitting her with a crutch. The old aunt falls down the steps of the porch, which she had so well guarded, and bruises her knees on the cement.

Pauline's liquor-store-owner friend dies and leaves her his savings. Her mother dies and leaves her alone. Pauline enrolls at the Yale School of Architecture.

The high school Yearbook for fifteen years had a black cover and Black graduates. This year it has an Arabic cover and Lebanese graduates. City University no longer enrolls whites. One has a choice of majors: Black Literature, Black Music, Black Arts, Black History, Urban Law as Related to the Third World, Third World Psychology, Third World Medicine, The Third World and Women, Third World Dance, Teaching Skills for the Third World.

Beatrix's past has fallen from the embankment.

She is thinking seriously of commencing Old Age.

# Looking for
# Shells

## The Sheller

This is a story.

It is feeding time. A man in tan shorts, whose hem has become unpressed, throws bread to the gulls. The gulls are noisier than the passing motorboats. Sandpipers, walking daintily into the surf, peck momentary holes in the sand. Pelicans, upside-down diving for fish, are long, long under water.

She walks the beach, Beatrix Palmer. From heel to toe shells are crunched, her soles scratched by gastropods. The Florida Cerith, a miniature Siamese tower, drills into her heel. The slipper shells collect between her toes. She picks up a red-veined slipper, turns it over, sees the pearly half-ledge, discards it, thinking someone else's heavy tread broke the other half of the ledge. It is not Beatrix Palmer's first mistake.

No letters arrive along with the *Key News*. No phone calls vibrate. At her window Australian pines drop their cones. An albino cat mews to be let in, then becomes frantic to go out again. From her window a blue heron perches on the wooden pilings.

She forgot to put the sand dollars into the sun. They are on the coffee table, like uncut cookie dough, with their five petals and five slashes cut into the off-white uneven circle. They are molding. Green almost obliterates the daisy-shape and speckles, like poppy seed, the slight hump of the animal. It is offensive to her to see that spreading mold. She turns it over. The shapes are inclusive on the flat back, like claws, fronds, like clusters of leaves. They remain upside down on her coffee table.

All is upside down—the diving birds, the sand dollars, and her day. For the sun is too hot to sun in, she discovered, lying on the sand, the sugary-white sand, that first day of arrival and burning her eyelids so that she had to wear sunglasses for a week. She looked puffy-lidded and Oriental, but then, when the puffiness deflated, the lids shriveled and she became older, like the leathery retirees around her.

So she covers herself tightly in the sun with a green overpriced cotton hat from the shopping center near Sarasota.

If she shells she stoops, rising suddenly. Far down on the public beach she thinks she sees green, green moving slowly toward her, expanding brightly, her own light-green hat, walking on a stick, on branches of legs. There are no eyes under the hat. The mouth is smiling; no, sneering.

There is another green hat tickling, like a blade of grass at the back of her neck. Years ago. A green paper crown cut out of bunting. Under it straggles a green-dyed mop, the strands separating over the shoulder, curling on a nylon curtain, dyed light green, over a green dress, whose cap sleeve is visible, as is the pinkish arm through the gossamer curtain. The hands are folded on the lap. The pink lips—is it the color film, too brownish?—are slightly separated and the light sparkles on a bit of a tooth. What has come into her head with the shimmering green queen? Is it Halloween? A St. Patrick's Day affair?

She stumbles over spiny shells, spiky shells, abalone fish scales, shells stuck inside of other shells until she is at her own efficiency apartment with its indoor-outdoor green carpeting (for grass in winter climates, for grass in sandy ones). She pulls the drapery cord against the sun and the aquamarine Gulf, purple further out where the sandy bottom is not visible.

210

She glues scallop shells to driftwood.

"Elmer's Glue," said the crackly voices at the Art Club. "That makes it really stick."

They glue their shells and sell each other their own arrangements.

Beatrix Palmer glues a white scallop shell with its finlike projections next to a red-ribbed scallop shell. The coloring is fading from the red shell as the shell dries, so Beatrix sprinkles water on the shell and bluish gray appears under the red. She fancies selling the shells with a circulating spray, a pump that will wet them so they can retain their sea color. The two shells, white and damp bluish gray under red, are turned sideways, facing the center. There, slightly elevated, is the most beautiful scallop of the beach—a sherbety peach with white edges and projections like whiskers.

The room darkens, a squall storm coming up. Rain—and more of her shells drying outside!

A storm is at another cottage. She reads, in a lettered rather than scripted hand:

You always hear seagulls and boats' horns and a little repair work on the docks in the morning. Right now the foghorn is booming every few seconds:

B-o-o-o-o-o-o-om.

B-o-o-o-o-o-o-om.

B-o-o-o-o-om.

B-o-o-o-om.

Pardon me, but due to an unquiet rest last night, the author of these reminiscences has just fallen asleep. Therefore, in the author's stead, I bring this odyssey to a close. Fin.

It was Lena, after a summer in London, during a summer in Maine.

The same cabin, some years before "the author" could write, could only print, could only print capital letters, Beatrix had a record of The Weeping Willow, The Seagulls, The Pretty Clouds, The Dark Room.

The Weeping Willow rested on tall grass, crayoned red green yellow blue green. The trunk was shaped like an ice cream cone and was colored blackish brown. The willow leaves were each a separate color, red, yellow, black, green alternating.

The Seagulls were plants of gulls with wings like leaves, with head and beak of flowers. The Pretty Clouds were more conventional, with purple-aquamarine-green-yellow-black-crayoned clouds. In the same order of color, flowers sprouted below.

The Dark Room had red dark walls, dark blue drapes, purple rug, dark green lamp, brown lamp cord, huge brown electrical outlet. Although Beatrix has now opened her drapes, in the light of the squall it is still The Dark Room.

To the tune of "Swanee River" ("The home of Stephen Foster," said the billboards on her way down through Ohio, Kentucky, and on to Florida), the oldies had sung: "Now we are gathered for Barney Greenstone, who's sixty-three."

He was also the baby of the group, a bouncy, overweight baby boy. They cuddled him, treasured him, would have glued him on driftwood to set their own memories of ten, twenty years before. He was also, until Beatrix arrived, the only Jew on Dolphin Key. He had widely spaced teeth, a moustache, and an aggressive stomach, and he aggressed toward Beatrix with his hairy mouth and aerated teeth.

He invites her into the pool of his condominium. But he is so busy greeting people at both the shallow and deep ends of this small pool and introducing her that she has no chance to swim. Mr. Greenstone is very social.

He calls to take her to Marina Jacks. They will view the sunset from that ideal spot, but he has been busy greeting people before he picks her up and they miss the sunset, park too far from the restaurant and have a several block walk. They do have a table overlooking the water but with no streaked sky or dramatic sun. It is better when twin lights go on above and then below, shimmering in the water. It is better when the green turtle soup arrives. It is *not* better when Barney talks about his *netsukes*. It is *not* better when he drives her back to his condominium to show them to her, Japanese toggles, behind an ornate glass case. Each is dwarfed, humped, a gargoyle; each is a scowling big-headed miniature; each is a peasant carrying fruit or a miniature baby. It is *not* better when Barney reads her their papers, the history of each toggle and of their carver.

He goes to get her a glass of wine. Beatrix is fast asleep on his couch, not leaning or stretching out but sitting stiffly, head erect and snoring.

The jingle shells around her jingle, common in these warm waters. She holds them in her palm, a monochromatic study ranging from pearly white, mottled bluish gray to a dark gray, about or less than an inch, none regular, none flat or in smooth circles.

She has collected ten eared-ark shells, heavy, clumsy, thickish things, strongly ribbed, irregularly marked. The rich black around the edge looks as if it were dipped in tar. The eared ark is less clumsy upside down with its regular fluted, toothed hinge line.

These smooth ears of shells.

The sun through Baby Lena's ear, a red sun, for Baby Lena has a port-wine stain.

"Nothing serious, just a cosmetic difficulty," Beatrix is told by her pediatrician.

When Baby Lena grows up and can see herself in the mirror, she never again allows her hair to be cut or her ears to show.

The squall storm is over. Light mottles the front yard of Australian pines. The pines clean their own grounds with fir needles. The sun mottles in her eyes.

There is Baby Lena by flecked light, ears projecting, eyes squinting, green gingham dress faded in the snapshot, green rattle faded in her mouth. The background, seen above the ledge of the yellow-lined carriage, is in splotches of greens and yellows and is not recognizable.

Before that. The baby stretching its arms on the couch.

"How big?"

"So big!"

The baby, not yet strong enough to sit up alone, leans over the balancing weight of her Buddha stomach and thickly diapered bottom. She has fallen backward in the yellow-lined

213

carriage. Her mouth is spread. Her ears are spread. Her hands hug each other. The belly button winks, and holes of cheek, elbow, and knee dimple.

That's when Beatrix had gained too much weight. She is in red jeans and red-checkered shirt. Her thick hair is fastened back. Her legs fill the jean pants. Her hips fill the pockets. Her breasts, milk-filled, stuff the red gingham shirt. She, although a young woman, has fatty pouches under her cheeks.

Black and white snap. She has her red shawl over one shoulder, her nursing shawl. It is dark gray in the photograph. Her hair is very black, pinned in place as befits a nursing mother. There is the soft black of new baby's hair against her hand. There is the receiving blanket, photographed white. There is the black cord of the watchband against her wrist, the white sparkling face of watch, the lipstick 1950s red, a beauty mark on her left cheek. There is her plaid pull-out couch losing a button. There is the infant's fist lost on the hill of the breast. There is the nipple a circle around the mouth. No one is reading the time on the watch. Harold Steiner has since disliked both faces, the watch's and her own.

She has a two-burner efficiency kitchen behind the blinds and reaches over her head to the shelves for a plate. She bought cheese and fruit at the supermarket, but the cheese is sweating and the fruit is molding.

There is a scramble on her hand, a leap, a scream. Who screamed? It could not have been that big South American cockroach that screamed. She chases it with a wet beach towel, slams it, kills it, and kills it again. She cannot let it go, not the tiniest quiver of the legs, of the antennae, the wings. It is curled and small when she flushes it down the toilet.

Barney's car drives up and he laughs at her breathless account of the hunt and the bagged game. He will take her to the Ringling Museum. It is still hot out. She puts on her green sun hat, a towel dress in greens and blues that she has worn every summer for ten years. She needs no bra for her breasts have not been milk-filled in many years.

"I can't identify everything," she tells Barney.

He can for, along with his condominium, he purchased *Golden Nature Guide, 475 Marine Subjects in Full Color*.

She can identify people along the beach.

They are, besides the oldies, a few bikinied grandchildren, golden rather than leathered. Surprisingly, there are the Amish, bonneted, bearded, suspendered, sitting near the hot dog stand and picnic tables, in the hot sun.

Do the Amish, through their beards and bonnet crowns, look at the smooth flesh of the bathers? Do those old men, with white shirts and black pants, see a colorful world beyond them, under the palms, away from the garish red of hot dogs, the falsely colored orange drink? Do they see that world of blue, green, brown of eye, pink of lips, curve of hips?

Beatrix Palmer's cheek.

Beatrix Palmer's cheek is to be scratched. On the day of the visit. It is to be a thin red vein of a scratch, as on the slipper shells. It is to be a thin rib of blood along her shell of cheek. The nail will catch her cheek, Lena's bitten, jagged nail, so that the mark on the cheek will not be a straight line but a dot-dashed one where the nail is or is bitten away.

Beatrix Palmer's face will have the scowl of Barney's *netsukes*. In a broken whirl, in sun that seems to glare from bits of mirror, Beatrix Palmer will strike back at the attacker and will catch the corner of an eye with her own sharp, mist-pink nail polish, and will pull Lena's eye Oriental.

Barney takes her into the hot sun of the Ringling Museum courtyard. They walk through a transplanted Roman villa, gauche, not grand, into the art gallery. Circuslike paintings, crowd-catching biblical scenes are playing. A particularly repeated theme is Judith with the Head of Holofernes.

There are large paintings of Rubens' bulging bodies from his body factory. There are those three circus rings of biblical scenes, everything visible from the top of the bleachers. There is Barney, stomach bouncing, hairs of moustache blowing as he explains, as he explains. Beatrix becomes thirsty and irritable.

"I can't write, I can't speak," said the loose-leaf sheet which Beatrix found after one of the disappearances and revisits. "I no longer think. Feeling and pictures have taken over. Now Mrs. Kennedy is pregnant with an eleventh child and there are the constant assassinations, assassinations as common as births. I cry & mother weeps, tears falling on my head in her lap. I don't understand and therefore no words, no logical, comprehending words come to calm me. I am 16 & it is unfair that people at 16 must think about the country's fate, must experience the pain.

"Come, Hades, give me a taste of your medicine. Cure me of the life force. Last week at Jim's I tried your medicine, powerful Hades. And mother found me and laughed and screamed, 'You are sick. If I had the money I'd put you in an institution,' and I, in my pain, hear her laughing scream, and she slaps me to show me how much she loves me, and the doctor on the radio tells of slapping Kennedy to hear a heartbeat and the pulse, and he hands the stethoscope to Ethel Kennedy to listen."

Barney goes into the carpentry shop to buy Mrs. Palmer a Coke. There is a box for dimes on top of the refrigerator. He helps himself, puts in his dimes and carries out the bottles. The guard stops him, so they drink the Cokes in the carpentry shop.

They drive back, Barney one hand on the wheel, the other holding Mrs. Palmer's. The waves are high and there are the high-pitched cries of the sandpipers. Barney parks the car at her rented efficiency and walks with her along the beach. Waves implode, a dull thud as of distant thunder. Later the waves slam against the groins that jut out from each beach home. The pilings have been built recently to stop the loss of the beach.

"That's forty thousand dollars worth of pilings," says Barney. "I don't know if the Gulf takes away more than it gives."

Shells are piled against each wooden beach barrier. There are the most delicate fingernail pink of shells, spirals of shells, jellyfish shimmering on the sand. When the sea recedes the shells are left behind like buttons on a mattress. Black-headed gulls stand on the water's edge.

Barney and Beatrix find tar on their sandals. The odor is brackish. Beatrix will not let Barney come into the apartment

216

for he has tar between his toes. They stretch out on the steps and wiggle their toes at each other. In the greening evening their toes are like seaweed.

Beatrix remarks on the Spanish moss draped on a neighbor's trees.

"Like lace shawls," says Beatrix.

"Like cannibals," says Barney. "They eat up the trees."

Moon shells are drying on the stoop, each a carnivore that engulfed and smothered other shellfish. Barney studies them with his porpoise eyes. There is the Shark Eye staring back at him.

Beatrix is proudest of her Florida Fighting Conches with their pagoda tops, the orange, golden, purple pearly interiors. She has found a West Indian Fighting Conch also.

Barney wants her to return with him to the condominium.

"Not *netsukes*," he promises. "I have the largest conches in the Crafts Club, twelve-inch Queen Conches, fourteen-inch Emperor Helmets. I have Giant Tuns. I have Fig Shells."

As she sits there, she again becomes sleepy and yawns. He is hurt and puts on his sandals. She is yawning too hard to apologize, but does wave as he drives away.


"NO THING UNITES US," said the outside of the airmail envelope, still capitals, all caps, no matter where the voyage overseas. But why write to say that? The yawning brought tears to Beatrix. The daughter had written to say more: a visit was pending, impending, rending.

Beatrix kept several ugly yet fascinating shells. One huge thing had barnacles all over it. Another was a thick, corroded, white oyster shell. Sand cemented small shells together. Beatrix kept a piece of sponge. And she kept letters, those corrosive letters.

"Was in Hawaii. Pretty uptight."

From some country whose postmark was obliterated:

"There's a cat on my lap listening. The light is dim afternoon before the rain. One auburn cow in all this green. Supersonic crickets. Everything that's still appears to be moving."

Months later, another card:

217

"One day a person entered a room feeling confused. I am nowhere. What can I do? A person answered saying when one is nowhere there is no thing to say and nothing to confuse. One is nowhere."

And where was Beatrix Palmer, who was considering investment in Old Age, in a condominium with her royalties, who was consulting a stock broker and a Dolphin Key bookmaker?

No child crossed her path. The oldies on the Key fled when a youngster approached. Their leases, Barney informed her, banned children under fifteen years of age. The few longhairs the Key people saw were hitchhikers on their way to Fort Lauderdale or Georgia kids down from Atlanta for a bit of warmth. The old drivers would grip the wheels of their cars tightly not to swerve suddenly upon them.

There was traffic through Dolphin Key, those schools of dolphins that leapt by in the early morning, the blue heron, coromorants, pelicans, and gulls. The oldies put these symbols on the doors of their houses, metal arching gulls, wrought-iron ships, tarpons, and dolphins.

The next morning Barney is by.

"Breakfast?" he grins.

"I have strawberries," says Beatrix, "cantaloupe, eggs."

She has not been spending her mornings writing. Afternoons she naps. Evenings there are social affairs.

"No," says Barney, "waffles, bacon, sausages."

It is a joyous thought for him, eating forbidden foods, bacon and pork sausages, the clams and lobsters from the other evening at Marina Jacks. He obeyed not Leviticus and set himself down in a condominium in this land of Gentiles.

In Beatrix Palmer's car were boxes of books. She took her research for *Unafraid Women*, her business contracts, her photo albums, her correspondence.

Last night Beatrix had opened her photo album. The album is of imitation leather with imitation golden tooling. She is kneeling in an early shot. Her arms are spread. She wears a black velvet or sleeveless blouse. Her hair looks like black velveteen. Everything is darkened and lightened. Her skin is light Northern. Her flared skirt is very white with large black polka dots. On one knee is her daughter's head, her daugh-

218

r's arms hugging that knee, the little girl's black hair a little
luer than the sleeveless black velveteen blouse that is its
ackdrop, the mouth closed but upturned, the eyes soft, the
irs protruding, the port wine stain almost as red as the red
nee socks. Mother and daughter are kneeling in the grass.

When had the sad pictures begun? The portents? The one
ith the red knitted hat that fastened under the chin, the red
nitted sweater with large white pearl buttons, where she is
ated on a furry pony and the pony's face, under its harness,
worried, not knowing who is on the saddle, on its velveteen
d blanket with silver stars. The little girl is clutching her
wn hands rather than the reins. Her face is almost serious
ough to be grim.

There is a picture in front of that screened-in cabin by the
ke, long ago. The wind is blowing. The mother's hair is
led on top of her head in curls. The daughter's hair has
osened from the ponytail. She is holding something. A
be? Beatrix Palmer thinks it might be a frozen ice cream
umstick. The mouth is twisted. Worry? The sun in her
yes? Or just because she's been eating the drumstick?

Younger still. Lena on a park bench. Someone took the
hoto, not Beatrix Palmer for there is Beatrix Palmer in the
ackground. A tiny part of Beatrix's rounded cheek, slender
ose, a bit of her red-lipsticked smiling mouth, three or four
pper teeth visible. Obscuring the rest of Beatrix's face is her
aughter's, one eye large and round with worry or fear or
esentment of the photographer. Lena's brows are knitted.
he mouth is definitely in pain, the hair in need of combing.
he dress is neatly ironed, the press marks showing on the
ap sleeves.

Another photo, Lena at six with six of her upper baby teeth
issing. Is that smile gay, impish, or malicious? Beatrix
almer never knew, would never know.

At the Howard Johnson: waffles, sausages, toast, pats of
utter, encapsulated marmalade, and old people.

In the next booth are a round-bellied, jeweled man with
ulldog face and his prune-faced wife. With the wife every-
ing had tightened to a scrunch; with the husband everything
as loosened.

219

Another old man nearby was tight-faced, a stretch-skinned man with cheekbones cutting through the skin. O of the window Beatrix Palmer saw a barrel of an old man wi tiny feet skimming along the sidewalk.

They heard two couples talking in the lobby, while th awaited their tables.

"You can't trust California for the earthquakes," said o old man.

"You can't trust Florida for the sudden freeze," said other.

"Trust Arizona," said one of the old ladies, holding purse handles. "It cools down at night in Arizona and you c sleep."

"Looking all over," said the couples, "for a place sleep."

Barney had listened, amused.

"Nobody dies in Florida," he tells Beatrix.

Beatrix Palmer will look down into the water. It will clear. She will see depressions under her eyes. She will the skin around her eye, left eye, is becoming cracked li mud. Too much sun? She will see several chins, or is slight hanging of the skin under the one chin? And a slig light growth of colorless hair on the chin that she will not able to see in the dark efficiency apartment, and therefo cannot pluck. Her forehead will be drying and lining. bathing cap will be pulled off by her opponent and hur away. Her hair will be pulled down toward the water by opponent. Her mouth will be open above the water, stretch so wide the loose skin of the chin is taut. Soon her upper te will be covered by her upper lip as she will sink toward water.

Barney has a surprise for her. A pen shell, a gross, u thing that he unwraps for her at the Howard Johnson table is almost a foot long, rough-shelled but inside it shines as were oil in sunlight, with glowing golds, bluish gree purplish blues, and silver.

"I have another," Barney says. "Even larger. You're depriving me of anything. Take it."

But does she want it?

"Do you want to watercolor with me on one of the other Keys?"

"I don't have paint or paper."

"You know me, old Barney from CIT."

"I know MIT. What's CIT?"

"Cleveland Institute of Technology."

"How well do I know you?"

"Well enough so that it will come as no surprise, after I pay the bill, leave the fifteen percent, that I came prepared with paper and watercolor paints."

They paint at the beach. She paints the froth of waves left against the groins of pilings, frothlike meringue, chiffon-jello. She paints the shells spilled to one side, the twinkling froth, sinking into the shell pile. She paints chips of shells, holes in bells. She paints brown seaweed, light green sea lettuce clinging like thin rubber.

He paints a little boy with a fishing pole, a little Black boy with a pail of worms, leaning over the bridge connecting the Keys. He paints the boats moored there. He paints an Amish man sitting on a rocking chair on the bridge.

There is a sudden bark. She drops her brush into the sand.

"Did my dog scare you?" asks the passing man. "She's exuberant this morning."

Beatrix's leg is bitten in a few minutes, the mean bite of a red ant.

He takes her to a cocktail party given at the Crafts Club. She is a new neighbor, maybe a permanent one. *The Saratoga Times* has listed her under Distinguished Visitors to the Keys and the Tampa paper has her in its column, Visitors Receiving Keys to the Kingdom.

The drinks are too strong. The men all look and sound like W. C. Fields. The women are sand-keeping machines, sweeping their men, flattening the white hair, tying their ties, dampening their faces, keeping their men in working order.

The men, freed of work, become the lives their women have always had to lead, frivolous, useless, full of crafts but not crafty, filling the time. Their bodies become their own floating rubber tubes in the condominium pools. They change clothes several times a day for changing social events.

221

No one hears the news or talks of it. No one reads the paper or talks of it, except for the listing of plays at the Ringling Museum, of movies in Tampa or Sarasota, of religious services, and those lists of visiting dignitaries to their Keys.

They discuss shelling with Beatrix. Only one man in the group works and he has to pay for it by missing the boating excursions, the craft classes, and the cocktail parties, or the swims in the heated pool.

They are proud that Beatrix has gathered a fairly rare gastropod, an olive shell with unusual markings, for the shell had cracked and had repaired itself. The shell is passed about.

Beatrix's hand will press down on the hair that is floating like seaweed and that, through the greenish water, is brown. Under water the strands separate like the strands of that St. Patrick's Day mop hair. Beatrix will press down more. Bubbles will appear and Beatrix will move her legs away from the scratching hands, the kicking legs. Beatrix will punch at the opened brown eyes, the gasping mouth, the stalk of neck. Beatrix's hand and face will become tired. The lines along her cheek will groove more deeply; the mouth will turn downward in strain.

One of the red-, swollen-nosed gentlemen of the Crafts Club is speaking to her.

"Your name's been bandied about, yes indeed, bandiieeed about."

The chairperson of the Crafts Club has clipped the items on Mrs. Palmer, encircling with magic marker the paragraph in which she's mentioned and obliterating the other names with the thick stroke.

In this world, Mrs. Palmer is decades younger than Barney, the baby.

"Come here, youngster," says Barney.

She is his exhibit, his seashell on driftwood, his enameled copper earrings and cuff links that he exhibits in the Crafts Members Gift Shop.

Beatrix will shell, walking as she always does, head down, early mornings or early evenings. She is becoming acquisitive and annoyed at another sheller's turkey wing or lovely pinkish tellin.

As she will walk head turned downward, there will be an obstinate shadow before her that will not move. She will step to one side. So will the shadow. She will look up into the eyes of a shadowed green sun hat, a bikini, a sneering smile, a daughter.

"I wondered where . . . I wondered when. . . ," says the mother.

"No where," says the daughter.

"Have you eaten?" asks Beatrix.

"Same mother," says Lena.

"Same daughter," says Beatrix.

They go into the efficiency. The daughter is a vegetarian so never mind the tuna or lamb chops. Now Beatrix has somebody to share the fruit, the too-soft avocado, the wilting greens. She wishes Lena would wash up, comb her hair. She wishes her daughter would take off the mother's green sun hat.

Beatrix rinses her hands, standing on the indoor-outdoor carpeting that extends from the wall kitchen into the bathroom.

Once there was a pink plastic birthday comb with a pink-framed mirror and a pink bow in Lena's hair. The pink comb combed the brown bangs. The eyes were looking at the mirror. The collar was frilled and fading into the neck. What color was that collar, was that dress? The mouth is open in concentration, almost in a smile at the mirror.

The mother can hear the Gulf, regular, splashing against the piles. They eat the salad, the fruit. The daughter finishes and laughs.

"I'm into meat again," she says.

"I can't please you," says the mother.

"That's right," says the daughter.

The night is full of: "Which of us is the kid?"
"Your cowardice or is it disinterest?"
"Answer me!"
"Are you afraid?"
"Who's your boyfriend this time?"

Who is talking? Beatrix cannot always tell.

"I still love you," Beatrix Palmer says to her daughter.

All the pain in the dressers of her bedrooms, all the pain that groaned with the opened drawer, the pain of notebooks filled with drawings of drawn women. Later, from other lands, the drawings are crying, the eyes have tears but the tears have become hearts, pearls, seashells. The drawings are in a lovely, hand-bound book (bound by her nowhere-bound daughter) from India. They are on soft paper and the ink of the Indian fantasies has spread slightly.

There will be a bite under water, the mouth will turn on the mother's arm and bite it until the hand lets go of the hair. The daughter will slowly ascend to the surface, floating upward while the mother will rub the teeth marks in her arm. Slowly, slowly the daughter will walk the water back to shore, back to the efficiency that housed a night of accusation. The daughter will pick up her mother's sun hat and put it on her wet hair.

The mother will be left, bereft. They had drowned each other first in tears and then had almost drowned each other. The daughter will leave, wearing the mother's favorite towel dress and the mother's overpriced light green sun hat. The daughter's thumbs will work the road. The oldies will pass her by until a Fort Lauderdale (probably) bound, long-haired blond boy will stop. The mother will watch from behind the Australian pines, from behind the neighbor's trees being consumed by Spanish moss.

"Where to?" the boy will ask.

"Wherever," the daughter will say.

Last shot. Window down, daughter staring straight ahead to the bridge connecting Dolphin Key to the other Keys. The daughter's mouth will be widely smiling.

Beatrix is now a retiree. She is now an oldie.

"What *do* these young people want? What *do* they want?"

There is a shadow on Beatrix's upper lip. The hairs there

are darkening. Will her stomach thicken? Should she attach herself to Barney? Would two retirees be less tired?

Would the sun be enough to make up for growing old? Will she spend her time gardening, trying to grow rosebushes in this sandy, salty soil, leaving the bushes in planters and bringing them in every night? Would she mother those thorny bushes as she could never adequately protect from sand and wind her daughter?

Was intent to murder equal in the eye of God to the commission of murder.

The insults, the vile insults, the slaps, the slaps returned, the punch, punch revisited, the flailing, kicking, scratching, uprooting of hair, ripping at cheeks, the attempts to destroy the photographs of face in the water.

Beatrix Palmer is still at the road, staring past departure. Had she wheeled the yellow-lined carriage into the Gulf? Was she strangling that baby with her red scarf when she nurtured her? Was she pressing that face into her chest to keep the nose from breathing?

All of that happened in the moment of immersion. At that pushing down of Lena's head through the water, albums were spilled and snapshots cracked. Ink ran from letters, stamps loosened, envelopes opened.

Beatrix destroyed the present, but, much worse, the past.

Did the sea surface with her to crack her against these pilings, shuck her, leave her with other empty shells of people?

She will lock firmly the luggage of her life, her typewriter, suitcase, cosmetic bag, and record nothing, accomplish no distance, alter no tired appearance.

A car comes down the road. Beatrix's vision is blurred. It honks. Noisy Barney?

Her green hat comes out of the car. Her green-and-blue towel dress comes walking toward her.

"No more assassinations," says Lena.

Birth me, Mothers. Carry me in the brine of your belly and your tears.

Let us sit on each others' laps, daughters and mothers.

We have hired our own hall. We hold hands. Our engagements rings do not scratch. Our wedding bands do not disband us. The musicians are women. The one ascending the podium is a woman.

"Mother, I'm pregnant with a baby girl."
"What is she doing?"
"She is singing."
"Why is she singing?"
"Because she's unafraid."

Acknowledgments: To more of my mothers, the following young girls and women who loved and sustained me

## Mothers Under Ten

Jenny Freedman, Haifa, Israel
Sarah Cole, Cambridge, Massachusetts
Effie Galnoor, Jerusalem, Israel

## Mothers Under Twenty

Nahama Broner, Detroit, Michigan
Tamar Weinstein, Englewood, New Jersey
Claudia Weinstein, Englewood, New Jersey
Susan Broner, West Hempstead, New York
Maya Sonenberg, New York, New York
Jill Brose, Highland Park, Michigan
Erica Bogin, New Rochelle, New York

## MOTHERS IN THEIR TWENTIES

Sari Broner, Detroit, Michigan
Finvola Drury, Jr., New York, New York
Aliza Masserman, Ann Arbor, Michigan
Lois Clamage, Detroit, Michigan
Doron Galnoor, Jerusalem, Israel
Cathy Bogin, New Rochelle, New York
Ilana Kanska, Jerusalem, Israel


## MOTHERS IN THEIR THIRTIES

Virginia Kelley, New York, New York
Davida Cohen, Hof HaCarmel, Israel
Julie Jensen, Detroit, Michigan
Marcia Freedman, Haifa, Israel
Arella Bar Lev, Tel Aviv, Israel
Sue Brose, Highland Park, Michigan
Karen Klein, Royal Oak, Michigan
Prof. Linda Jaron, Providence, Rhode Island
Marylou Zieve, Bloomfield Hills, Michigan
Prof. Elizabeth Meese, New Brunswick, New Jersey
Prof. Jane Eberwein, Rochester, Michigan
Marian Wood, New York, New York
Sally Lund, New York, New York
Nomi Nimrod, Haifa, Israel


## MOTHERS IN THEIR FORTIES

Joan Weinstein, Englewood, New Jersey
Evelyn Orbach, Detroit, Michigan
Dina Saxer Margolis, Toronto, Canada
Margaret Lowinger, San Francisco, California
Rina Kimche, Hof HaCarmel, Israel
Phoebe Hellman Sonenberg, New York, New York
Lucille Field, Providence, Rhode Island
Joyce Weckstein, Mouthfield, Michigan
June Snow, Detroit, Michigan

Dr. Elizabeth Kubler-Ross, Flossmoor, Illinois
Barbara Fussiner, New Haven, Connecticut
Ruth Kroll, Detroit, Michigan
Prof. Alice Shalvi, Jerusalem, Israel

## Mothers in Their Fifties

Dr. Sylvia Fried, Tenafly, New Jersey
Malverne Reisman, Southfield, Michigan
Judith Lieber, New York, New York
Annette Freedman, Southfield, Michigan
Eleanor Torrey West, Bloomfield Hills, Michigan
Sylvia Gingold, Teaneck, New Jersey
Harriet Berg, Detroit, Michigan
Nancy Bogin, New Rochelle, New York
Miriam Ben Arie, Jerusalem, Israel
Elizabeth Weiss, Oak Park, Michigan

## Mothers in Their Sixties

Ilse Schrag, New York, New York
Hannah Pokempner, Detroit, Michigan
Dr. Hansi Mark, Oak Park, Michigan
Phyllis Bowman, New York, New York
Priscilla Merritt, Deer Isle, Maine
Florence Crowther, White Plains, New York
Evelyn Scheyer, Detroit, Michigan

## Mothers in Their Seventies

Beatrice Masserman, Oak Park, Michigan
Pearl Sternlight, New York, New York
Antoinette Opperman, South Bend, Indiana
Agnes Bruenton, Detroit, Michigan

# THE BEST IN FICTION FROM BERKLEY

**COMING TO**      (K3046 — $1.75)
  by Alan Brody

**DEKKER**      (D3079 — $1.50)
  by Lou Cameron

**SWITCH**      (Z3082 — $1.25)
  by Mike Jahn

**WATERS OF DECISION**      (K3075 — $1.75)
  by Warren Adler

**NASHVILLE LADY**      (Z3088 — $1.25)
  by B. C. Hall

**TWYLA**      (N3076 — 95¢)
  by Pamela Walker

**THE SAND CASTLES**      (T3130 — $1.95)
  by Louise Montague

Send for a *free* list of all our books in print

These books are available at your local bookstore, or send
price indicated plus 30¢ per copy to cover mailing costs to:
Berkley Publishing Corporation
200 Madison Avenue
New York, New York 10016

## MORE CONTEMPORARY FICTION
## YOU'LL ENJOY FROM BERKLEY